CHAPTER ONE: BOOK BANDIT

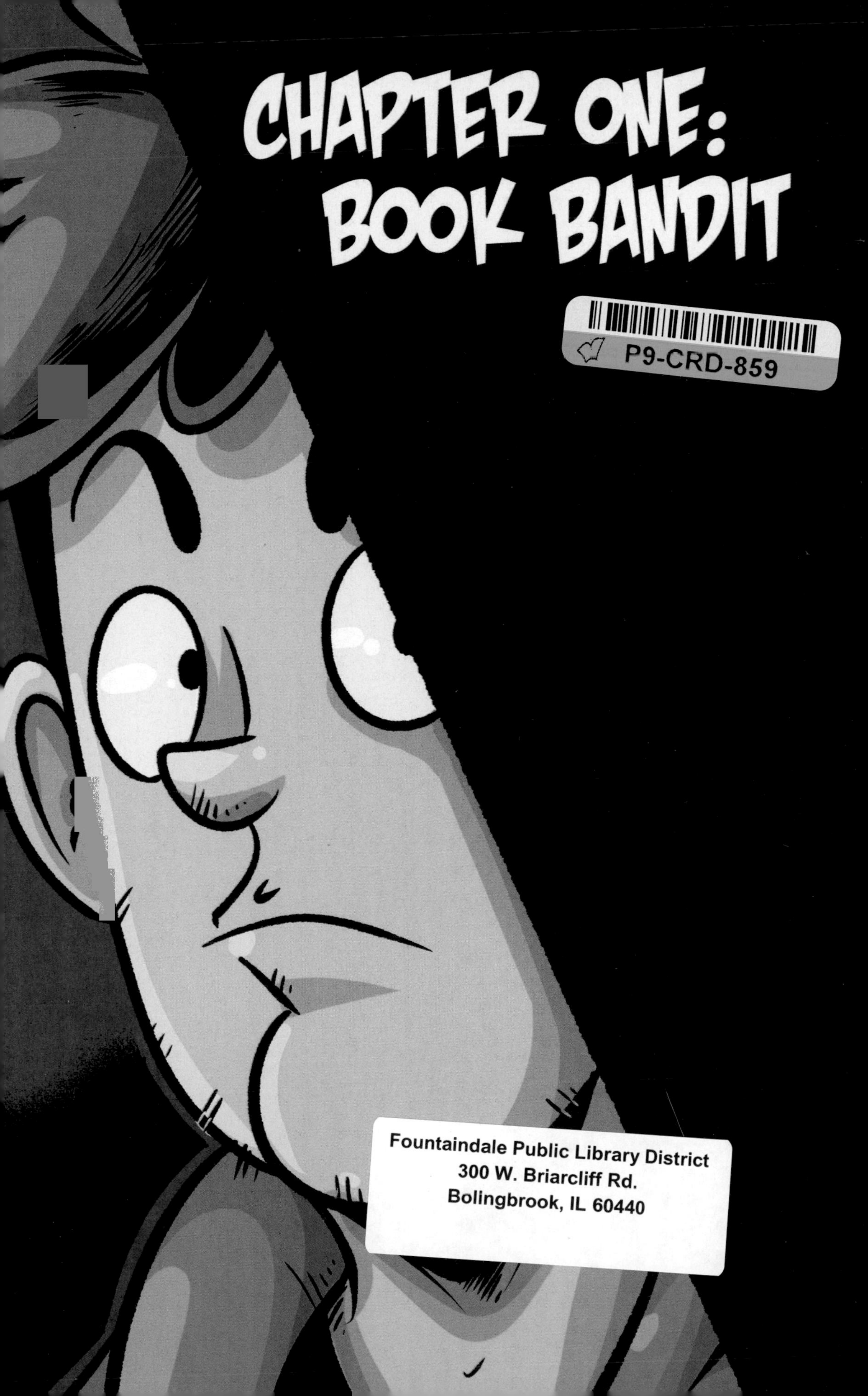

SASQUATCH
IN LOVE

JASON NUTT
Writer

ALEXIS VIVALLO
Artist

JOSH SOUTHALL
Letterer

Special thanks to David Nutt
and David Anaxagoras

For Olivia and
Eureka
- Jason

To Alexis,
20 years ago
- Alexis

Bryan Seaton: Publisher/CEO
Shawn Gabborin: Editor In Chief
Jason Martin: Publisher-Danger Zone
Nicole D'Andria: Marketing Director/Editor
Danielle Davison: Executive Administrator
Chad Cicconi: ~~Bigfoot~~ Sasquatch Wrangler
Shawn Pryor: President of Creator Relations

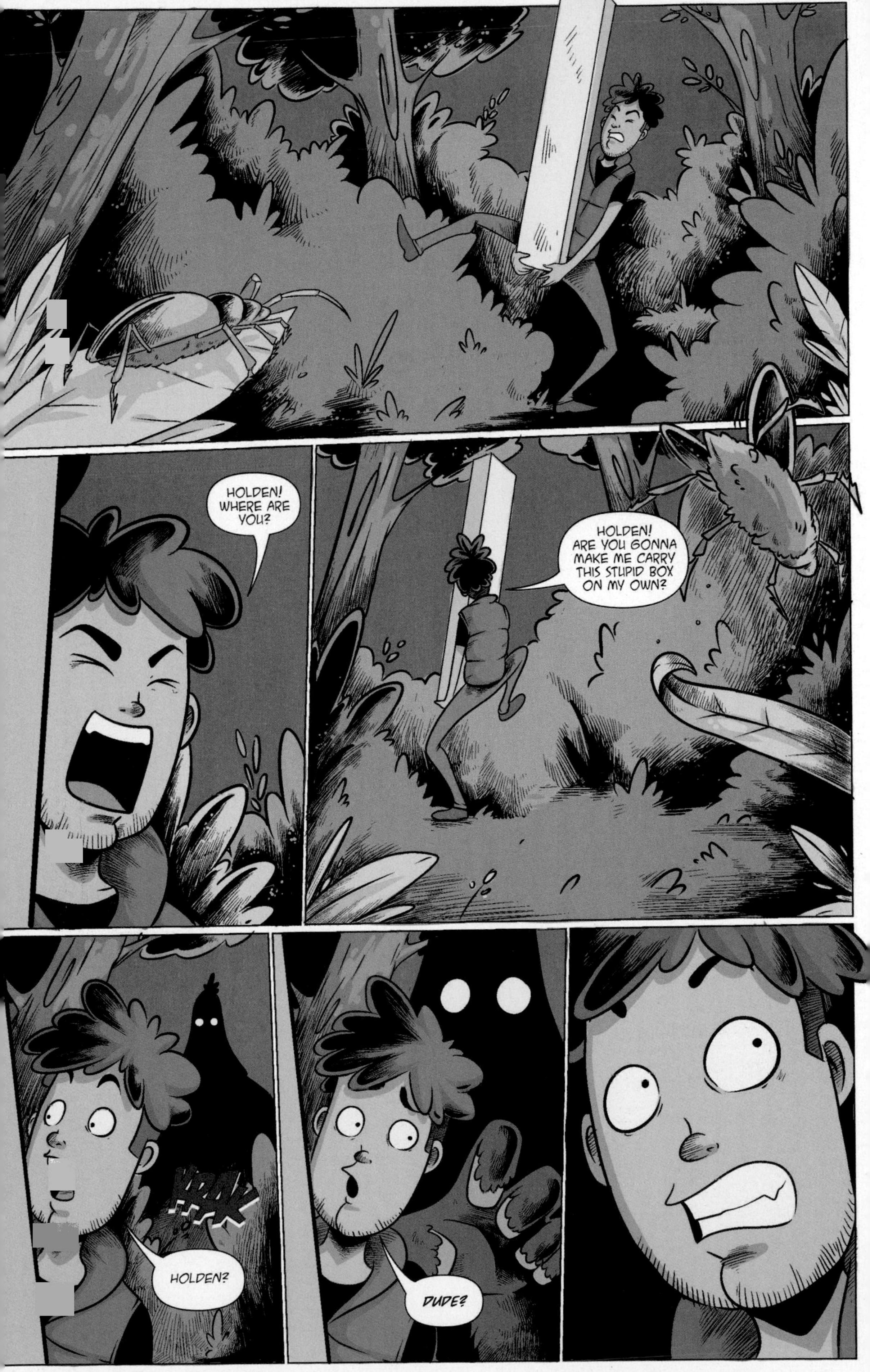
HOLDEN! WHERE ARE YOU?
HOLDEN! ARE YOU GONNA MAKE ME CARRY THIS STUPID BOX ON MY OWN?
HOLDEN?
DUDE?

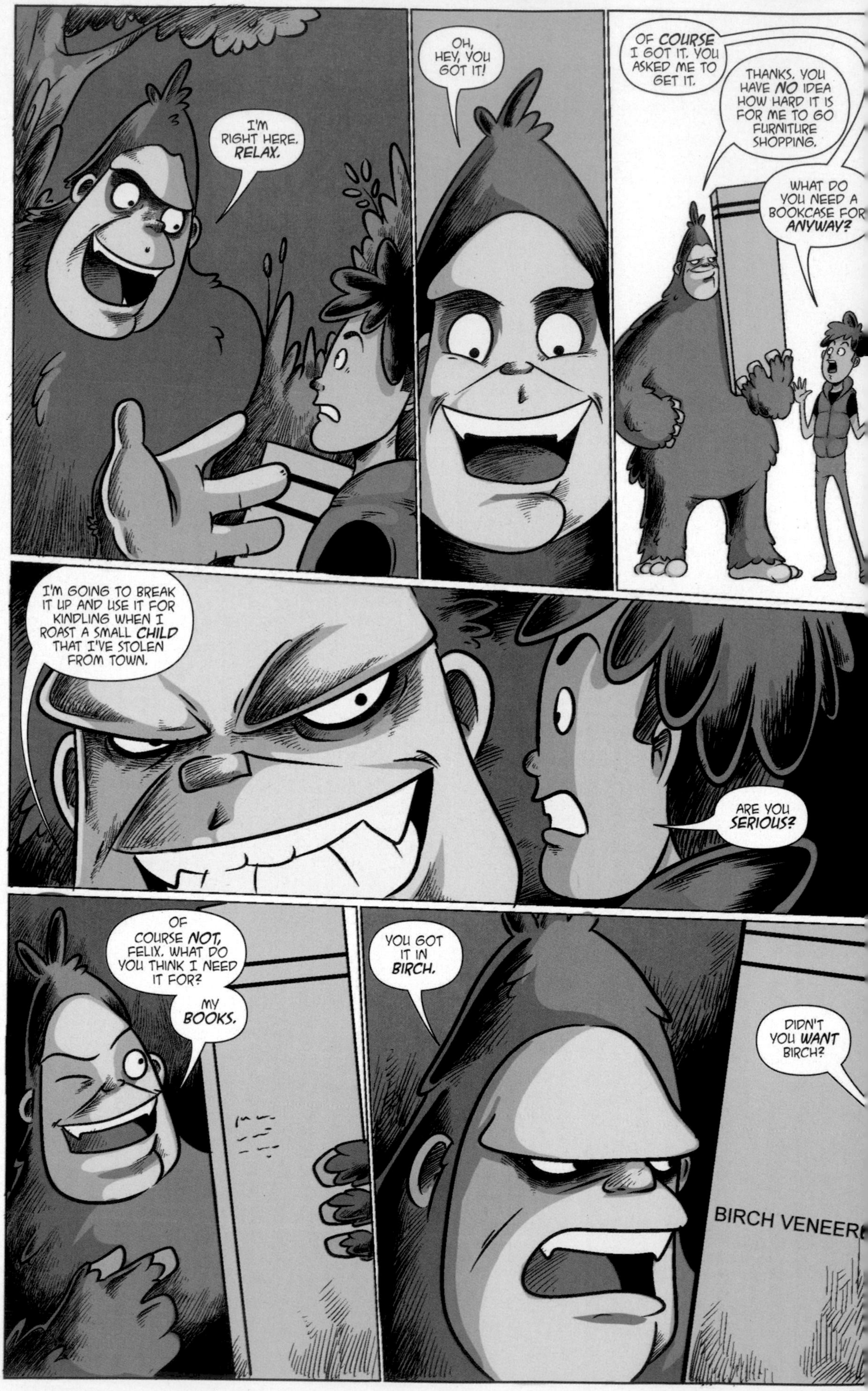
I'M RIGHT HERE. RELAX.
OH, HEY, YOU GOT IT!
OF COURSE I GOT IT. YOU ASKED ME TO GET IT.
THANKS. YOU HAVE NO IDEA HOW HARD IT IS FOR ME TO GO FURNITURE SHOPPING.
WHAT DO YOU NEED A BOOKCASE FOR ANYWAY?
I'M GOING TO BREAK IT UP AND USE IT FOR KINDLING WHEN I ROAST A SMALL CHILD THAT I'VE STOLEN FROM TOWN.
ARE YOU SERIOUS?
OF COURSE NOT, FELIX. WHAT DO YOU THINK I NEED IT FOR?
MY BOOKS.
YOU GOT IT IN BIRCH.
DIDN'T YOU WANT BIRCH?
BIRCH VENEER

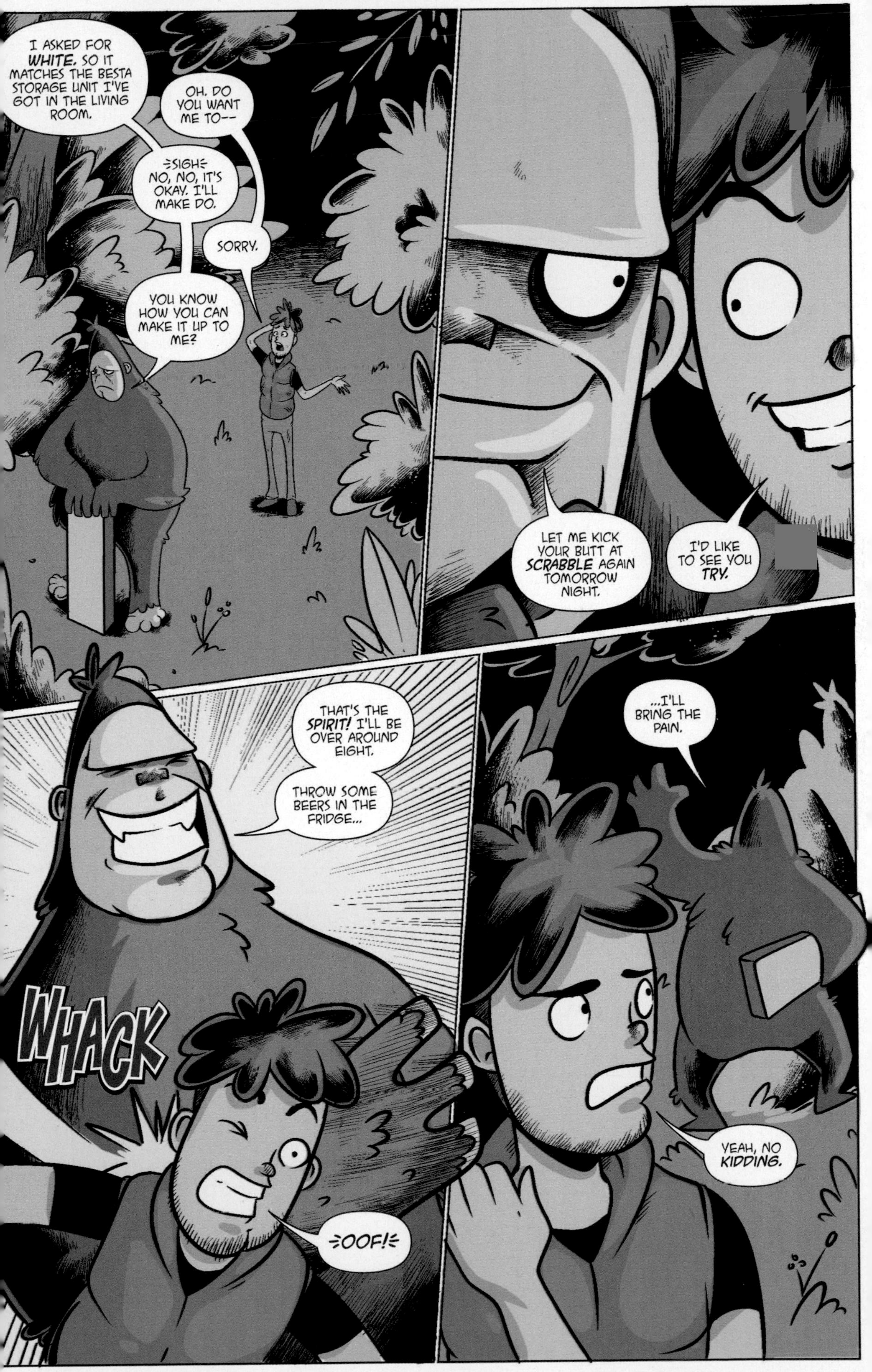
I ASKED FOR WHITE. SO IT MATCHES THE BESTA STORAGE UNIT I'VE GOT IN THE LIVING ROOM.
OH. DO YOU WANT ME TO--
=SIGH= NO, NO, IT'S OKAY. I'LL MAKE DO.
SORRY.
YOU KNOW HOW YOU CAN MAKE IT UP TO ME?
LET ME KICK YOUR BUTT AT SCRABBLE AGAIN TOMORROW NIGHT.
I'D LIKE TO SEE YOU TRY.
THAT'S THE SPIRIT! I'LL BE OVER AROUND EIGHT.
THROW SOME BEERS IN THE FRIDGE...
WHACK
=OOF!=
...I'LL BRING THE PAIN.
YEAH, NO KIDDING.

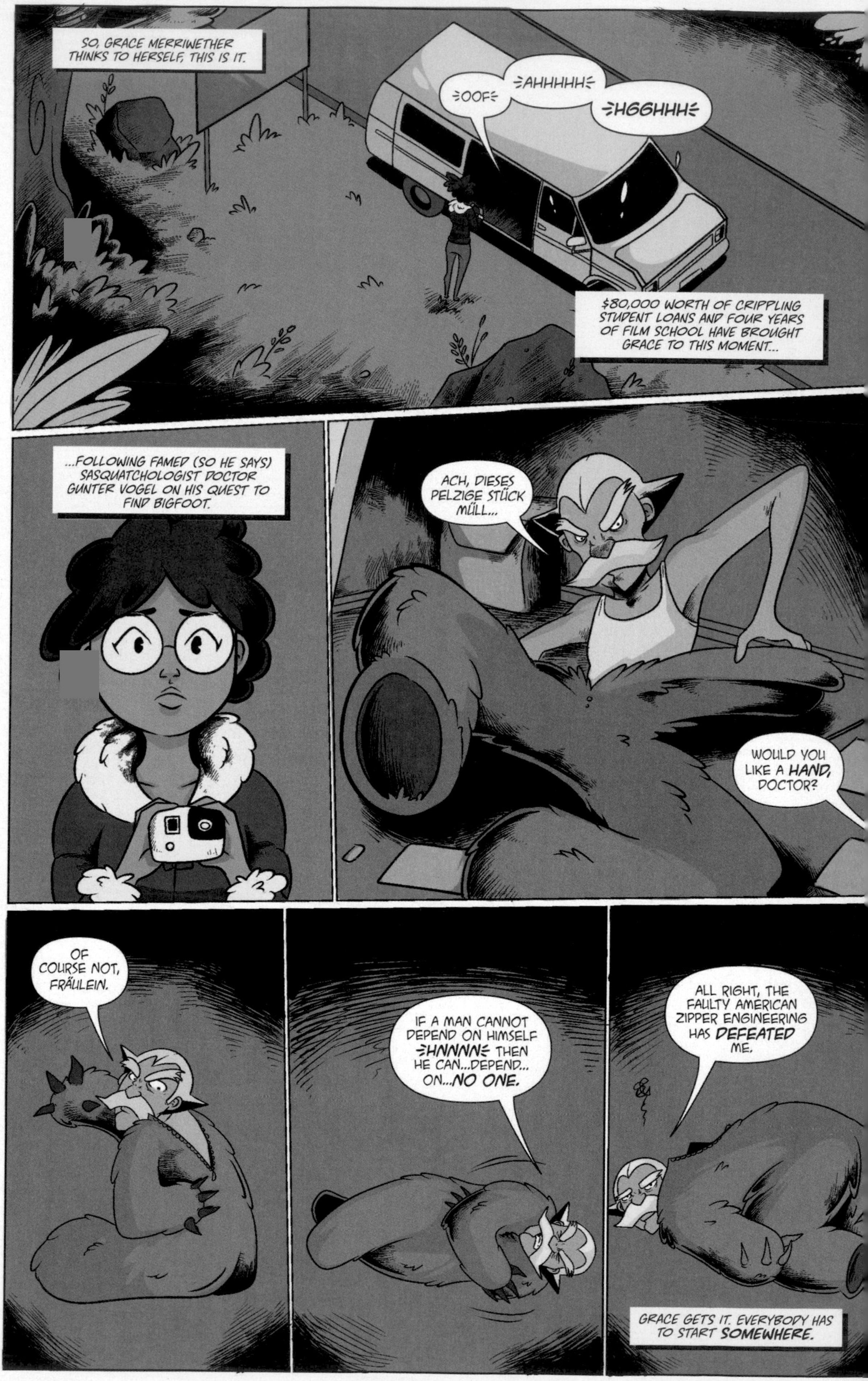
SO, GRACE MERRIWETHER THINKS TO HERSELF, THIS IS IT.
OOF
AHHHHH
HGGHHH
$80,000 WORTH OF CRIPPLING STUDENT LOANS AND FOUR YEARS OF FILM SCHOOL HAVE BROUGHT GRACE TO THIS MOMENT...
...FOLLOWING FAMED (SO HE SAYS) SASQUATCHOLOGIST DOCTOR GUNTER VOGEL ON HIS QUEST TO FIND BIGFOOT.
ACH, DIESES PELZIGE STÜCK MÜLL...
WOULD YOU LIKE A HAND, DOCTOR?
OF COURSE NOT, FRÄULEIN.
IF A MAN CANNOT DEPEND ON HIMSELF HNNNN THEN HE CAN...DEPEND... ON...NO ONE.
ALL RIGHT, THE FAULTY AMERICAN ZIPPER ENGINEERING HAS DEFEATED ME.
GRACE GETS IT. EVERYBODY HAS TO START SOMEWHERE.

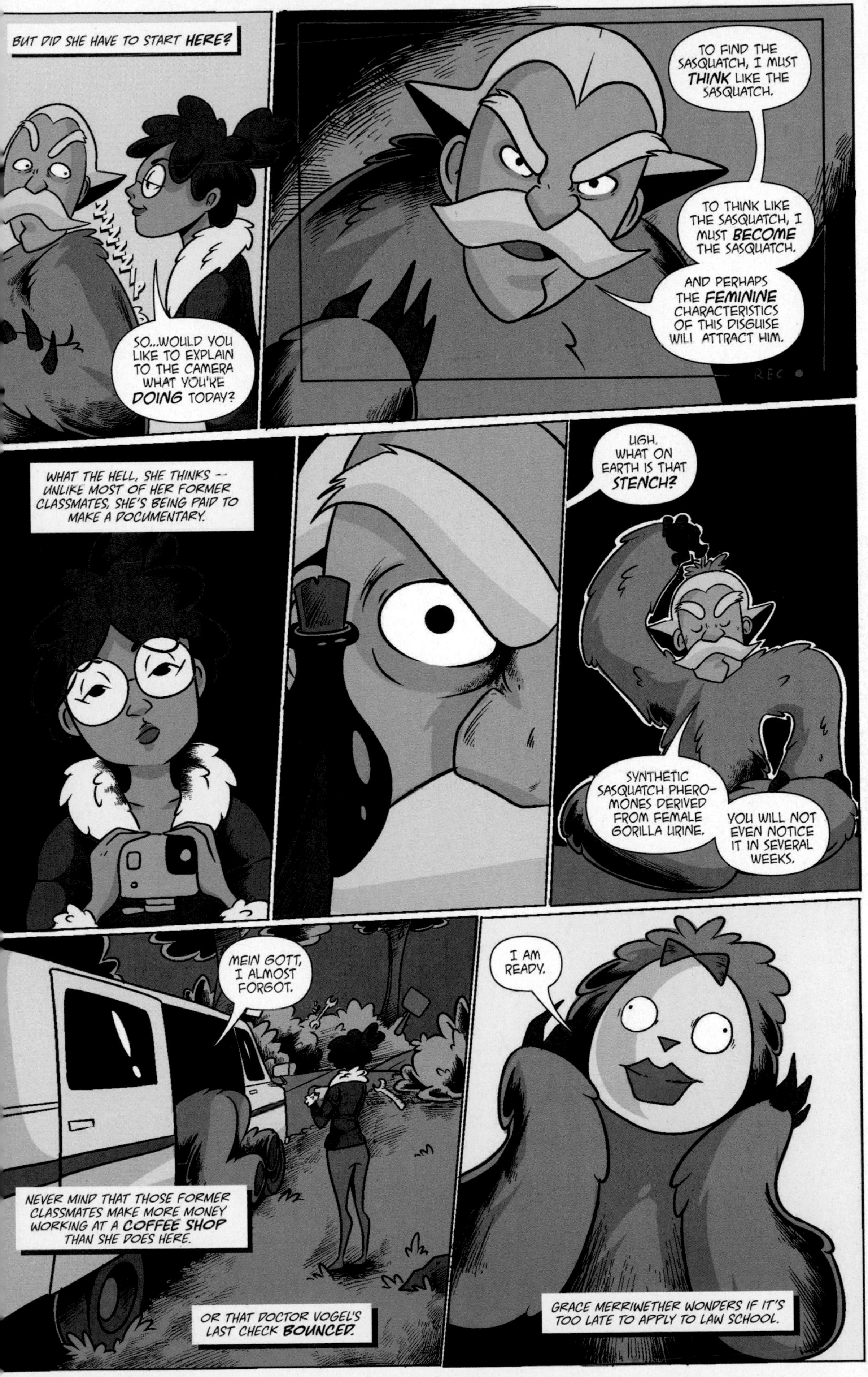
BUT DID SHE HAVE TO START HERE?
SO...WOULD YOU LIKE TO EXPLAIN TO THE CAMERA WHAT YOU'RE DOING TODAY?
TO FIND THE SASQUATCH, I MUST THINK LIKE THE SASQUATCH.
TO THINK LIKE THE SASQUATCH, I MUST BECOME THE SASQUATCH.
AND PERHAPS THE FEMININE CHARACTERISTICS OF THIS DISGUISE WILL ATTRACT HIM.
REC
WHAT THE HELL, SHE THINKS -- UNLIKE MOST OF HER FORMER CLASSMATES, SHE'S BEING PAID TO MAKE A DOCUMENTARY.
UGH, WHAT ON EARTH IS THAT STENCH?
SYNTHETIC SASQUATCH PHEROMONES DERIVED FROM FEMALE GORILLA URINE.
YOU WILL NOT EVEN NOTICE IT IN SEVERAL WEEKS.
MEIN GOTT, I ALMOST FORGOT.
NEVER MIND THAT THOSE FORMER CLASSMATES MAKE MORE MONEY WORKING AT A COFFEE SHOP THAN SHE DOES HERE.
OR THAT DOCTOR VOGEL'S LAST CHECK BOUNCED.
I AM READY.
GRACE MERRIWETHER WONDERS IF IT'S TOO LATE TO APPLY TO LAW SCHOOL.

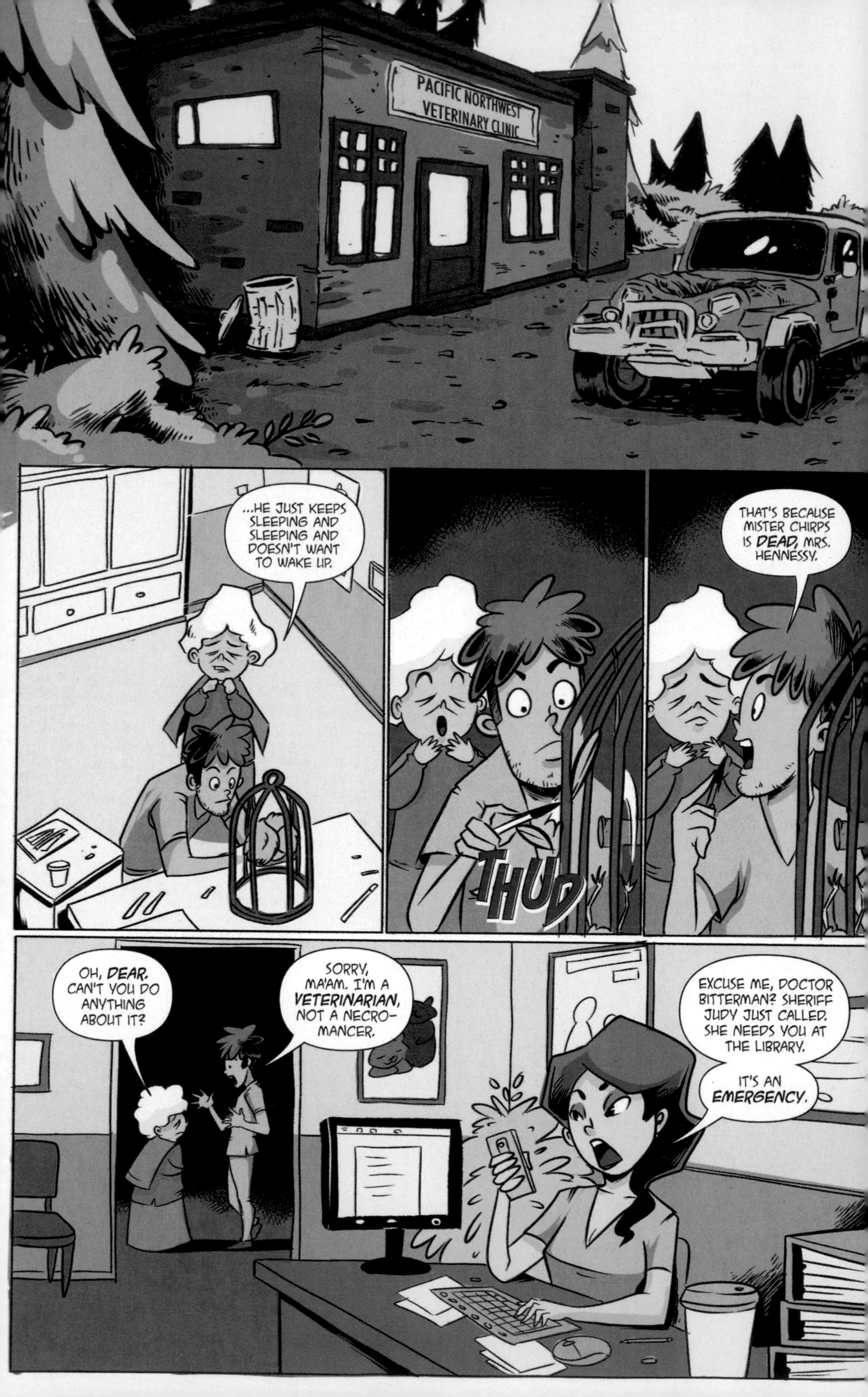
PACIFIC NORTHWEST VETERINARY CLINIC
...HE JUST KEEPS SLEEPING AND SLEEPING AND DOESN'T WANT TO WAKE UP.
THUD
THAT'S BECAUSE MISTER CHIRPS IS DEAD, MRS. HENNESSY.
OH, DEAR. CAN'T YOU DO ANYTHING ABOUT IT?
SORRY, MA'AM. I'M A VETERINARIAN, NOT A NECRO-MANCER.
EXCUSE ME, DOCTOR BITTERMAN? SHERIFF JUDY JUST CALLED. SHE NEEDS YOU AT THE LIBRARY.
IT'S AN EMERGENCY.

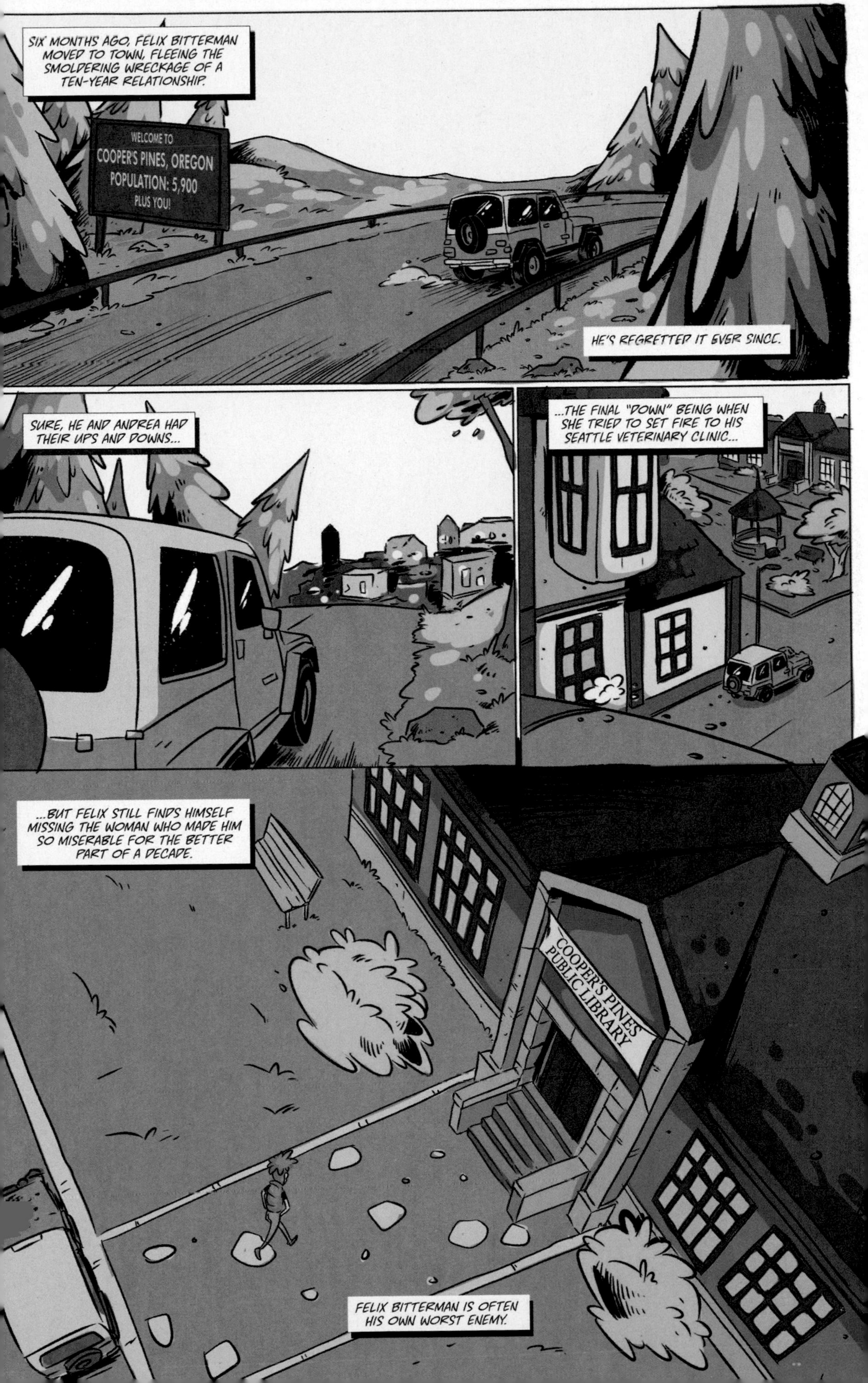
SIX MONTHS AGO, FELIX BITTERMAN MOVED TO TOWN, FLEEING THE SMOLDERING WRECKAGE OF A TEN-YEAR RELATIONSHIP.
WELCOME TO COOPER'S PINES, OREGON POPULATION: 5,900 PLUS YOU!
HE'S REGRETTED IT EVER SINCE.
SURE, HE AND ANDREA HAD THEIR UPS AND DOWNS...
...THE FINAL "DOWN" BEING WHEN SHE TRIED TO SET FIRE TO HIS SEATTLE VETERINARY CLINIC...
...BUT FELIX STILL FINDS HIMSELF MISSING THE WOMAN WHO MADE HIM SO MISERABLE FOR THE BETTER PART OF A DECADE.
COOPER'S PINES PUBLIC LIBRARY
FELIX BITTERMAN IS OFTEN HIS OWN WORST ENEMY.

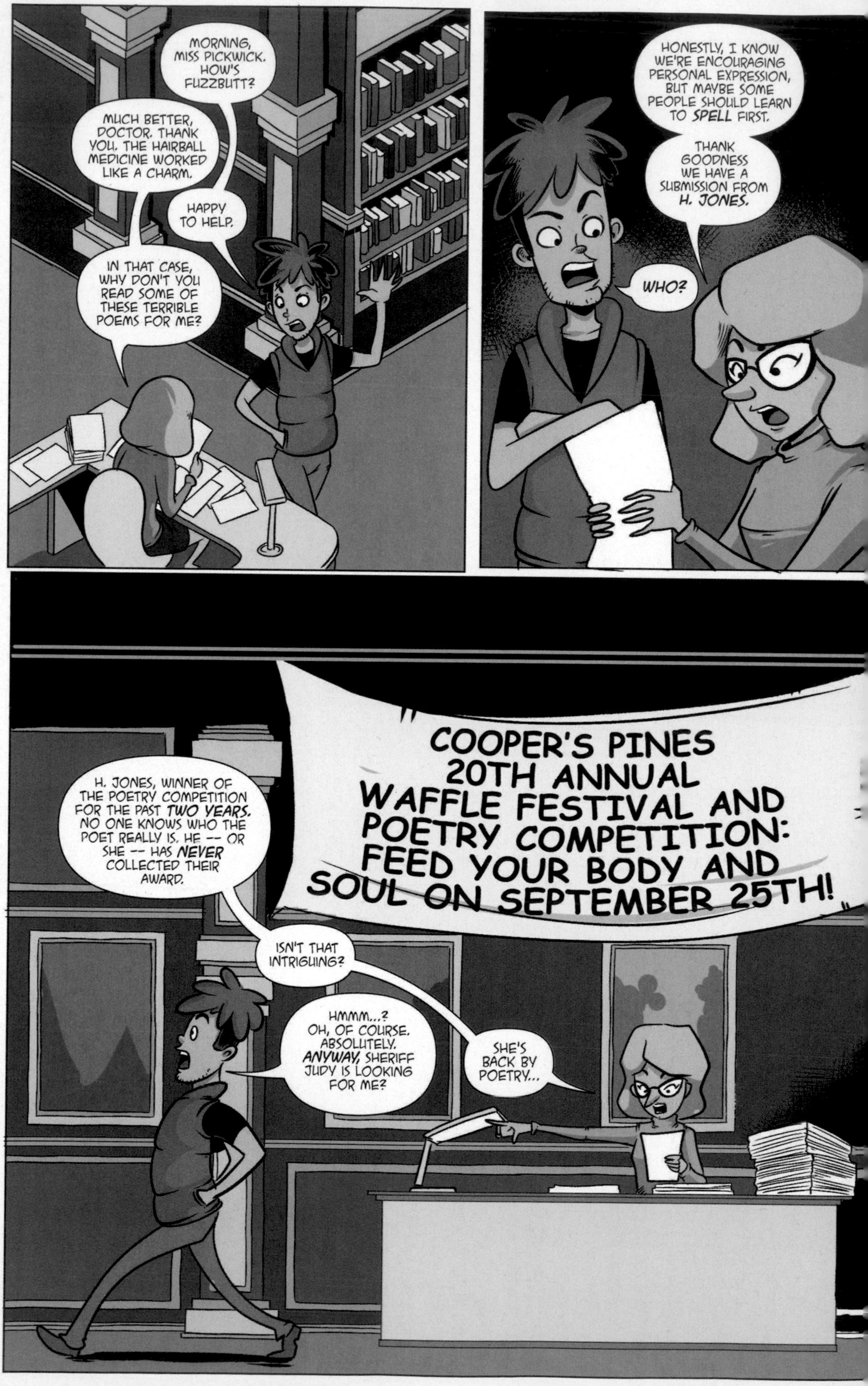
MORNING, MISS PICKWICK. HOW'S FUZZBUTT?
MUCH BETTER, DOCTOR. THANK YOU. THE HAIRBALL MEDICINE WORKED LIKE A CHARM.
HAPPY TO HELP.
IN THAT CASE, WHY DON'T YOU READ SOME OF THESE TERRIBLE POEMS FOR ME?
HONESTLY, I KNOW WE'RE ENCOURAGING PERSONAL EXPRESSION, BUT MAYBE SOME PEOPLE SHOULD LEARN TO SPELL FIRST.
THANK GOODNESS WE HAVE A SUBMISSION FROM H. JONES.
WHO?
COOPER'S PINES 20TH ANNUAL WAFFLE FESTIVAL AND POETRY COMPETITION: FEED YOUR BODY AND SOUL ON SEPTEMBER 25TH!
H. JONES, WINNER OF THE POETRY COMPETITION FOR THE PAST TWO YEARS. NO ONE KNOWS WHO THE POET REALLY IS. HE -- OR SHE -- HAS NEVER COLLECTED THEIR AWARD.
ISN'T THAT INTRIGUING?
HMMM...? OH, OF COURSE. ABSOLUTELY. ANYWAY, SHERIFF JUDY IS LOOKING FOR ME?
SHE'S BACK BY POETRY...

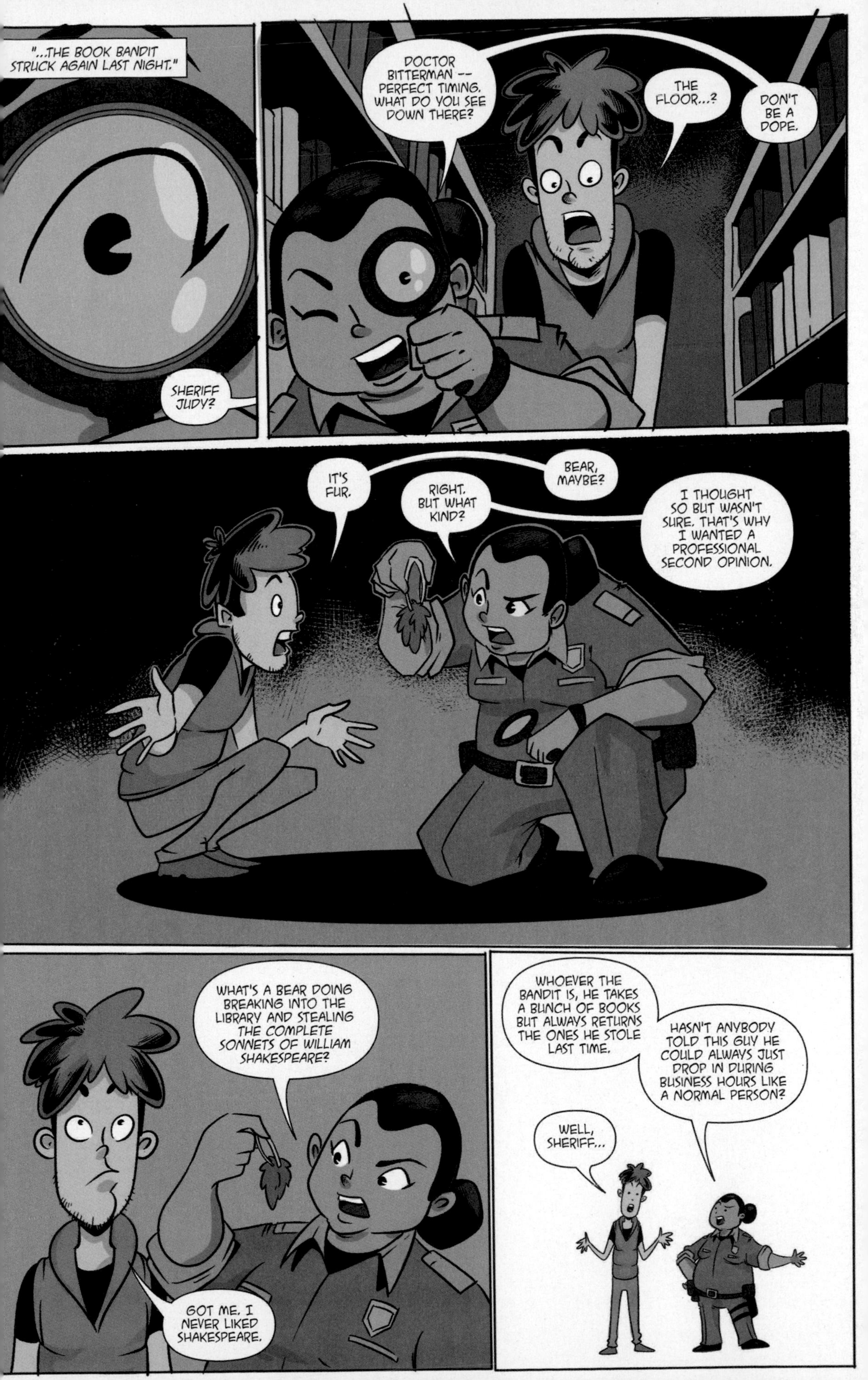
"...THE BOOK BANDIT STRUCK AGAIN LAST NIGHT."
SHERIFF JUDY?
DOCTOR BITTERMAN -- PERFECT TIMING. WHAT DO YOU SEE DOWN THERE?
THE FLOOR...?
DON'T BE A DOPE.
IT'S FUR.
RIGHT. BUT WHAT KIND?
BEAR, MAYBE?
I THOUGHT SO BUT WASN'T SURE. THAT'S WHY I WANTED A PROFESSIONAL SECOND OPINION.
WHAT'S A BEAR DOING BREAKING INTO THE LIBRARY AND STEALING THE COMPLETE SONNETS OF WILLIAM SHAKESPEARE?
GOT ME. I NEVER LIKED SHAKESPEARE.
WHOEVER THE BANDIT IS, HE TAKES A BUNCH OF BOOKS BUT ALWAYS RETURNS THE ONES HE STOLE LAST TIME.
HASN'T ANYBODY TOLD THIS GUY HE COULD ALWAYS JUST DROP IN DURING BUSINESS HOURS LIKE A NORMAL PERSON?
WELL, SHERIFF...

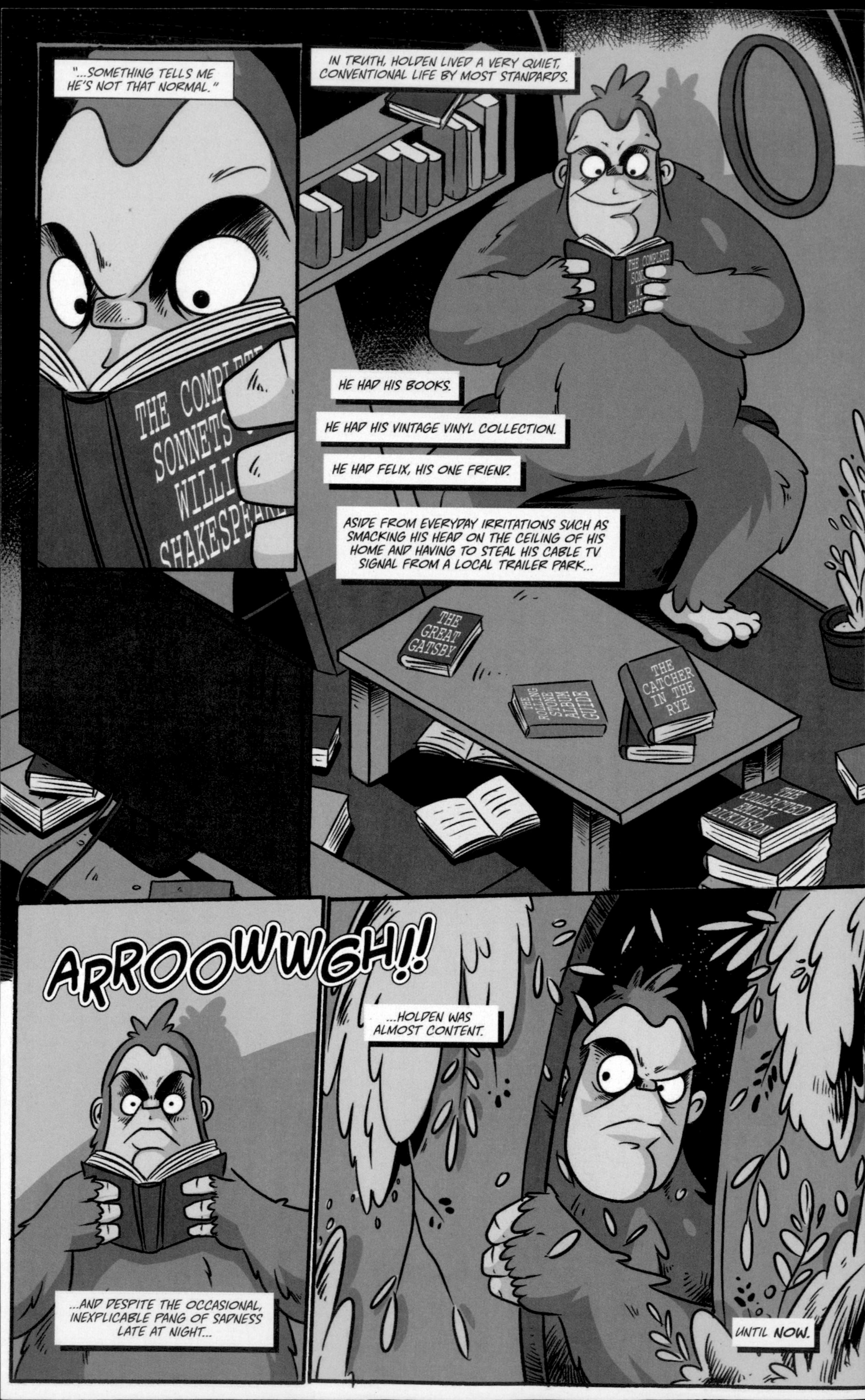
"...SOMETHING TELLS ME HE'S NOT THAT NORMAL."
THE COMPLETE SONNETS OF WILLIAM SHAKESPEARE
IN TRUTH, HOLDEN LIVED A VERY QUIET, CONVENTIONAL LIFE BY MOST STANDARDS.
HE HAD HIS BOOKS.
HE HAD HIS VINTAGE VINYL COLLECTION.
HE HAD FELIX, HIS ONE FRIEND.
ASIDE FROM EVERYDAY IRRITATIONS SUCH AS SMACKING HIS HEAD ON THE CEILING OF HIS HOME AND HAVING TO STEAL HIS CABLE TV SIGNAL FROM A LOCAL TRAILER PARK...
THE GREAT GATSBY
THE ROLLING STONE ALBUM GUIDE
THE CATCHER IN THE RYE
THE COLLECTED EMILY DICKINSON
ARROOWWGH!!
...AND DESPITE THE OCCASIONAL, INEXPLICABLE PANG OF SADNESS LATE AT NIGHT...
...HOLDEN WAS ALMOST CONTENT.
UNTIL NOW.

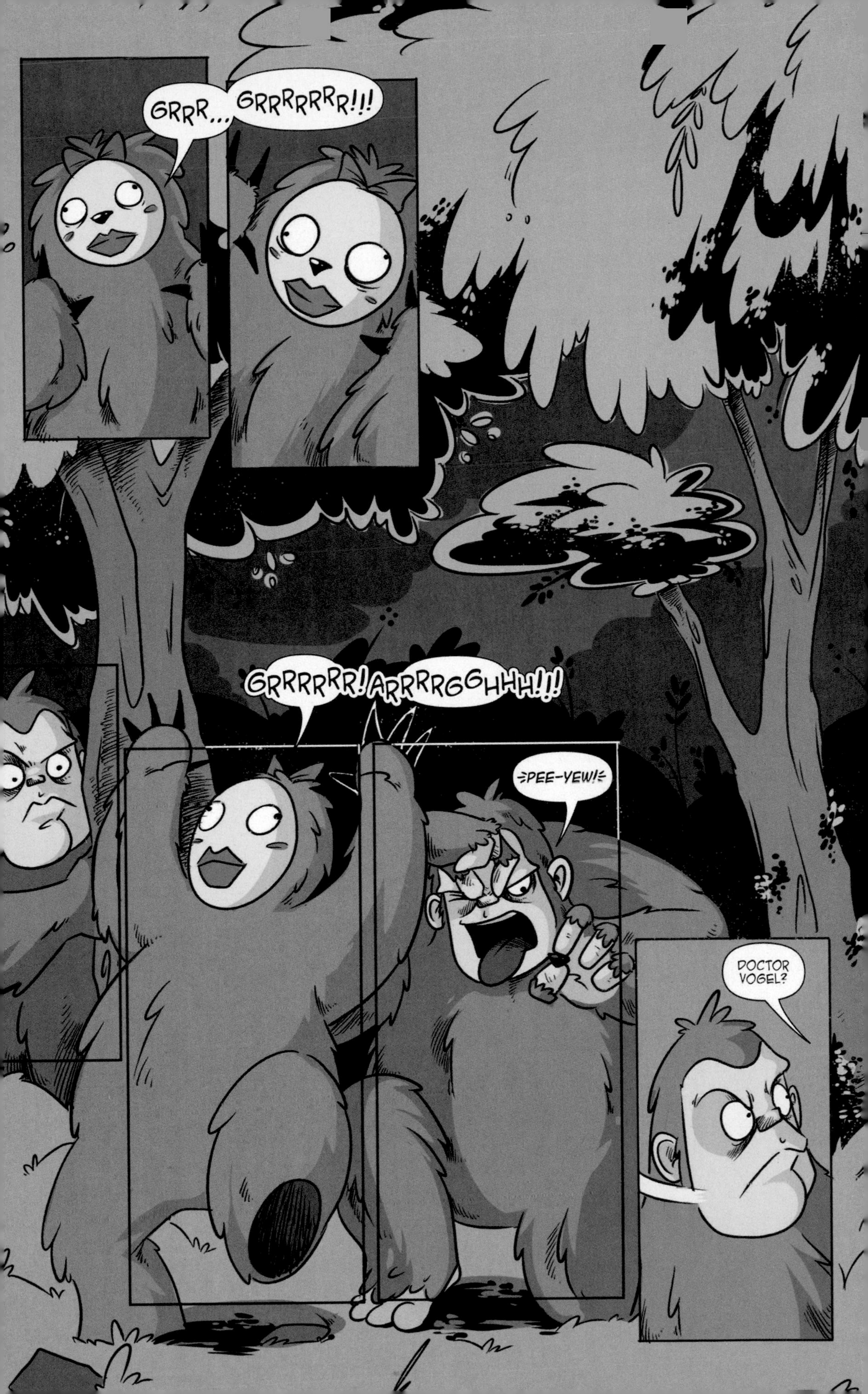
GRRR...
GRRRRRRR!!!
GRRRRRR! ARRRRGGHHH!!!
PEE-YEW!
DOCTOR VOGEL?

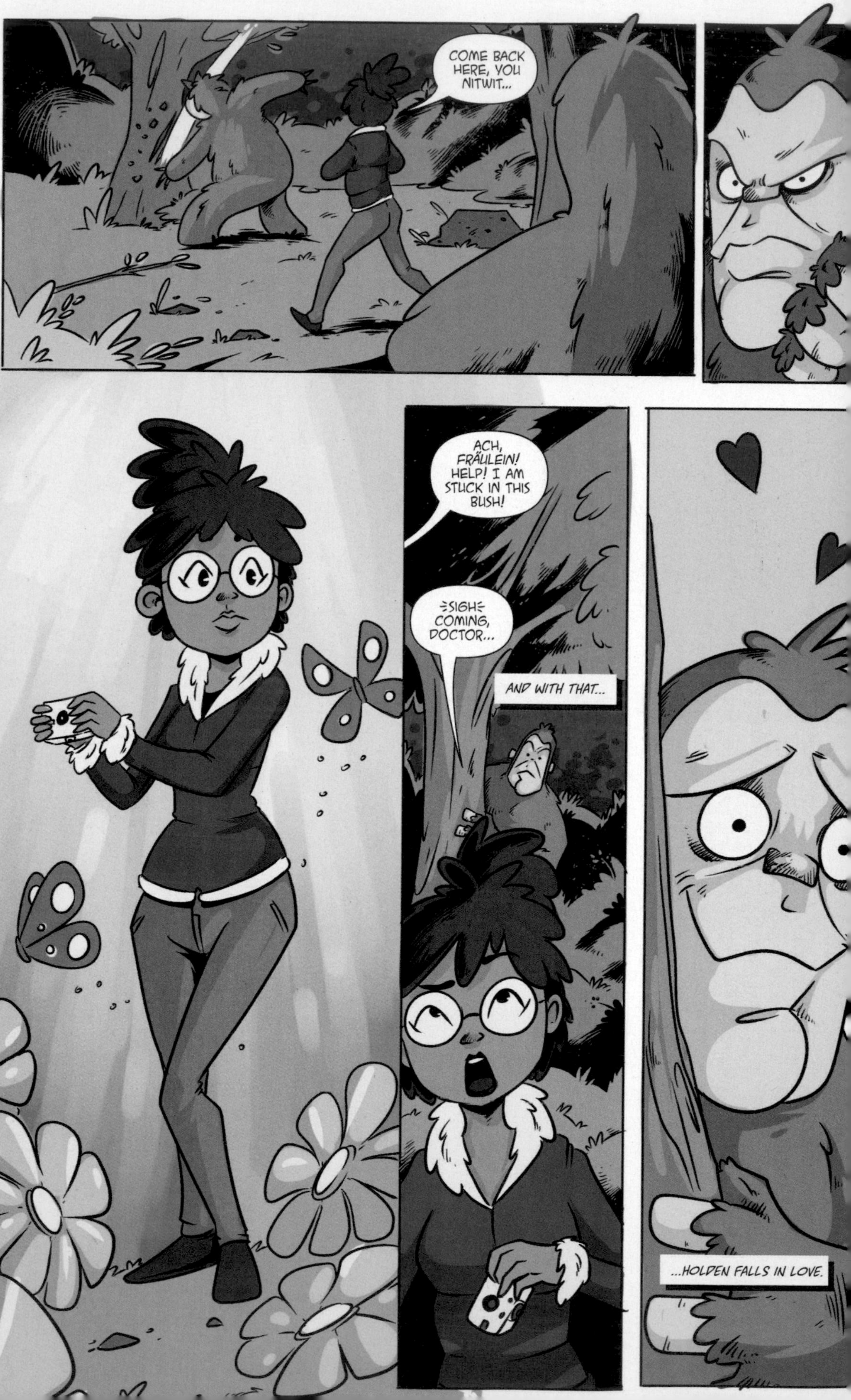
COME BACK HERE, YOU NITWIT...
ACH, FRÄULEIN! HELP! I AM STUCK IN THIS BUSH!
=SIGH= COMING, DOCTOR...
AND WITH THAT...
...HOLDEN FALLS IN LOVE.

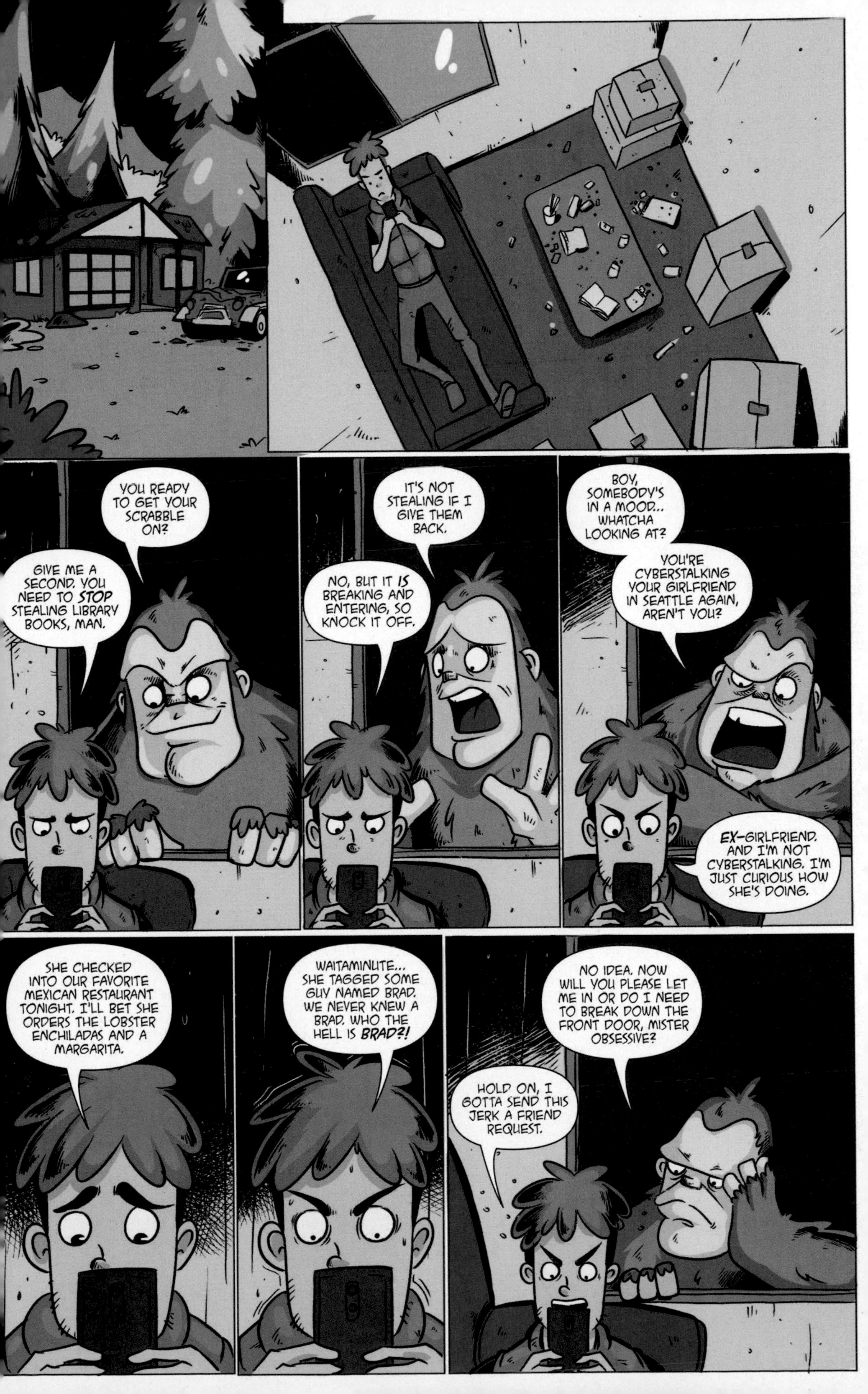

YOU READY TO GET YOUR SCRABBLE ON?
GIVE ME A SECOND. YOU NEED TO STOP STEALING LIBRARY BOOKS, MAN.
IT'S NOT STEALING IF I GIVE THEM BACK.
NO, BUT IT IS BREAKING AND ENTERING, SO KNOCK IT OFF.
BOY, SOMEBODY'S IN A MOOD... WHATCHA LOOKING AT?
YOU'RE CYBERSTALKING YOUR GIRLFRIEND IN SEATTLE AGAIN, AREN'T YOU?
EX-GIRLFRIEND. AND I'M NOT CYBERSTALKING. I'M JUST CURIOUS HOW SHE'S DOING.
SHE CHECKED INTO OUR FAVORITE MEXICAN RESTAURANT TONIGHT. I'LL BET SHE ORDERS THE LOBSTER ENCHILADAS AND A MARGARITA.
WAITAMINUTE... SHE TAGGED SOME GUY NAMED BRAD. WE NEVER KNEW A BRAD. WHO THE HELL IS BRAD?!
NO IDEA. NOW WILL YOU PLEASE LET ME IN OR DO I NEED TO BREAK DOWN THE FRONT DOOR, MISTER OBSESSIVE?
HOLD ON, I GOTTA SEND THIS JERK A FRIEND REQUEST.

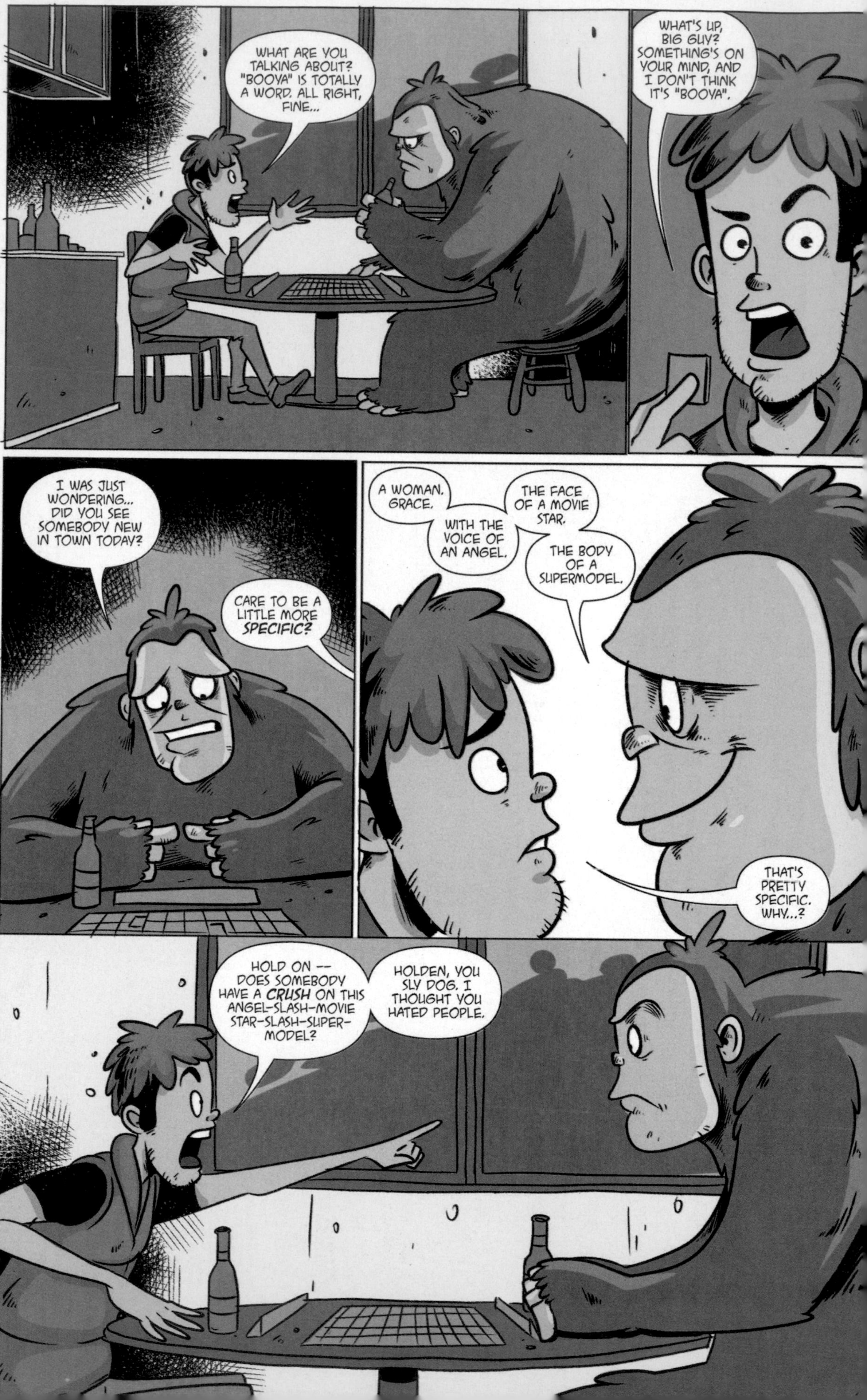
WHAT ARE YOU TALKING ABOUT? "BOOYA" IS TOTALLY A WORD. ALL RIGHT, FINE...
WHAT'S UP, BIG GUY? SOMETHING'S ON YOUR MIND, AND I DON'T THINK IT'S "BOOYA".
I WAS JUST WONDERING... DID YOU SEE SOMEBODY NEW IN TOWN TODAY?
CARE TO BE A LITTLE MORE *SPECIFIC?*
A WOMAN. GRACE.
WITH THE VOICE OF AN ANGEL.
THE FACE OF A MOVIE STAR.
THE BODY OF A SUPERMODEL.
THAT'S PRETTY SPECIFIC. WHY...?
HOLD ON -- DOES SOMEBODY HAVE A **CRUSH** ON THIS ANGEL-SLASH-MOVIE STAR-SLASH-SUPER-MODEL?
HOLDEN, YOU SLY DOG. I THOUGHT YOU HATED PEOPLE.

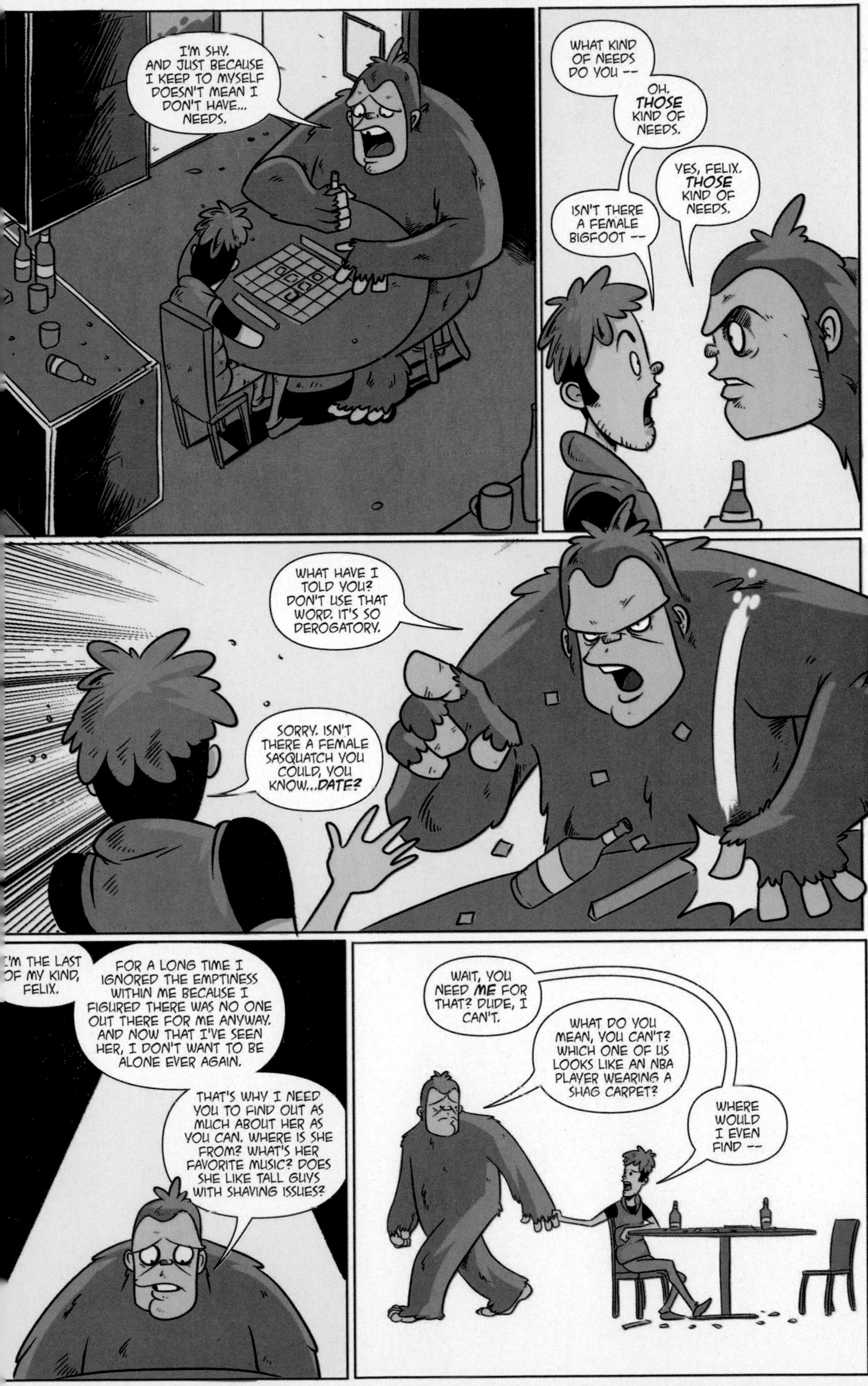
I'M SHY. AND JUST BECAUSE I KEEP TO MYSELF DOESN'T MEAN I DON'T HAVE... NEEDS.
WHAT KIND OF NEEDS DO YOU --
OH. THOSE KIND OF NEEDS.
ISN'T THERE A FEMALE BIGFOOT --
YES, FELIX. THOSE KIND OF NEEDS.
WHAT HAVE I TOLD YOU? DON'T USE THAT WORD. IT'S SO DEROGATORY.
SORRY. ISN'T THERE A FEMALE SASQUATCH YOU COULD, YOU KNOW...DATE?
I'M THE LAST OF MY KIND, FELIX.
FOR A LONG TIME I IGNORED THE EMPTINESS WITHIN ME BECAUSE I FIGURED THERE WAS NO ONE OUT THERE FOR ME ANYWAY. AND NOW THAT I'VE SEEN HER, I DON'T WANT TO BE ALONE EVER AGAIN.
THAT'S WHY I NEED YOU TO FIND OUT AS MUCH ABOUT HER AS YOU CAN. WHERE IS SHE FROM? WHAT'S HER FAVORITE MUSIC? DOES SHE LIKE TALL GUYS WITH SHAVING ISSUES?
WAIT, YOU NEED ME FOR THAT? DUDE, I CAN'T.
WHAT DO YOU MEAN, YOU CAN'T? WHICH ONE OF US LOOKS LIKE AN NBA PLAYER WEARING A SHAG CARPET?
WHERE WOULD I EVEN FIND --

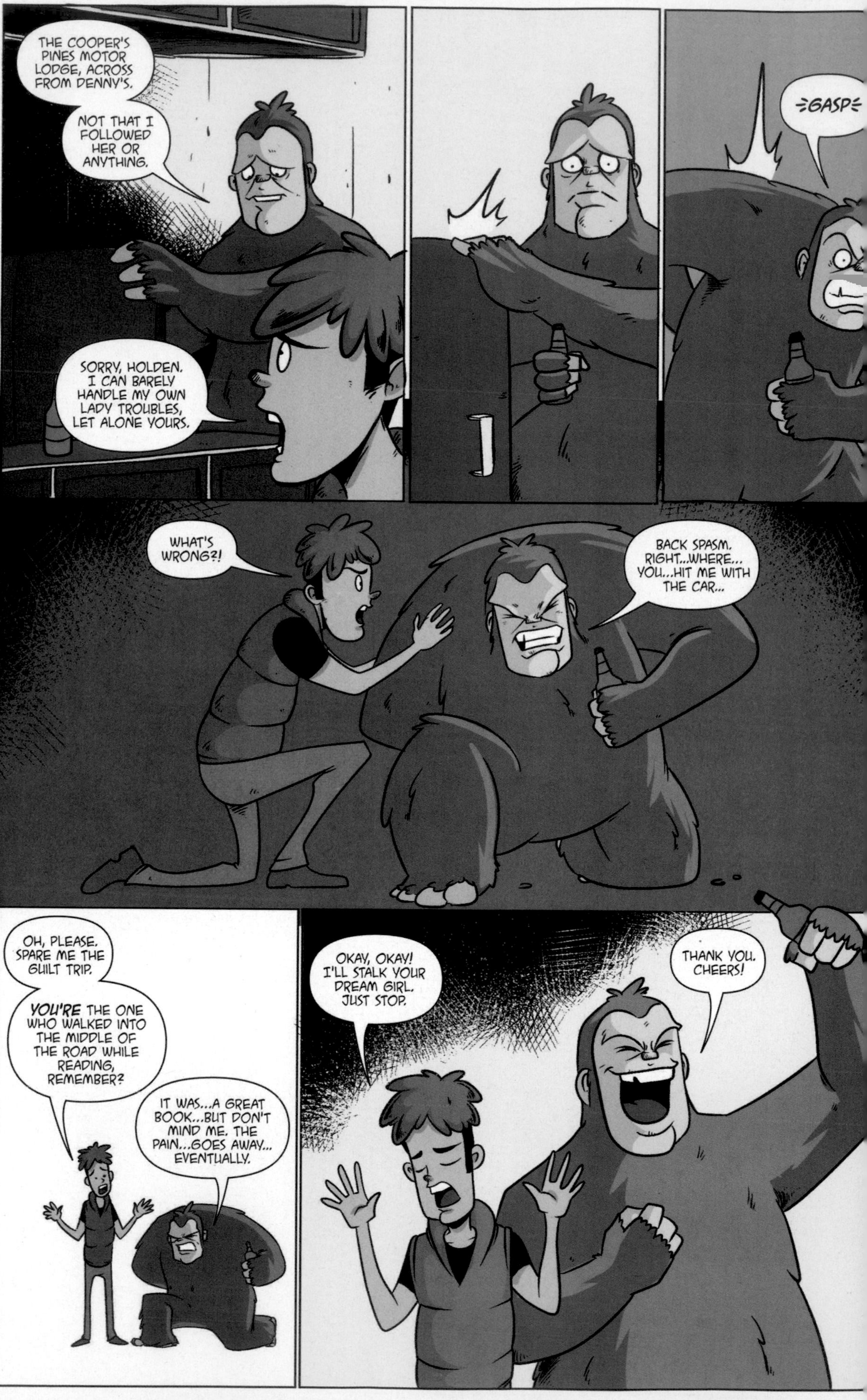
THE COOPER'S PINES MOTOR LODGE, ACROSS FROM DENNY'S.
NOT THAT I FOLLOWED HER OR ANYTHING.
SORRY, HOLDEN. I CAN BARELY HANDLE MY OWN LADY TROUBLES, LET ALONE YOURS.
GASP
WHAT'S WRONG?!
BACK SPASM. RIGHT...WHERE... YOU...HIT ME WITH THE CAR...
OH, PLEASE. SPARE ME THE GUILT TRIP.
YOU'RE THE ONE WHO WALKED INTO THE MIDDLE OF THE ROAD WHILE READING, REMEMBER?
IT WAS...A GREAT BOOK...BUT DON'T MIND ME. THE PAIN...GOES AWAY... EVENTUALLY.
OKAY, OKAY! I'LL STALK YOUR DREAM GIRL. JUST STOP.
THANK YOU. CHEERS!

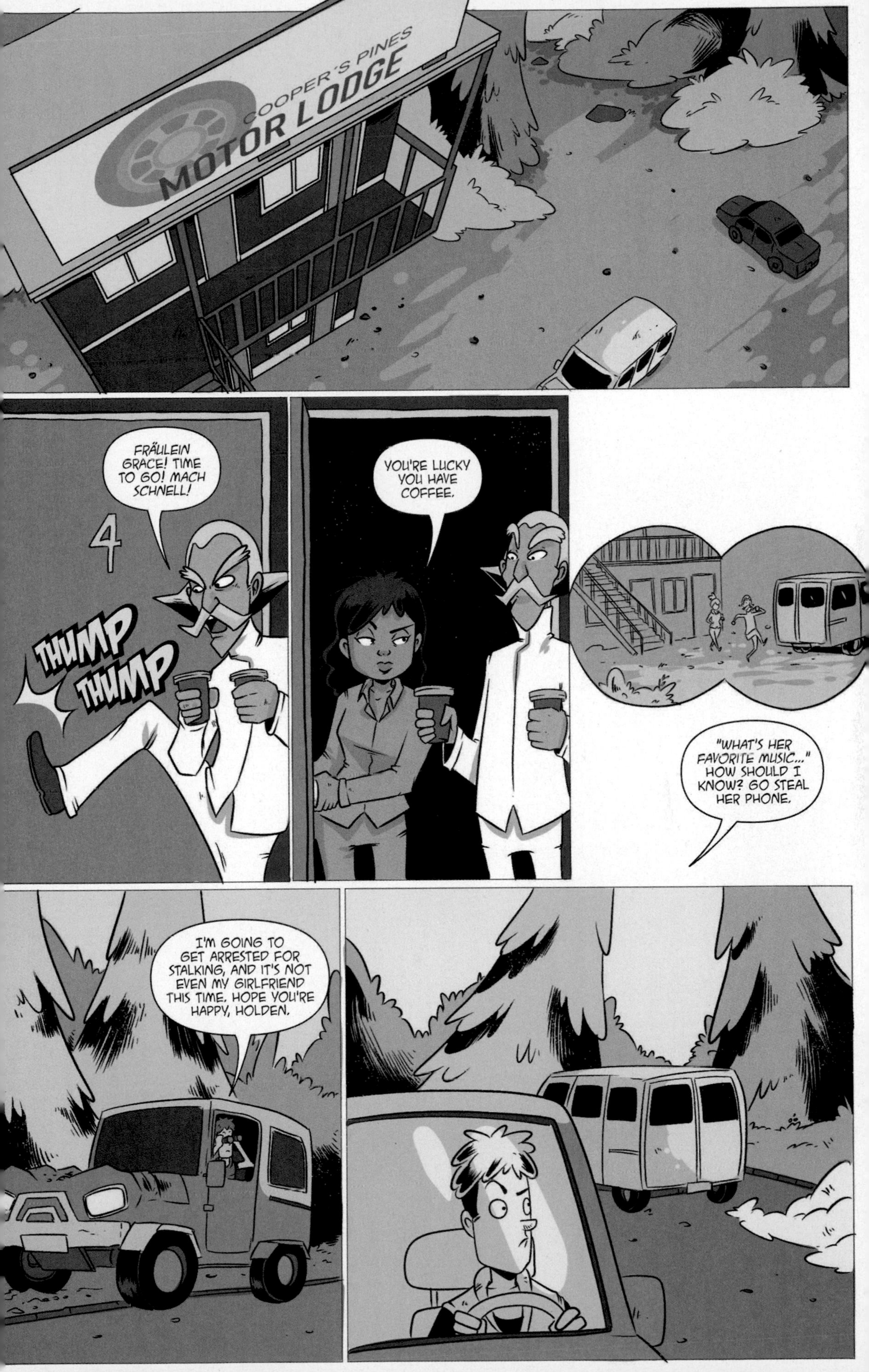

COOPER'S PINES
MOTOR LODGE
FRÄULEIN GRACE! TIME TO GO! MACH SCHNELL!
4
THUMP THUMP
YOU'RE LUCKY YOU HAVE COFFEE.
"WHAT'S HER FAVORITE MUSIC..." HOW SHOULD I KNOW? GO STEAL HER PHONE.
I'M GOING TO GET ARRESTED FOR STALKING, AND IT'S NOT EVEN MY GIRLFRIEND THIS TIME. HOPE YOU'RE HAPPY, HOLDEN.

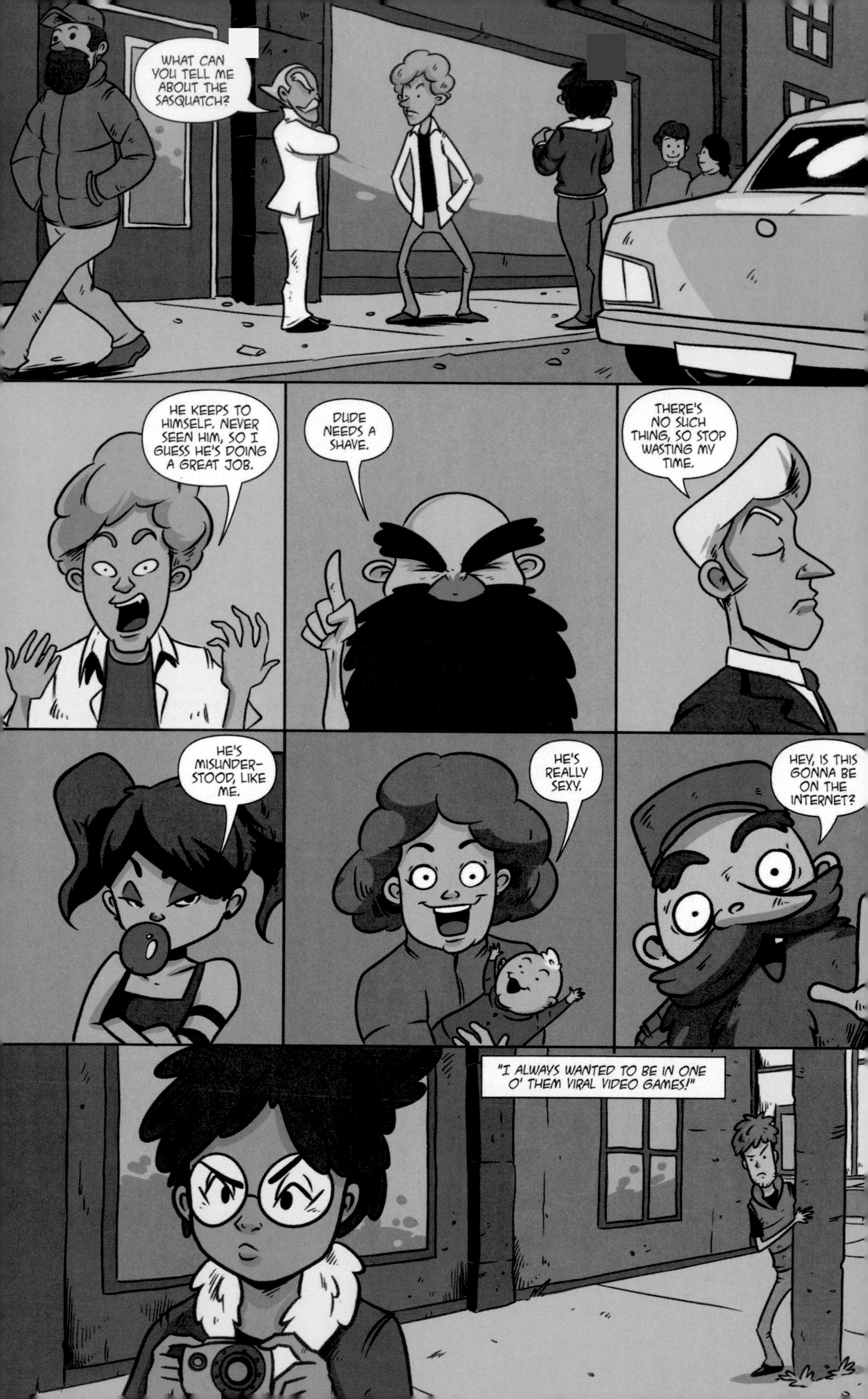
WHAT CAN YOU TELL ME ABOUT THE SASQUATCH?
HE KEEPS TO HIMSELF. NEVER SEEN HIM, SO I GUESS HE'S DOING A GREAT JOB.
DUDE NEEDS A SHAVE.
THERE'S NO SUCH THING, SO STOP WASTING MY TIME.
HE'S MISUNDER-STOOD, LIKE ME.
HE'S REALLY SEXY.
HEY, IS THIS GONNA BE ON THE INTERNET?
"I ALWAYS WANTED TO BE IN ONE O' THEM VIRAL VIDEO GAMES!"

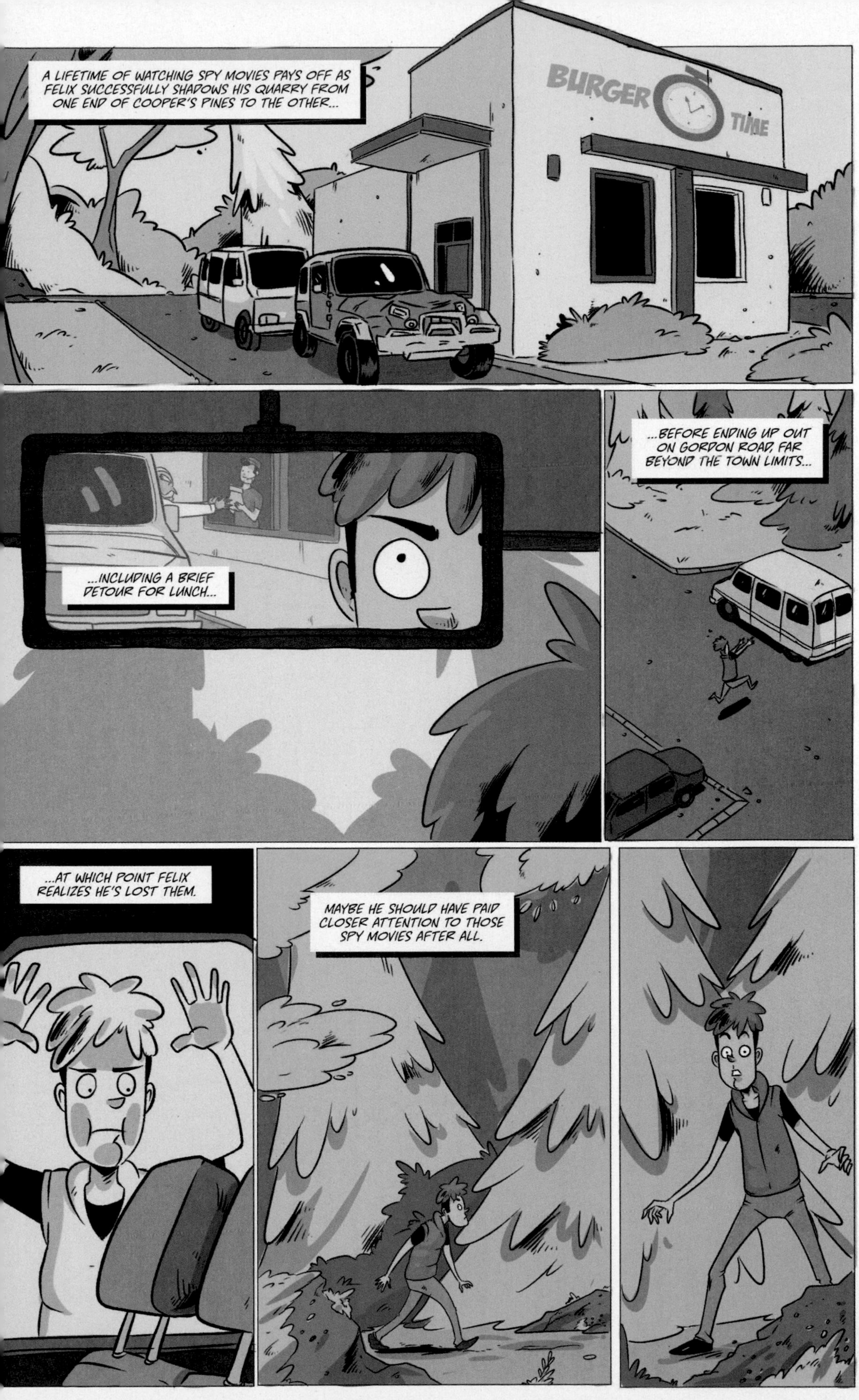
A LIFETIME OF WATCHING SPY MOVIES PAYS OFF AS FELIX SUCCESSFULLY SHADOWS HIS QUARRY FROM ONE END OF COOPER'S PINES TO THE OTHER...
BURGER TIME
...INCLUDING A BRIEF DETOUR FOR LUNCH...
...BEFORE ENDING UP OUT ON GORDON ROAD, FAR BEYOND THE TOWN LIMITS...
...AT WHICH POINT FELIX REALIZES HE'S LOST THEM.
MAYBE HE SHOULD HAVE PAID CLOSER ATTENTION TO THOSE SPY MOVIES AFTER ALL.

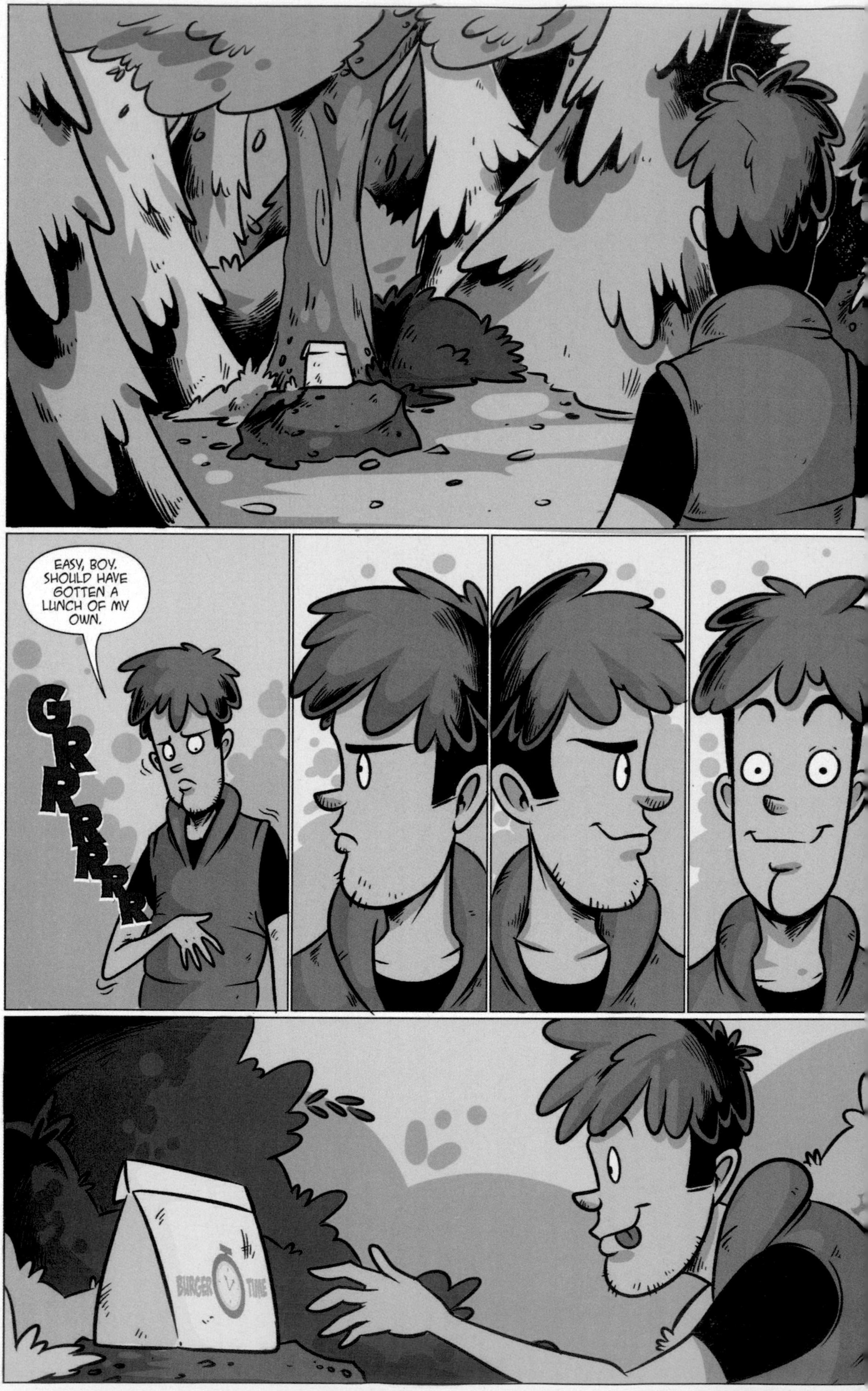
EASY, BOY. SHOULD HAVE GOTTEN A LUNCH OF MY OWN.
GRRRRRR
BURGER TIME

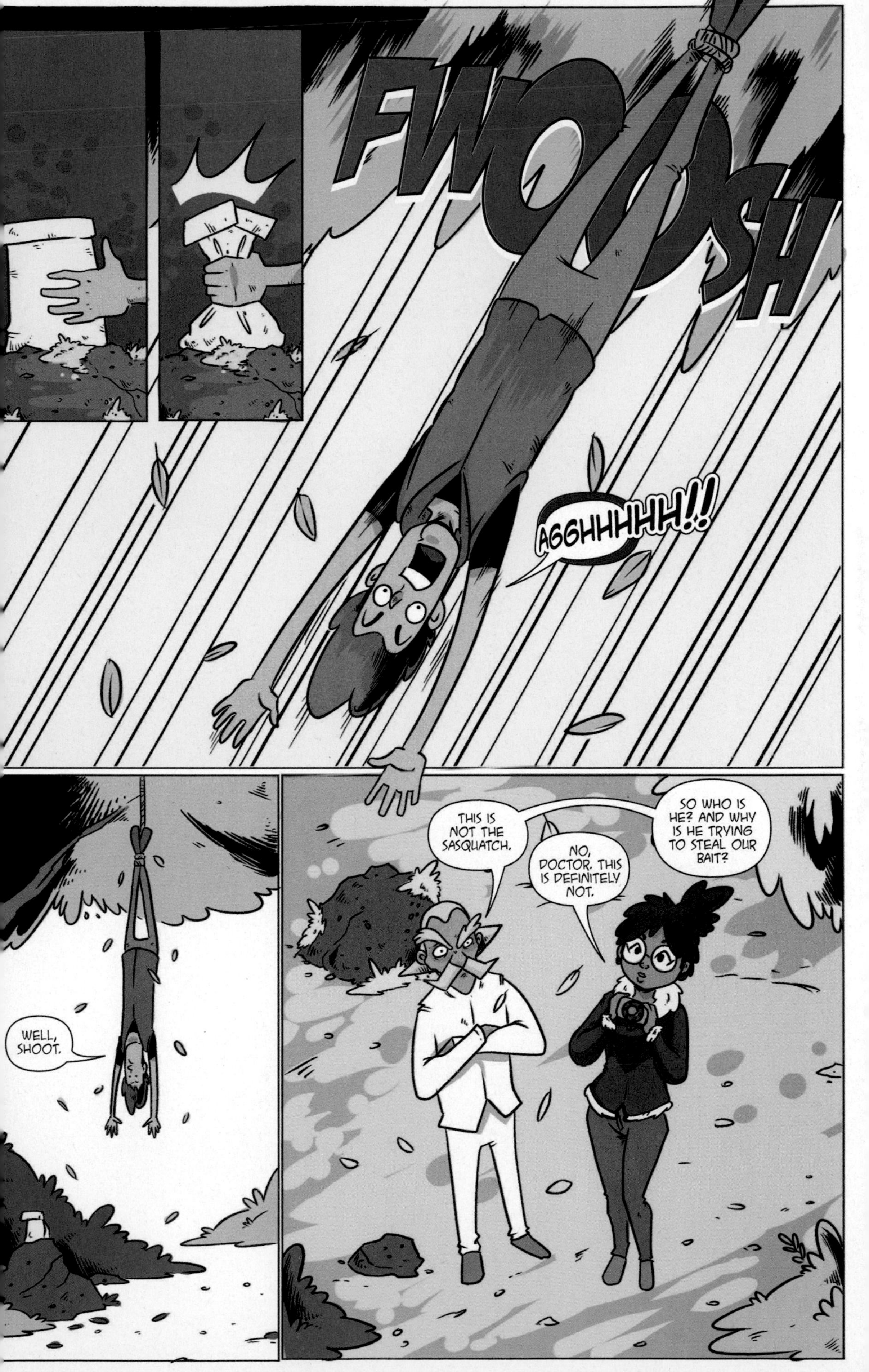
FWOOSH
AGGHHHHH!!
WELL, SHOOT.
THIS IS NOT THE SASQUATCH.
NO, DOCTOR. THIS IS DEFINITELY NOT.
SO WHO IS HE? AND WHY IS HE TRYING TO STEAL OUR BAIT?

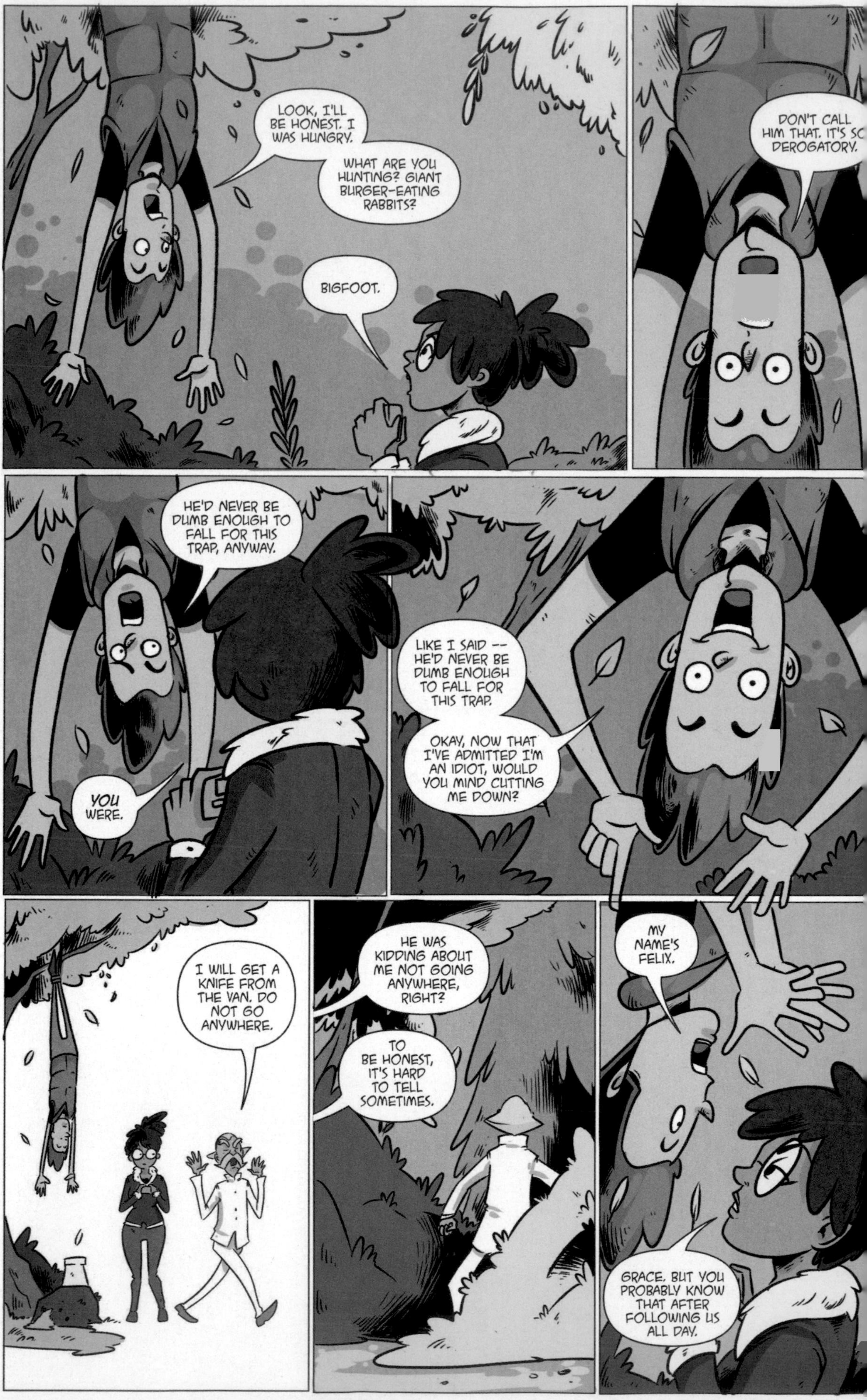
LOOK, I'LL BE HONEST. I WAS HUNGRY.
WHAT ARE YOU HUNTING? GIANT BURGER-EATING RABBITS?
BIGFOOT.
DON'T CALL HIM THAT. IT'S SO DEROGATORY.
HE'D NEVER BE DUMB ENOUGH TO FALL FOR THIS TRAP, ANYWAY.
YOU WERE.
LIKE I SAID -- HE'D NEVER BE DUMB ENOUGH TO FALL FOR THIS TRAP.
OKAY, NOW THAT I'VE ADMITTED I'M AN IDIOT, WOULD YOU MIND CUTTING ME DOWN?
I WILL GET A KNIFE FROM THE VAN. DO NOT GO ANYWHERE.
HE WAS KIDDING ABOUT ME NOT GOING ANYWHERE, RIGHT?
TO BE HONEST, IT'S HARD TO TELL SOMETIMES.
MY NAME'S FELIX.
GRACE. BUT YOU PROBABLY KNOW THAT AFTER FOLLOWING US ALL DAY.

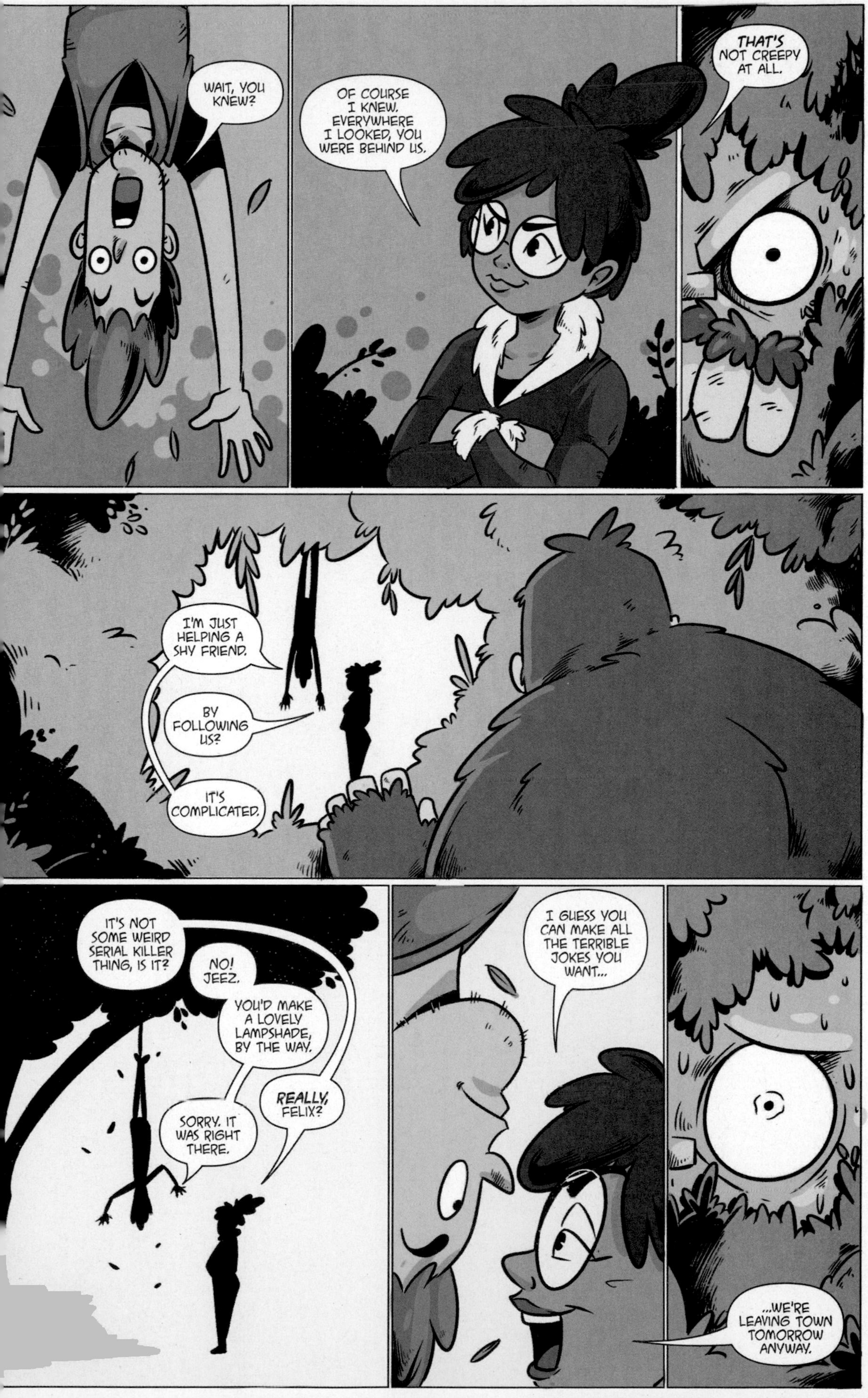
WAIT, YOU KNEW?
OF COURSE I KNEW. EVERYWHERE I LOOKED, YOU WERE BEHIND US.
THAT'S NOT CREEPY AT ALL.
I'M JUST HELPING A SHY FRIEND.
BY FOLLOWING US?
IT'S COMPLICATED.
IT'S NOT SOME WEIRD SERIAL KILLER THING, IS IT?
NO! JEEZ.
YOU'D MAKE A LOVELY LAMPSHADE, BY THE WAY.
SORRY. IT WAS RIGHT THERE.
REALLY, FELIX?
I GUESS YOU CAN MAKE ALL THE TERRIBLE JOKES YOU WANT...
...WE'RE LEAVING TOWN TOMORROW ANYWAY.

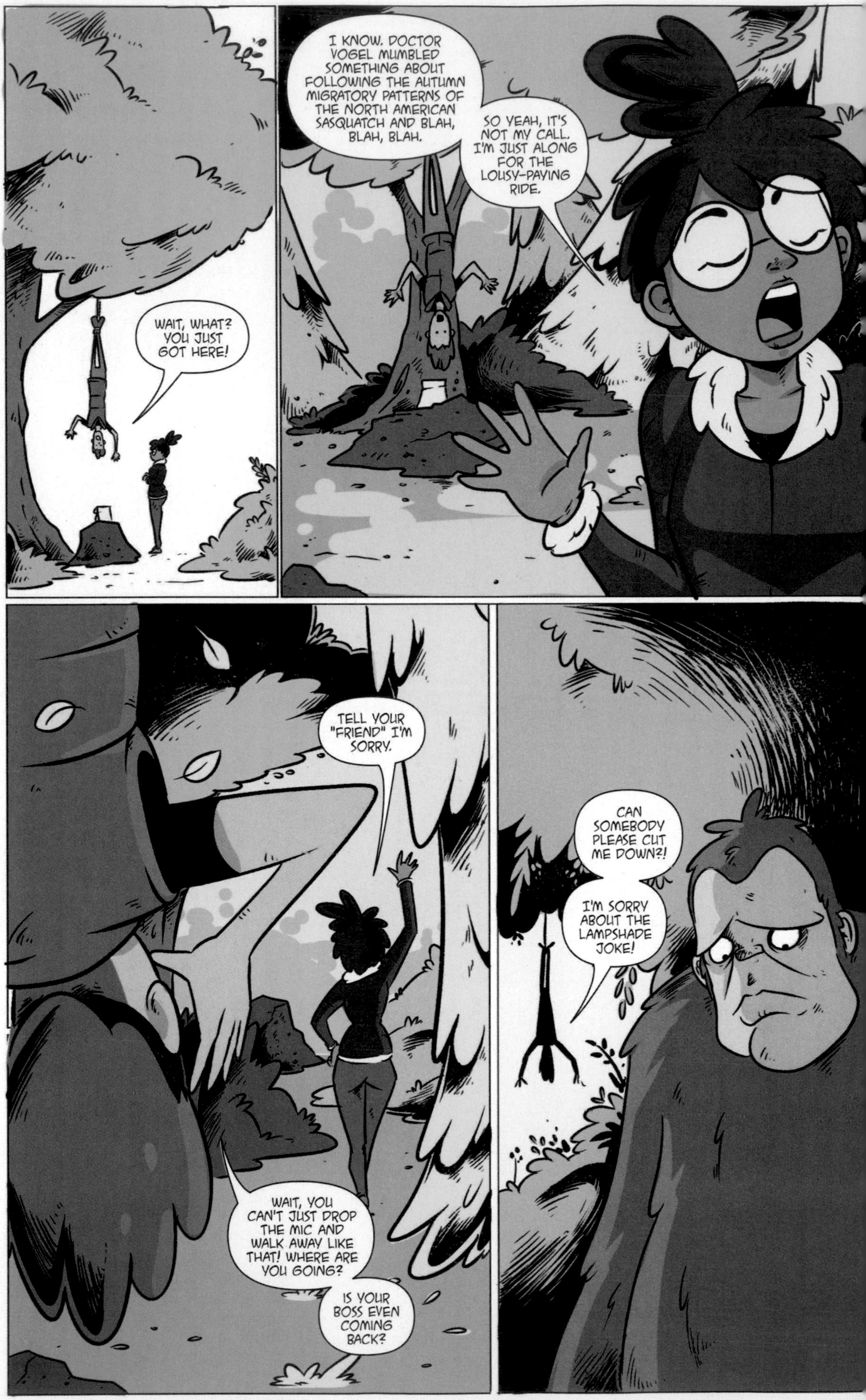
WAIT, WHAT? YOU JUST GOT HERE!
I KNOW. DOCTOR VOGEL MUMBLED SOMETHING ABOUT FOLLOWING THE AUTUMN MIGRATORY PATTERNS OF THE NORTH AMERICAN SASQUATCH AND BLAH, BLAH, BLAH.
SO YEAH, IT'S NOT MY CALL. I'M JUST ALONG FOR THE LOUSY-PAYING RIDE.
TELL YOUR "FRIEND" I'M SORRY.
WAIT, YOU CAN'T JUST DROP THE MIC AND WALK AWAY LIKE THAT! WHERE ARE YOU GOING?
IS YOUR BOSS EVEN COMING BACK?
CAN SOMEBODY PLEASE CUT ME DOWN?!
I'M SORRY ABOUT THE LAMPSHADE JOKE!

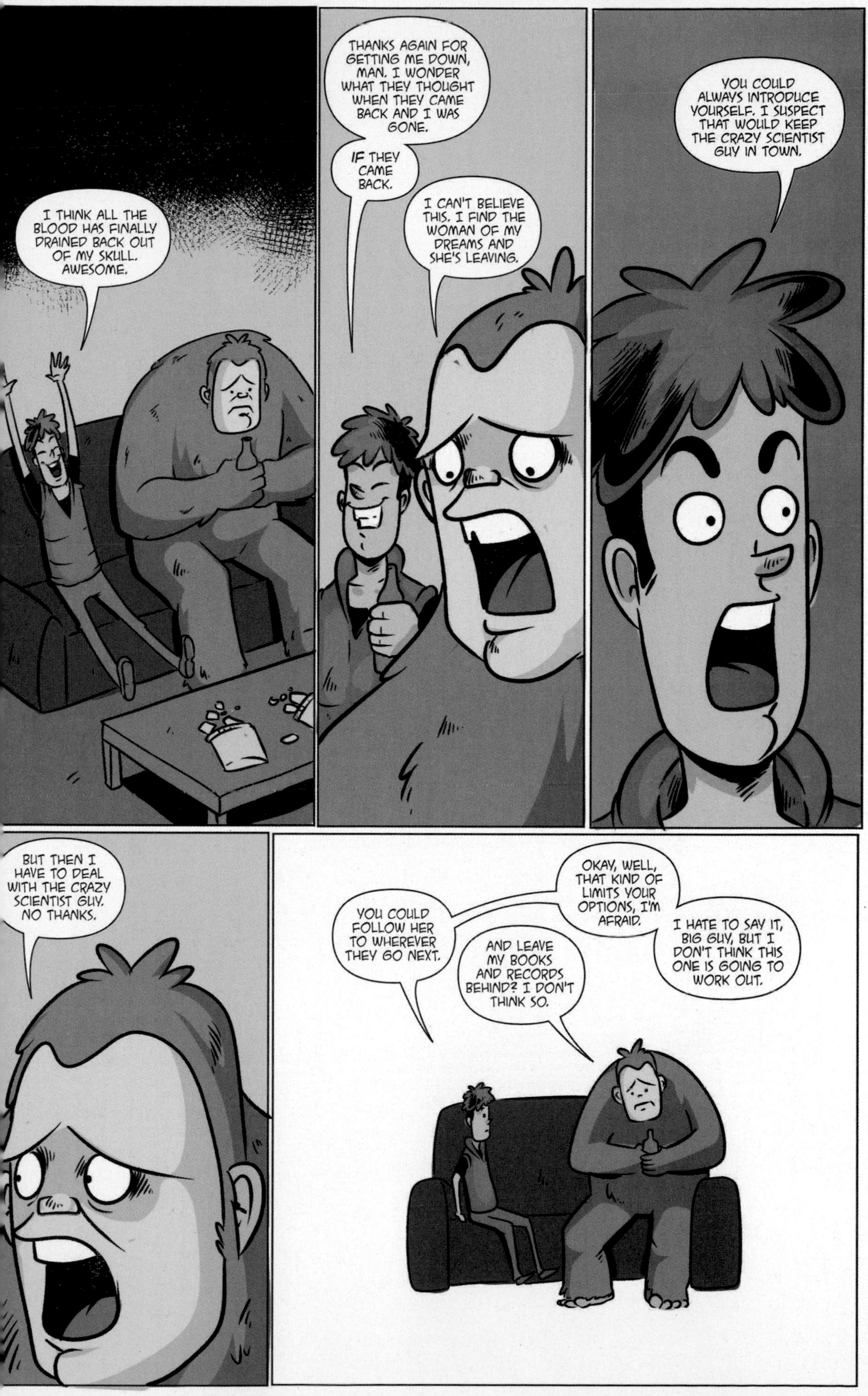
I THINK ALL THE BLOOD HAS FINALLY DRAINED BACK OUT OF MY SKULL. AWESOME.
THANKS AGAIN FOR GETTING ME DOWN, MAN. I WONDER WHAT THEY THOUGHT WHEN THEY CAME BACK AND I WAS GONE.
IF THEY CAME BACK.
I CAN'T BELIEVE THIS. I FIND THE WOMAN OF MY DREAMS AND SHE'S LEAVING.
YOU COULD ALWAYS INTRODUCE YOURSELF. I SUSPECT THAT WOULD KEEP THE CRAZY SCIENTIST GUY IN TOWN.
BUT THEN I HAVE TO DEAL WITH THE CRAZY SCIENTIST GUY. NO THANKS.
YOU COULD FOLLOW HER TO WHEREVER THEY GO NEXT.
AND LEAVE MY BOOKS AND RECORDS BEHIND? I DON'T THINK SO.
OKAY, WELL, THAT KIND OF LIMITS YOUR OPTIONS, I'M AFRAID.
I HATE TO SAY IT, BIG GUY, BUT I DON'T THINK THIS ONE IS GOING TO WORK OUT.

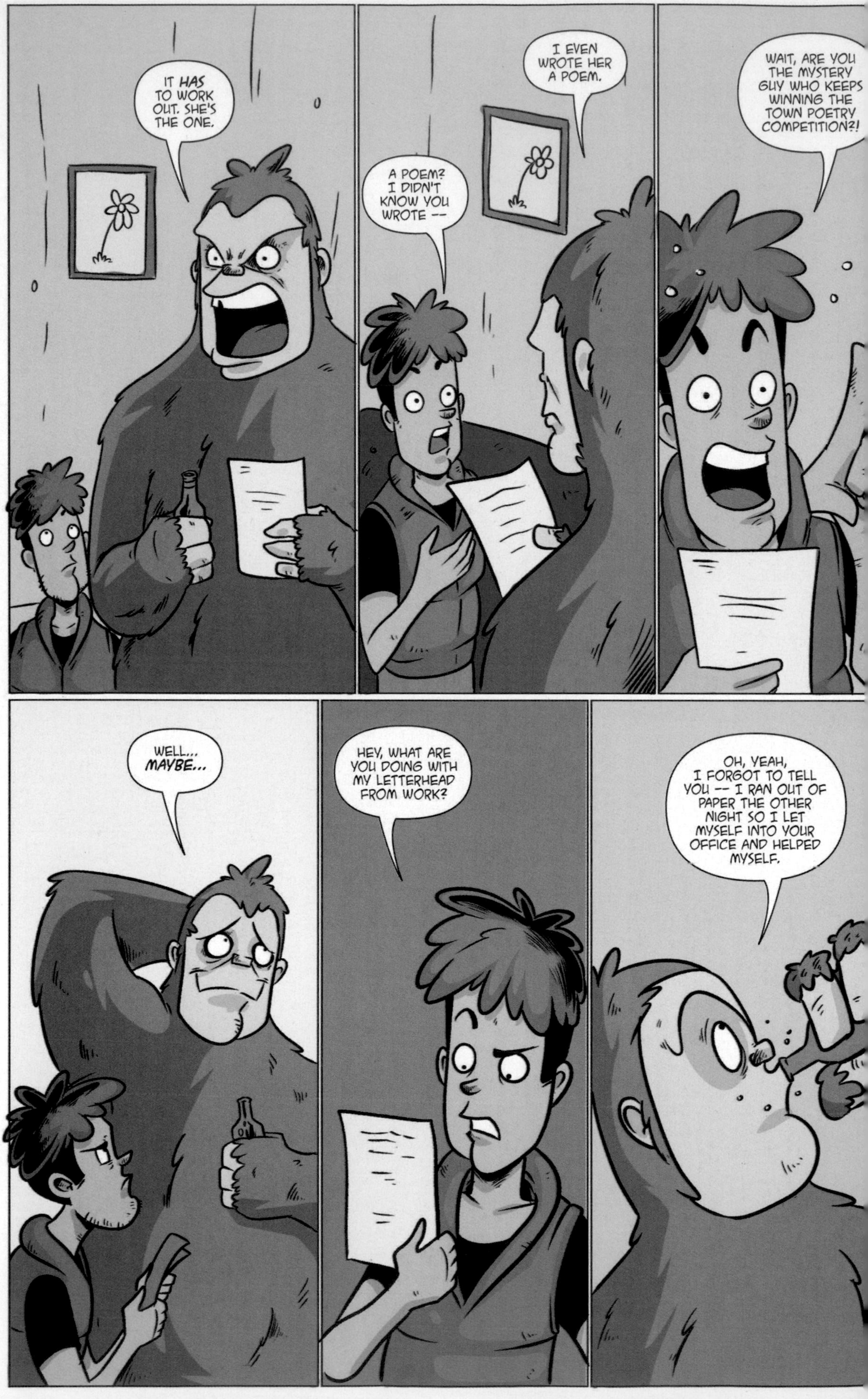
IT HAS TO WORK OUT. SHE'S THE ONE.
I EVEN WROTE HER A POEM.
A POEM? I DIDN'T KNOW YOU WROTE --
WAIT, ARE YOU THE MYSTERY GUY WHO KEEPS WINNING THE TOWN POETRY COMPETITION?!
WELL... MAYBE...
HEY, WHAT ARE YOU DOING WITH MY LETTERHEAD FROM WORK?
OH, YEAH, I FORGOT TO TELL YOU -- I RAN OUT OF PAPER THE OTHER NIGHT SO I LET MYSELF INTO YOUR OFFICE AND HELPED MYSELF.

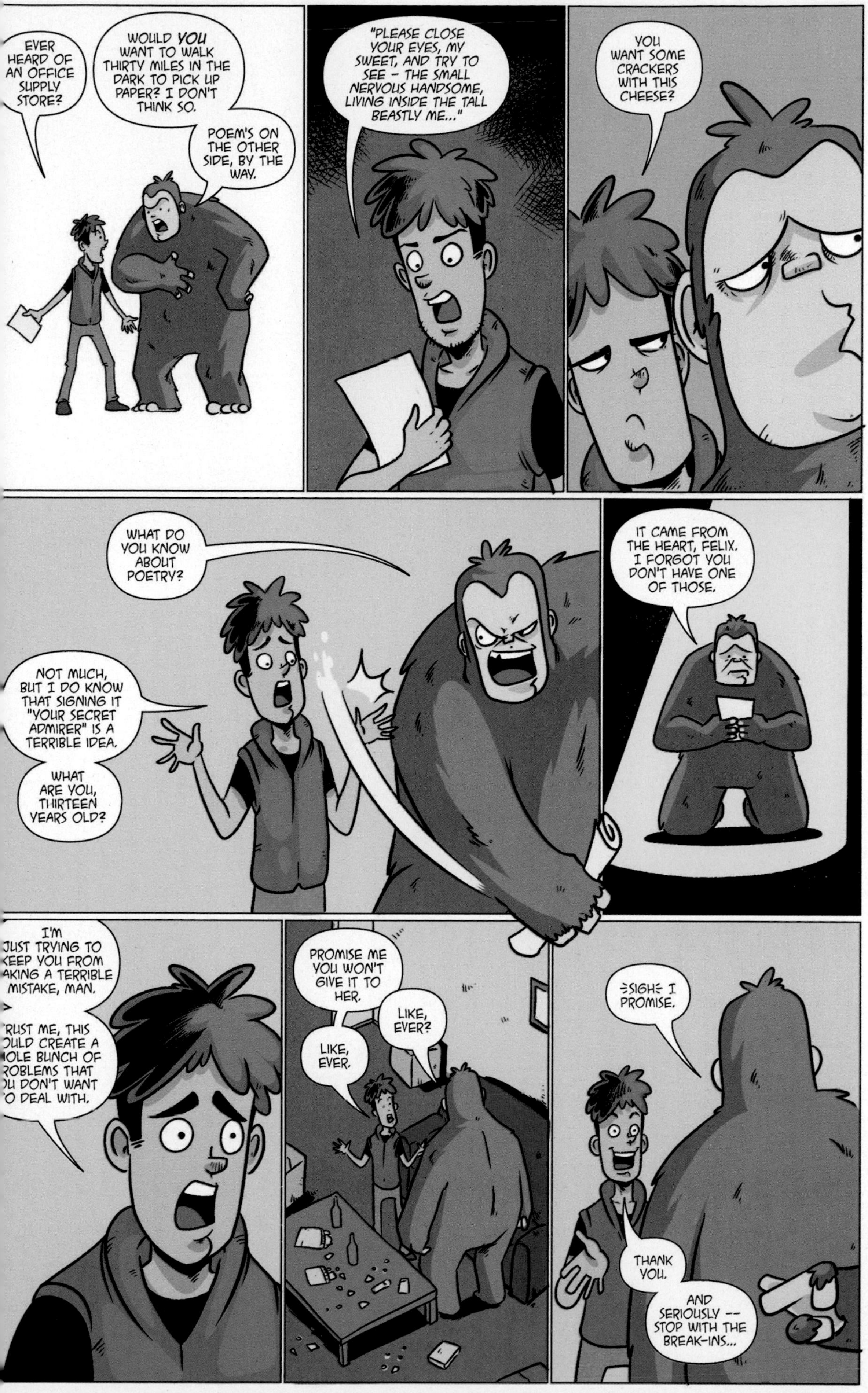
EVER HEARD OF AN OFFICE SUPPLY STORE?
WOULD YOU WANT TO WALK THIRTY MILES IN THE DARK TO PICK UP PAPER? I DON'T THINK SO.
POEM'S ON THE OTHER SIDE, BY THE WAY.
"PLEASE CLOSE YOUR EYES, MY SWEET, AND TRY TO SEE – THE SMALL NERVOUS HANDSOME, LIVING INSIDE THE TALL BEASTLY ME..."
YOU WANT SOME CRACKERS WITH THIS CHEESE?
WHAT DO YOU KNOW ABOUT POETRY?
NOT MUCH, BUT I DO KNOW THAT SIGNING IT "YOUR SECRET ADMIRER" IS A TERRIBLE IDEA.
WHAT ARE YOU, THIRTEEN YEARS OLD?
IT CAME FROM THE HEART, FELIX. I FORGOT YOU DON'T HAVE ONE OF THOSE.
I'M JUST TRYING TO KEEP YOU FROM MAKING A TERRIBLE MISTAKE, MAN.
TRUST ME, THIS COULD CREATE A WHOLE BUNCH OF PROBLEMS THAT YOU DON'T WANT TO DEAL WITH.
PROMISE ME YOU WON'T GIVE IT TO HER.
LIKE, EVER.
LIKE, EVER?
SIGH I PROMISE.
THANK YOU.
AND SERIOUSLY -- STOP WITH THE BREAK-INS...

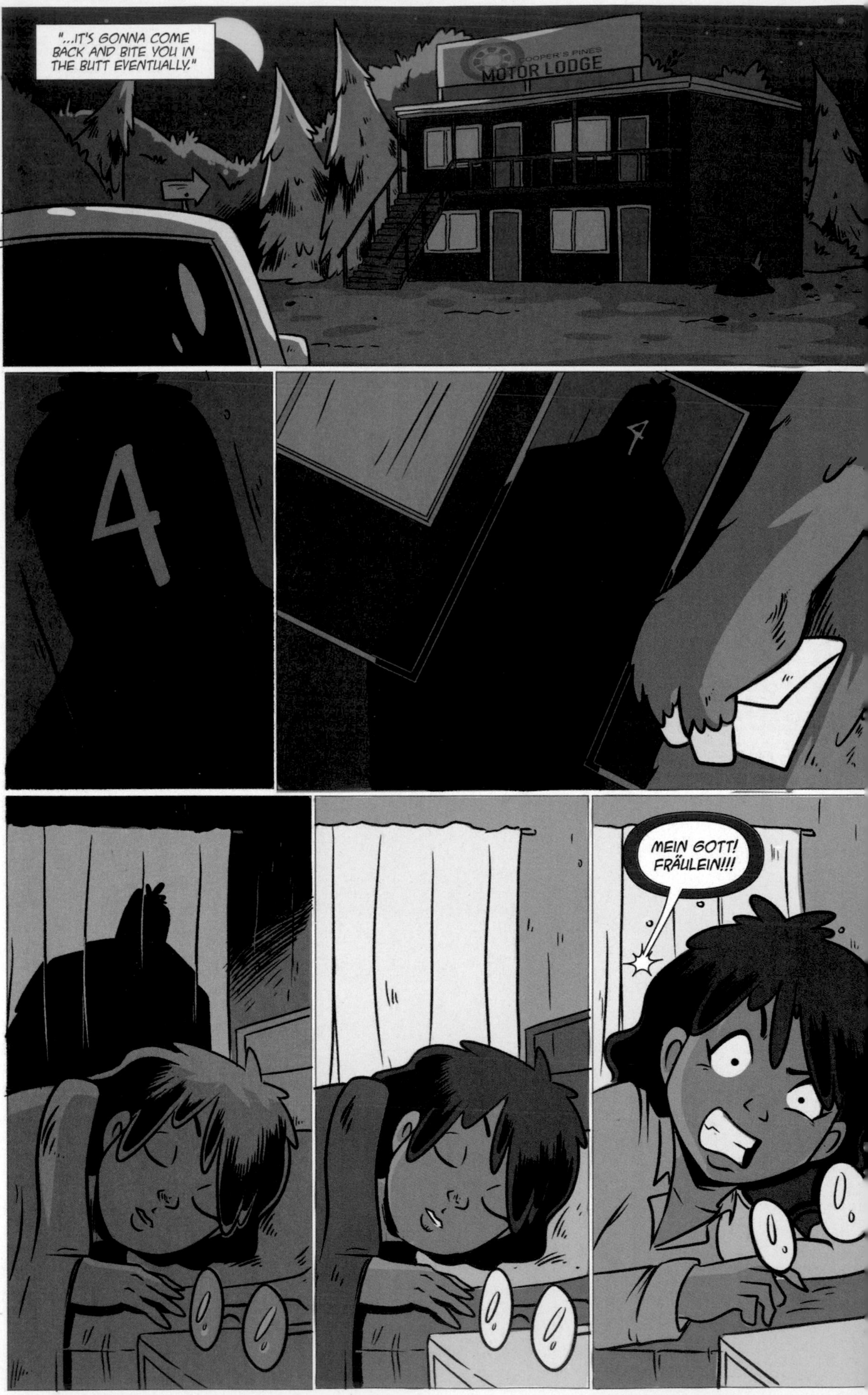
"...IT'S GONNA COME BACK AND BITE YOU IN THE BUTT EVENTUALLY."
COOPER'S PINES MOTOR LODGE
4
MEIN GOTT! FRÄULEIN!!!

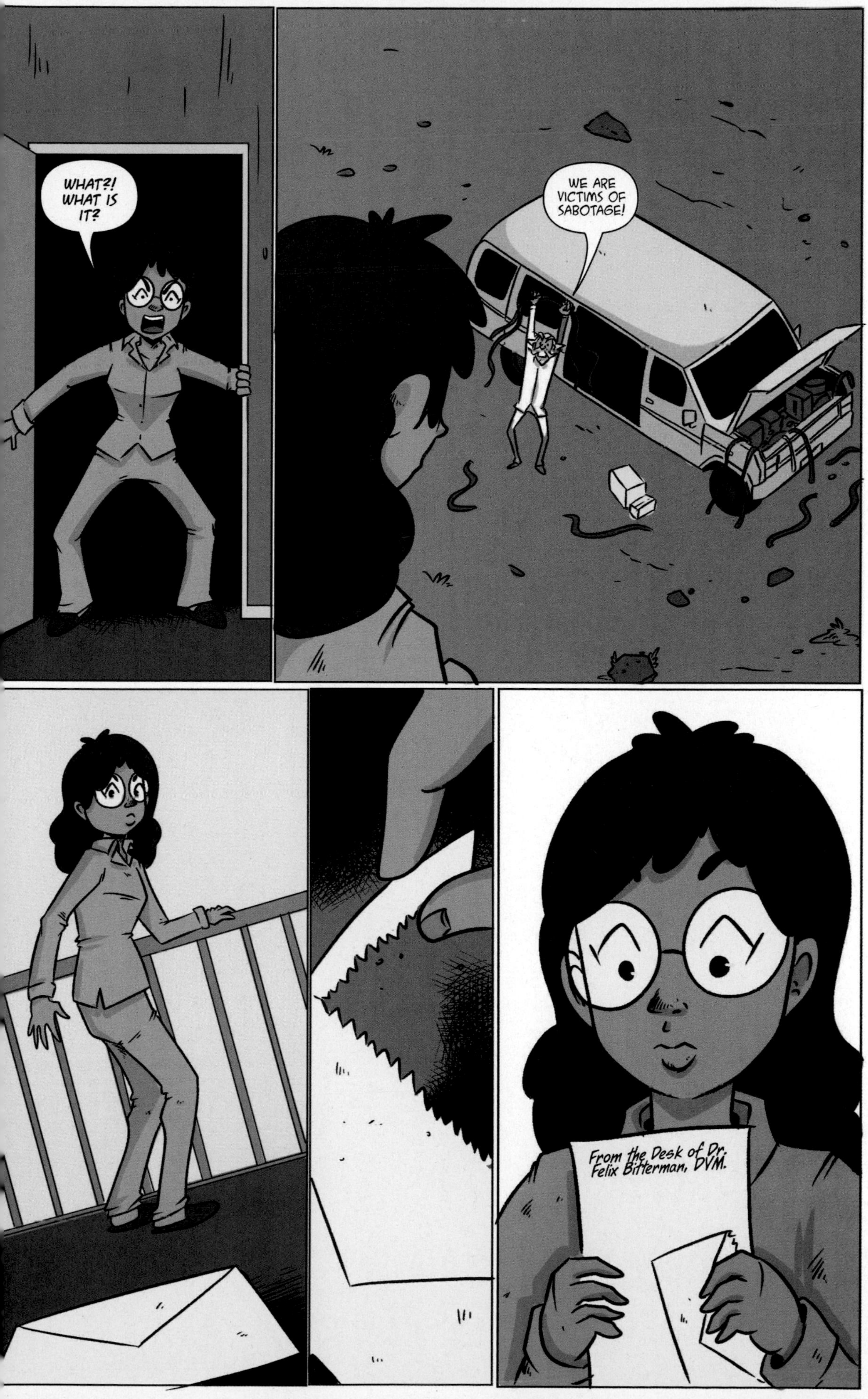
WHAT?! WHAT IS IT?
WE ARE VICTIMS OF SABOTAGE!
From the Desk of Dr. Felix Bitterman, DVM.

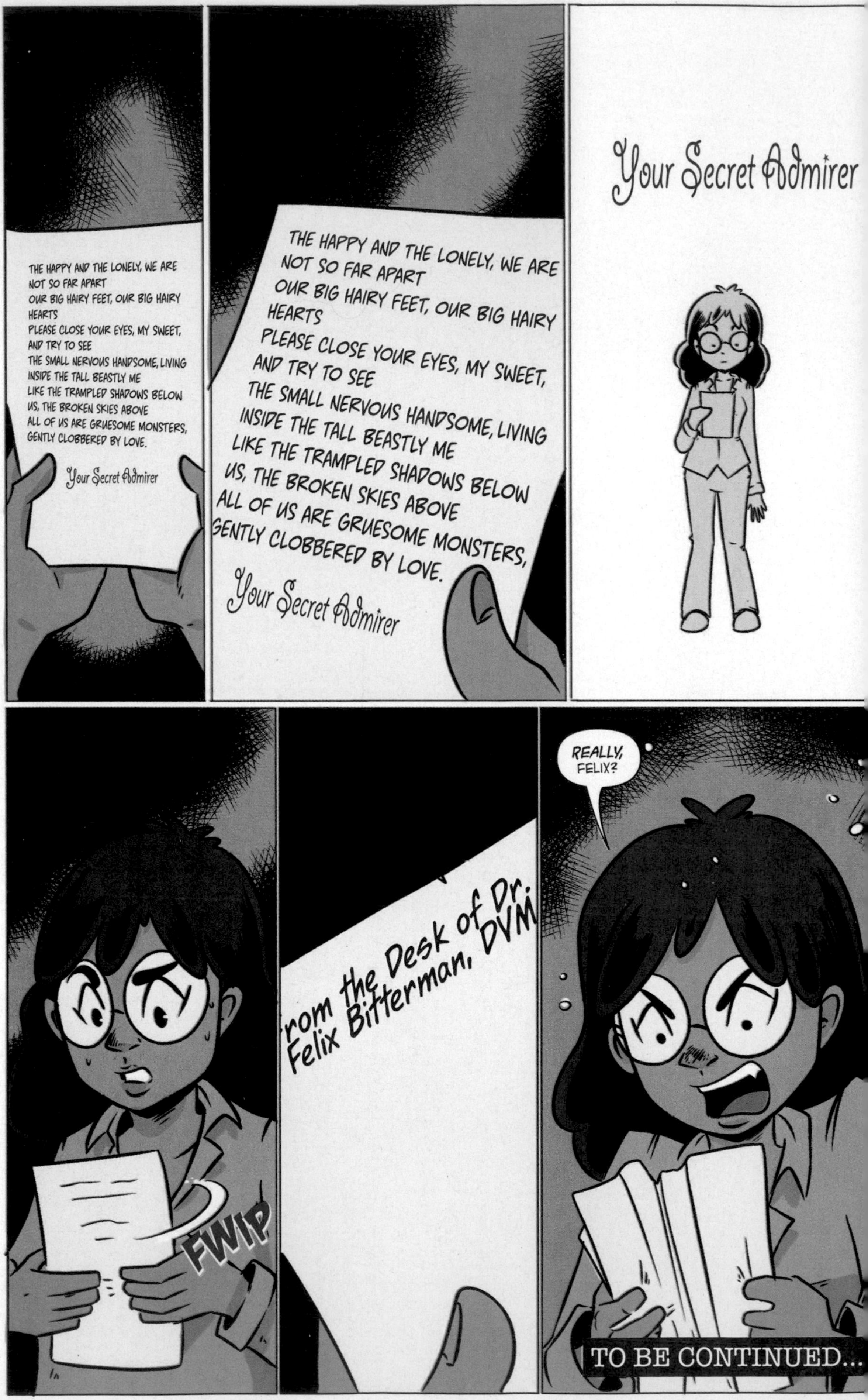

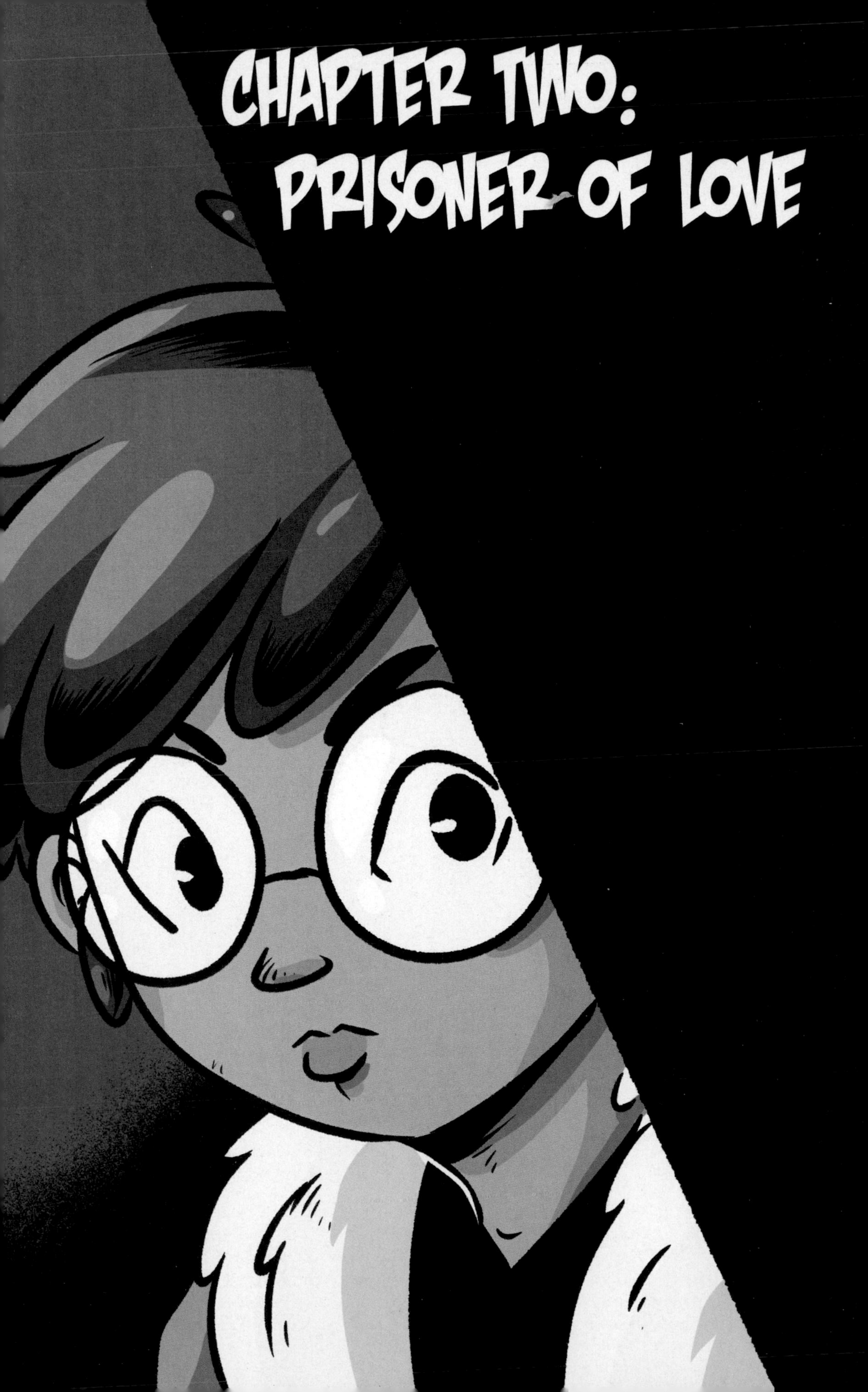
CHAPTER TWO:
PRISONER OF LOVE

SASQUATCH
IN LOVE

JASON NUTT
Writer

ALEXIS VIVALLO
Artist

JOSH SOUTHALL
Letterer

Bryan Seaton: Publisher/CEO
Shawn Gabborin: Editor In Chief
Jason Martin: Publisher-Danger Zone
Nicole D'Andria: Marketing Director/Editor
Danielle Davison: Executive Administrator
Chad Cicconi: Assistant Waffle Taster
Shawn Pryor: President of Creator Relations

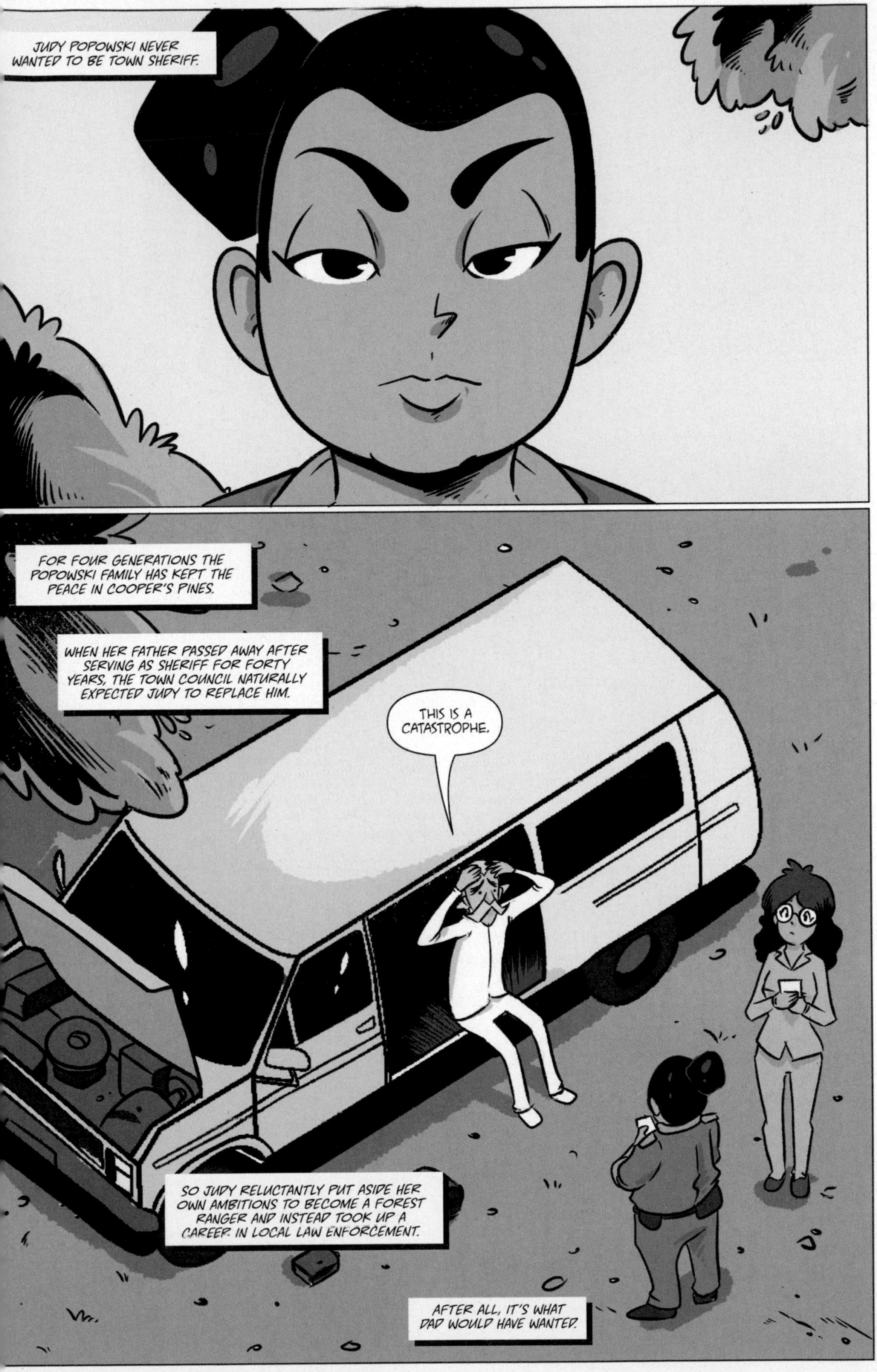
JUDY POPOWSKI NEVER WANTED TO BE TOWN SHERIFF.
FOR FOUR GENERATIONS THE POPOWSKI FAMILY HAS KEPT THE PEACE IN COOPER'S PINES.
WHEN HER FATHER PASSED AWAY AFTER SERVING AS SHERIFF FOR FORTY YEARS, THE TOWN COUNCIL NATURALLY EXPECTED JUDY TO REPLACE HIM.
THIS IS A CATASTROPHE.
SO JUDY RELUCTANTLY PUT ASIDE HER OWN AMBITIONS TO BECOME A FOREST RANGER AND INSTEAD TOOK UP A CAREER IN LOCAL LAW ENFORCEMENT.
AFTER ALL, IT'S WHAT DAD WOULD HAVE WANTED.

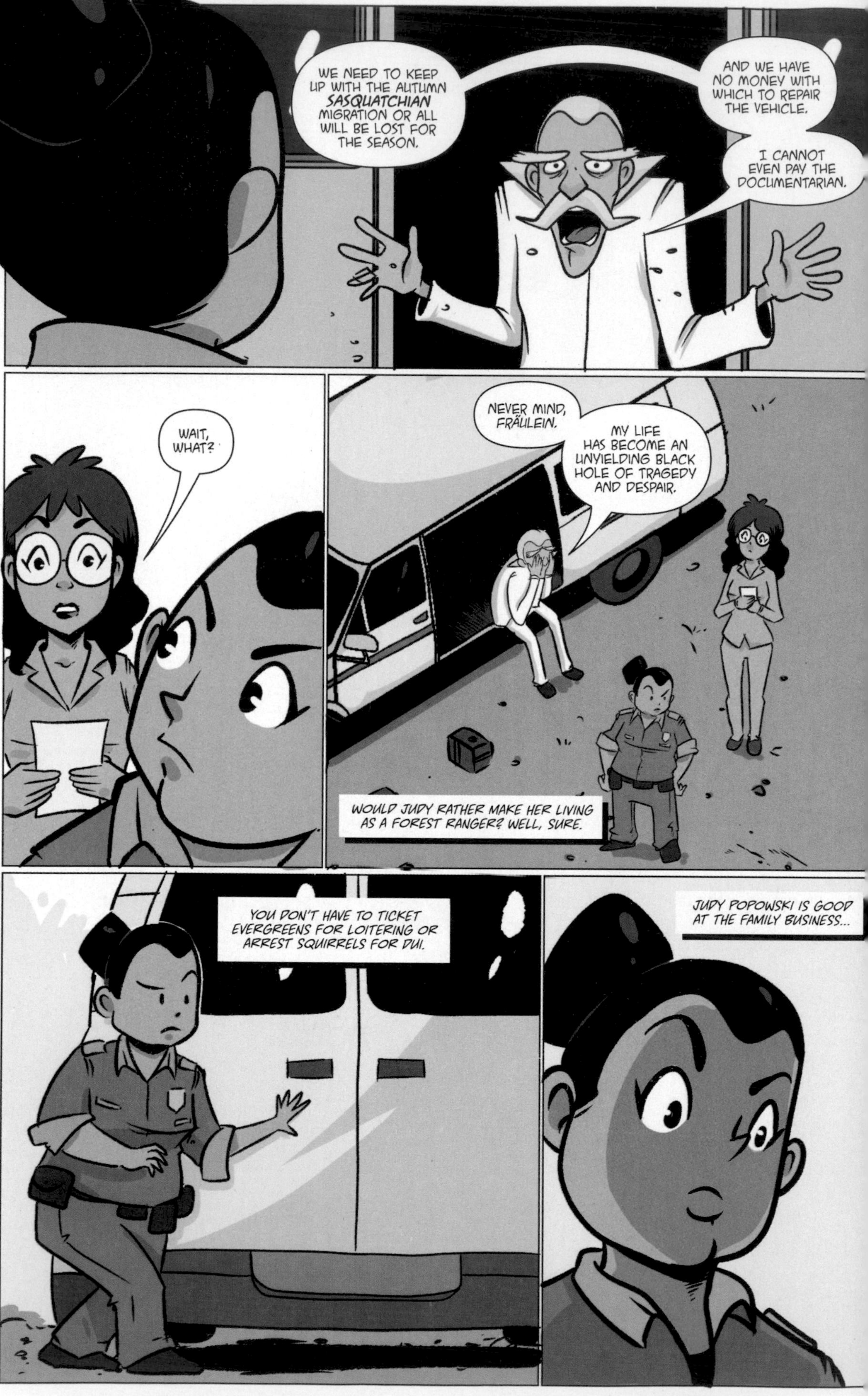
WE NEED TO KEEP UP WITH THE AUTUMN SASQUATCHIAN MIGRATION OR ALL WILL BE LOST FOR THE SEASON.
AND WE HAVE NO MONEY WITH WHICH TO REPAIR THE VEHICLE.
I CANNOT EVEN PAY THE DOCUMENTARIAN.
WAIT, WHAT?
NEVER MIND, FRÄULEIN.
MY LIFE HAS BECOME AN UNYIELDING BLACK HOLE OF TRAGEDY AND DESPAIR.
WOULD JUDY RATHER MAKE HER LIVING AS A FOREST RANGER? WELL, SURE.
YOU DON'T HAVE TO TICKET EVERGREENS FOR LOITERING OR ARREST SQUIRRELS FOR DUI.
JUDY POPOWSKI IS GOOD AT THE FAMILY BUSINESS...

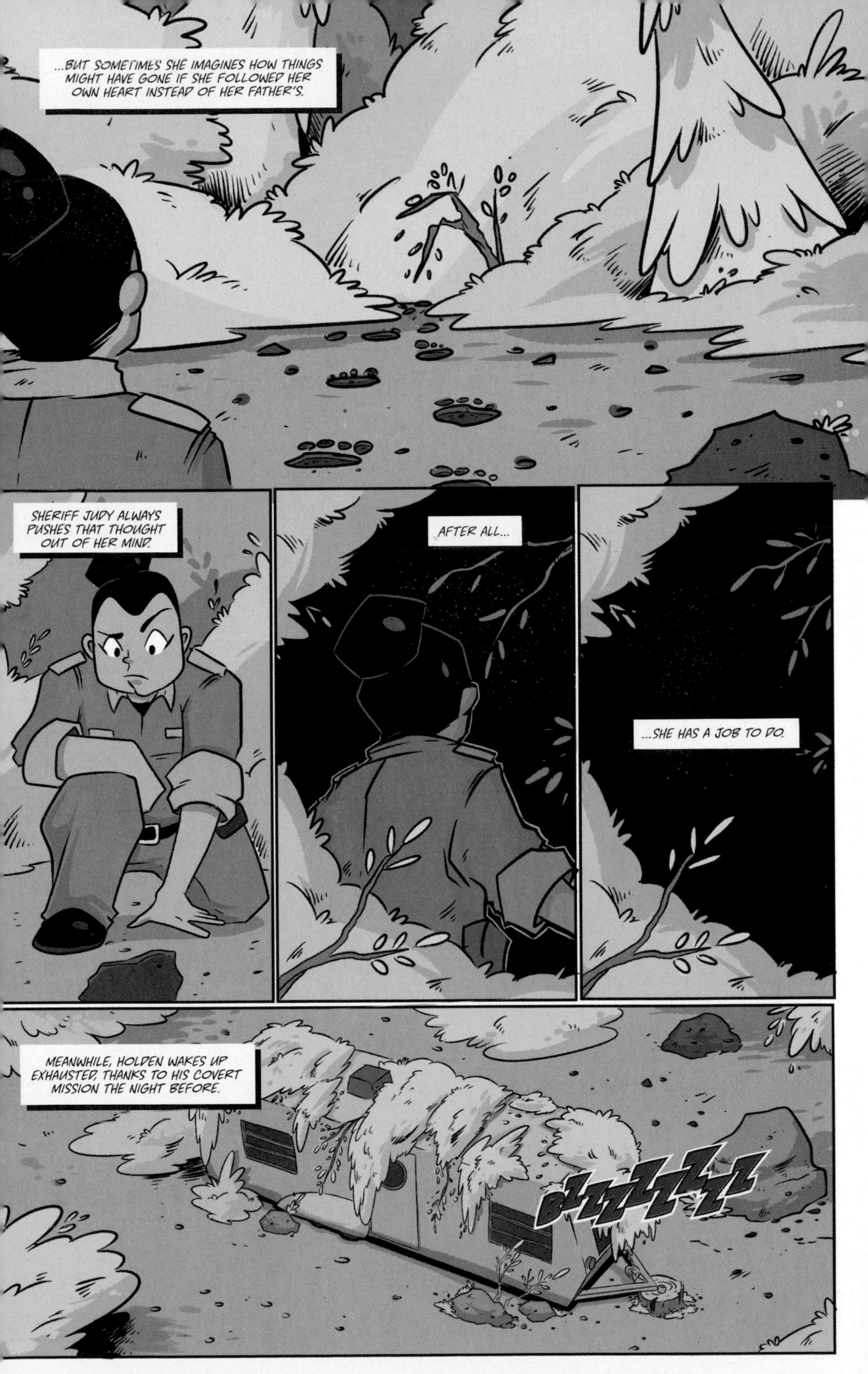
...BUT SOMETIMES SHE IMAGINES HOW THINGS MIGHT HAVE GONE IF SHE FOLLOWED HER OWN HEART INSTEAD OF HER FATHER'S.
SHERIFF JUDY ALWAYS PUSHES THAT THOUGHT OUT OF HER MIND.
AFTER ALL...
...SHE HAS A JOB TO DO.
MEANWHILE, HOLDEN WAKES UP EXHAUSTED, THANKS TO HIS COVERT MISSION THE NIGHT BEFORE.
BZZZZZZZZ

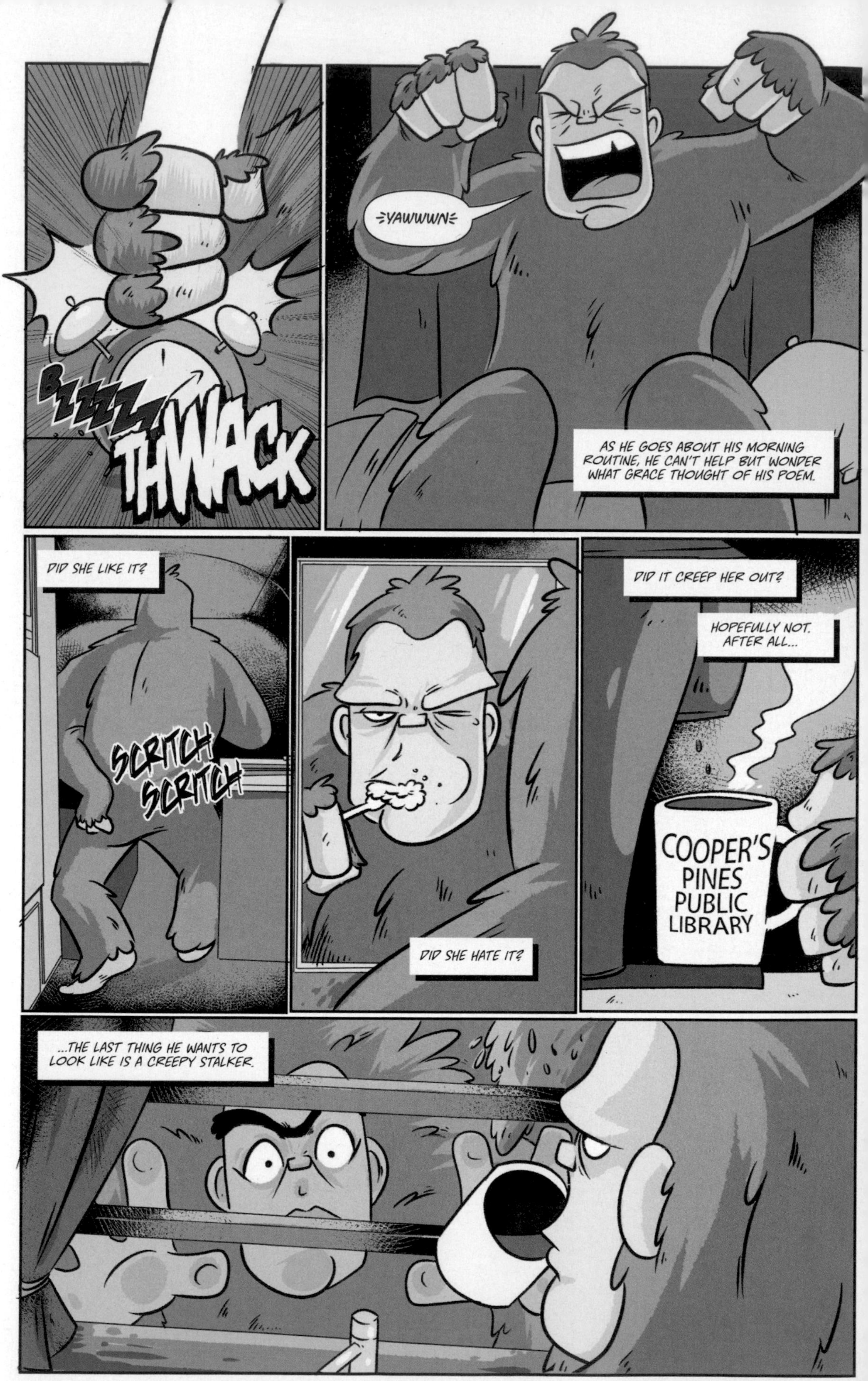
BZZZZ
THWACK
YAWWWN
AS HE GOES ABOUT HIS MORNING ROUTINE, HE CAN'T HELP BUT WONDER WHAT GRACE THOUGHT OF HIS POEM.
DID SHE LIKE IT?
SCRITCH SCRITCH
DID SHE HATE IT?
DID IT CREEP HER OUT?
HOPEFULLY NOT. AFTER ALL...
COOPER'S PINES PUBLIC LIBRARY
...THE LAST THING HE WANTS TO LOOK LIKE IS A CREEPY STALKER.

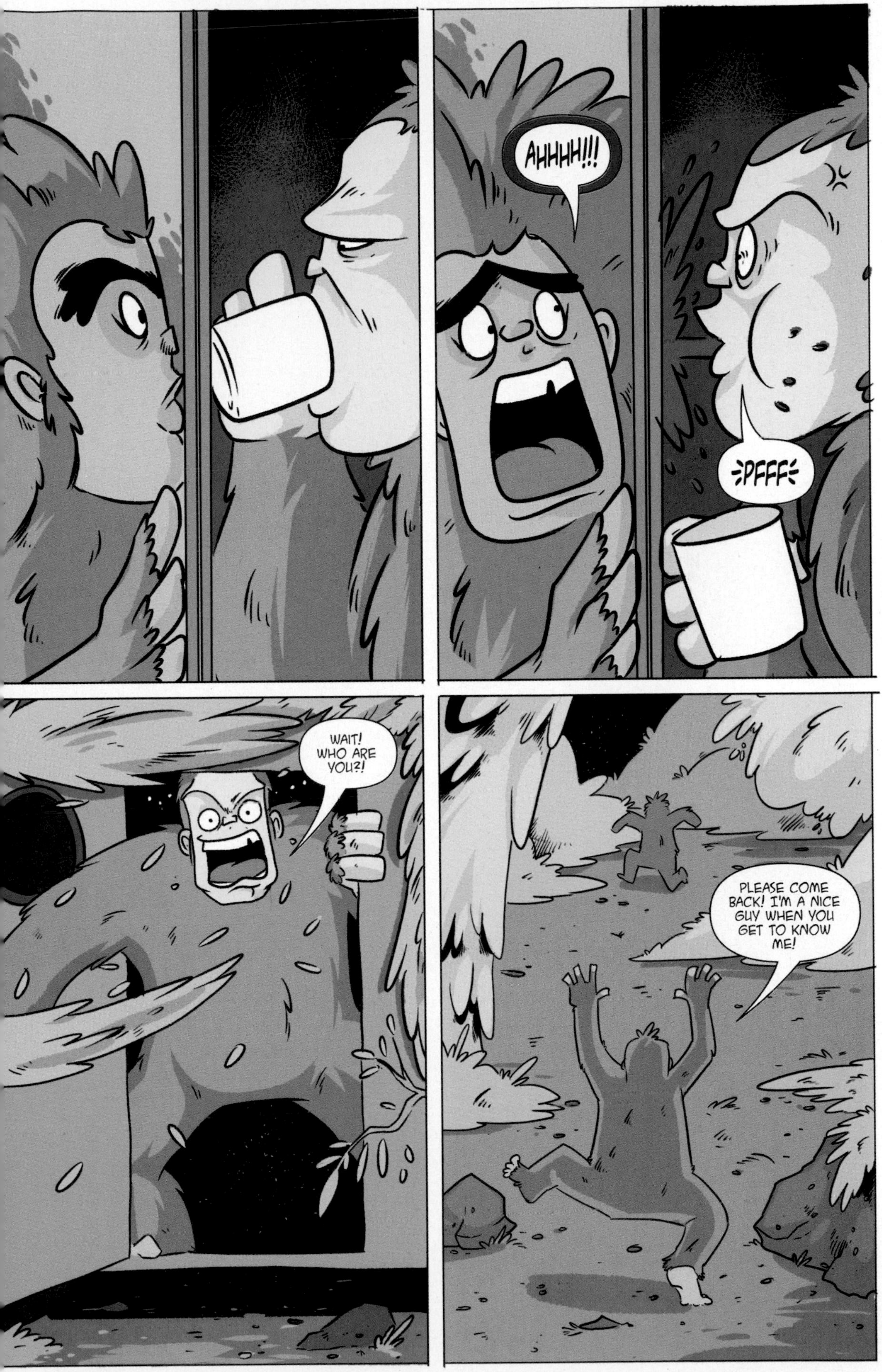
AHHHH!!!
PFFF
WAIT! WHO ARE YOU?!
PLEASE COME BACK! I'M A NICE GUY WHEN YOU GET TO KNOW ME!

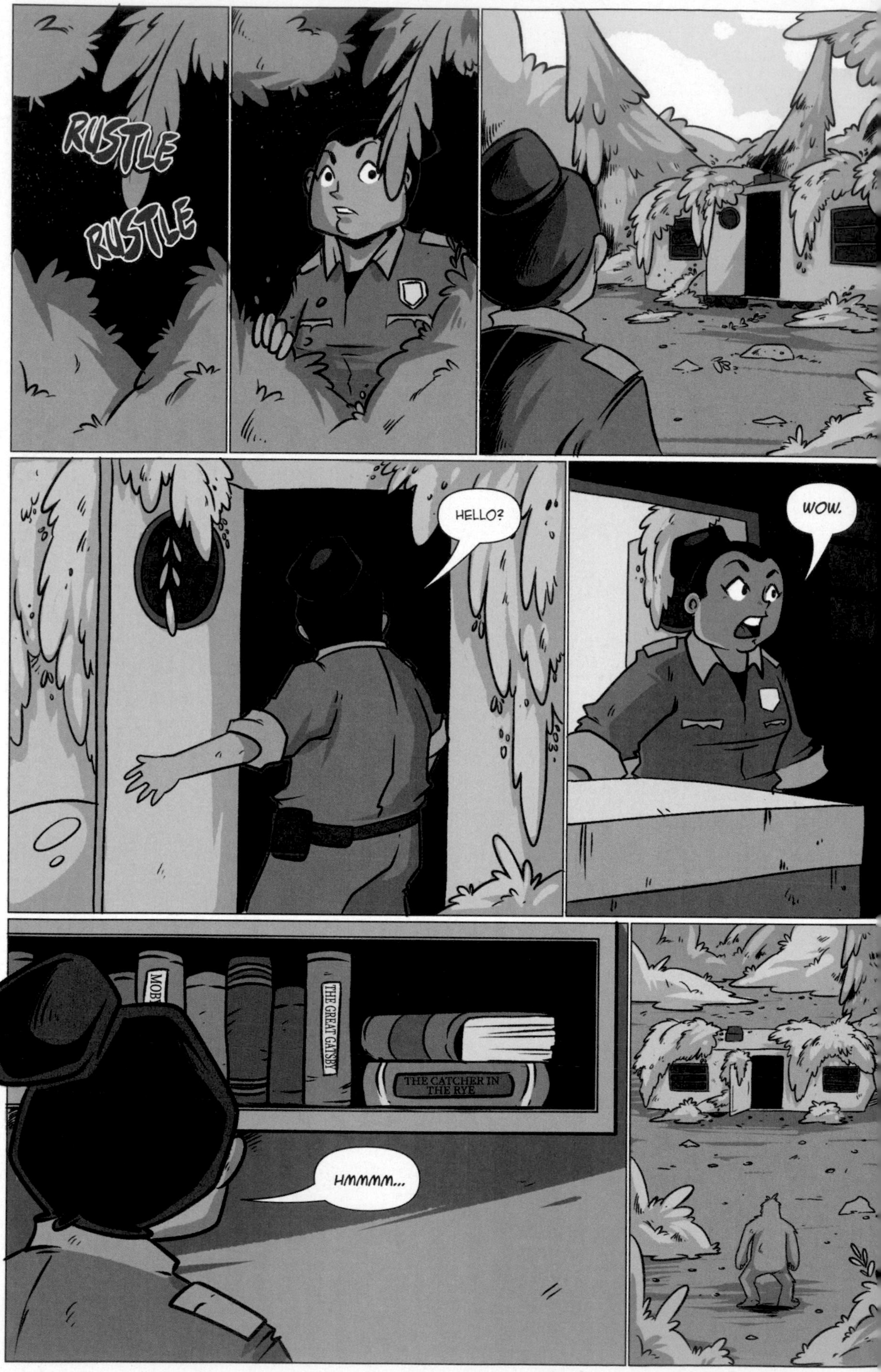
RUSTLE
RUSTLE
HELLO?
WOW.
MOBY
THE GREAT GATSBY
THE CATCHER IN THE RYE
HMMMM...

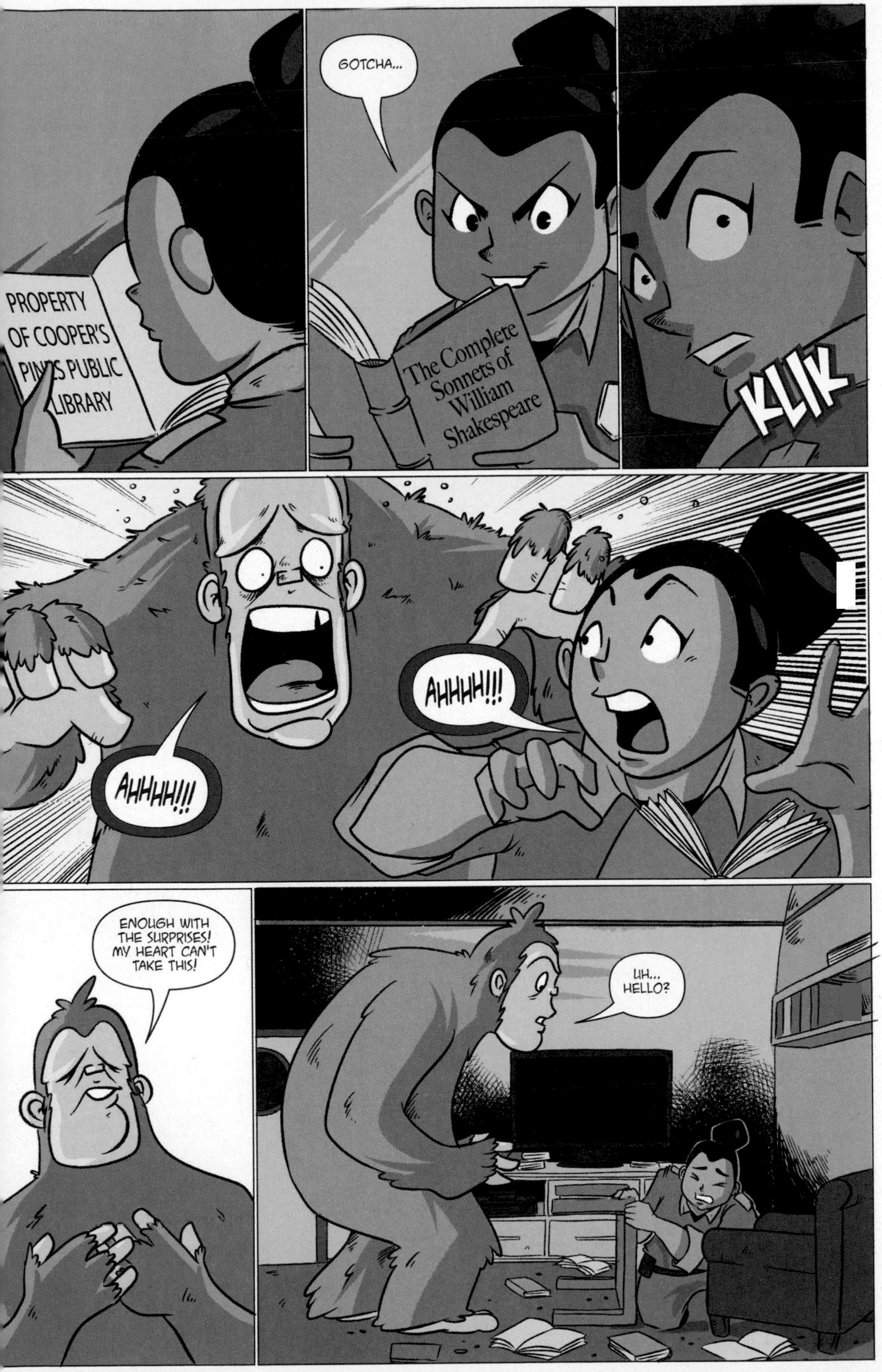
PROPERTY
OF COOPER'S
PINES PUBLIC
LIBRARY
GOTCHA...
The Complete Sonnets of William Shakespeare
KLIK
AHHHH!!!
AHHHH!!!
ENOUGH WITH THE SURPRISES! MY HEART CAN'T TAKE THIS!
UH... HELLO?

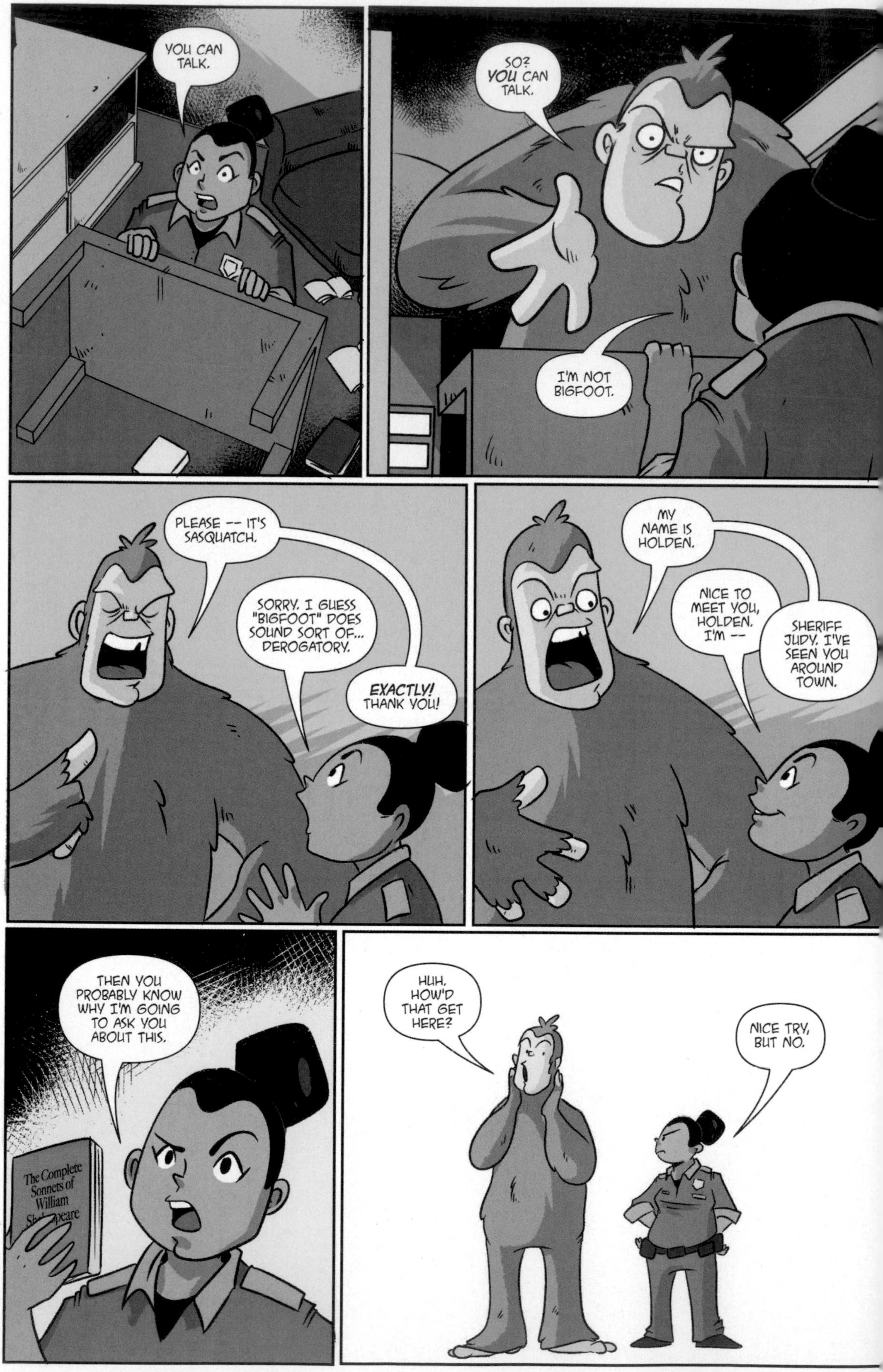

YOU CAN TALK.
SO? YOU CAN TALK.
I'M NOT BIGFOOT.
PLEASE -- IT'S SASQUATCH.
SORRY. I GUESS "BIGFOOT" DOES SOUND SORT OF... DEROGATORY.
EXACTLY! THANK YOU!
MY NAME IS HOLDEN.
NICE TO MEET YOU, HOLDEN. I'M --
SHERIFF JUDY. I'VE SEEN YOU AROUND TOWN.
THEN YOU PROBABLY KNOW WHY I'M GOING TO ASK YOU ABOUT THIS.
The Complete Sonnets of William Shakespeare
HUH. HOW'D THAT GET HERE?
NICE TRY, BUT NO.

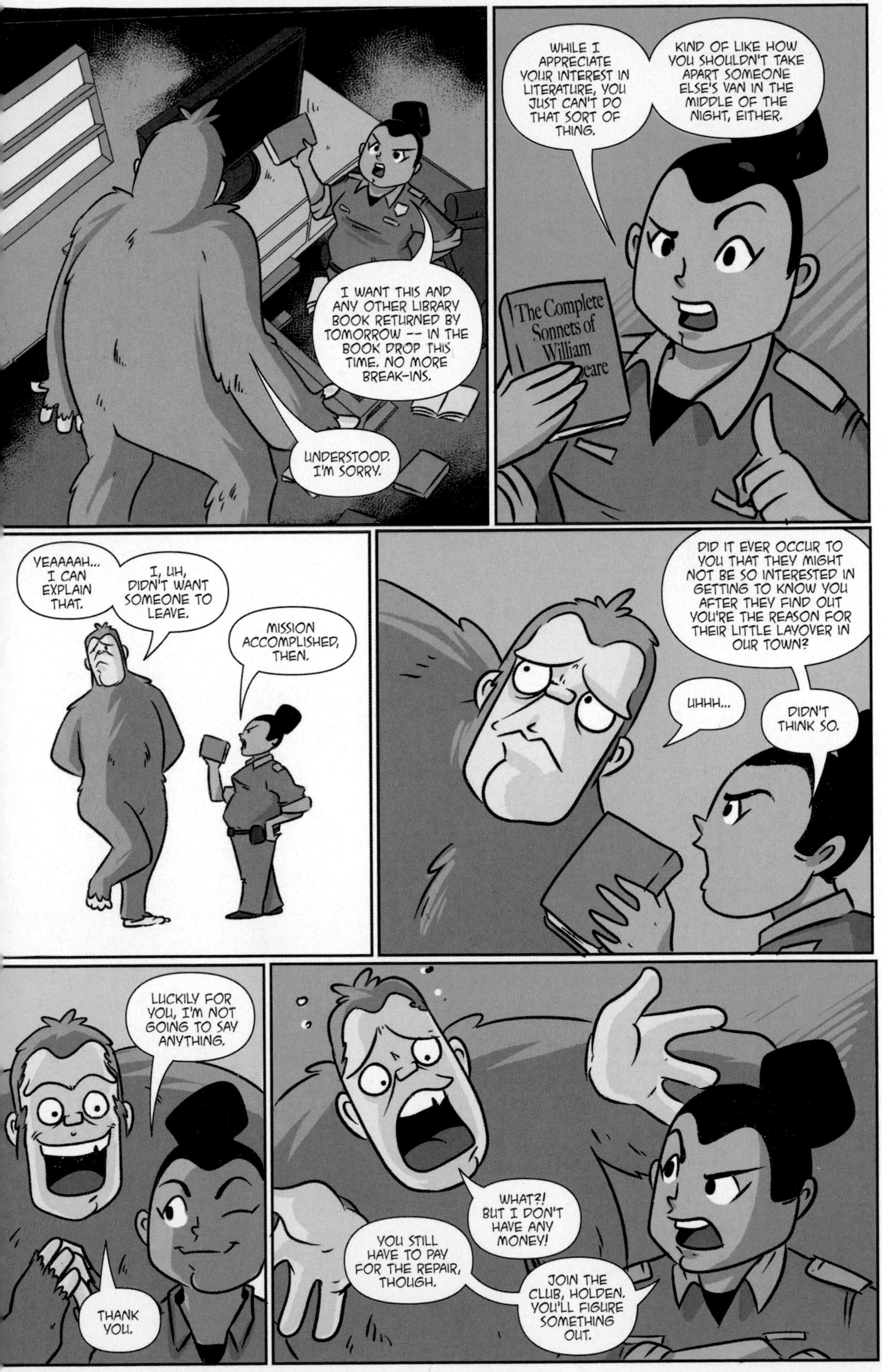
I WANT THIS AND ANY OTHER LIBRARY BOOK RETURNED BY TOMORROW -- IN THE BOOK DROP THIS TIME. NO MORE BREAK-INS.
UNDERSTOOD. I'M SORRY.
WHILE I APPRECIATE YOUR INTEREST IN LITERATURE, YOU JUST CAN'T DO THAT SORT OF THING.
KIND OF LIKE HOW YOU SHOULDN'T TAKE APART SOMEONE ELSE'S VAN IN THE MIDDLE OF THE NIGHT, EITHER.
The Complete Sonnets of William
YEAAAAH... I CAN EXPLAIN THAT.
I, UH, DIDN'T WANT SOMEONE TO LEAVE.
MISSION ACCOMPLISHED, THEN.
DID IT EVER OCCUR TO YOU THAT THEY MIGHT NOT BE SO INTERESTED IN GETTING TO KNOW YOU AFTER THEY FIND OUT YOU'RE THE REASON FOR THEIR LITTLE LAYOVER IN OUR TOWN?
UHHH...
DIDN'T THINK SO.
LUCKILY FOR YOU, I'M NOT GOING TO SAY ANYTHING.
THANK YOU.
YOU STILL HAVE TO PAY FOR THE REPAIR, THOUGH.
WHAT?! BUT I DON'T HAVE ANY MONEY!
JOIN THE CLUB, HOLDEN. YOU'LL FIGURE SOMETHING OUT.

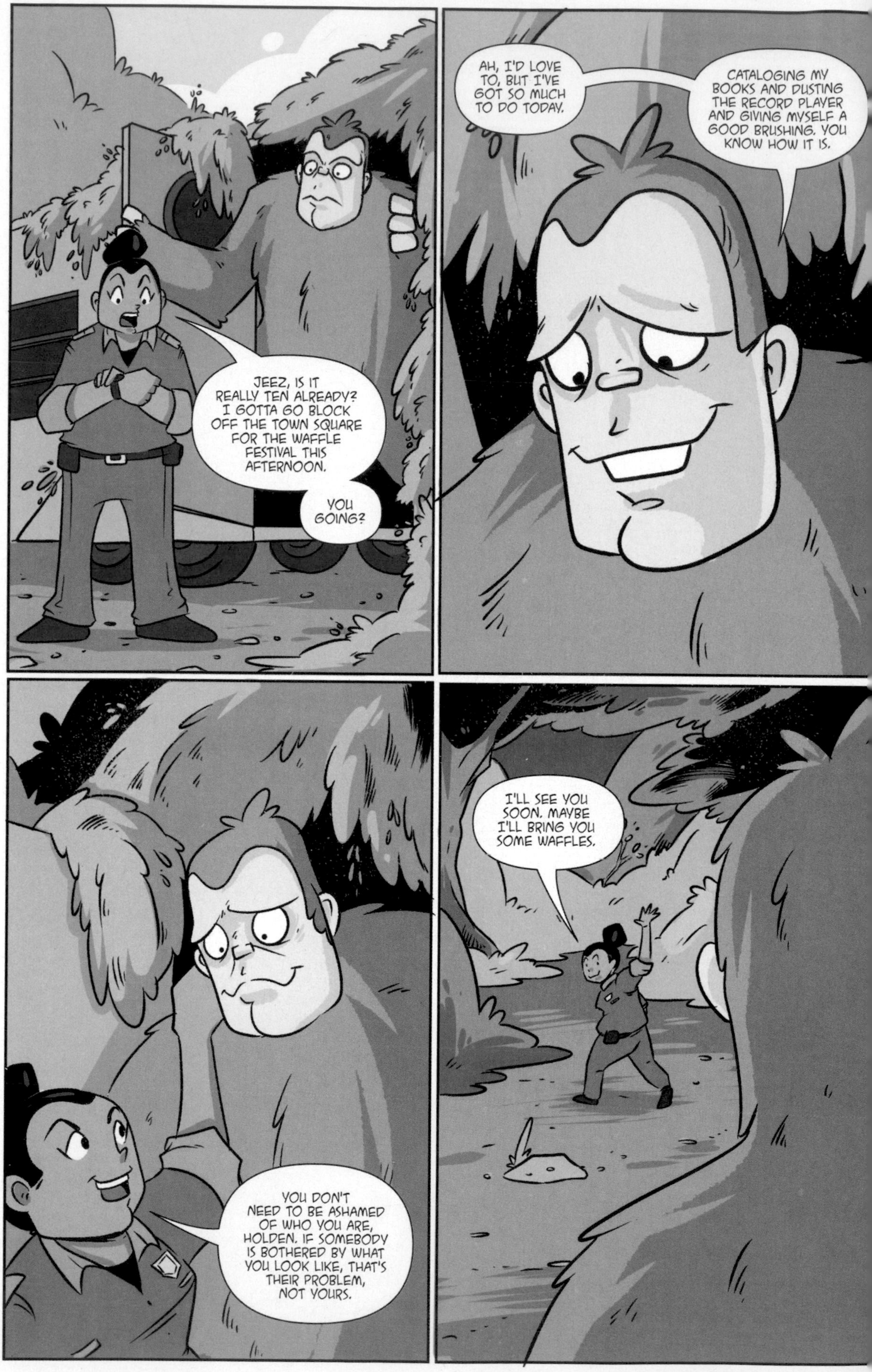
JEEZ, IS IT REALLY TEN ALREADY? I GOTTA GO BLOCK OFF THE TOWN SQUARE FOR THE WAFFLE FESTIVAL THIS AFTERNOON.
YOU GOING?
AH, I'D LOVE TO, BUT I'VE GOT SO MUCH TO DO TODAY.
CATALOGING MY BOOKS AND DUSTING THE RECORD PLAYER AND GIVING MYSELF A GOOD BRUSHING. YOU KNOW HOW IT IS.
YOU DON'T NEED TO BE ASHAMED OF WHO YOU ARE, HOLDEN. IF SOMEBODY IS BOTHERED BY WHAT YOU LOOK LIKE, THAT'S THEIR PROBLEM, NOT YOURS.
I'LL SEE YOU SOON. MAYBE I'LL BRING YOU SOME WAFFLES.

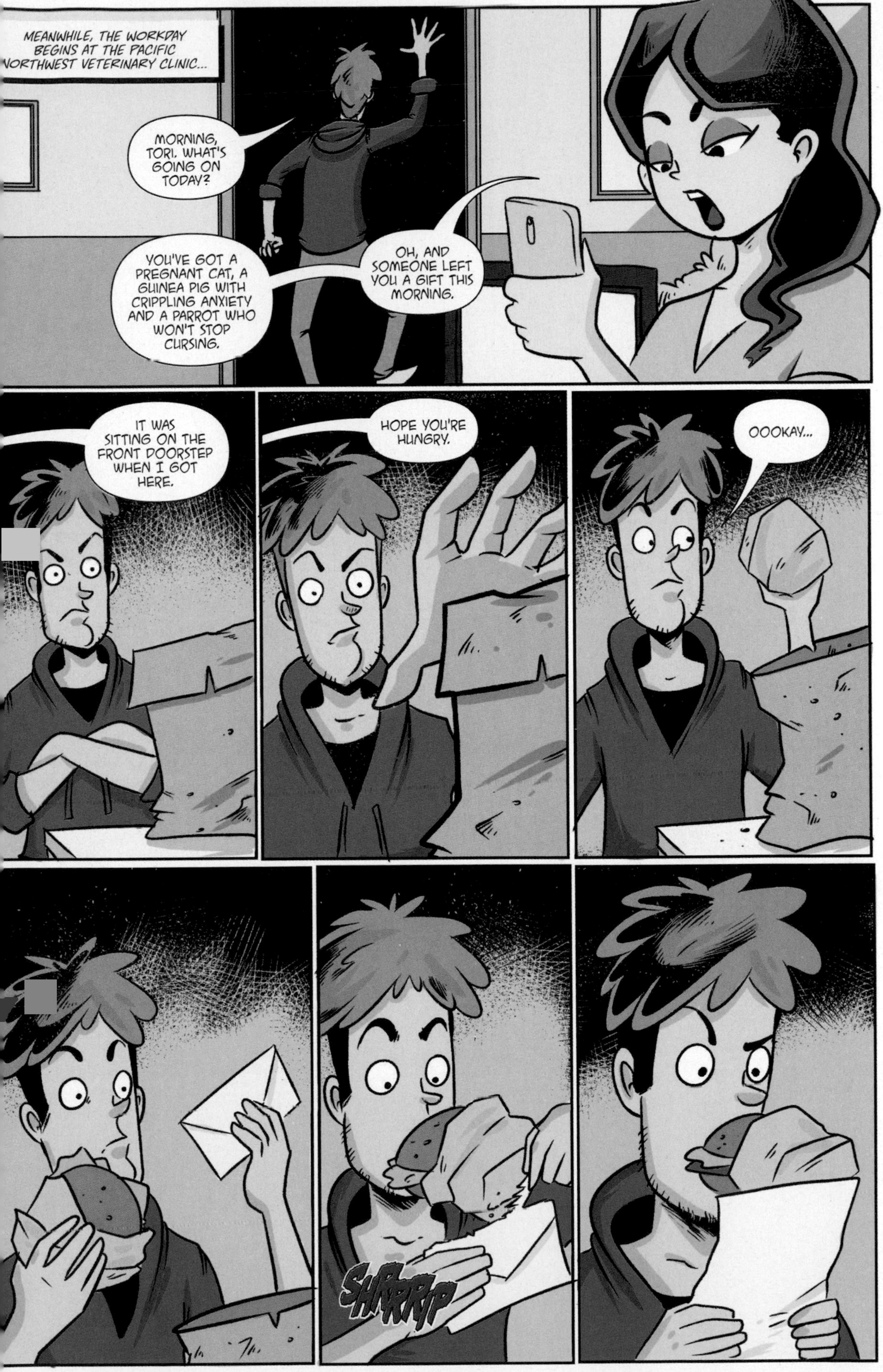
MEANWHILE, THE WORKDAY BEGINS AT THE PACIFIC NORTHWEST VETERINARY CLINIC...
MORNING, TORI. WHAT'S GOING ON TODAY?
YOU'VE GOT A PREGNANT CAT, A GUINEA PIG WITH CRIPPLING ANXIETY AND A PARROT WHO WON'T STOP CURSING.
OH, AND SOMEONE LEFT YOU A GIFT THIS MORNING.
IT WAS SITTING ON THE FRONT DOORSTEP WHEN I GOT HERE.
HOPE YOU'RE HUNGRY.
OOOKAY...
SHRRRIP

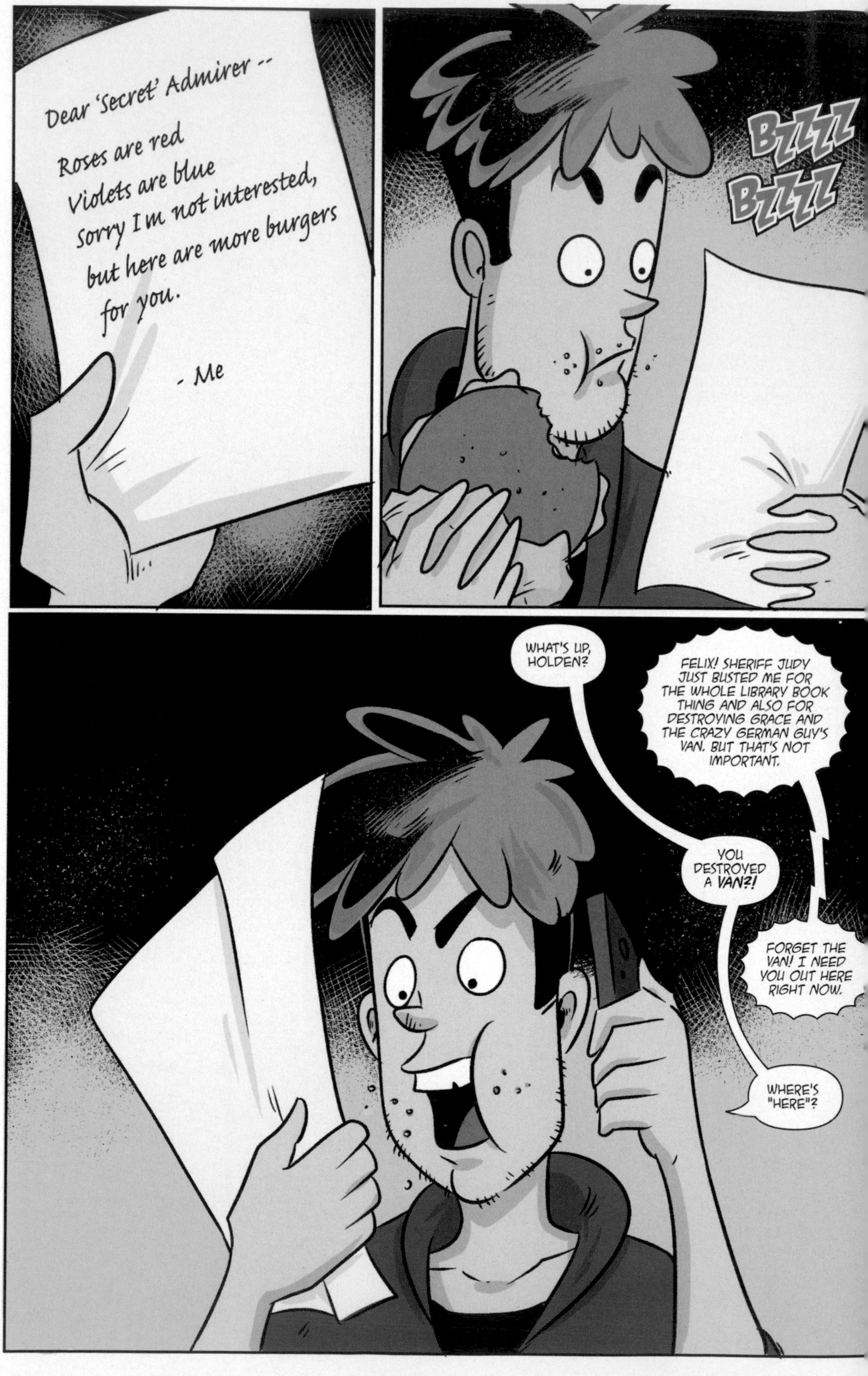
Dear 'Secret' Admirer --
Roses are red
Violets are blue
Sorry I'm not interested,
but here are more burgers
for you.
- Me
BZZZZ
BZZZZ
WHAT'S UP, HOLDEN?
FELIX! SHERIFF JUDY JUST BUSTED ME FOR THE WHOLE LIBRARY BOOK THING AND ALSO FOR DESTROYING GRACE AND THE CRAZY GERMAN GUY'S VAN. BUT THAT'S NOT IMPORTANT.
YOU DESTROYED A VAN?!
FORGET THE VAN! I NEED YOU OUT HERE RIGHT NOW.
WHERE'S "HERE"?

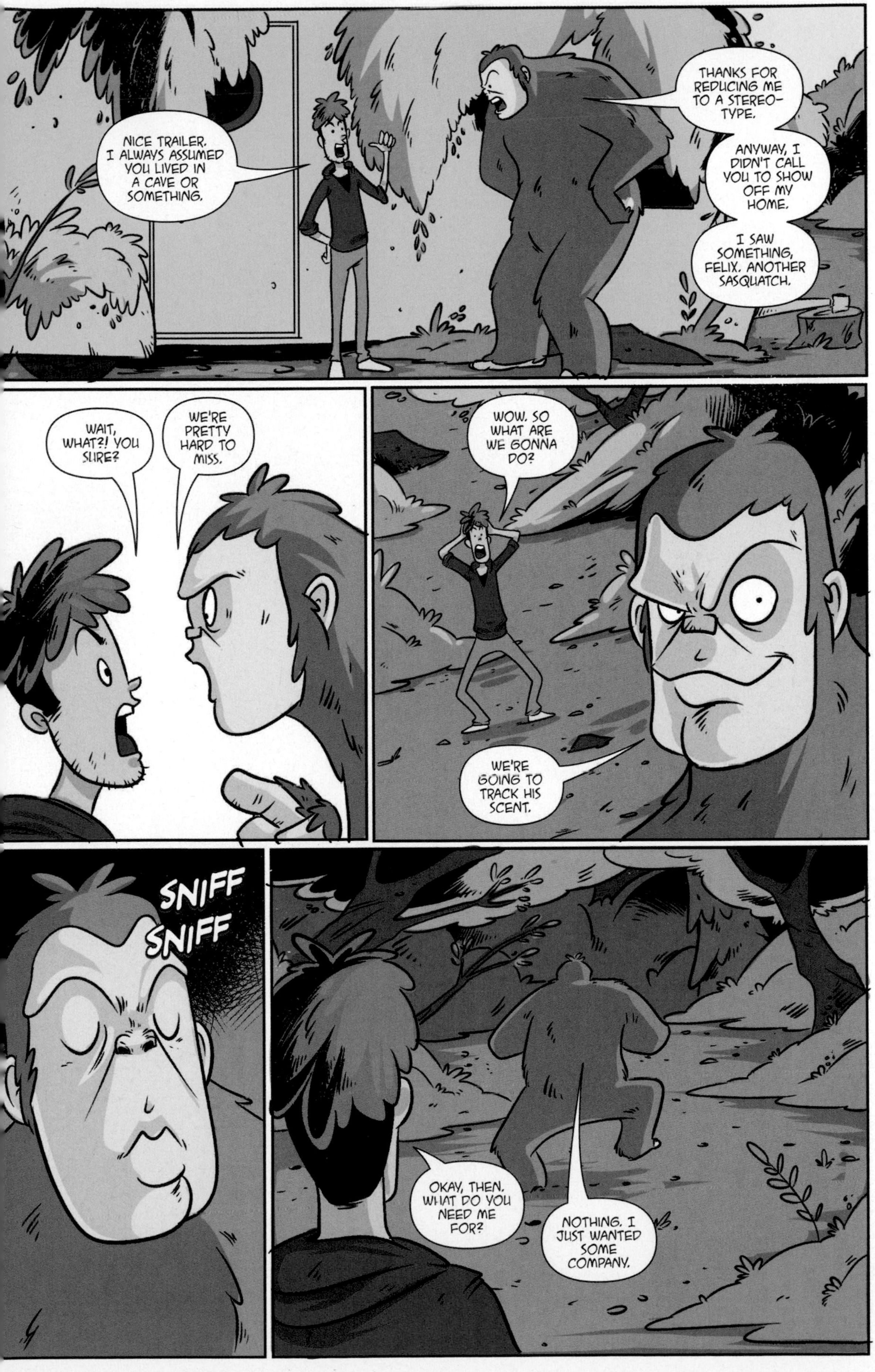
NICE TRAILER. I ALWAYS ASSUMED YOU LIVED IN A CAVE OR SOMETHING.
THANKS FOR REDUCING ME TO A STEREO-TYPE.
ANYWAY, I DIDN'T CALL YOU TO SHOW OFF MY HOME.
I SAW SOMETHING, FELIX. ANOTHER SASQUATCH.
WAIT, WHAT?! YOU SURE?
WE'RE PRETTY HARD TO MISS.
WOW. SO WHAT ARE WE GONNA DO?
WE'RE GOING TO TRACK HIS SCENT.
SNIFF
SNIFF
OKAY, THEN. WHAT DO YOU NEED ME FOR?
NOTHING. I JUST WANTED SOME COMPANY.

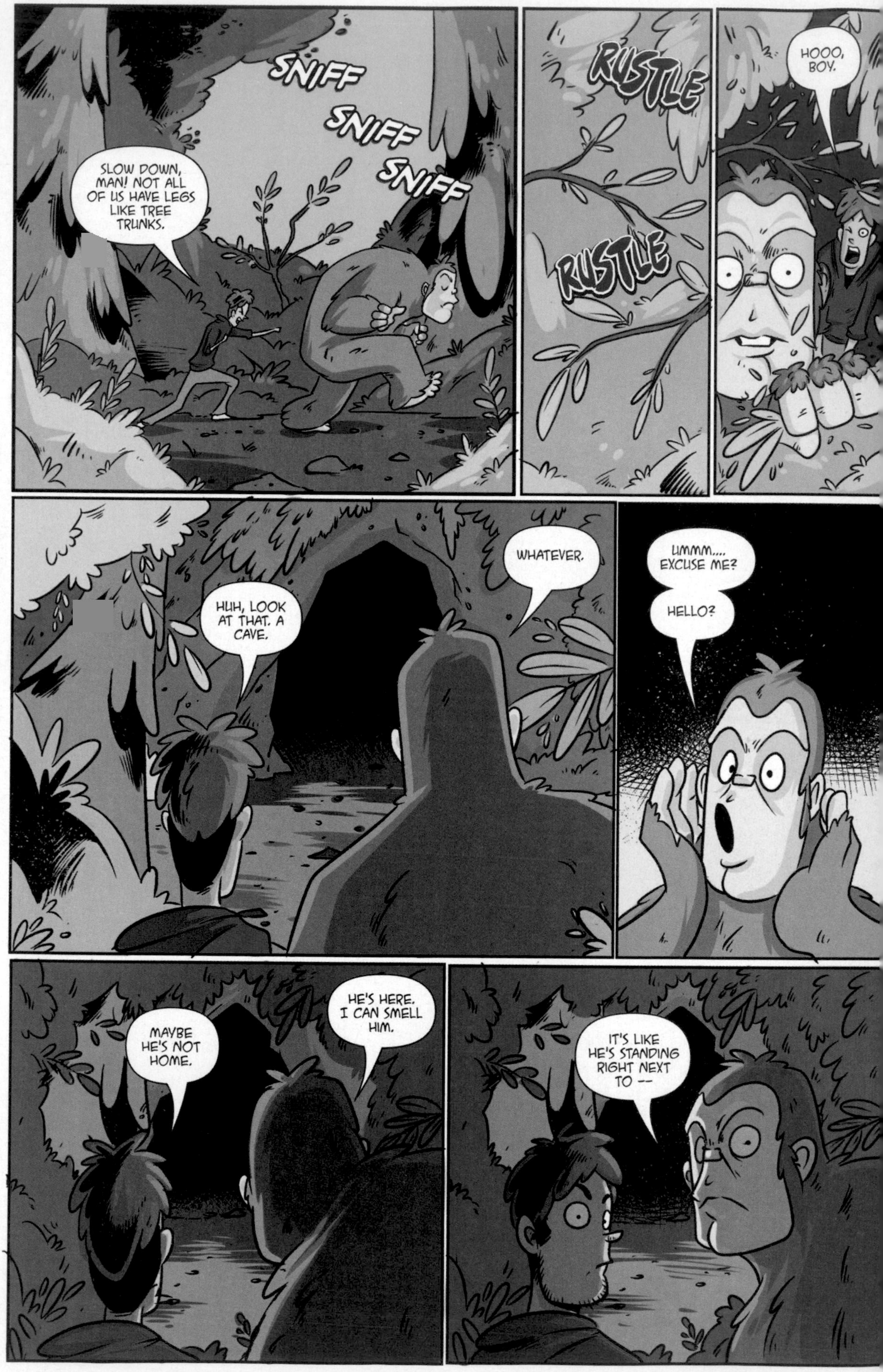
SNIFF
SNIFF
SNIFF
SLOW DOWN, MAN! NOT ALL OF US HAVE LEGS LIKE TREE TRUNKS.
RUSTLE
RUSTLE
HOOO, BOY.
HUH, LOOK AT THAT. A CAVE.
WHATEVER.
UMMM.... EXCUSE ME?
HELLO?
MAYBE HE'S NOT HOME.
HE'S HERE. I CAN SMELL HIM.
IT'S LIKE HE'S STANDING RIGHT NEXT TO --

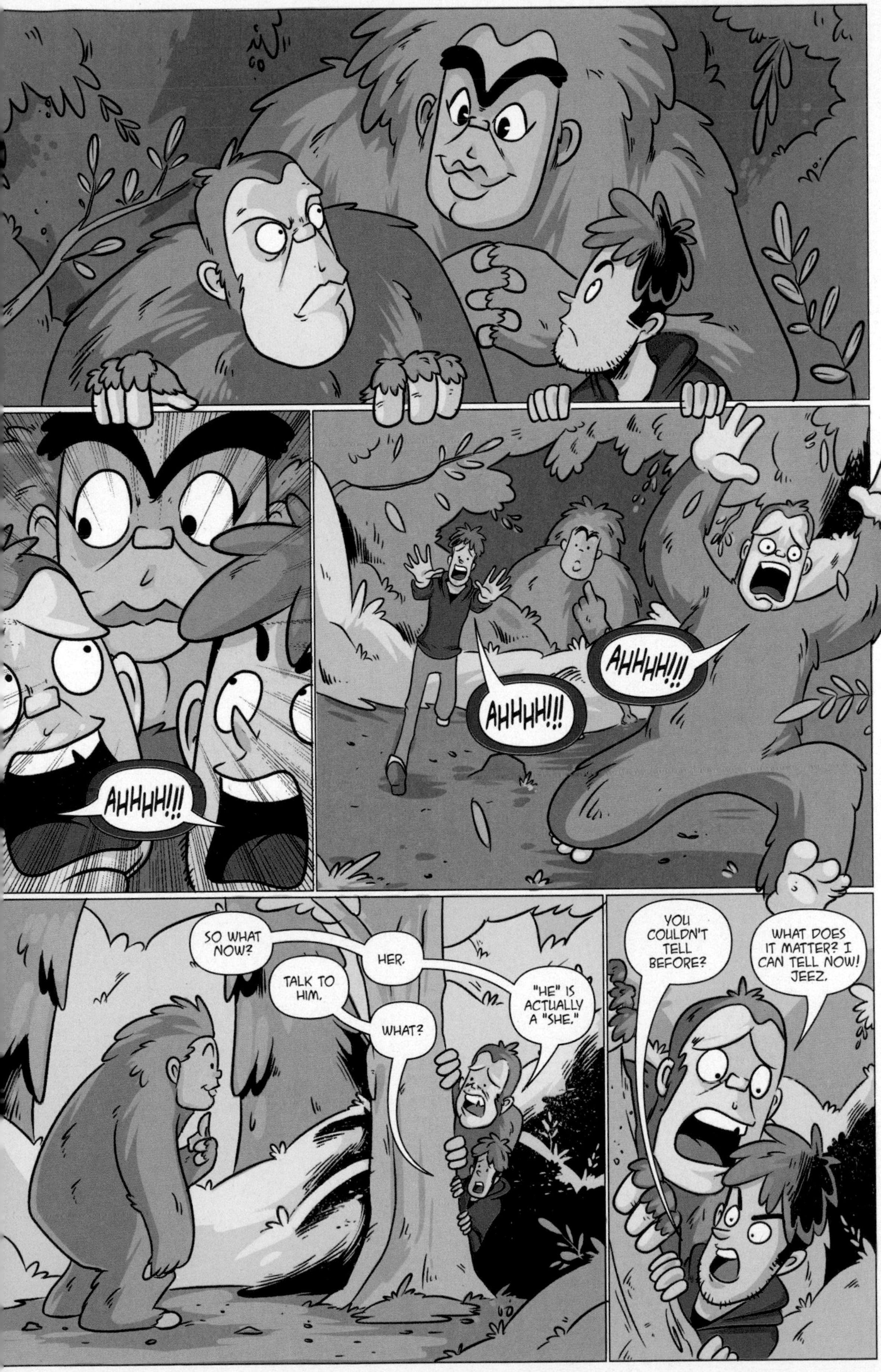
AHHHH!!!
AHHHH!!!
AHHHH!!!
SO WHAT NOW?
HER.
TALK TO HIM.
WHAT?
"HE" IS ACTUALLY A "SHE."
YOU COULDN'T TELL BEFORE?
WHAT DOES IT MATTER? I CAN TELL NOW! JEEZ.

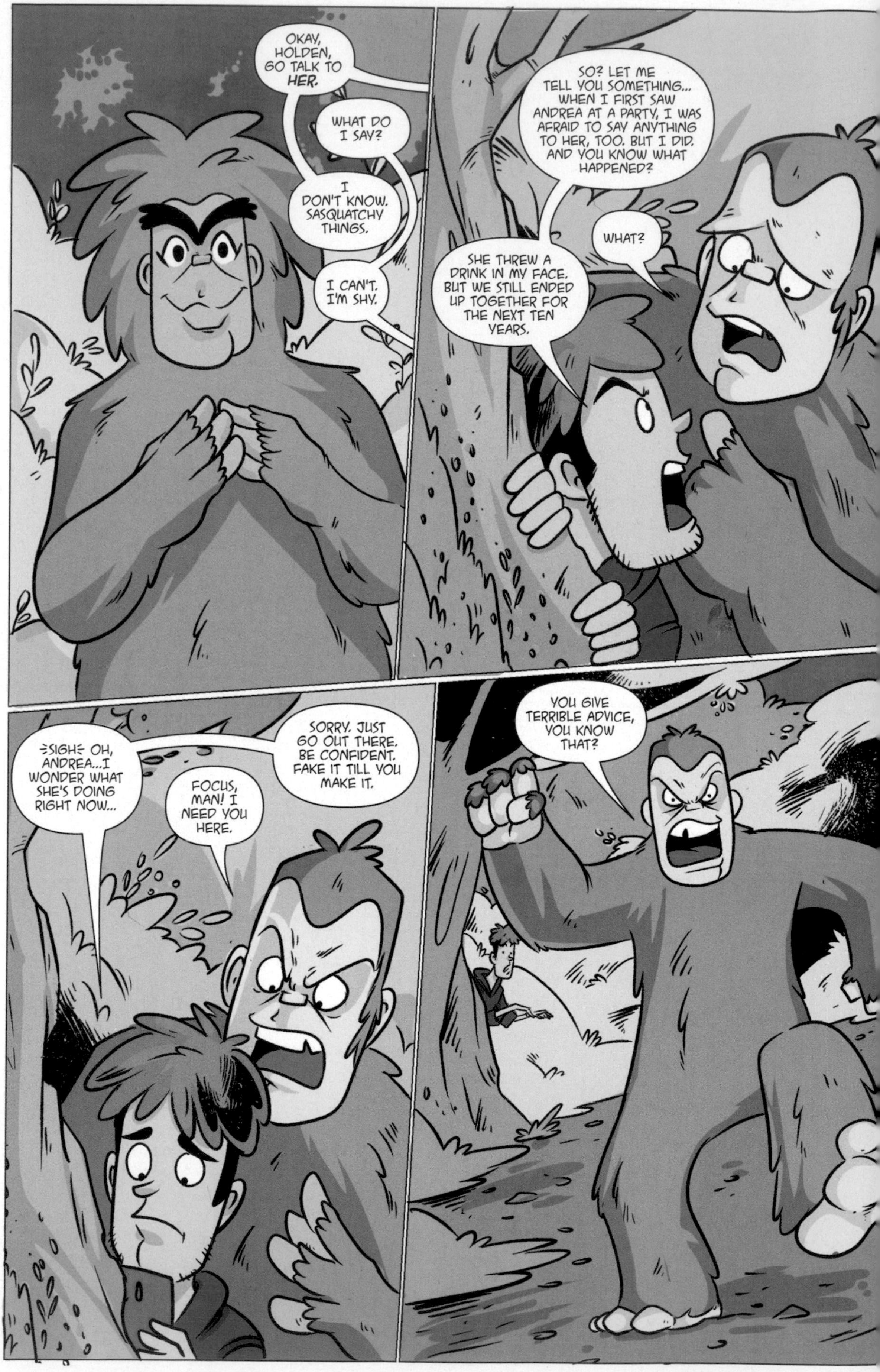
OKAY, HOLDEN, GO TALK TO **HER.**
WHAT DO I SAY?
I DON'T KNOW. SASQUATCHY THINGS.
I CAN'T. I'M SHY.
SO? LET ME TELL YOU SOMETHING... WHEN I FIRST SAW ANDREA AT A PARTY, I WAS AFRAID TO SAY ANYTHING TO HER, TOO. BUT I DID. AND YOU KNOW WHAT HAPPENED?
WHAT?
SHE THREW A DRINK IN MY FACE. BUT WE STILL ENDED UP TOGETHER FOR THE NEXT TEN YEARS.
=SIGH= OH, ANDREA...I WONDER WHAT SHE'S DOING RIGHT NOW...
FOCUS, MAN! I NEED YOU HERE.
SORRY. JUST GO OUT THERE. BE CONFIDENT. FAKE IT TILL YOU MAKE IT.
YOU GIVE TERRIBLE ADVICE, YOU KNOW THAT?

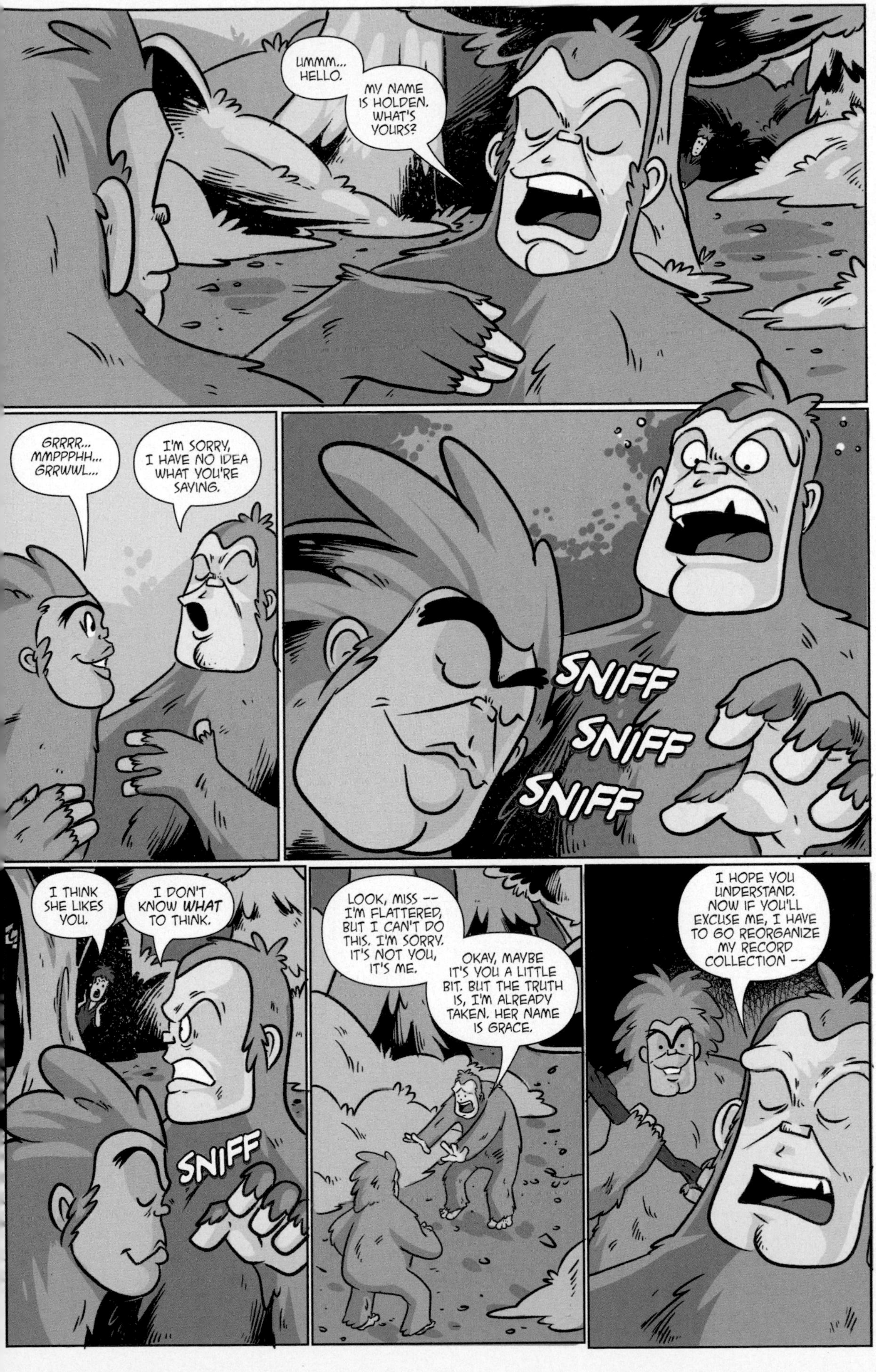
UMMM... HELLO.
MY NAME IS HOLDEN. WHAT'S YOURS?
GRRRR... MMPPPHH... GRRWWL...
I'M SORRY, I HAVE NO IDEA WHAT YOU'RE SAYING.
SNIFF
SNIFF
SNIFF
I THINK SHE LIKES YOU.
I DON'T KNOW **WHAT** TO THINK.
SNIFF
LOOK, MISS -- I'M FLATTERED, BUT I CAN'T DO THIS. I'M SORRY. IT'S NOT YOU, IT'S ME.
OKAY, MAYBE IT'S YOU A LITTLE BIT. BUT THE TRUTH IS, I'M ALREADY TAKEN. HER NAME IS GRACE.
I HOPE YOU UNDERSTAND. NOW IF YOU'LL EXCUSE ME, I HAVE TO GO REORGANIZE MY RECORD COLLECTION --

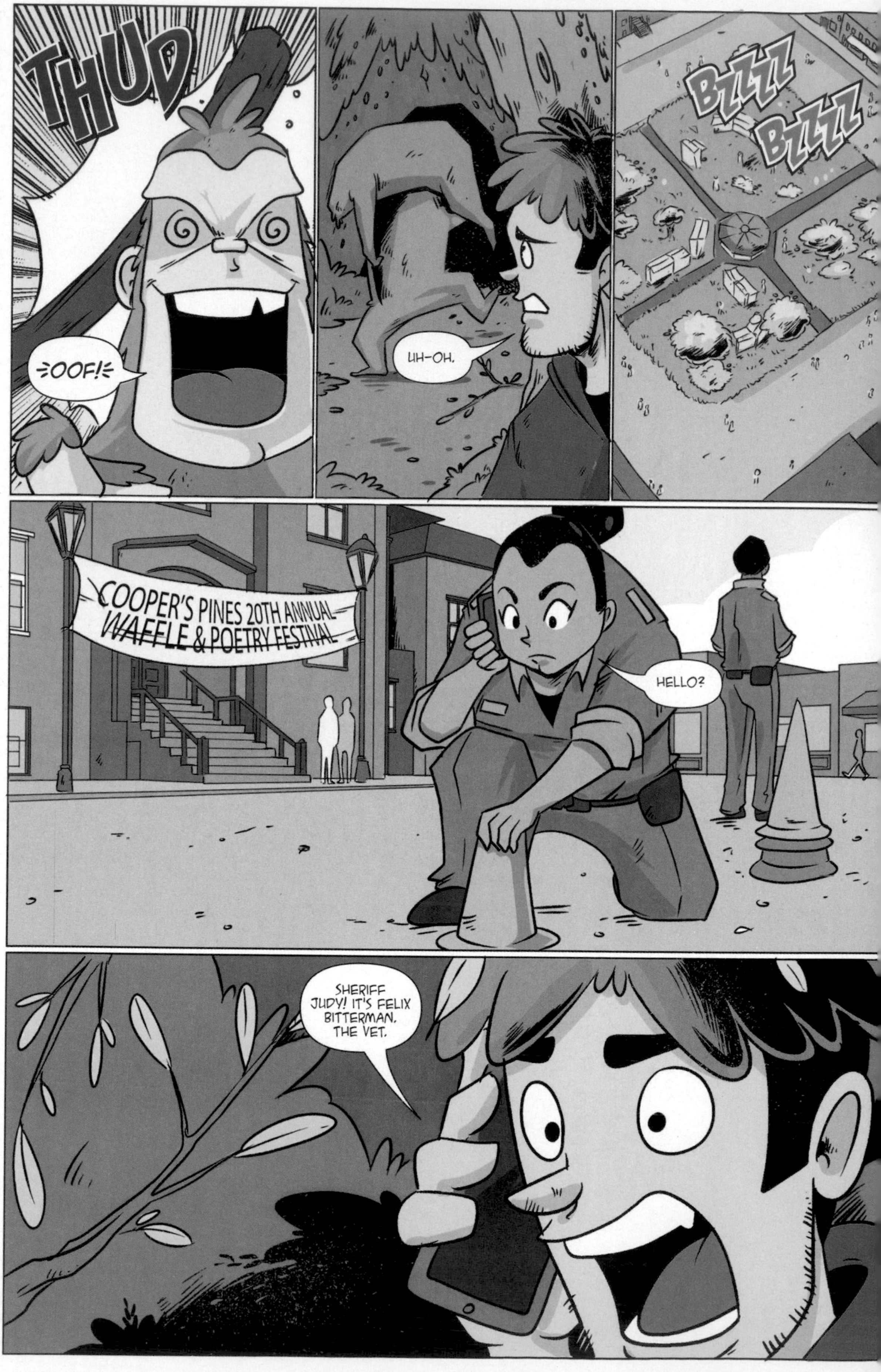
THUD
OOF!
UH-OH.
BZZZZ
BZZZZ
COOPER'S PINES 20TH ANNUAL WAFFLE & POETRY FESTIVAL
HELLO?
SHERIFF JUDY! IT'S FELIX BITTERMAN, THE VET.

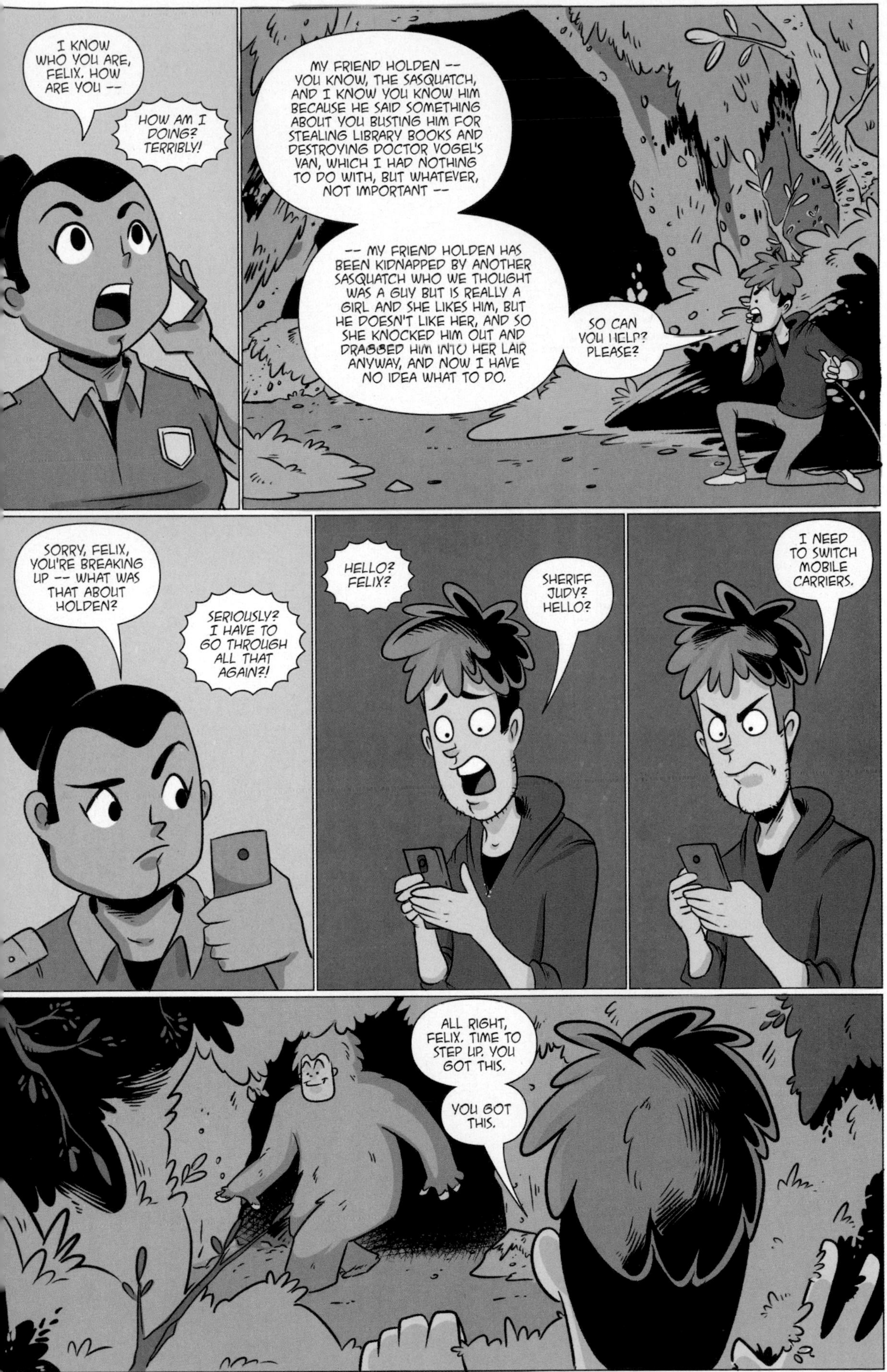
I KNOW WHO YOU ARE, FELIX. HOW ARE YOU --
HOW AM I DOING? TERRIBLY!
MY FRIEND HOLDEN -- YOU KNOW, THE SASQUATCH, AND I KNOW YOU KNOW HIM BECAUSE HE SAID SOMETHING ABOUT YOU BUSTING HIM FOR STEALING LIBRARY BOOKS AND DESTROYING DOCTOR VOGEL'S VAN, WHICH I HAD NOTHING TO DO WITH, BUT WHATEVER, NOT IMPORTANT --
-- MY FRIEND HOLDEN HAS BEEN KIDNAPPED BY ANOTHER SASQUATCH WHO WE THOUGHT WAS A GUY BUT IS REALLY A GIRL AND SHE LIKES HIM, BUT HE DOESN'T LIKE HER, AND SO SHE KNOCKED HIM OUT AND DRAGGED HIM INTO HER LAIR ANYWAY, AND NOW I HAVE NO IDEA WHAT TO DO.
SO CAN YOU HELP? PLEASE?
SORRY, FELIX, YOU'RE BREAKING UP -- WHAT WAS THAT ABOUT HOLDEN?
SERIOUSLY? I HAVE TO GO THROUGH ALL THAT AGAIN?!
HELLO? FELIX?
SHERIFF JUDY? HELLO?
I NEED TO SWITCH MOBILE CARRIERS.
ALL RIGHT, FELIX. TIME TO STEP UP. YOU GOT THIS.
YOU GOT THIS.

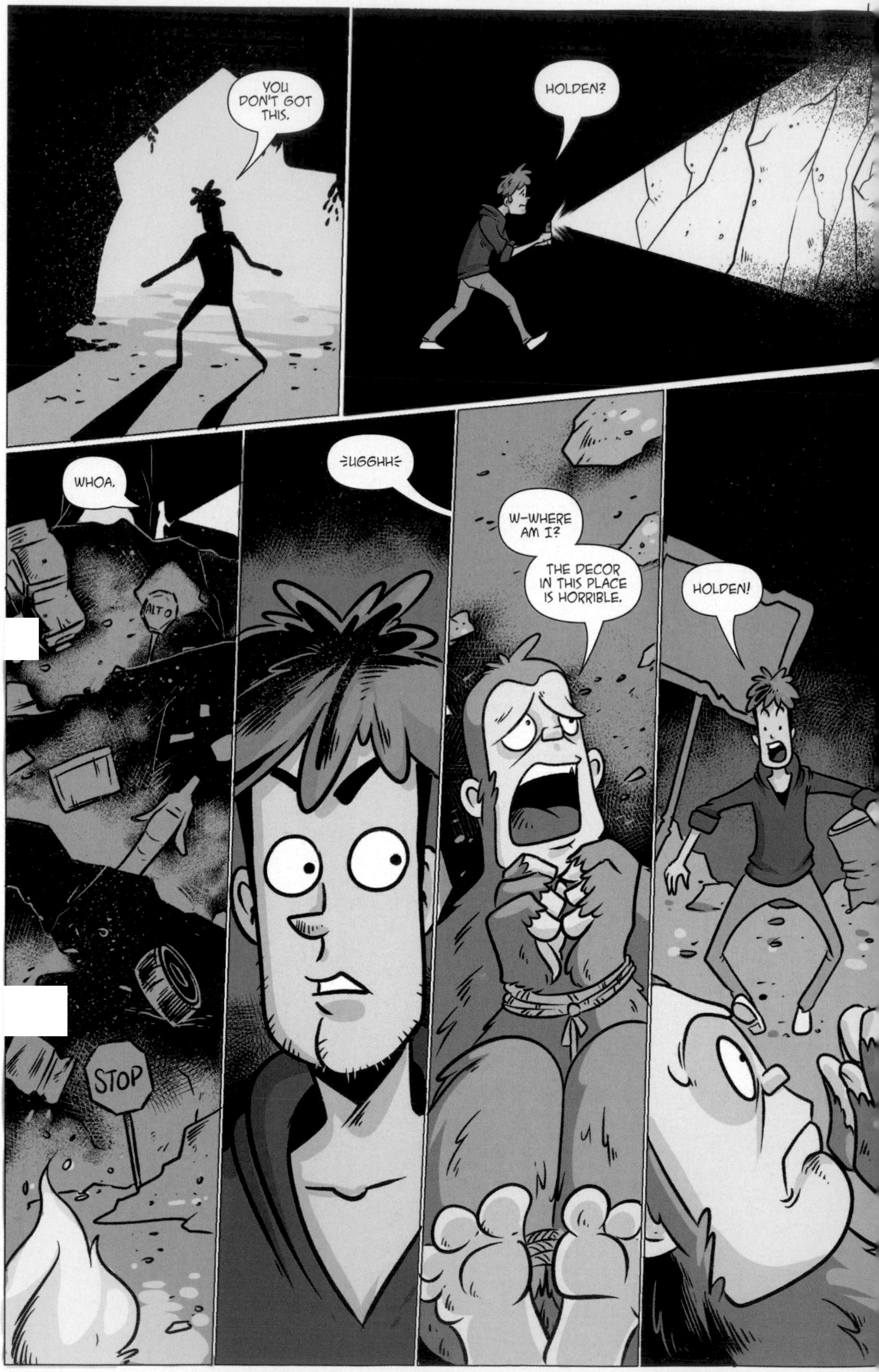

YOU DON'T GOT THIS.
HOLDEN?
WHOA.
ALTO
STOP
=UGGHH=
W-WHERE AM I?
THE DECOR IN THIS PLACE IS HORRIBLE.
HOLDEN!

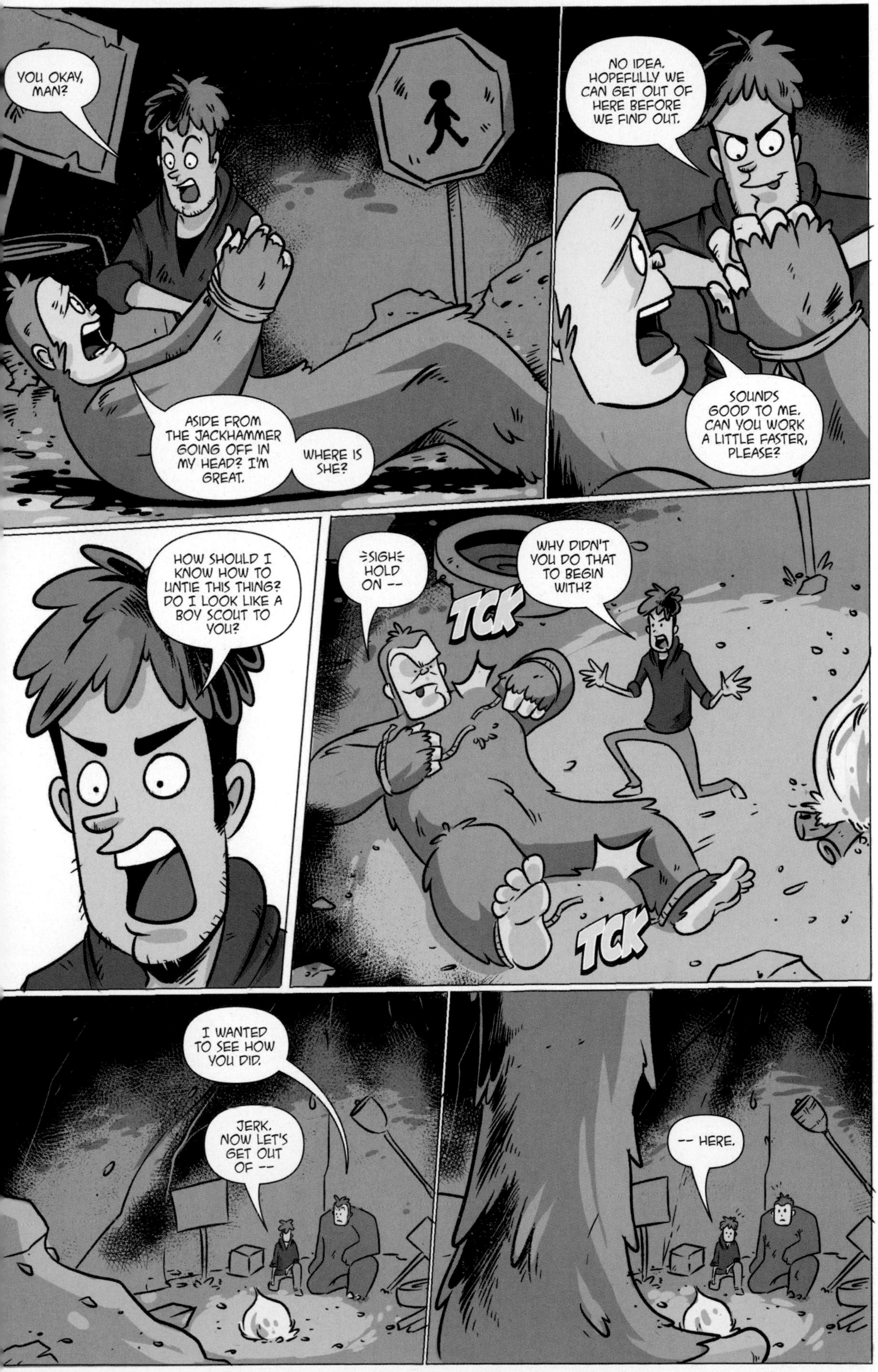
YOU OKAY, MAN?
ASIDE FROM THE JACKHAMMER GOING OFF IN MY HEAD? I'M GREAT.
WHERE IS SHE?
NO IDEA. HOPEFULLY WE CAN GET OUT OF HERE BEFORE WE FIND OUT.
SOUNDS GOOD TO ME. CAN YOU WORK A LITTLE FASTER, PLEASE?
HOW SHOULD I KNOW HOW TO UNTIE THIS THING? DO I LOOK LIKE A BOY SCOUT TO YOU?
=SIGH= HOLD ON --
TCK
WHY DIDN'T YOU DO THAT TO BEGIN WITH?
TCK
I WANTED TO SEE HOW YOU DID.
JERK. NOW LET'S GET OUT OF --
-- HERE.

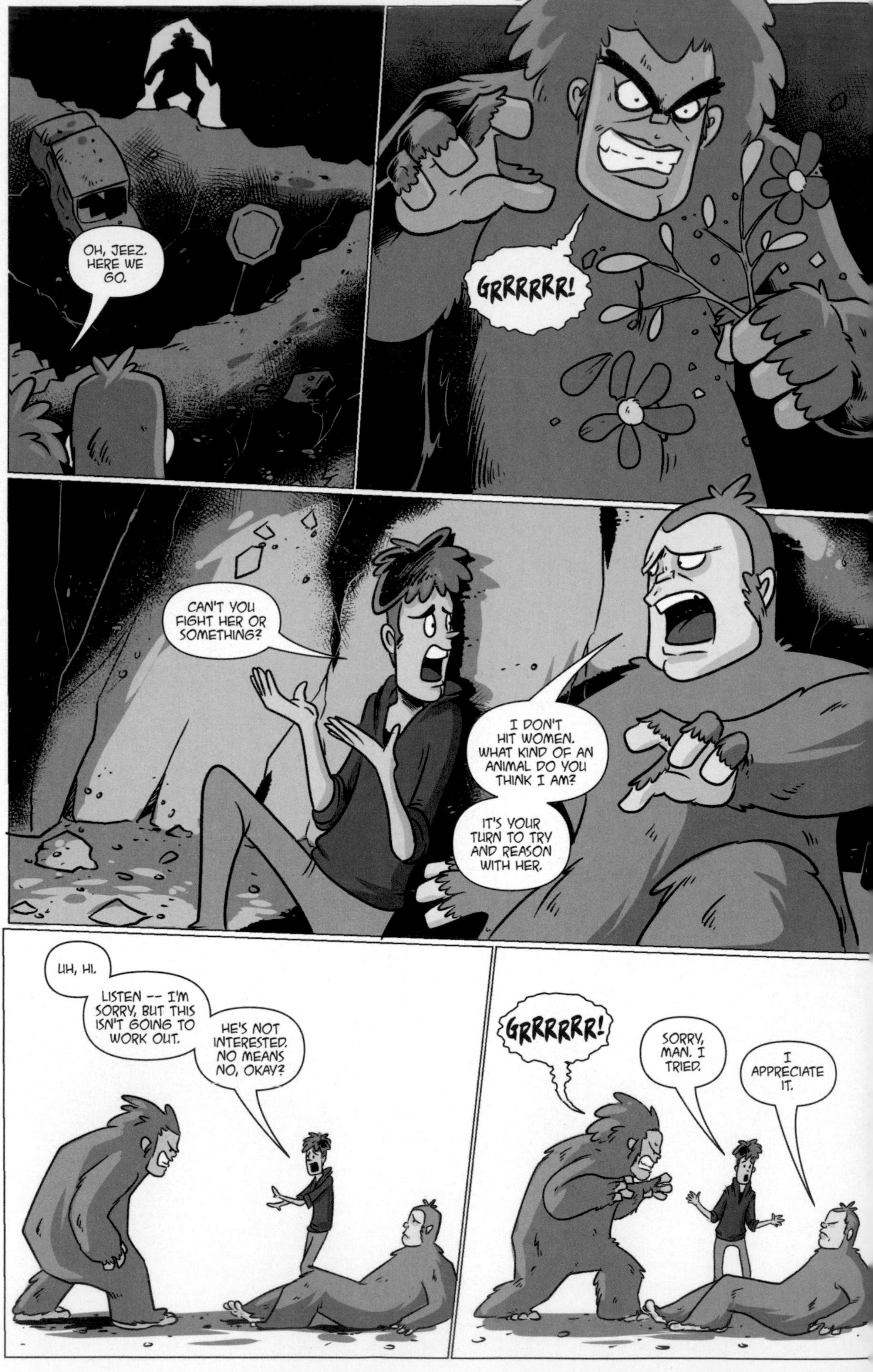
OH, JEEZ. HERE WE GO.
GRRRRRR!
CAN'T YOU FIGHT HER OR SOMETHING?
I DON'T HIT WOMEN. WHAT KIND OF AN ANIMAL DO YOU THINK I AM?
IT'S YOUR TURN TO TRY AND REASON WITH HER.
UH, HI.
LISTEN -- I'M SORRY, BUT THIS ISN'T GOING TO WORK OUT.
HE'S NOT INTERESTED. NO MEANS NO, OKAY?
GRRRRRR!
SORRY, MAN. I TRIED.
I APPRECIATE IT.

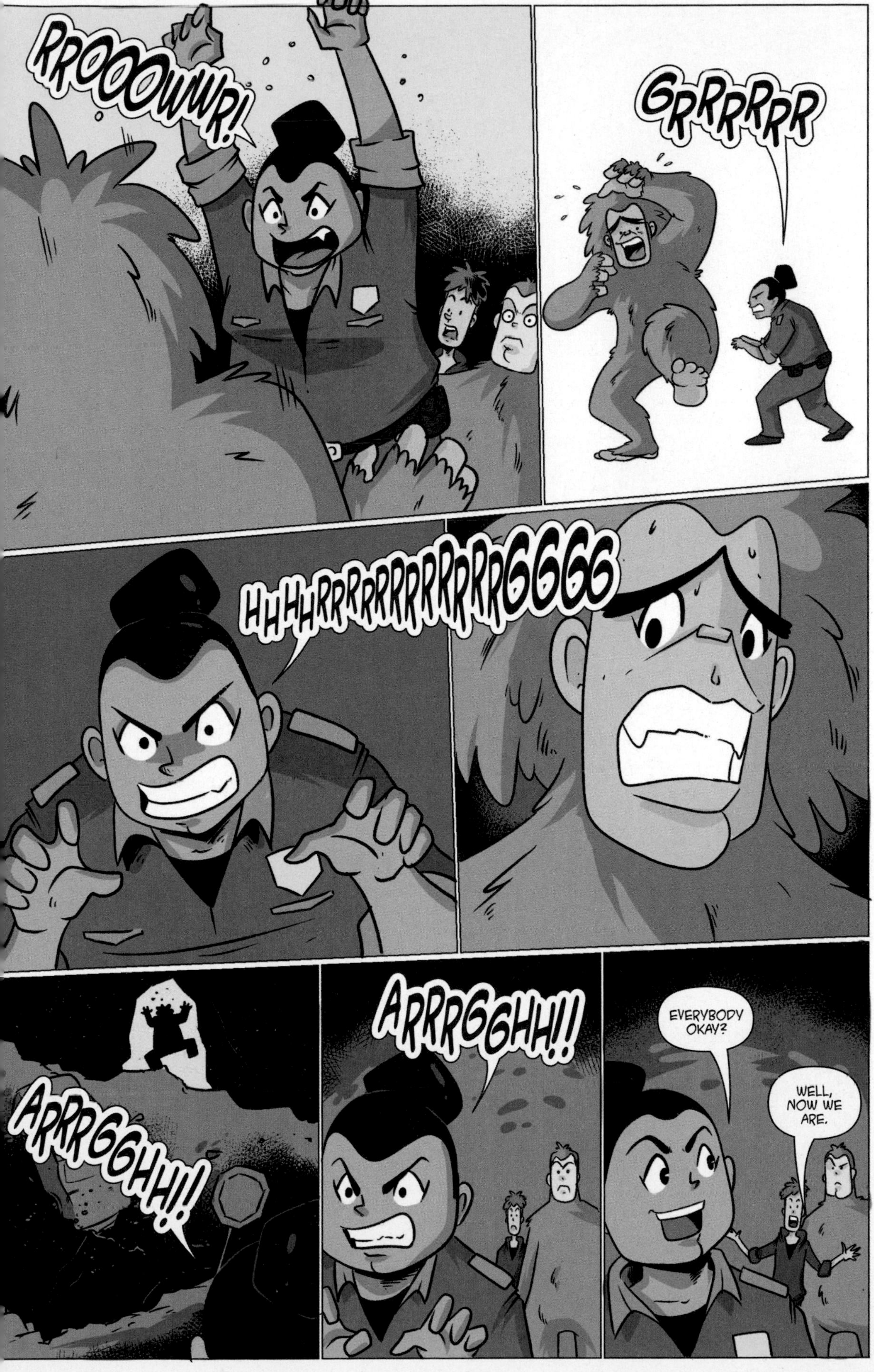
RROOOWWR!
GRRRRRR
HHHHRRRRRRRRRRRGGGG
ARRRGGHH!!
ARRRGGHH!!
EVERYBODY OKAY?
WELL, NOW WE ARE.

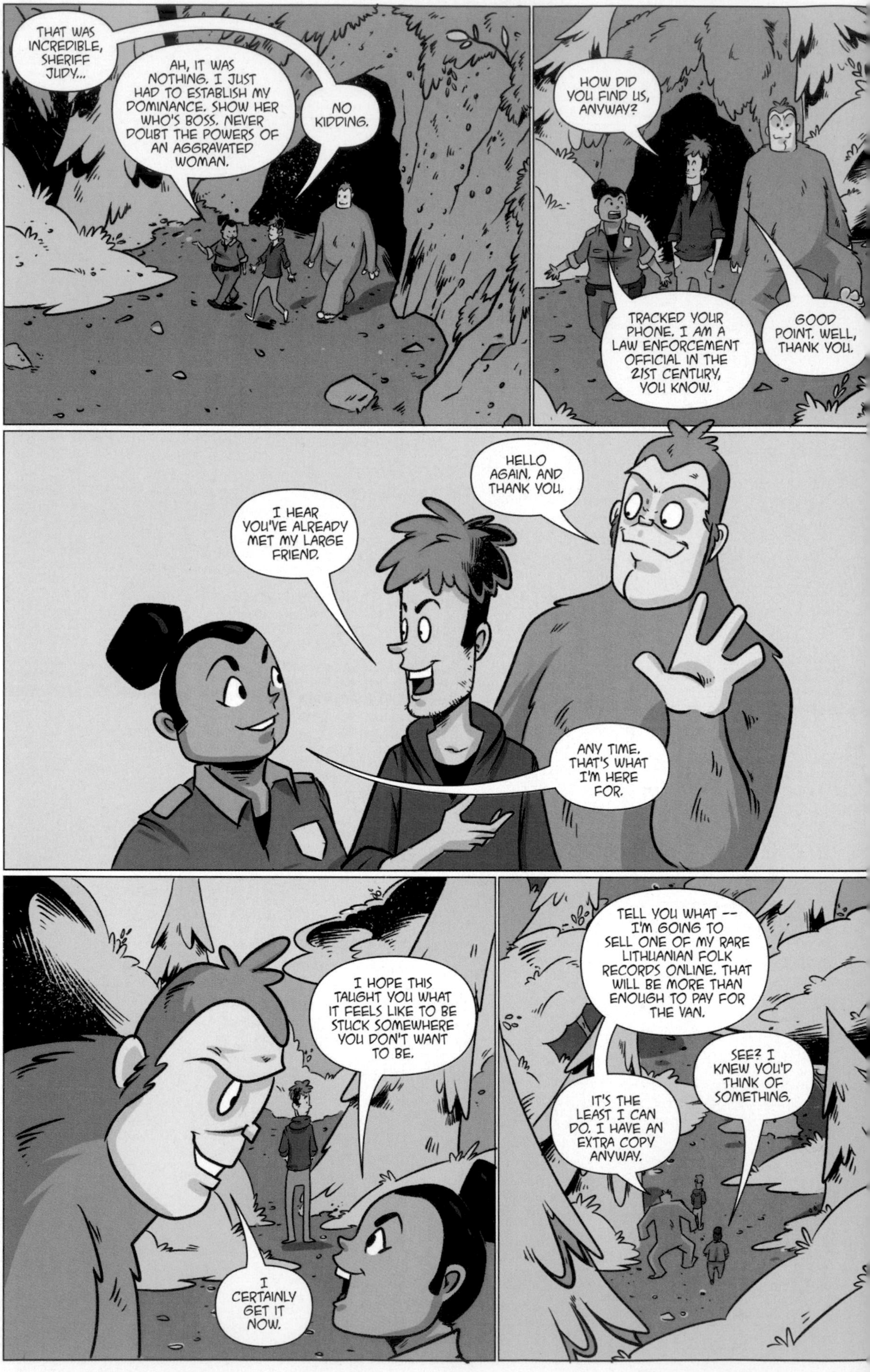
THAT WAS INCREDIBLE, SHERIFF JUDY...
AH, IT WAS NOTHING. I JUST HAD TO ESTABLISH MY DOMINANCE. SHOW HER WHO'S BOSS. NEVER DOUBT THE POWERS OF AN AGGRAVATED WOMAN.
NO KIDDING.
HOW DID YOU FIND US, ANYWAY?
TRACKED YOUR PHONE. I AM A LAW ENFORCEMENT OFFICIAL IN THE 21ST CENTURY, YOU KNOW.
GOOD POINT. WELL, THANK YOU.
I HEAR YOU'VE ALREADY MET MY LARGE FRIEND.
HELLO AGAIN. AND THANK YOU.
ANY TIME. THAT'S WHAT I'M HERE FOR.
I HOPE THIS TAUGHT YOU WHAT IT FEELS LIKE TO BE STUCK SOMEWHERE YOU DON'T WANT TO BE.
I CERTAINLY GET IT NOW.
TELL YOU WHAT -- I'M GOING TO SELL ONE OF MY RARE LITHUANIAN FOLK RECORDS ONLINE. THAT WILL BE MORE THAN ENOUGH TO PAY FOR THE VAN.
IT'S THE LEAST I CAN DO. I HAVE AN EXTRA COPY ANYWAY.
SEE? I KNEW YOU'D THINK OF SOMETHING.

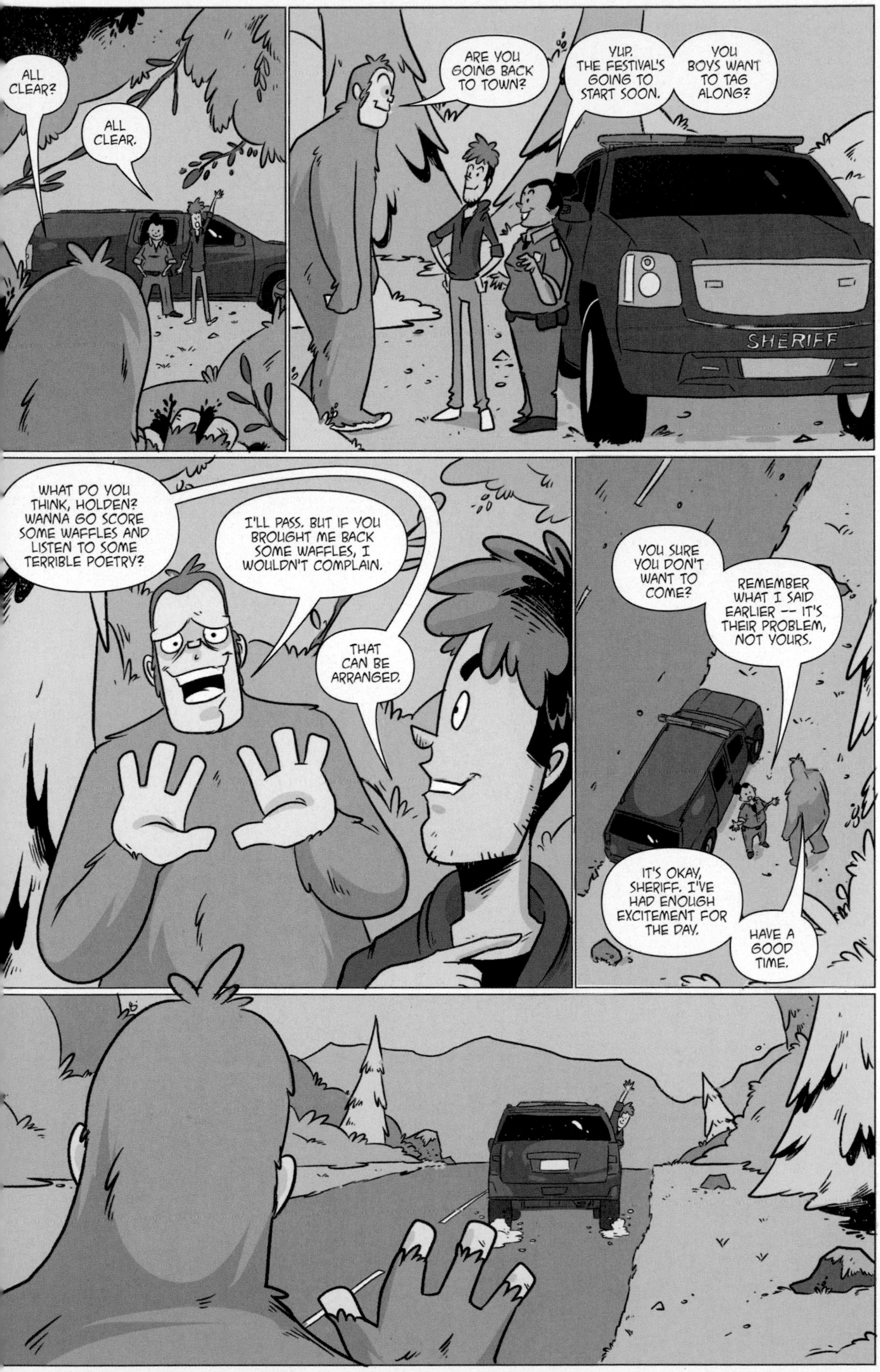
ALL CLEAR?
ALL CLEAR.
ARE YOU GOING BACK TO TOWN?
YUP. THE FESTIVAL'S GOING TO START SOON.
YOU BOYS WANT TO TAG ALONG?
SHERIFF
WHAT DO YOU THINK, HOLDEN? WANNA GO SCORE SOME WAFFLES AND LISTEN TO SOME TERRIBLE POETRY?
I'LL PASS. BUT IF YOU BROUGHT ME BACK SOME WAFFLES, I WOULDN'T COMPLAIN.
THAT CAN BE ARRANGED.
YOU SURE YOU DON'T WANT TO COME?
REMEMBER WHAT I SAID EARLIER -- IT'S THEIR PROBLEM, NOT YOURS.
IT'S OKAY, SHERIFF. I'VE HAD ENOUGH EXCITEMENT FOR THE DAY.
HAVE A GOOD TIME.

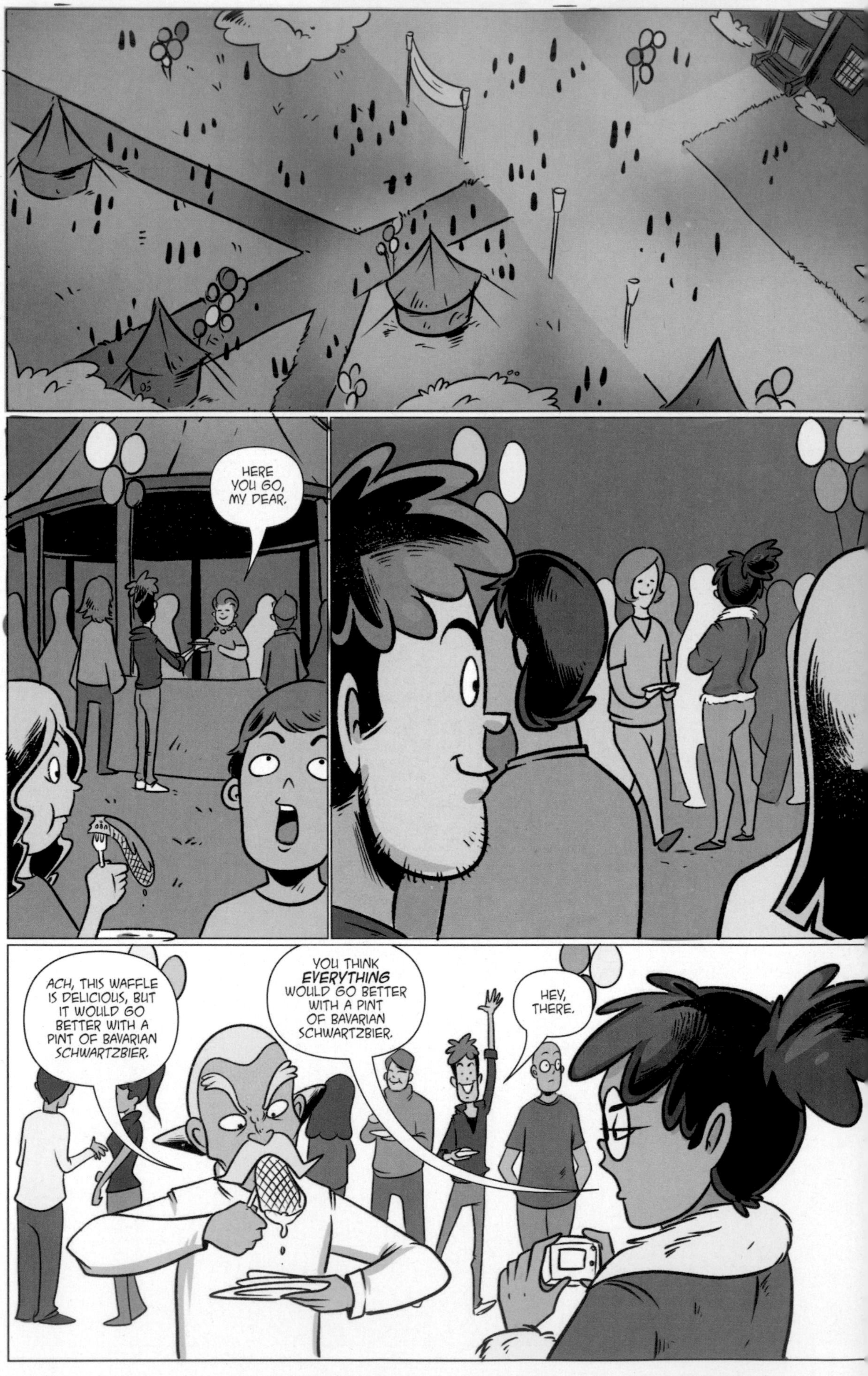
HERE YOU GO, MY DEAR.
ACH, THIS WAFFLE IS DELICIOUS, BUT IT WOULD GO BETTER WITH A PINT OF BAVARIAN SCHWARTZBIER.
YOU THINK EVERYTHING WOULD GO BETTER WITH A PINT OF BAVARIAN SCHWARTZBIER.
HEY, THERE.

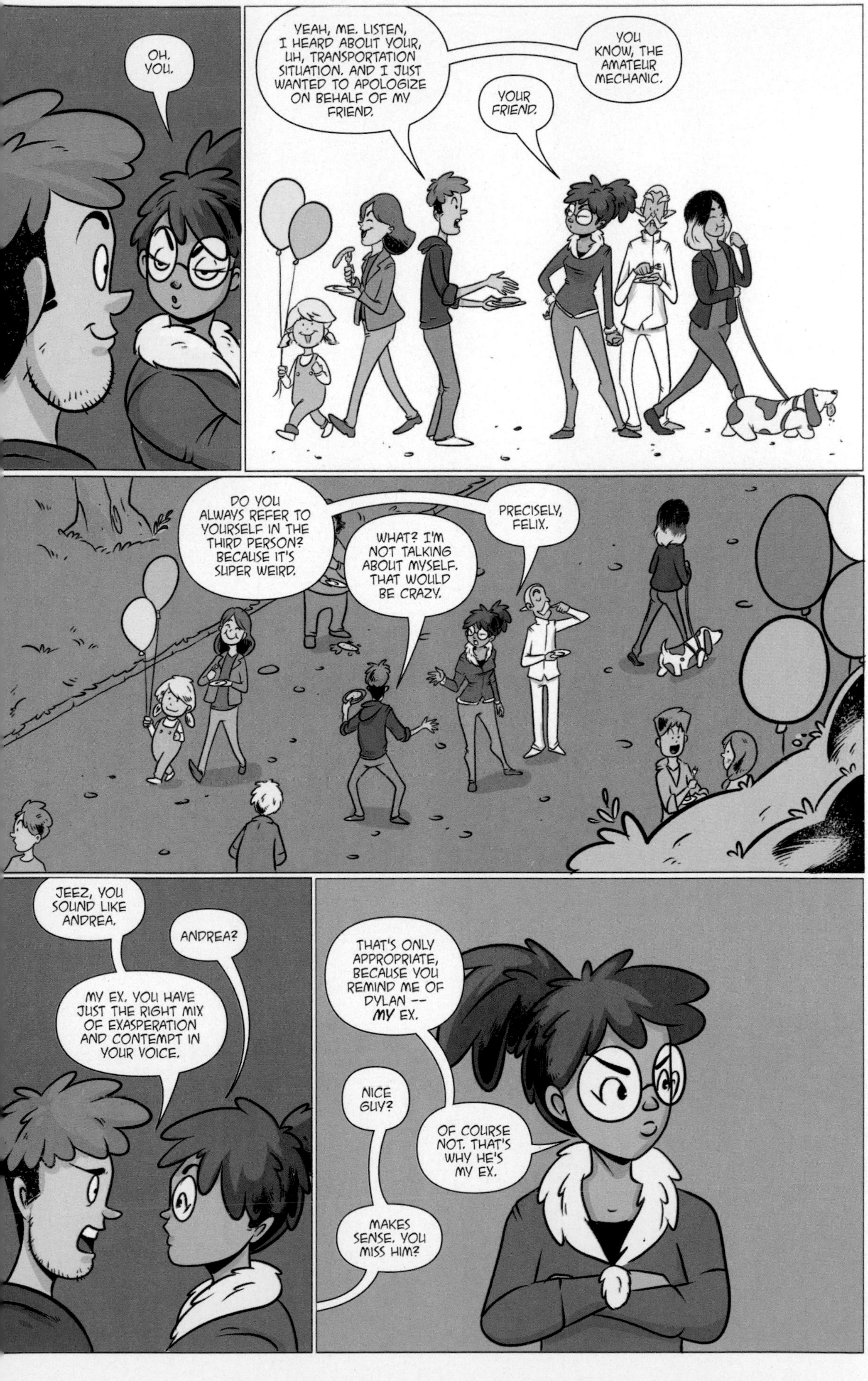
OH. YOU.
YEAH, ME. LISTEN, I HEARD ABOUT YOUR, UH, TRANSPORTATION SITUATION. AND I JUST WANTED TO APOLOGIZE ON BEHALF OF MY FRIEND.
YOU KNOW, THE AMATEUR MECHANIC.
YOUR FRIEND.
DO YOU ALWAYS REFER TO YOURSELF IN THE THIRD PERSON? BECAUSE IT'S SUPER WEIRD.
WHAT? I'M NOT TALKING ABOUT MYSELF. THAT WOULD BE CRAZY.
PRECISELY, FELIX.
JEEZ, YOU SOUND LIKE ANDREA.
ANDREA?
MY EX. YOU HAVE JUST THE RIGHT MIX OF EXASPERATION AND CONTEMPT IN YOUR VOICE.
THAT'S ONLY APPROPRIATE, BECAUSE YOU REMIND ME OF DYLAN -- MY EX.
NICE GUY?
OF COURSE NOT. THAT'S WHY HE'S MY EX.
MAKES SENSE. YOU MISS HIM?

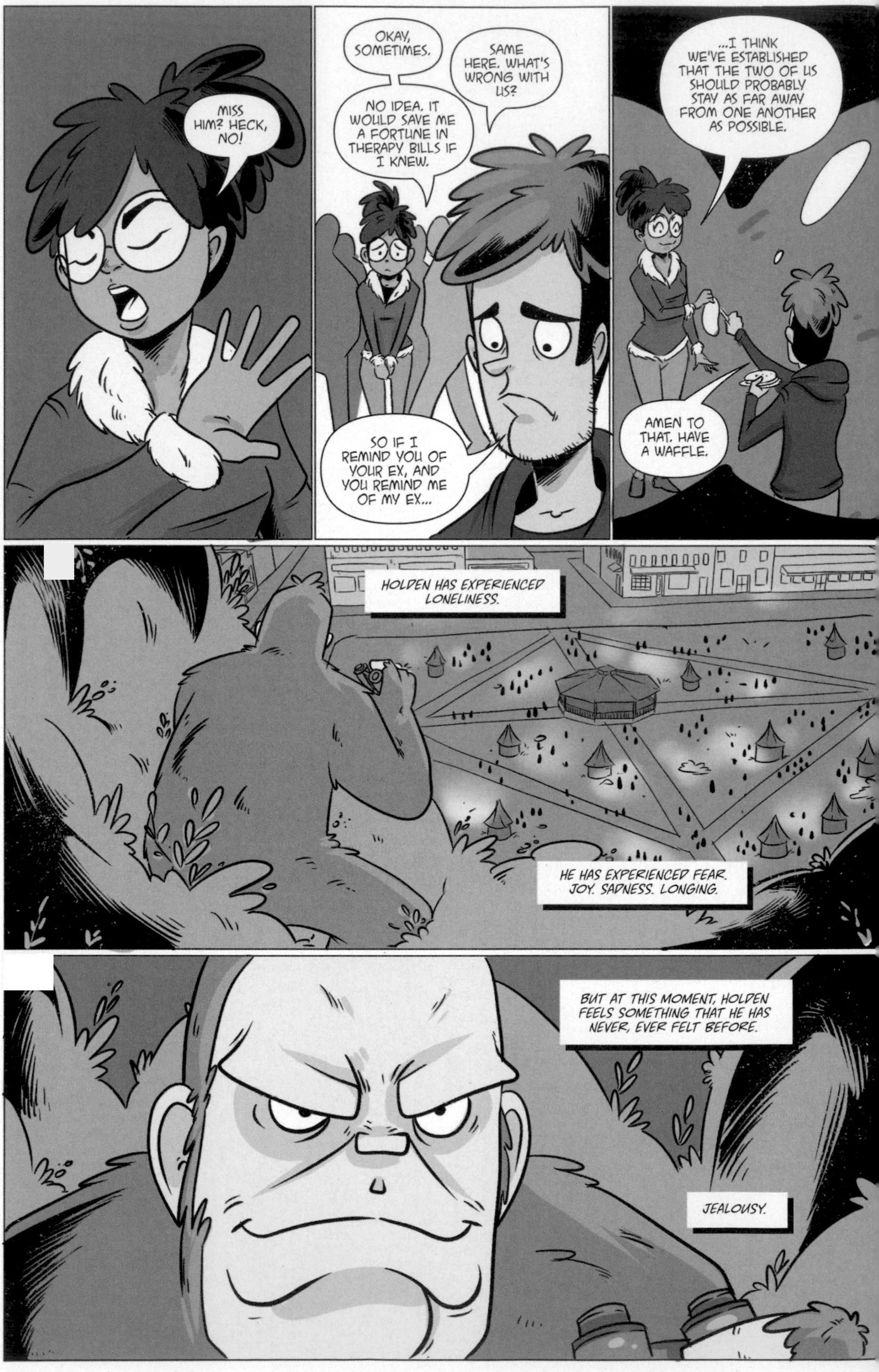
MISS HIM? HECK, NO!
OKAY, SOMETIMES.
NO IDEA. IT WOULD SAVE ME A FORTUNE IN THERAPY BILLS IF I KNEW.
SAME HERE. WHAT'S WRONG WITH US?
SO IF I REMIND YOU OF YOUR EX, AND YOU REMIND ME OF MY EX...
...I THINK WE'VE ESTABLISHED THAT THE TWO OF US SHOULD PROBABLY STAY AS FAR AWAY FROM ONE ANOTHER AS POSSIBLE.
AMEN TO THAT. HAVE A WAFFLE.
HOLDEN HAS EXPERIENCED LONELINESS.
HE HAS EXPERIENCED FEAR. JOY. SADNESS. LONGING.
BUT AT THIS MOMENT, HOLDEN FEELS SOMETHING THAT HE HAS NEVER, EVER FELT BEFORE.
JEALOUSY.

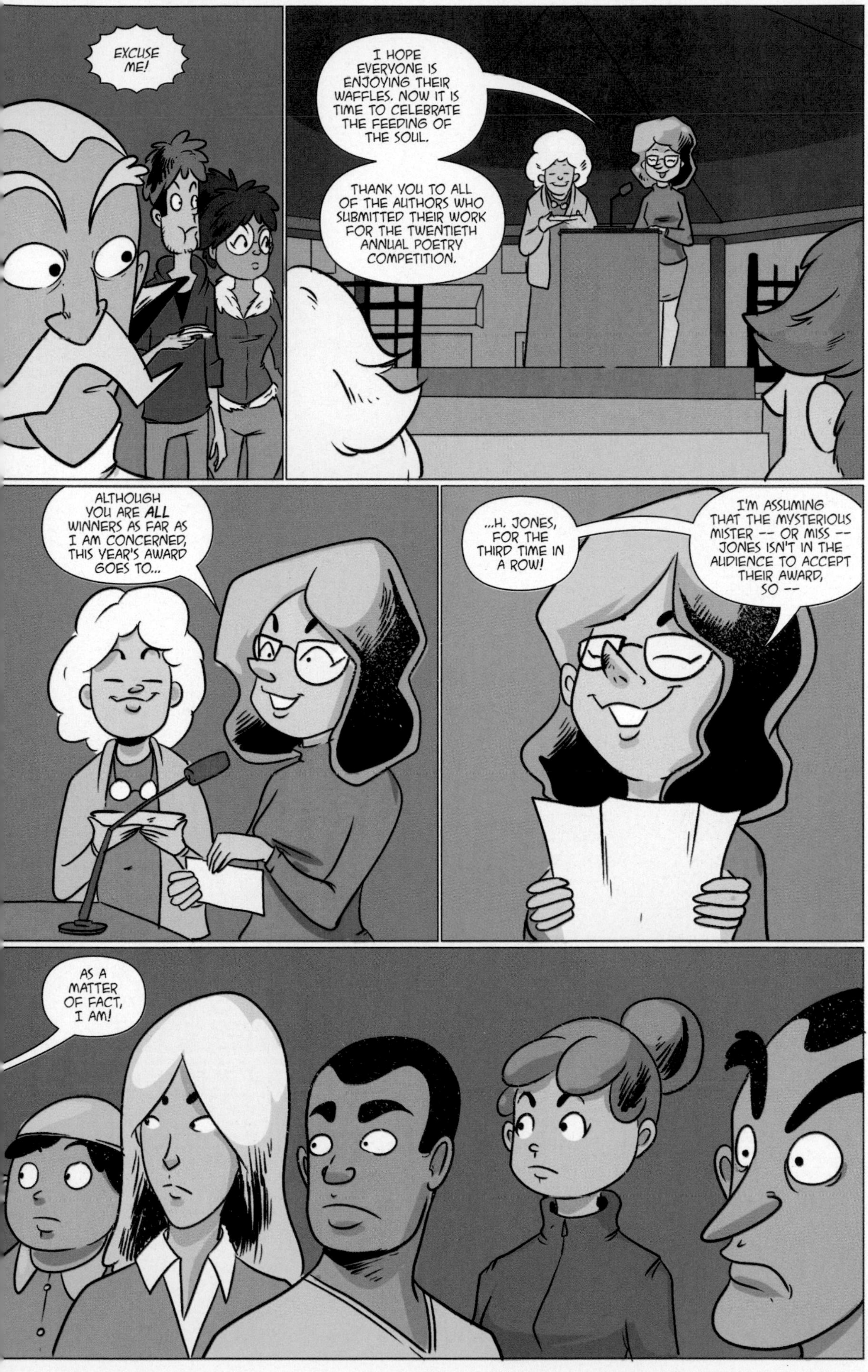
EXCUSE ME!
I HOPE EVERYONE IS ENJOYING THEIR WAFFLES. NOW IT IS TIME TO CELEBRATE THE FEEDING OF THE SOUL.
THANK YOU TO ALL OF THE AUTHORS WHO SUBMITTED THEIR WORK FOR THE TWENTIETH ANNUAL POETRY COMPETITION.
ALTHOUGH YOU ARE ALL WINNERS AS FAR AS I AM CONCERNED, THIS YEAR'S AWARD GOES TO...
...H. JONES, FOR THE THIRD TIME IN A ROW!
I'M ASSUMING THAT THE MYSTERIOUS MISTER -- OR MISS -- JONES ISN'T IN THE AUDIENCE TO ACCEPT THEIR AWARD, SO --
AS A MATTER OF FACT, I AM!

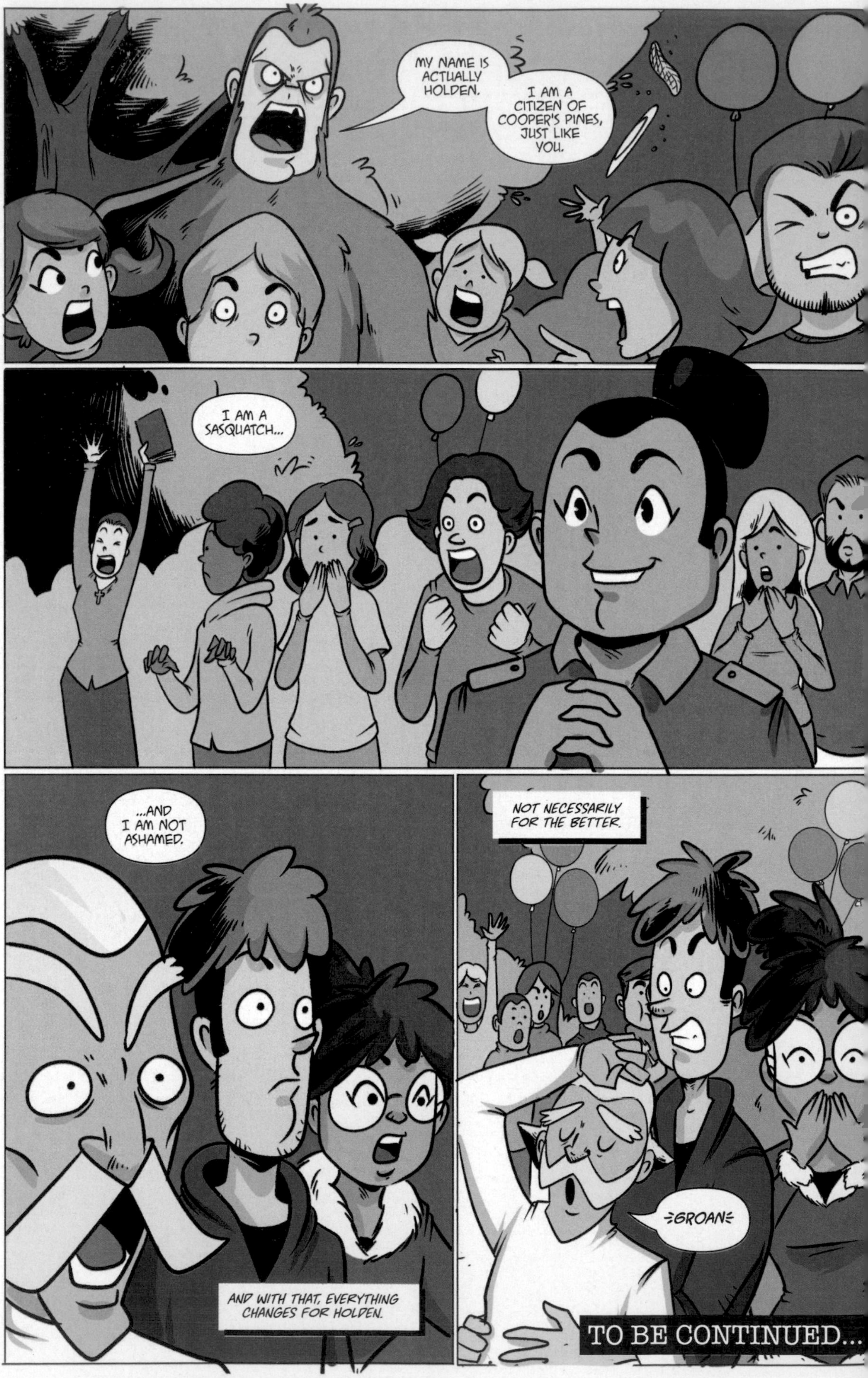
MY NAME IS ACTUALLY HOLDEN.
I AM A CITIZEN OF COOPER'S PINES, JUST LIKE YOU.
I AM A SASQUATCH...
...AND I AM NOT ASHAMED.
AND WITH THAT, EVERYTHING CHANGES FOR HOLDEN.
NOT NECESSARILY FOR THE BETTER.
GROAN
TO BE CONTINUED...

CHAPTER THREE: CITIZEN HOLDEN

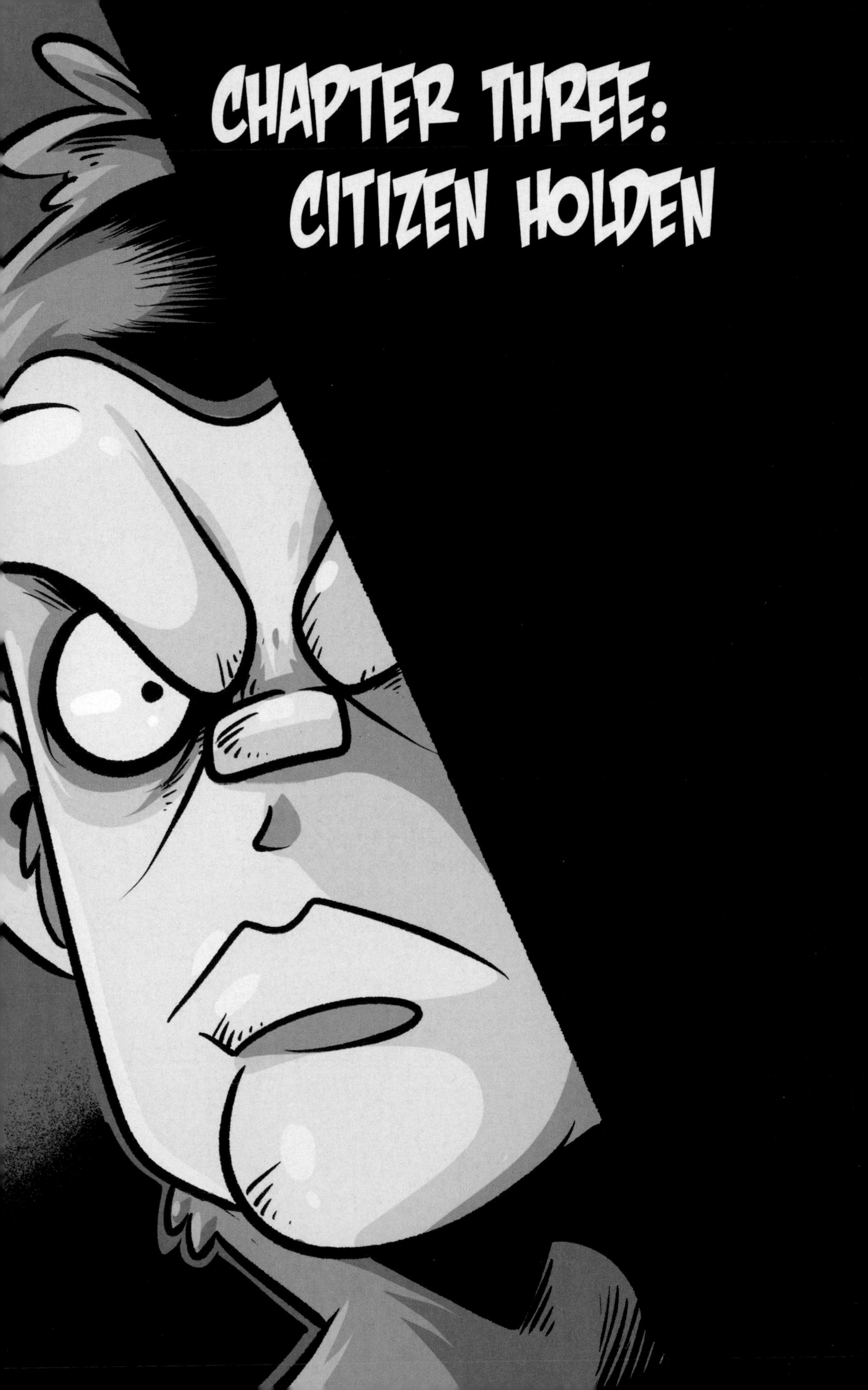

JASON NUTT
Writer

ALEXIS VIVALLO
Artist

DAVID ANAXAGORAS
Flatter

JOSH SOUTHALL
Letterer

Bryan Seaton: Publisher/CEO
Vito Delsante: Editor In Chief
Jason Martin: Publisher-Danger Zone
Chad Cicconi: Automotive Stunt Coordinator

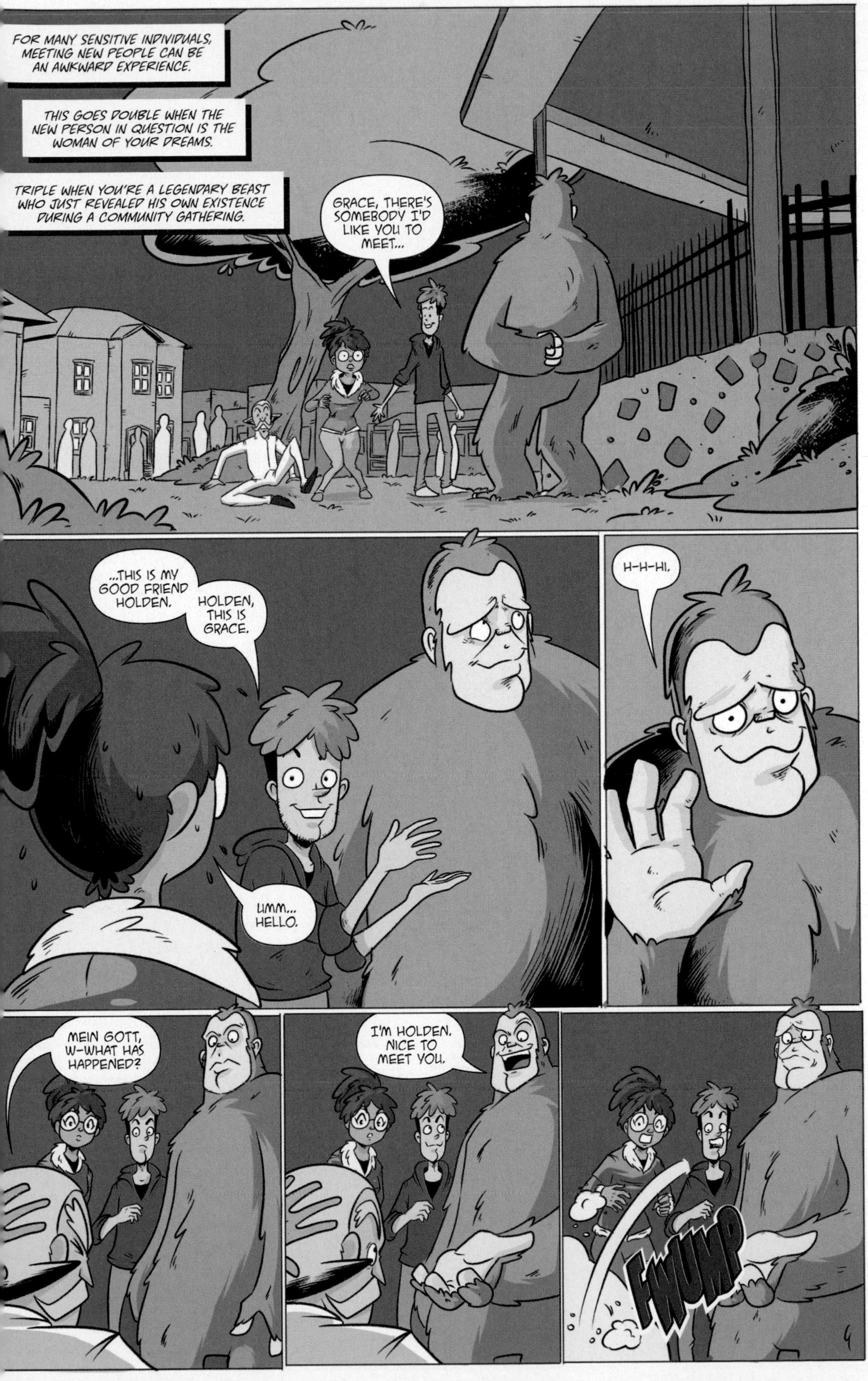

FOR MANY SENSITIVE INDIVIDUALS, MEETING NEW PEOPLE CAN BE AN AWKWARD EXPERIENCE.
THIS GOES DOUBLE WHEN THE NEW PERSON IN QUESTION IS THE WOMAN OF YOUR DREAMS.
TRIPLE WHEN YOU'RE A LEGENDARY BEAST WHO JUST REVEALED HIS OWN EXISTENCE DURING A COMMUNITY GATHERING.
GRACE, THERE'S SOMEBODY I'D LIKE YOU TO MEET...
...THIS IS MY GOOD FRIEND HOLDEN.
HOLDEN, THIS IS GRACE.
UMM... HELLO.
H-H-HI.
MEIN GOTT, W-WHAT HAS HAPPENED?
I'M HOLDEN. NICE TO MEET YOU.
FWUMP

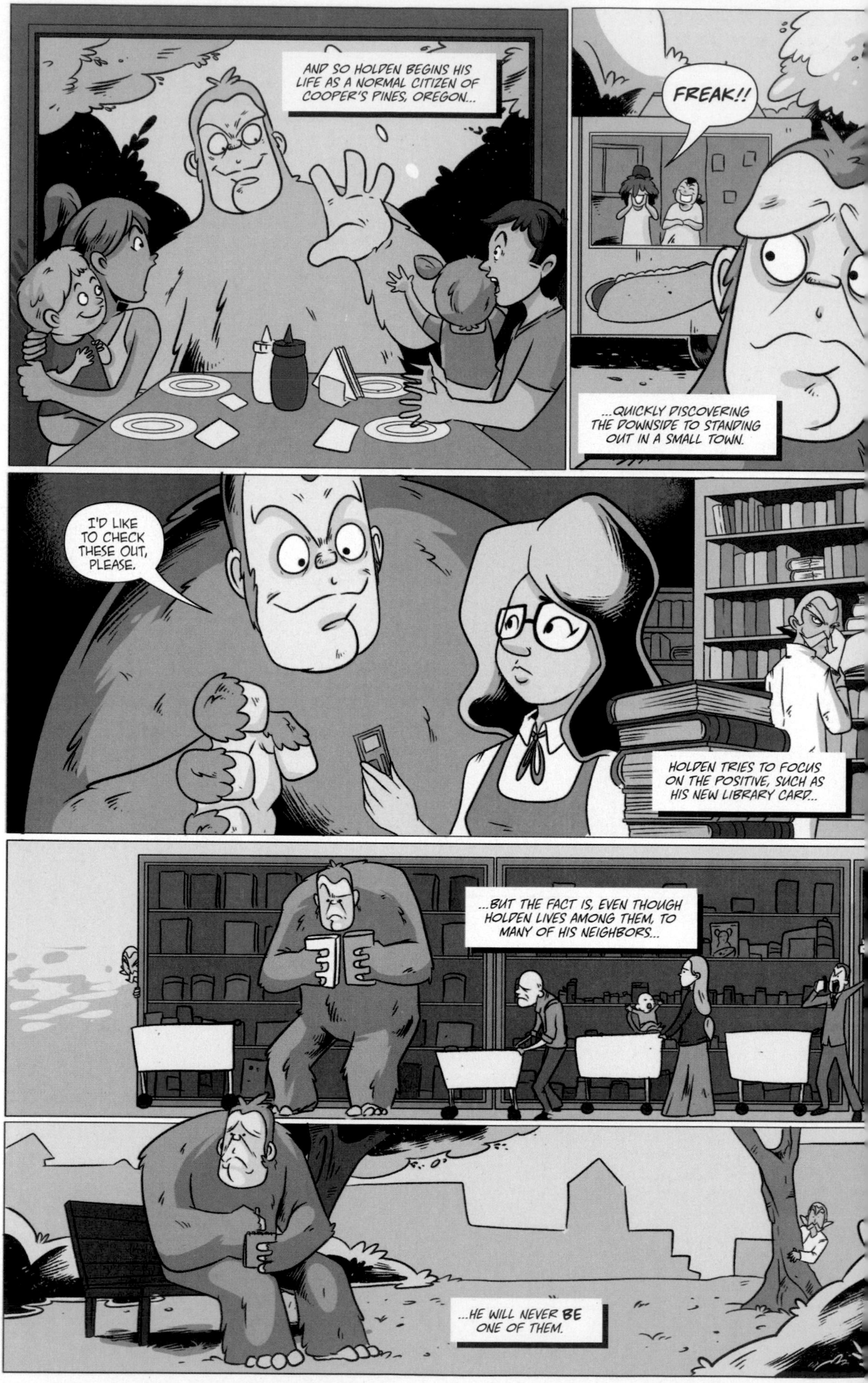
AND SO HOLDEN BEGINS HIS LIFE AS A NORMAL CITIZEN OF COOPER'S PINES, OREGON...
FREAK!!
...QUICKLY DISCOVERING THE DOWNSIDE TO STANDING OUT IN A SMALL TOWN.
I'D LIKE TO CHECK THESE OUT, PLEASE.
HOLDEN TRIES TO FOCUS ON THE POSITIVE, SUCH AS HIS NEW LIBRARY CARD...
...BUT THE FACT IS, EVEN THOUGH HOLDEN LIVES AMONG THEM, TO MANY OF HIS NEIGHBORS...
...HE WILL NEVER BE ONE OF THEM.

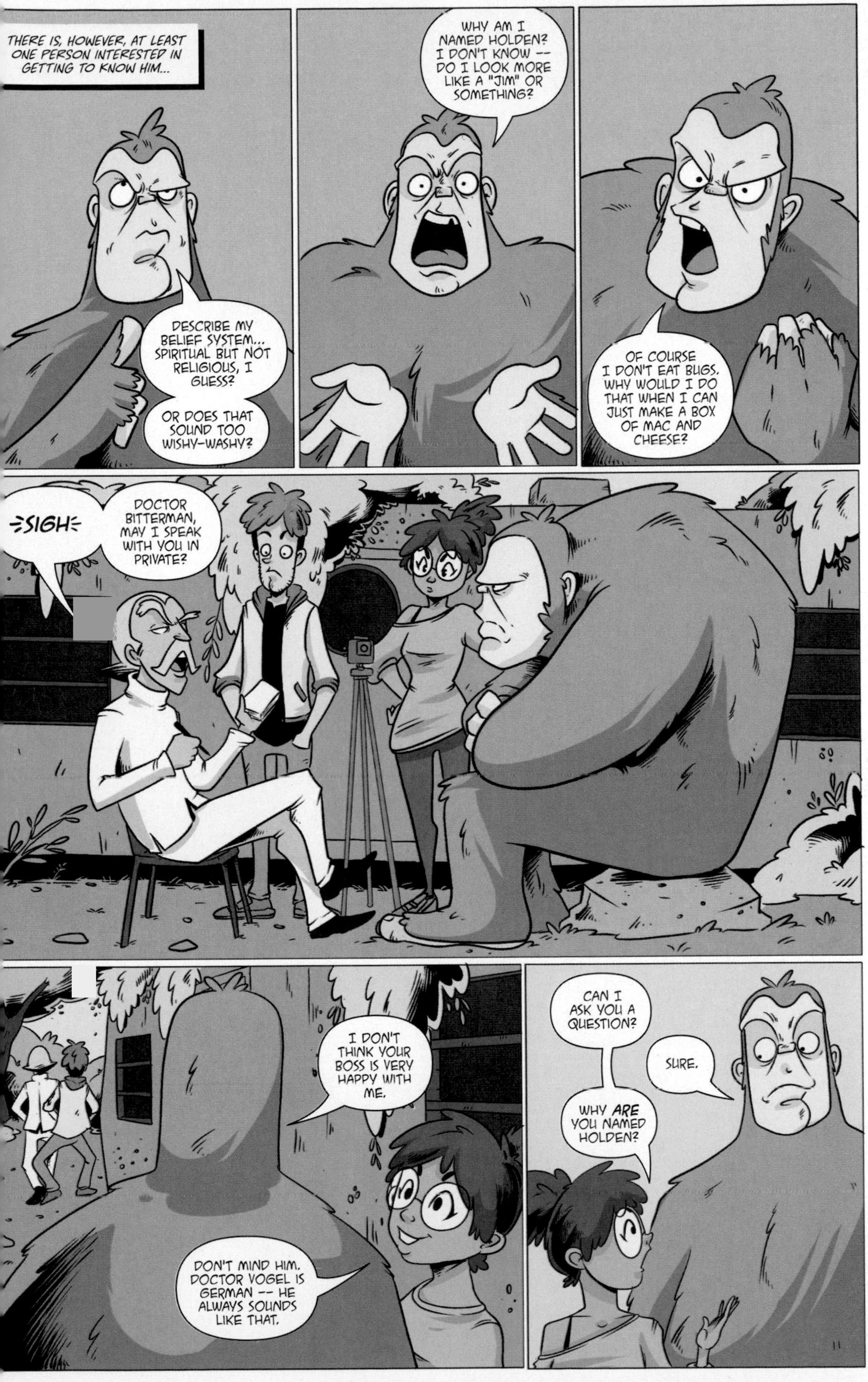
THERE IS, HOWEVER, AT LEAST ONE PERSON INTERESTED IN GETTING TO KNOW HIM...
DESCRIBE MY BELIEF SYSTEM... SPIRITUAL BUT NOT RELIGIOUS, I GUESS?
OR DOES THAT SOUND TOO WISHY-WASHY?
WHY AM I NAMED HOLDEN? I DON'T KNOW -- DO I LOOK MORE LIKE A "JIM" OR SOMETHING?
OF COURSE I DON'T EAT BUGS. WHY WOULD I DO THAT WHEN I CAN JUST MAKE A BOX OF MAC AND CHEESE?
SIGH
DOCTOR BITTERMAN, MAY I SPEAK WITH YOU IN PRIVATE?
I DON'T THINK YOUR BOSS IS VERY HAPPY WITH ME.
DON'T MIND HIM. DOCTOR VOGEL IS GERMAN -- HE ALWAYS SOUNDS LIKE THAT.
CAN I ASK YOU A QUESTION?
SURE.
WHY ARE YOU NAMED HOLDEN?

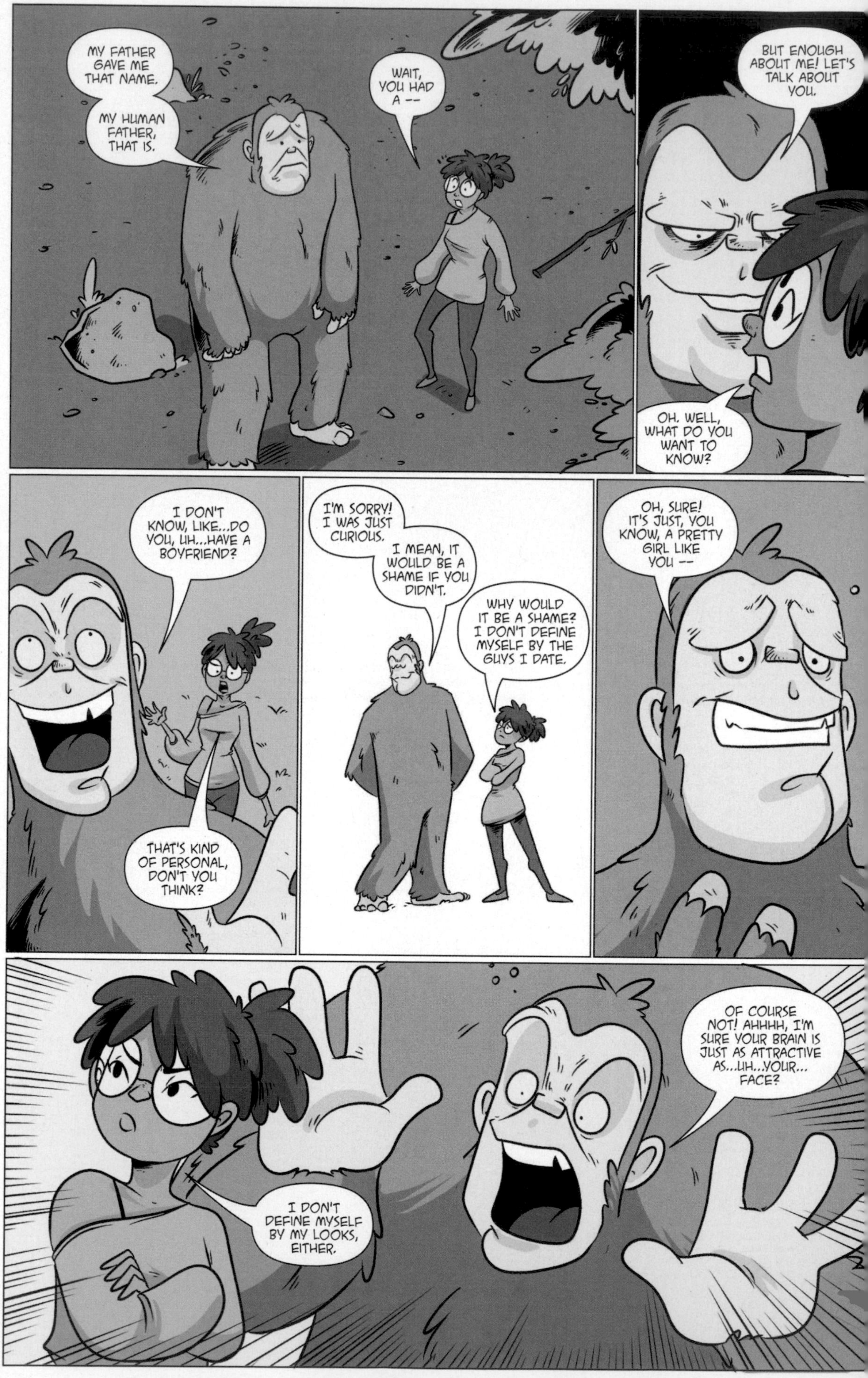
MY FATHER GAVE ME THAT NAME.
MY HUMAN FATHER, THAT IS.
WAIT, YOU HAD A --
BUT ENOUGH ABOUT ME! LET'S TALK ABOUT YOU.
OH. WELL, WHAT DO YOU WANT TO KNOW?
I DON'T KNOW, LIKE...DO YOU, UH...HAVE A BOYFRIEND?
THAT'S KIND OF PERSONAL, DON'T YOU THINK?
I'M SORRY! I WAS JUST CURIOUS.
I MEAN, IT WOULD BE A SHAME IF YOU DIDN'T.
WHY WOULD IT BE A SHAME? I DON'T DEFINE MYSELF BY THE GUYS I DATE.
OH, SURE! IT'S JUST, YOU KNOW, A PRETTY GIRL LIKE YOU --
I DON'T DEFINE MYSELF BY MY LOOKS, EITHER.
OF COURSE NOT! AHHHH, I'M SURE YOUR BRAIN IS JUST AS ATTRACTIVE AS...UH...YOUR... FACE?

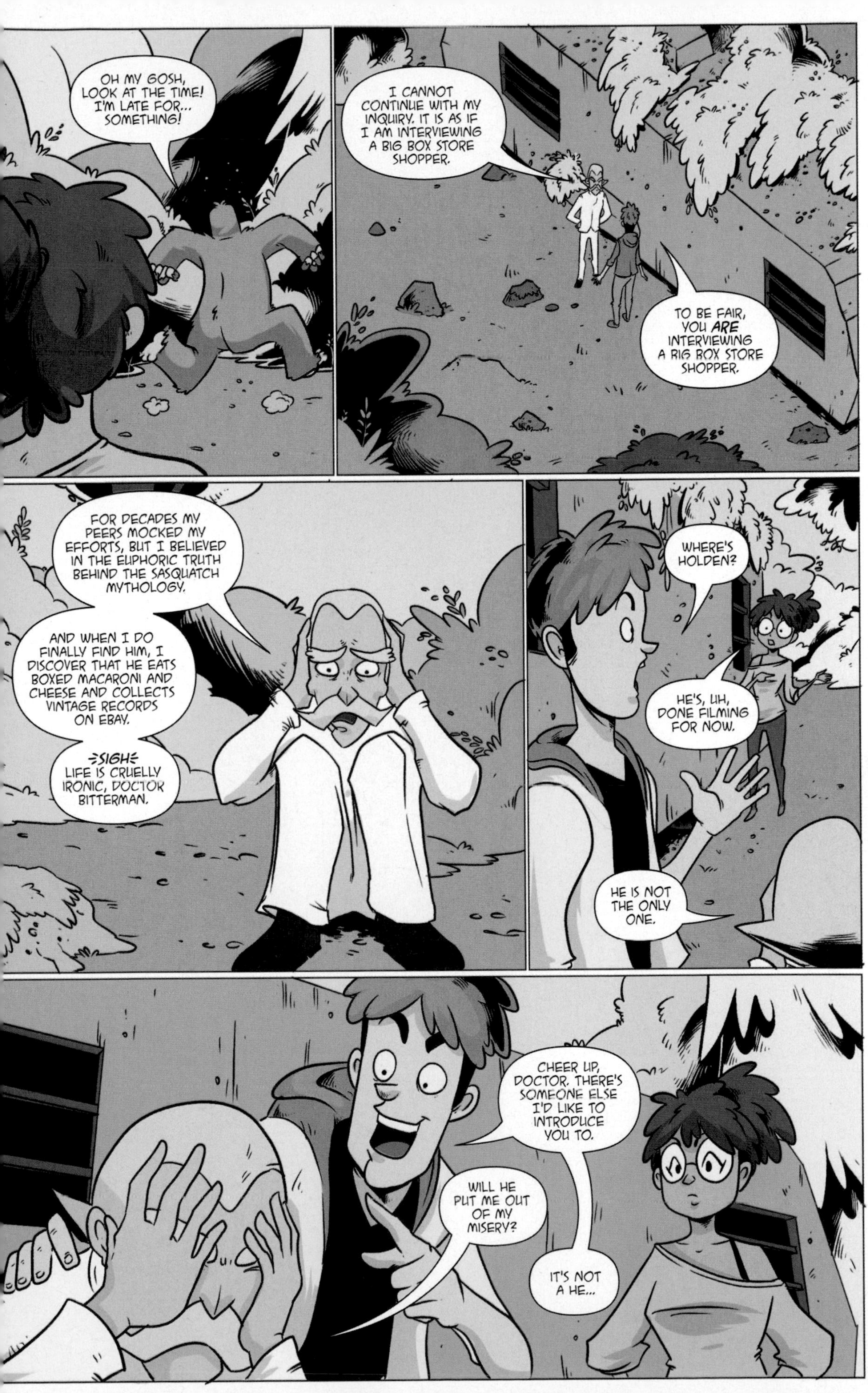
OH MY GOSH, LOOK AT THE TIME! I'M LATE FOR... SOMETHING!
I CANNOT CONTINUE WITH MY INQUIRY. IT IS AS IF I AM INTERVIEWING A BIG BOX STORE SHOPPER.
TO BE FAIR, YOU *ARE* INTERVIEWING A BIG BOX STORE SHOPPER.
FOR DECADES MY PEERS MOCKED MY EFFORTS, BUT I BELIEVED IN THE EUPHORIC TRUTH BEHIND THE SASQUATCH MYTHOLOGY.
AND WHEN I DO FINALLY FIND HIM, I DISCOVER THAT HE EATS BOXED MACARONI AND CHEESE AND COLLECTS VINTAGE RECORDS ON EBAY.
SIGH
LIFE IS CRUELLY IRONIC, DOCTOR BITTERMAN.
WHERE'S HOLDEN?
HE'S, UH, DONE FILMING FOR NOW.
HE IS NOT THE ONLY ONE.
CHEER UP, DOCTOR. THERE'S SOMEONE ELSE I'D LIKE TO INTRODUCE YOU TO.
WILL HE PUT ME OUT OF MY MISERY?
IT'S NOT A HE...

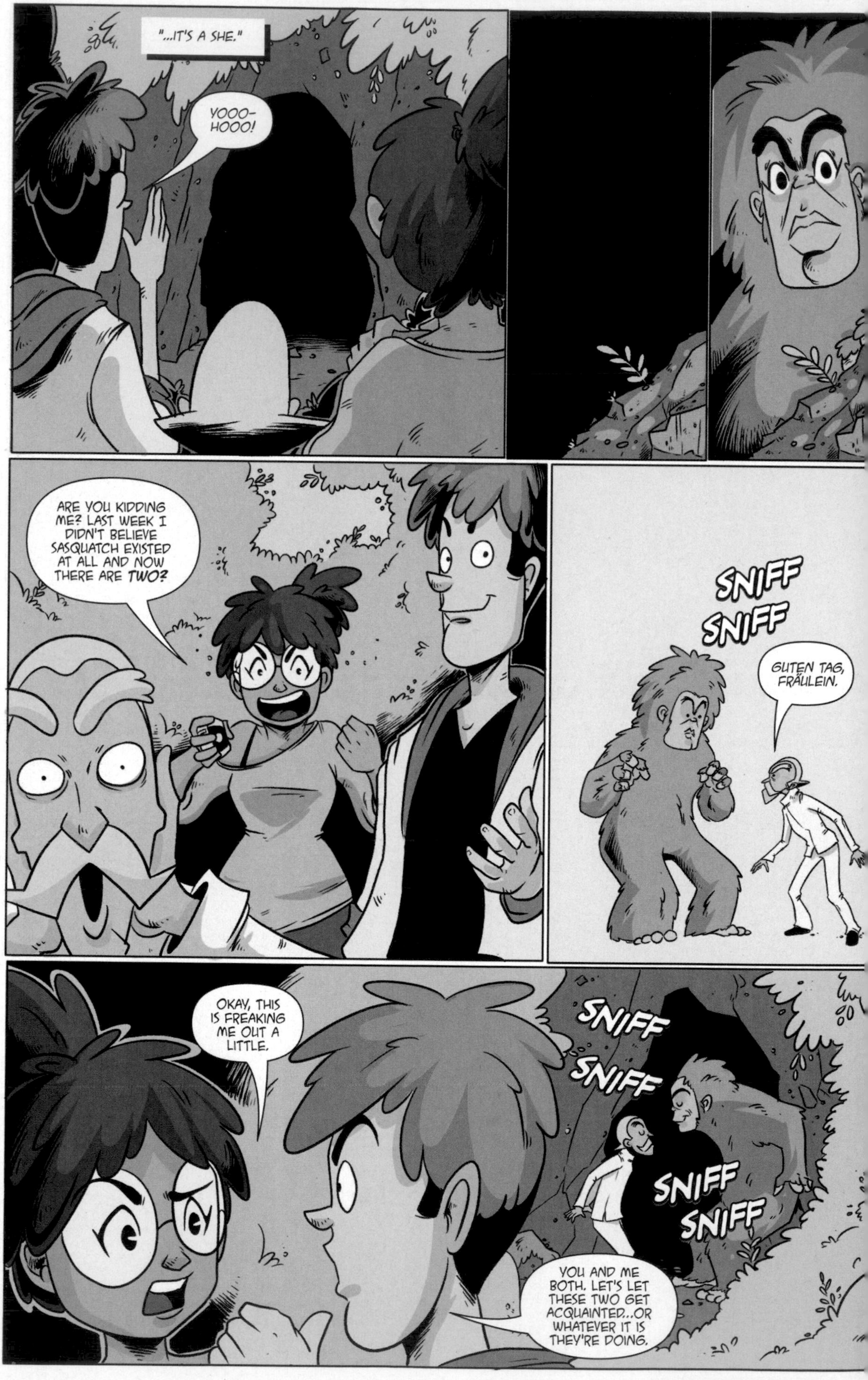
"...IT'S A SHE."
YOOO-HOOO!
ARE YOU KIDDING ME? LAST WEEK I DIDN'T BELIEVE SASQUATCH EXISTED AT ALL AND NOW THERE ARE *TWO*?
SNIFF SNIFF
GUTEN TAG, FRÄULEIN.
OKAY, THIS IS FREAKING ME OUT A LITTLE.
SNIFF SNIFF
SNIFF SNIFF
YOU AND ME BOTH. LET'S LET THESE TWO GET ACQUAINTED...OR WHATEVER IT IS THEY'RE DOING.

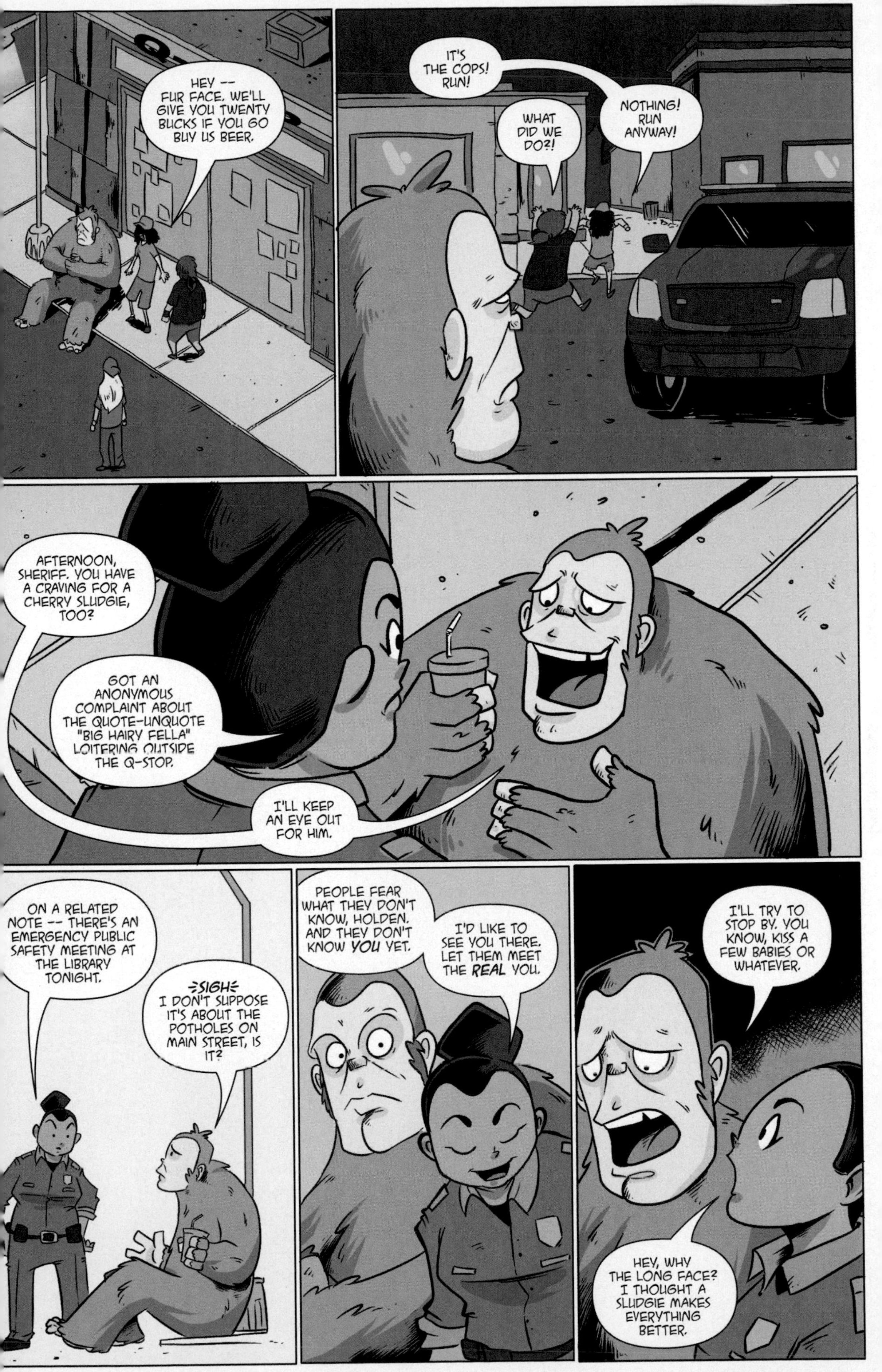
HEY -- FUR FACE. WE'LL GIVE YOU TWENTY BUCKS IF YOU GO BUY US BEER.
IT'S THE COPS! RUN!
WHAT DID WE DO?!
NOTHING! RUN ANYWAY!
AFTERNOON, SHERIFF. YOU HAVE A CRAVING FOR A CHERRY SLUDGIE, TOO?
GOT AN ANONYMOUS COMPLAINT ABOUT THE QUOTE-UNQUOTE "BIG HAIRY FELLA" LOITERING OUTSIDE THE Q-STOP.
I'LL KEEP AN EYE OUT FOR HIM.
ON A RELATED NOTE -- THERE'S AN EMERGENCY PUBLIC SAFETY MEETING AT THE LIBRARY TONIGHT.
SIGH
I DON'T SUPPOSE IT'S ABOUT THE POTHOLES ON MAIN STREET, IS IT?
PEOPLE FEAR WHAT THEY DON'T KNOW, HOLDEN. AND THEY DON'T KNOW YOU YET.
I'D LIKE TO SEE YOU THERE. LET THEM MEET THE REAL YOU.
I'LL TRY TO STOP BY. YOU KNOW, KISS A FEW BABIES OR WHATEVER.
HEY, WHY THE LONG FACE? I THOUGHT A SLUDGIE MAKES EVERYTHING BETTER.

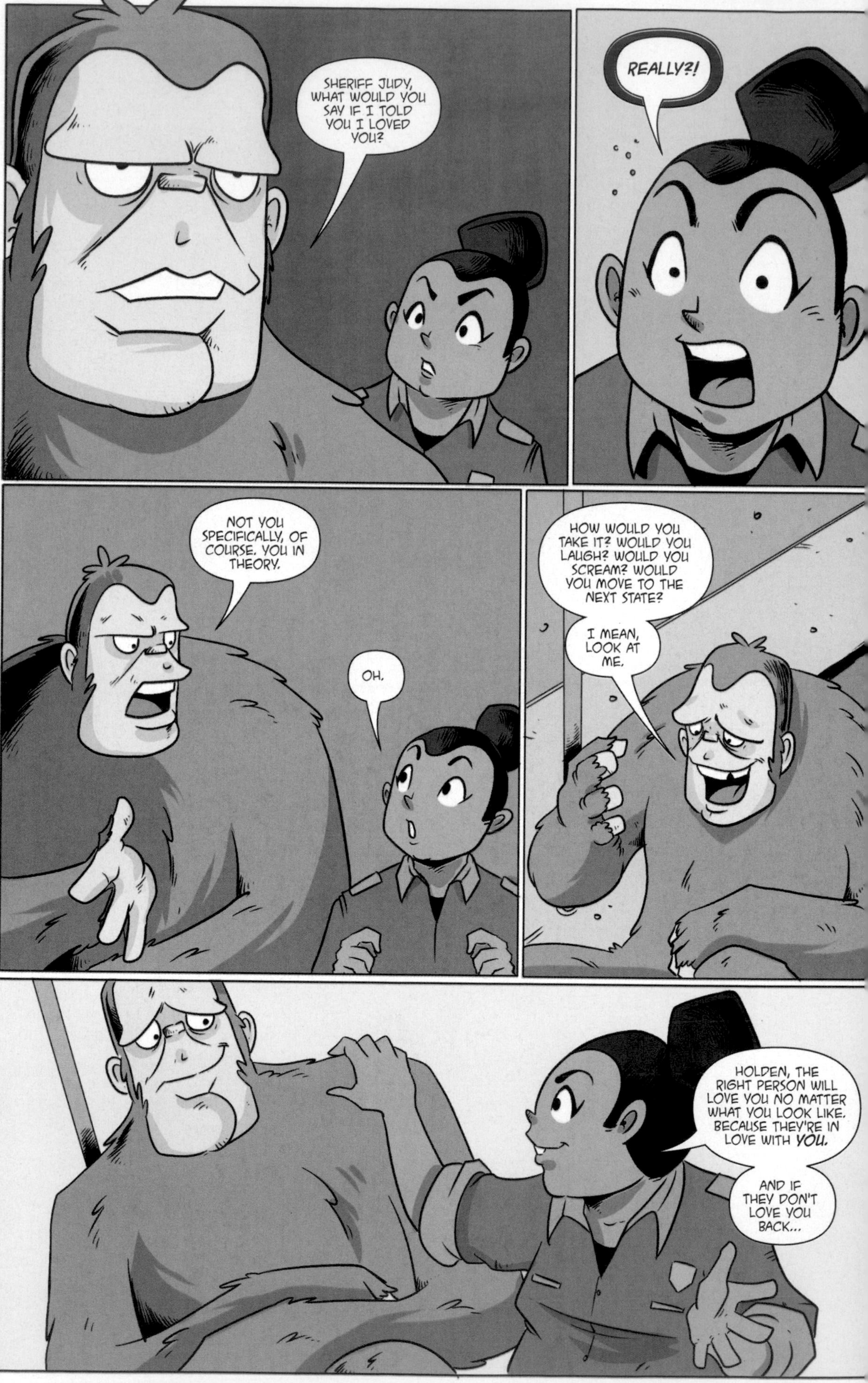
SHERIFF JUDY, WHAT WOULD YOU SAY IF I TOLD YOU I LOVED YOU?
REALLY?!
NOT YOU SPECIFICALLY, OF COURSE. YOU IN THEORY.
OH.
HOW WOULD YOU TAKE IT? WOULD YOU LAUGH? WOULD YOU SCREAM? WOULD YOU MOVE TO THE NEXT STATE?
I MEAN, LOOK AT ME.
HOLDEN, THE RIGHT PERSON WILL LOVE YOU NO MATTER WHAT YOU LOOK LIKE. BECAUSE THEY'RE IN LOVE WITH *YOU.*
AND IF THEY DON'T LOVE YOU BACK...

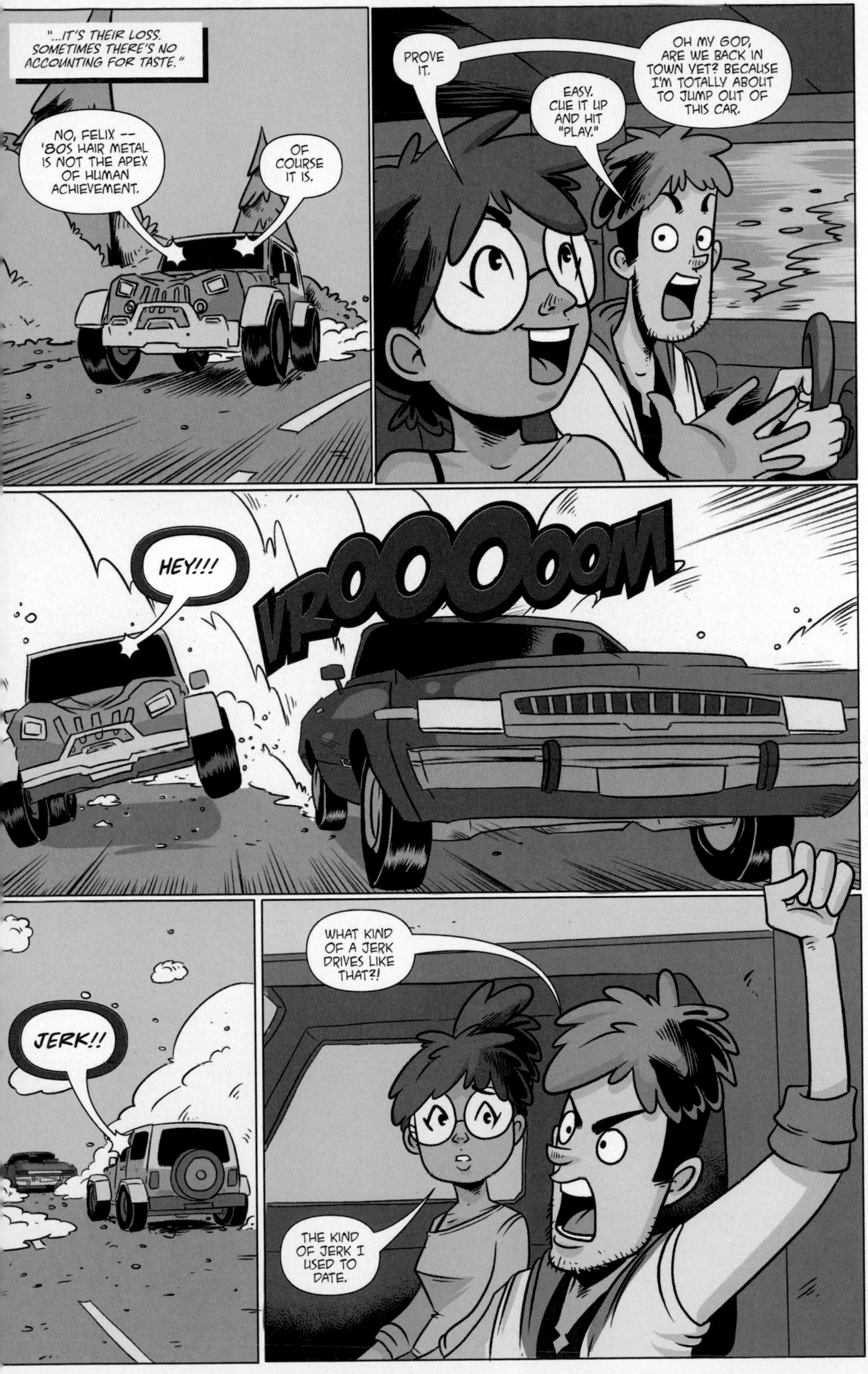
"...IT'S THEIR LOSS. SOMETIMES THERE'S NO ACCOUNTING FOR TASTE."
NO, FELIX -- '80S HAIR METAL IS NOT THE APEX OF HUMAN ACHIEVEMENT.
OF COURSE IT IS.
PROVE IT.
EASY. CUE IT UP AND HIT "PLAY."
OH MY GOD, ARE WE BACK IN TOWN YET? BECAUSE I'M TOTALLY ABOUT TO JUMP OUT OF THIS CAR.
HEY!!!
VROOOOoom
JERK!!
WHAT KIND OF A JERK DRIVES LIKE THAT?!
THE KIND OF JERK I USED TO DATE.

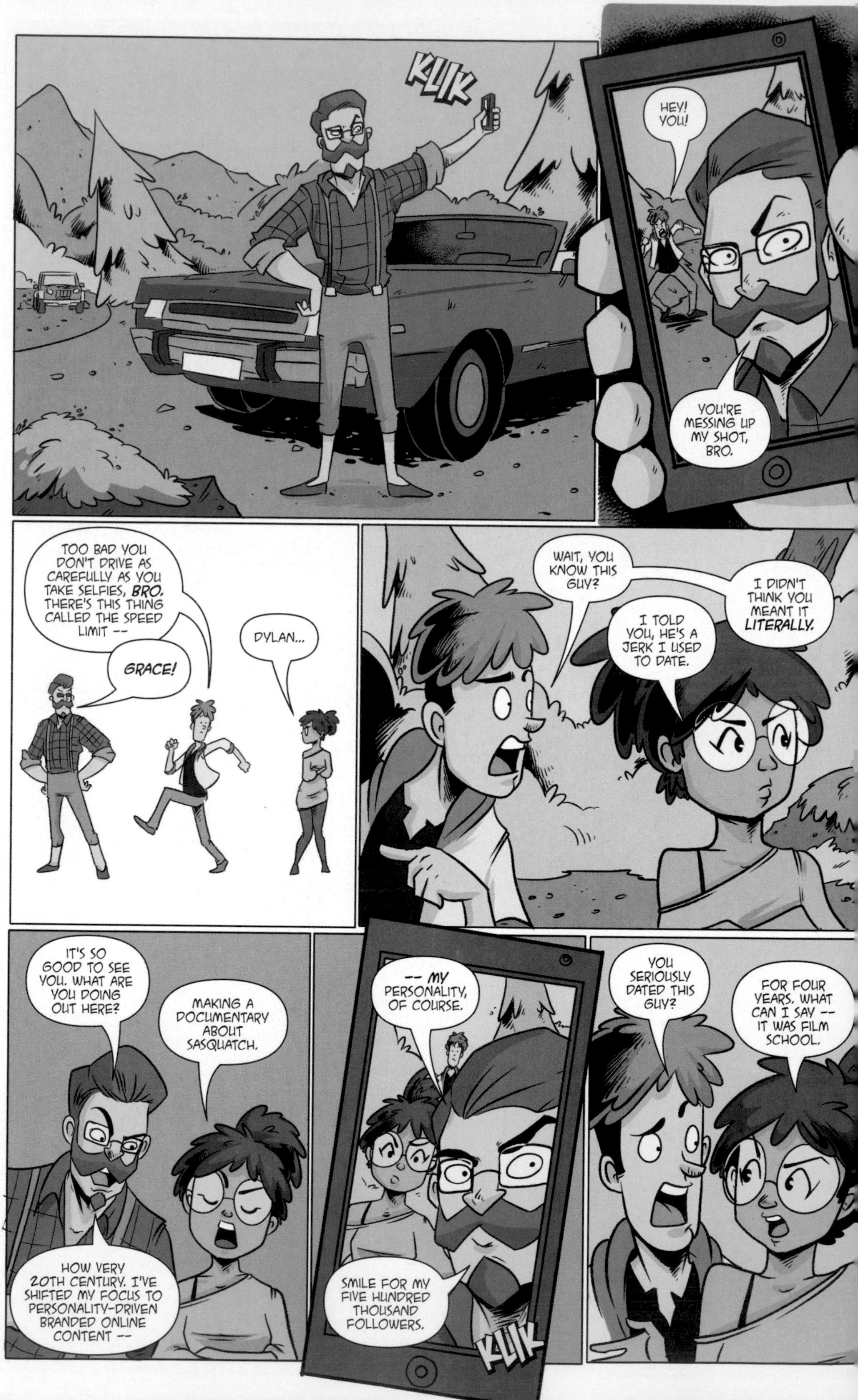
KLIK
HEY! YOU!
YOU'RE MESSING UP MY SHOT, BRO.
TOO BAD YOU DON'T DRIVE AS CAREFULLY AS YOU TAKE SELFIES, BRO. THERE'S THIS THING CALLED THE SPEED LIMIT --
GRACE!
DYLAN...
WAIT, YOU KNOW THIS GUY?
I TOLD YOU, HE'S A JERK I USED TO DATE.
I DIDN'T THINK YOU MEANT IT LITERALLY.
IT'S SO GOOD TO SEE YOU. WHAT ARE YOU DOING OUT HERE?
MAKING A DOCUMENTARY ABOUT SASQUATCH.
HOW VERY 20TH CENTURY. I'VE SHIFTED MY FOCUS TO PERSONALITY-DRIVEN BRANDED ONLINE CONTENT --
-- MY PERSONALITY, OF COURSE.
SMILE FOR MY FIVE HUNDRED THOUSAND FOLLOWERS.
KLIK
YOU SERIOUSLY DATED THIS GUY?
FOR FOUR YEARS. WHAT CAN I SAY -- IT WAS FILM SCHOOL.

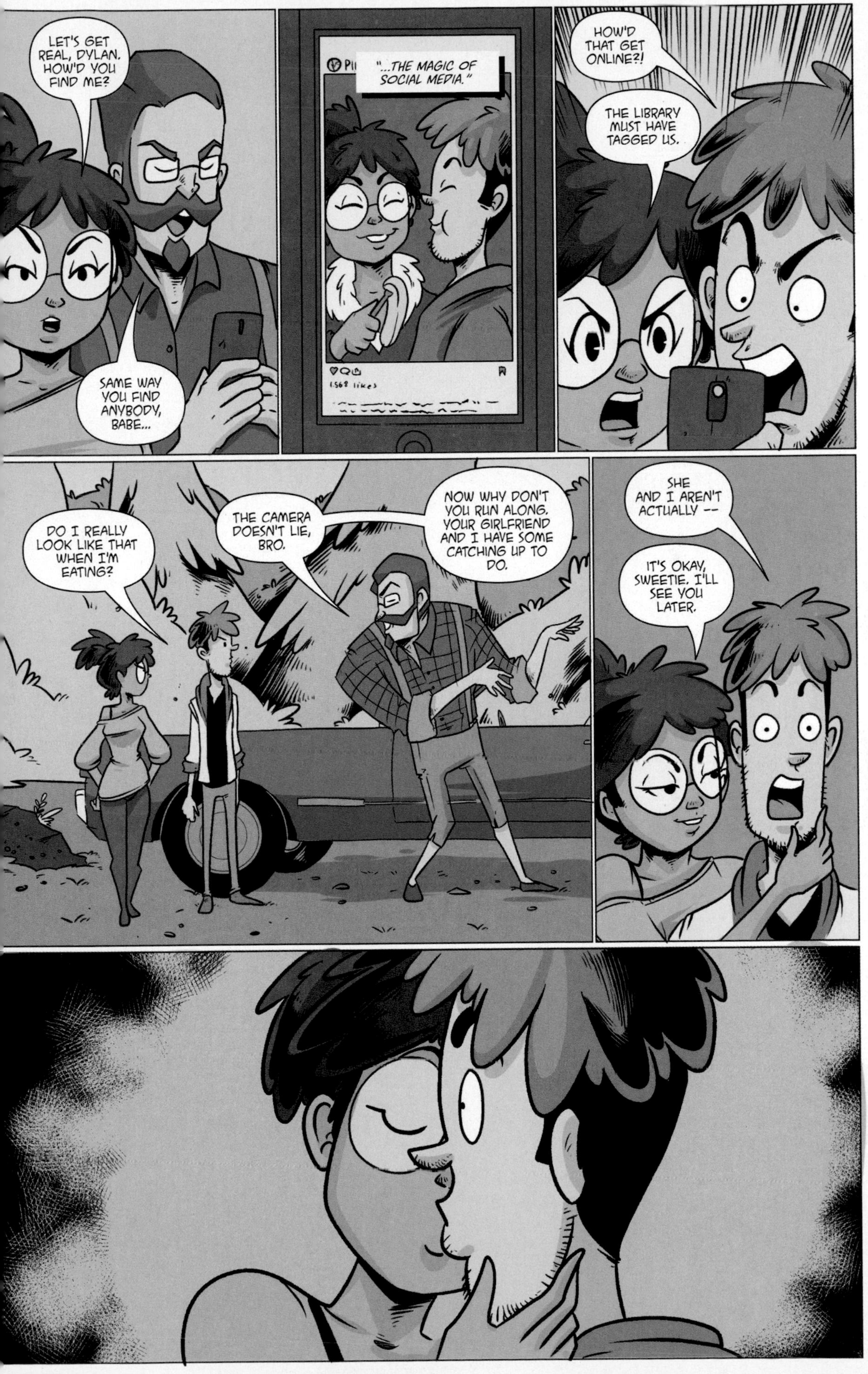
LET'S GET REAL, DYLAN. HOW'D YOU FIND ME?
SAME WAY YOU FIND ANYBODY, BABE...
"...THE MAGIC OF SOCIAL MEDIA."
1,568 likes
HOW'D THAT GET ONLINE?!
THE LIBRARY MUST HAVE TAGGED US.
DO I REALLY LOOK LIKE THAT WHEN I'M EATING?
THE CAMERA DOESN'T LIE, BRO.
NOW WHY DON'T YOU RUN ALONG. YOUR GIRLFRIEND AND I HAVE SOME CATCHING UP TO DO.
SHE AND I AREN'T ACTUALLY --
IT'S OKAY, SWEETIE. I'LL SEE YOU LATER.

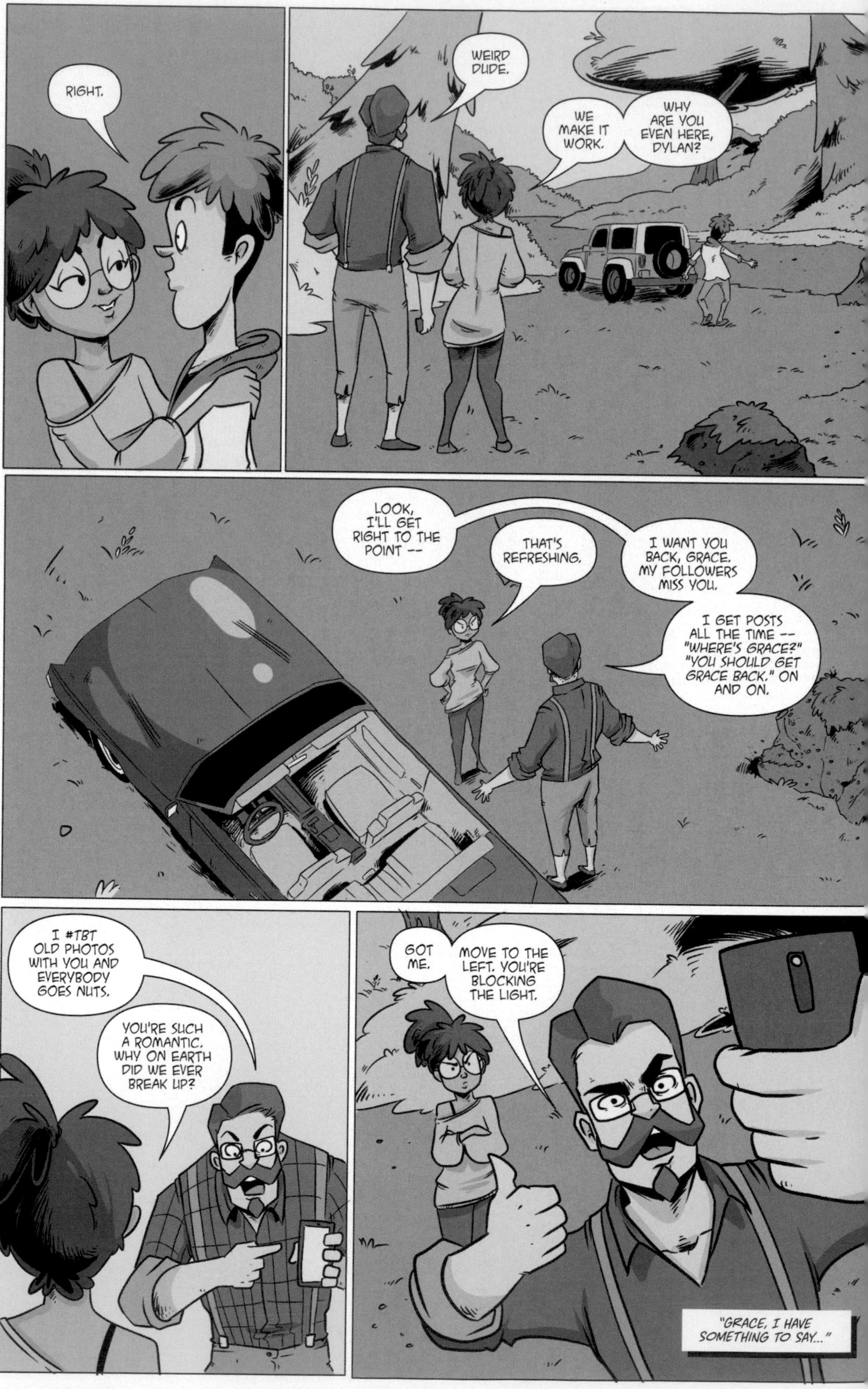
RIGHT.
WEIRD DUDE.
WE MAKE IT WORK.
WHY ARE YOU EVEN HERE, DYLAN?
LOOK, I'LL GET RIGHT TO THE POINT --
THAT'S REFRESHING.
I WANT YOU BACK, GRACE. MY FOLLOWERS MISS YOU.
I GET POSTS ALL THE TIME -- "WHERE'S GRACE?" "YOU SHOULD GET GRACE BACK." ON AND ON.
I #TBT OLD PHOTOS WITH YOU AND EVERYBODY GOES NUTS.
YOU'RE SUCH A ROMANTIC. WHY ON EARTH DID WE EVER BREAK UP?
GOT ME.
MOVE TO THE LEFT. YOU'RE BLOCKING THE LIGHT.
"GRACE, I HAVE SOMETHING TO SAY..."

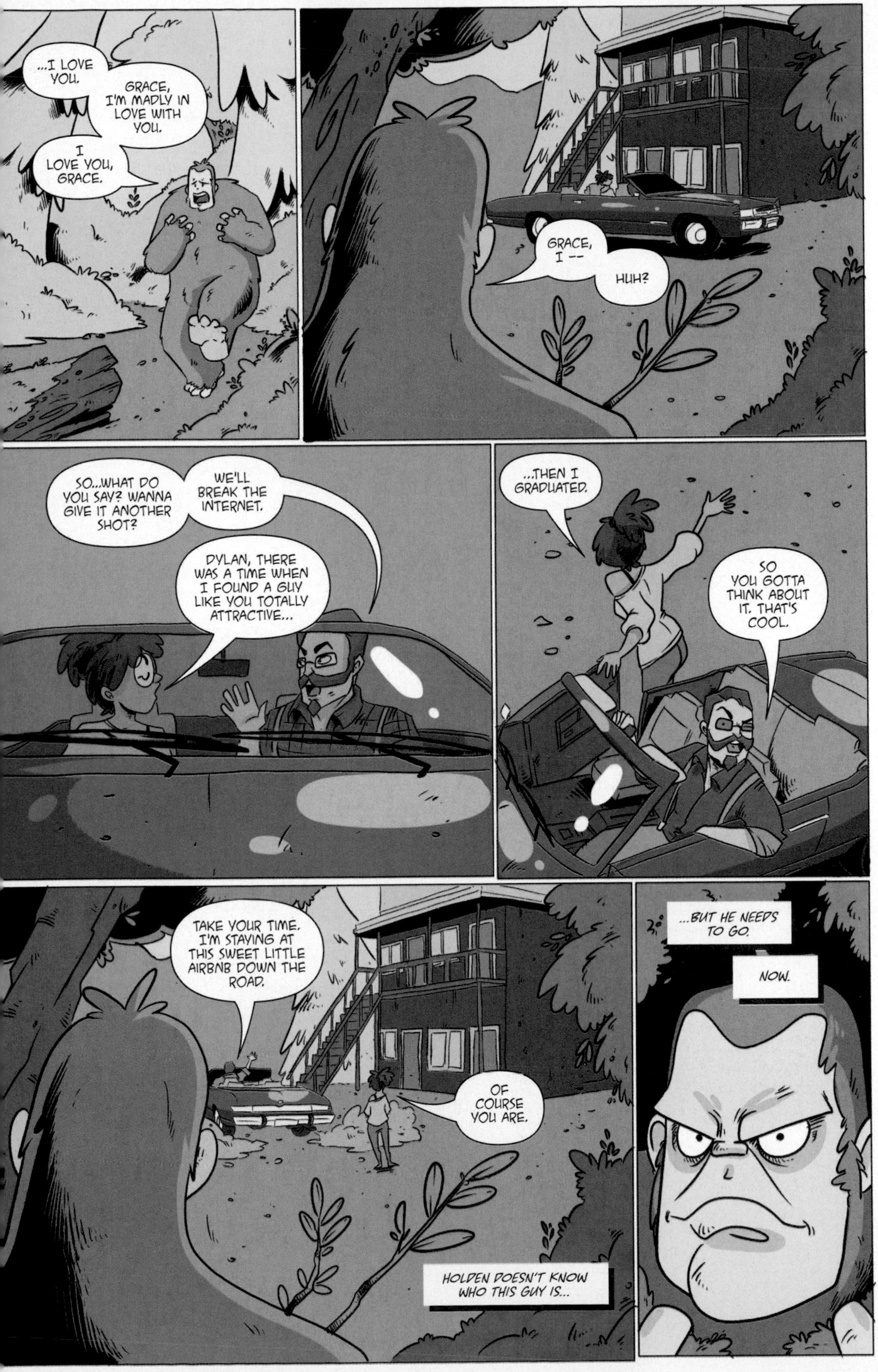
...I LOVE YOU.
GRACE, I'M MADLY IN LOVE WITH YOU.
I LOVE YOU, GRACE.
GRACE, I --
HUH?
SO...WHAT DO YOU SAY? WANNA GIVE IT ANOTHER SHOT?
WE'LL BREAK THE INTERNET.
DYLAN, THERE WAS A TIME WHEN I FOUND A GUY LIKE YOU TOTALLY ATTRACTIVE...
...THEN I GRADUATED.
SO YOU GOTTA THINK ABOUT IT. THAT'S COOL.
TAKE YOUR TIME. I'M STAYING AT THIS SWEET LITTLE AIRBNB DOWN THE ROAD.
OF COURSE YOU ARE.
HOLDEN DOESN'T KNOW WHO THIS GUY IS...
...BUT HE NEEDS TO GO.
NOW.

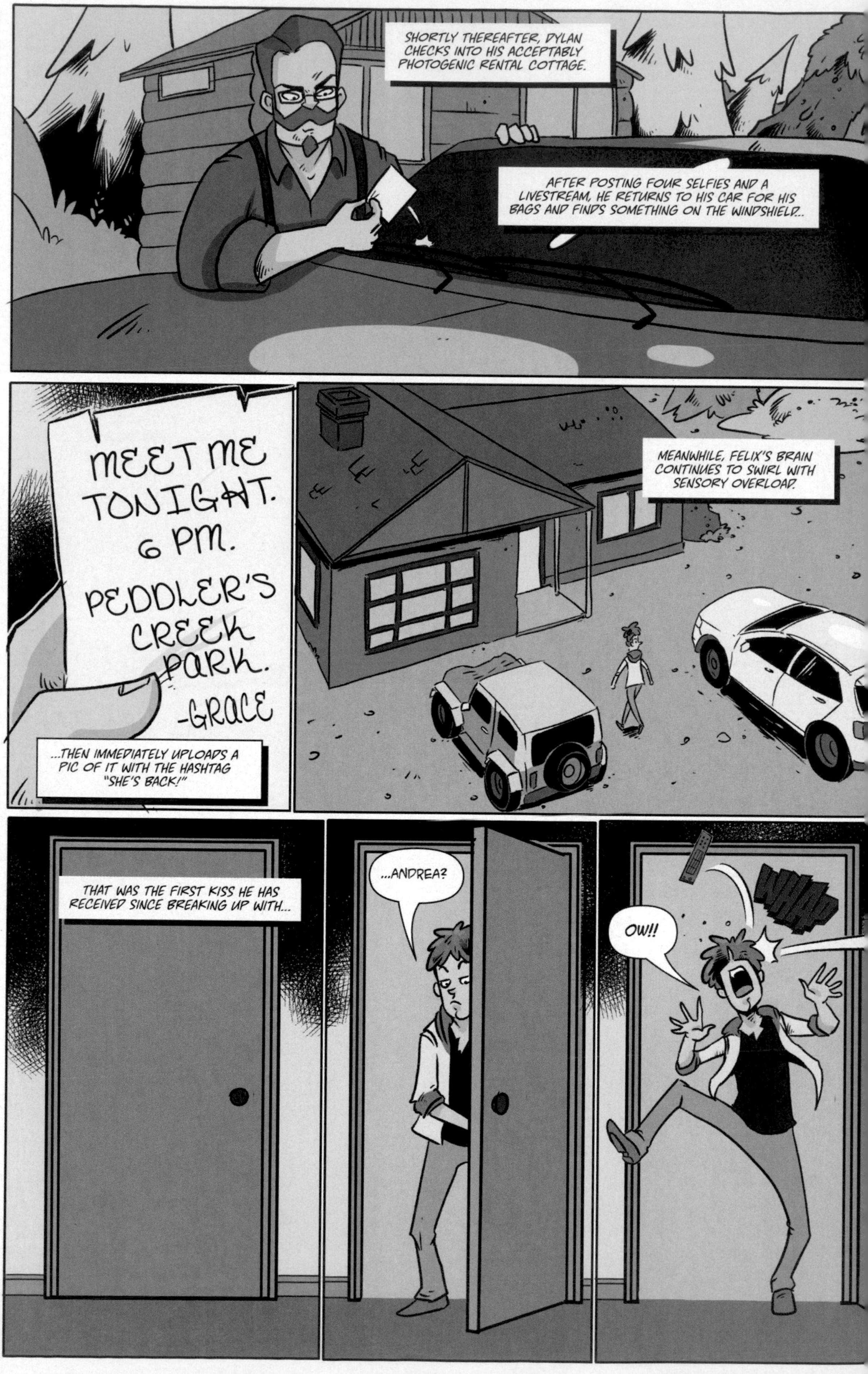
SHORTLY THEREAFTER, DYLAN CHECKS INTO HIS ACCEPTABLY PHOTOGENIC RENTAL COTTAGE.
AFTER POSTING FOUR SELFIES AND A LIVESTREAM, HE RETURNS TO HIS CAR FOR HIS BAGS AND FINDS SOMETHING ON THE WINDSHIELD...
MEET ME TONIGHT. 6 PM. PEDDLER'S CREEK PARK. -GRACE
...THEN IMMEDIATELY UPLOADS A PIC OF IT WITH THE HASHTAG "SHE'S BACK!"
MEANWHILE, FELIX'S BRAIN CONTINUES TO SWIRL WITH SENSORY OVERLOAD.
THAT WAS THE FIRST KISS HE HAS RECEIVED SINCE BREAKING UP WITH...
...ANDREA?
WHAP
OW!!

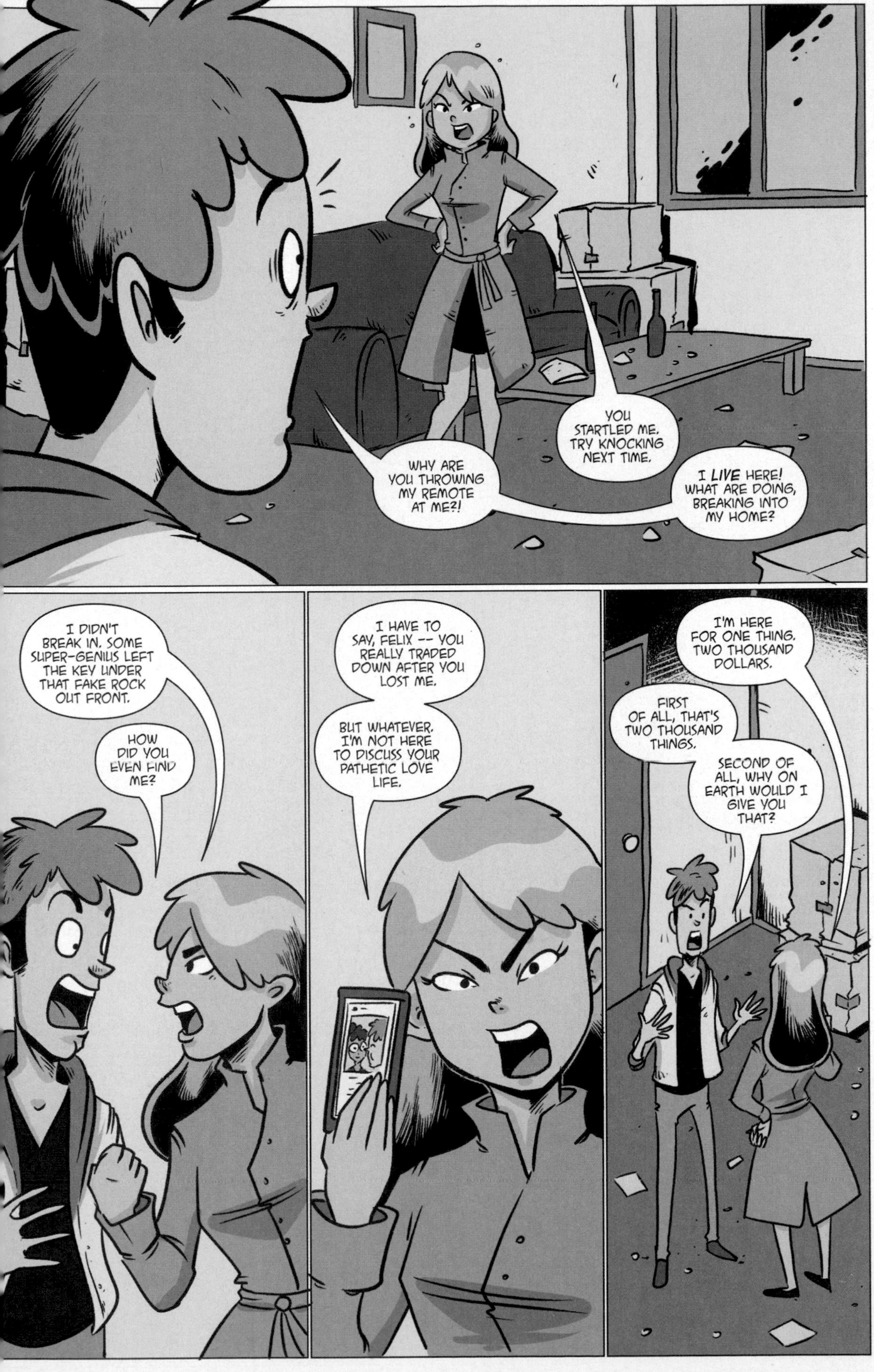
YOU STARTLED ME. TRY KNOCKING NEXT TIME.
WHY ARE YOU THROWING MY REMOTE AT ME?!
I LIVE HERE! WHAT ARE DOING, BREAKING INTO MY HOME?
I DIDN'T BREAK IN. SOME SUPER-GENIUS LEFT THE KEY UNDER THAT FAKE ROCK OUT FRONT.
HOW DID YOU EVEN FIND ME?
I HAVE TO SAY, FELIX -- YOU REALLY TRADED DOWN AFTER YOU LOST ME.
BUT WHATEVER. I'M NOT HERE TO DISCUSS YOUR PATHETIC LOVE LIFE.
I'M HERE FOR ONE THING. TWO THOUSAND DOLLARS.
FIRST OF ALL, THAT'S TWO THOUSAND THINGS.
SECOND OF ALL, WHY ON EARTH WOULD I GIVE YOU THAT?

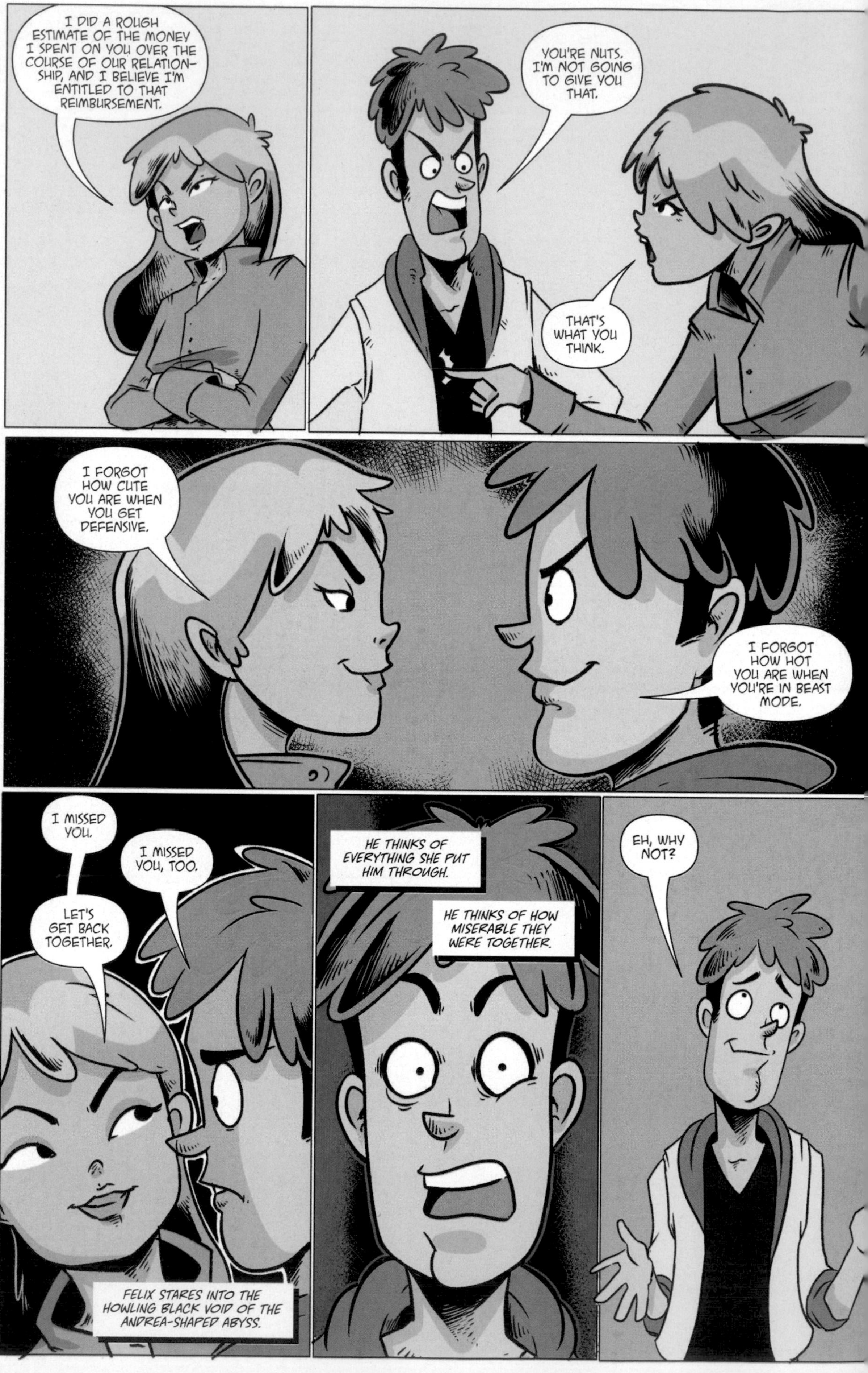
I DID A ROUGH ESTIMATE OF THE MONEY I SPENT ON YOU OVER THE COURSE OF OUR RELATIONSHIP, AND I BELIEVE I'M ENTITLED TO THAT REIMBURSEMENT.
YOU'RE NUTS. I'M NOT GOING TO GIVE YOU THAT.
THAT'S WHAT YOU THINK.
I FORGOT HOW CUTE YOU ARE WHEN YOU GET DEFENSIVE.
I FORGOT HOW HOT YOU ARE WHEN YOU'RE IN BEAST MODE.
I MISSED YOU.
I MISSED YOU, TOO.
LET'S GET BACK TOGETHER.
FELIX STARES INTO THE HOWLING BLACK VOID OF THE ANDREA-SHAPED ABYSS.
HE THINKS OF EVERYTHING SHE PUT HIM THROUGH.
HE THINKS OF HOW MISERABLE THEY WERE TOGETHER.
EH, WHY NOT?

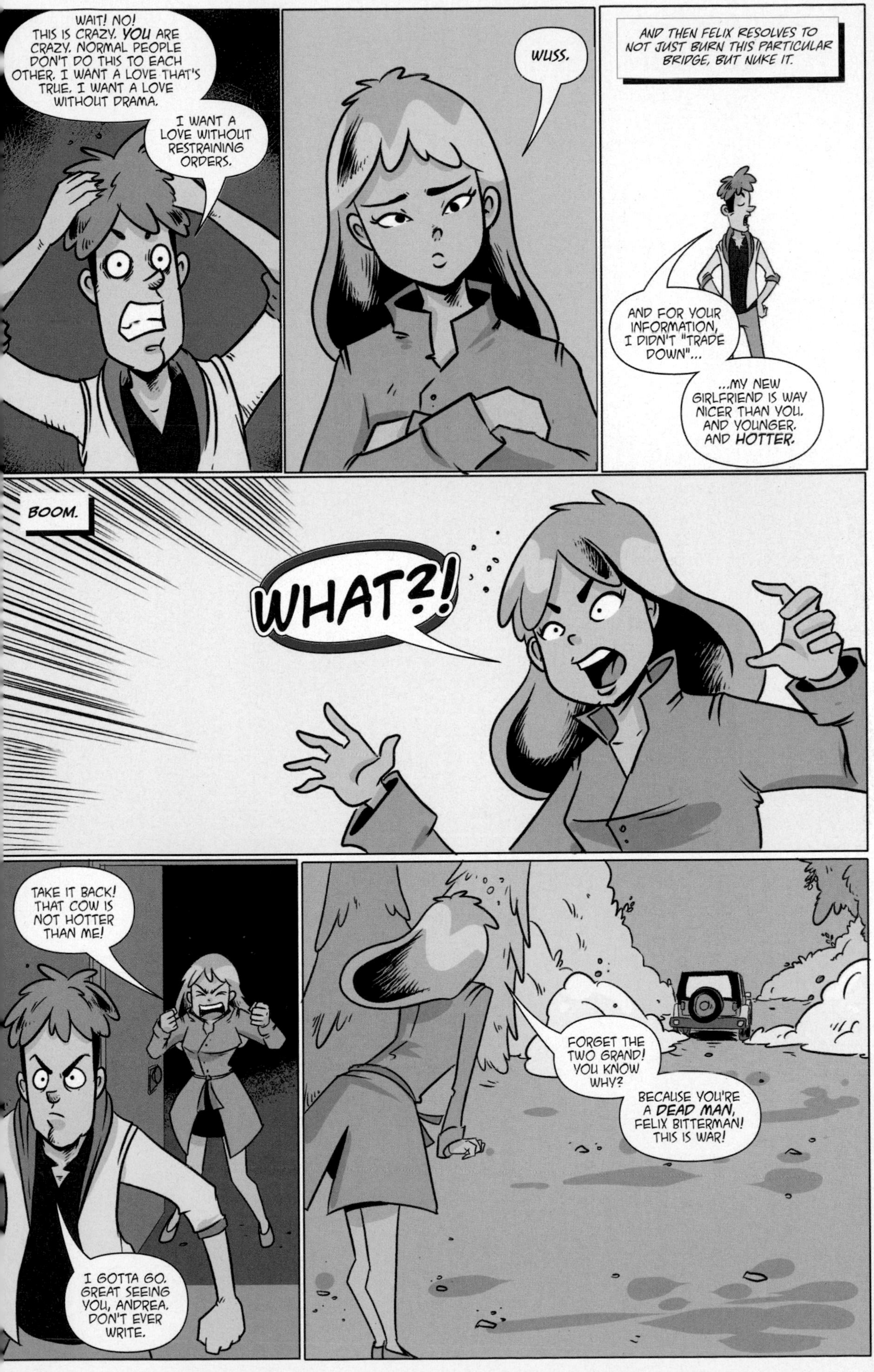
WAIT! NO! THIS IS CRAZY. YOU ARE CRAZY. NORMAL PEOPLE DON'T DO THIS TO EACH OTHER. I WANT A LOVE THAT'S TRUE. I WANT A LOVE WITHOUT DRAMA.
I WANT A LOVE WITHOUT RESTRAINING ORDERS.
WUSS.
AND THEN FELIX RESOLVES TO NOT JUST BURN THIS PARTICULAR BRIDGE, BUT NUKE IT.
AND FOR YOUR INFORMATION, I DIDN'T "TRADE DOWN"...
...MY NEW GIRLFRIEND IS WAY NICER THAN YOU. AND YOUNGER. AND HOTTER.
BOOM.
WHAT?!
TAKE IT BACK! THAT COW IS NOT HOTTER THAN ME!
I GOTTA GO. GREAT SEEING YOU, ANDREA. DON'T EVER WRITE.
FORGET THE TWO GRAND! YOU KNOW WHY?
BECAUSE YOU'RE A DEAD MAN, FELIX BITTERMAN! THIS IS WAR!

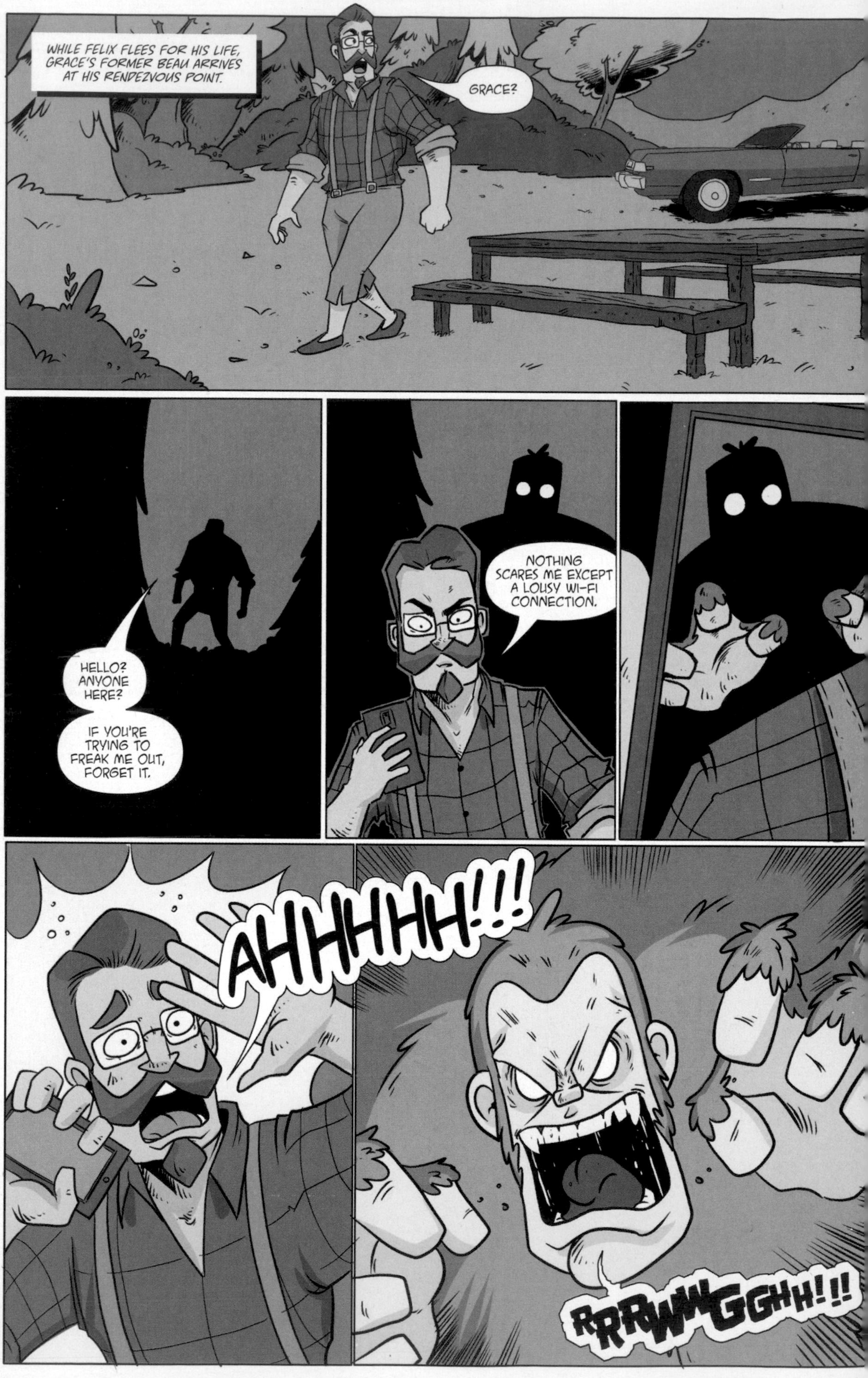
WHILE FELIX FLEES FOR HIS LIFE, GRACE'S FORMER BEAU ARRIVES AT HIS RENDEZVOUS POINT.
GRACE?
HELLO? ANYONE HERE?
IF YOU'RE TRYING TO FREAK ME OUT, FORGET IT.
NOTHING SCARES ME EXCEPT A LOUSY WI-FI CONNECTION.
AHHHHH!!!
RRRWWGGHH!!!

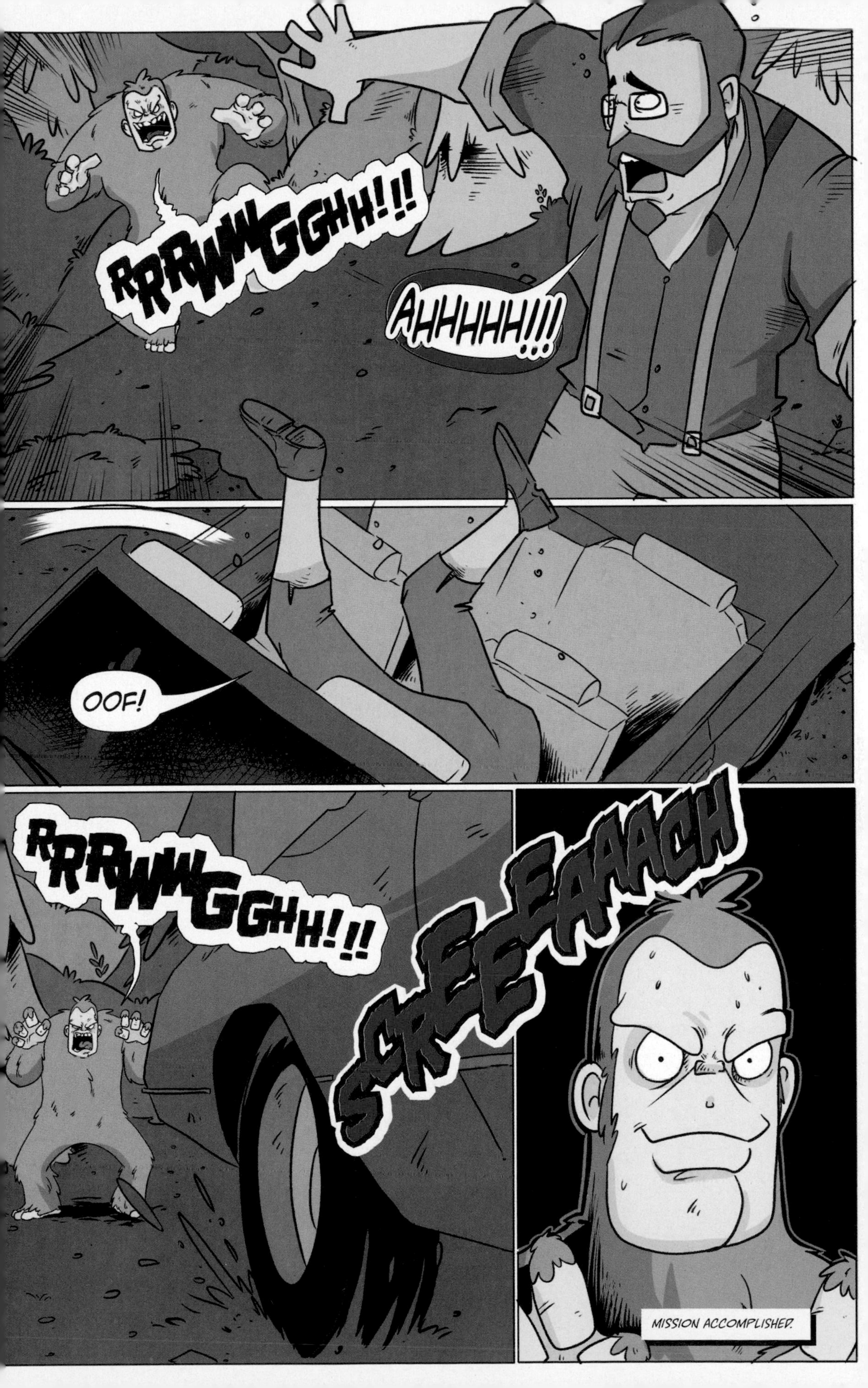
RRRWWGGHH!!!
AHHHHH!!!
OOF!
RRRWWGGHH!!!
SCREEEAAACH
MISSION ACCOMPLISHED.

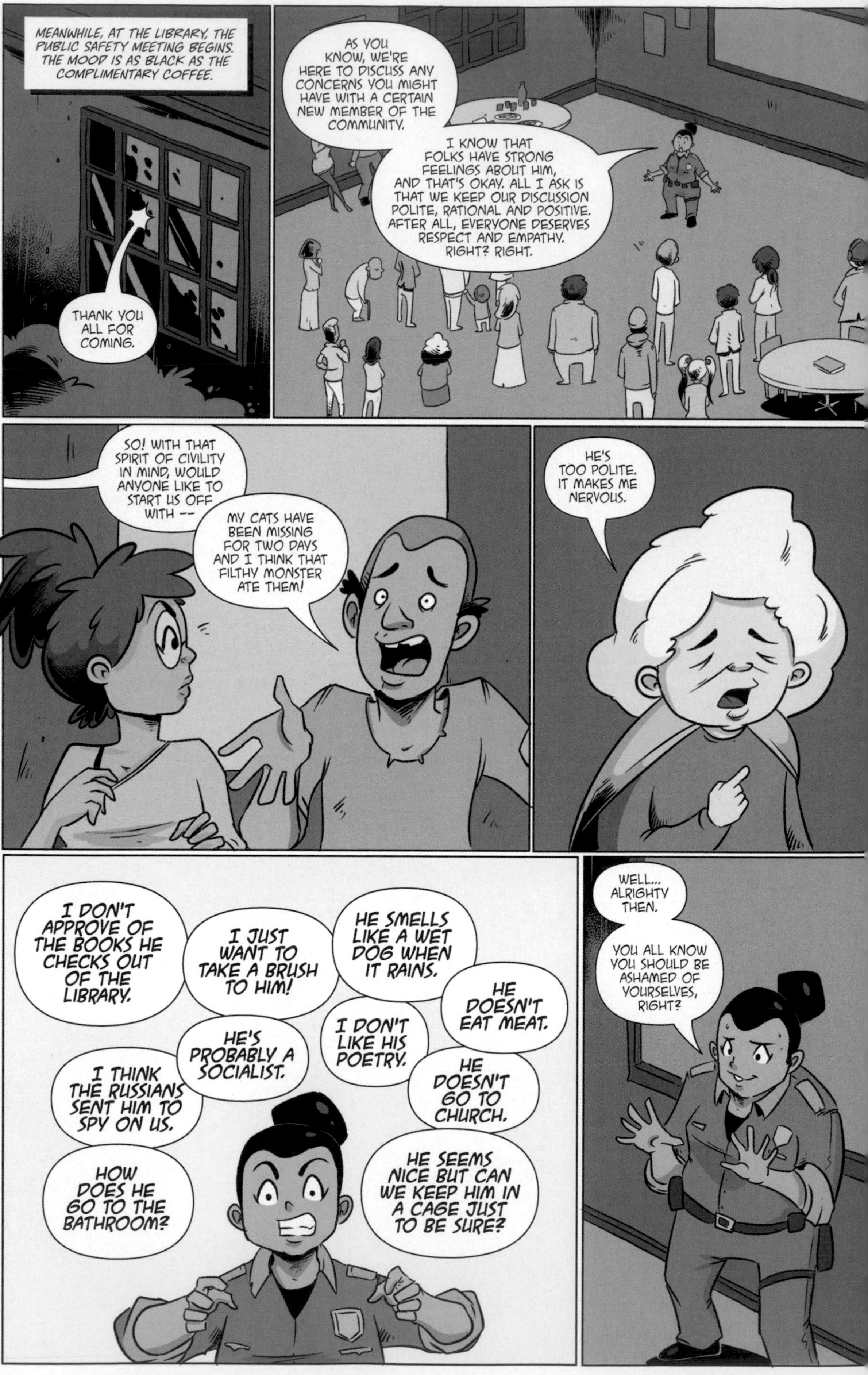
MEANWHILE, AT THE LIBRARY, THE PUBLIC SAFETY MEETING BEGINS. THE MOOD IS AS BLACK AS THE COMPLIMENTARY COFFEE.
THANK YOU ALL FOR COMING.
AS YOU KNOW, WE'RE HERE TO DISCUSS ANY CONCERNS YOU MIGHT HAVE WITH A CERTAIN NEW MEMBER OF THE COMMUNITY.
I KNOW THAT FOLKS HAVE STRONG FEELINGS ABOUT HIM, AND THAT'S OKAY. ALL I ASK IS THAT WE KEEP OUR DISCUSSION POLITE, RATIONAL AND POSITIVE. AFTER ALL, EVERYONE DESERVES RESPECT AND EMPATHY. RIGHT? RIGHT.
SO! WITH THAT SPIRIT OF CIVILITY IN MIND, WOULD ANYONE LIKE TO START US OFF WITH --
MY CATS HAVE BEEN MISSING FOR TWO DAYS AND I THINK THAT FILTHY MONSTER ATE THEM!
HE'S TOO POLITE. IT MAKES ME NERVOUS.
I DON'T APPROVE OF THE BOOKS HE CHECKS OUT OF THE LIBRARY.
I JUST WANT TO TAKE A BRUSH TO HIM!
HE SMELLS LIKE A WET DOG WHEN IT RAINS.
HE DOESN'T EAT MEAT.
HE'S PROBABLY A SOCIALIST.
I DON'T LIKE HIS POETRY.
I THINK THE RUSSIANS SENT HIM TO SPY ON US.
HE DOESN'T GO TO CHURCH.
HOW DOES HE GO TO THE BATHROOM?
HE SEEMS NICE BUT CAN WE KEEP HIM IN A CAGE JUST TO BE SURE?
WELL... ALRIGHTY THEN.
YOU ALL KNOW YOU SHOULD BE ASHAMED OF YOURSELVES, RIGHT?

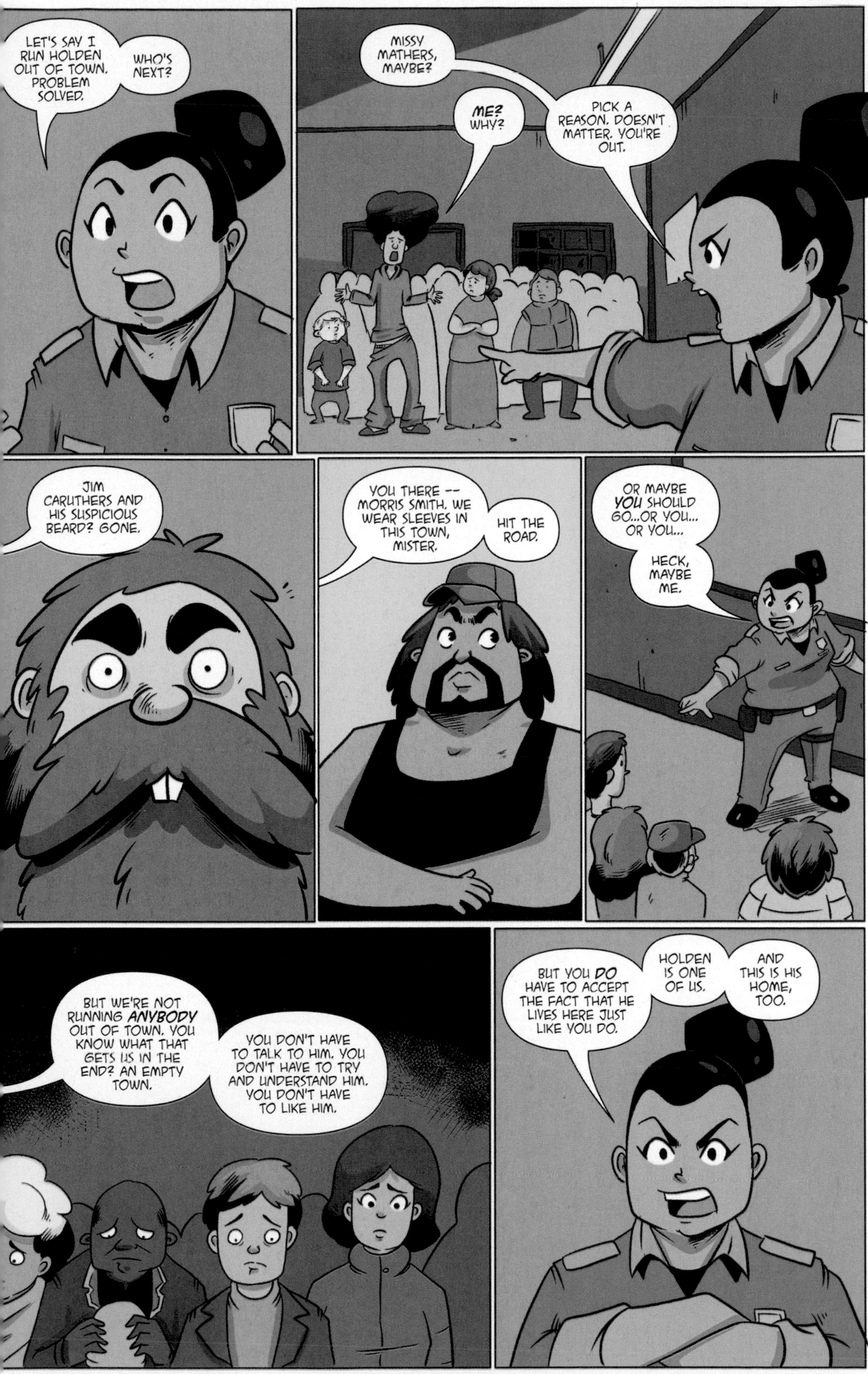
LET'S SAY I RUN HOLDEN OUT OF TOWN. PROBLEM SOLVED.
WHO'S NEXT?
MISSY MATHERS, MAYBE?
ME? WHY?
PICK A REASON. DOESN'T MATTER. YOU'RE OUT.
JIM CARUTHERS AND HIS SUSPICIOUS BEARD? GONE.
YOU THERE -- MORRIS SMITH. WE WEAR SLEEVES IN THIS TOWN, MISTER.
HIT THE ROAD.
OR MAYBE YOU SHOULD GO...OR YOU... OR YOU...
HECK, MAYBE ME.
BUT WE'RE NOT RUNNING ANYBODY OUT OF TOWN. YOU KNOW WHAT THAT GETS US IN THE END? AN EMPTY TOWN.
YOU DON'T HAVE TO TALK TO HIM. YOU DON'T HAVE TO TRY AND UNDERSTAND HIM. YOU DON'T HAVE TO LIKE HIM.
BUT YOU DO HAVE TO ACCEPT THE FACT THAT HE LIVES HERE JUST LIKE YOU DO.
HOLDEN IS ONE OF US.
AND THIS IS HIS HOME, TOO.

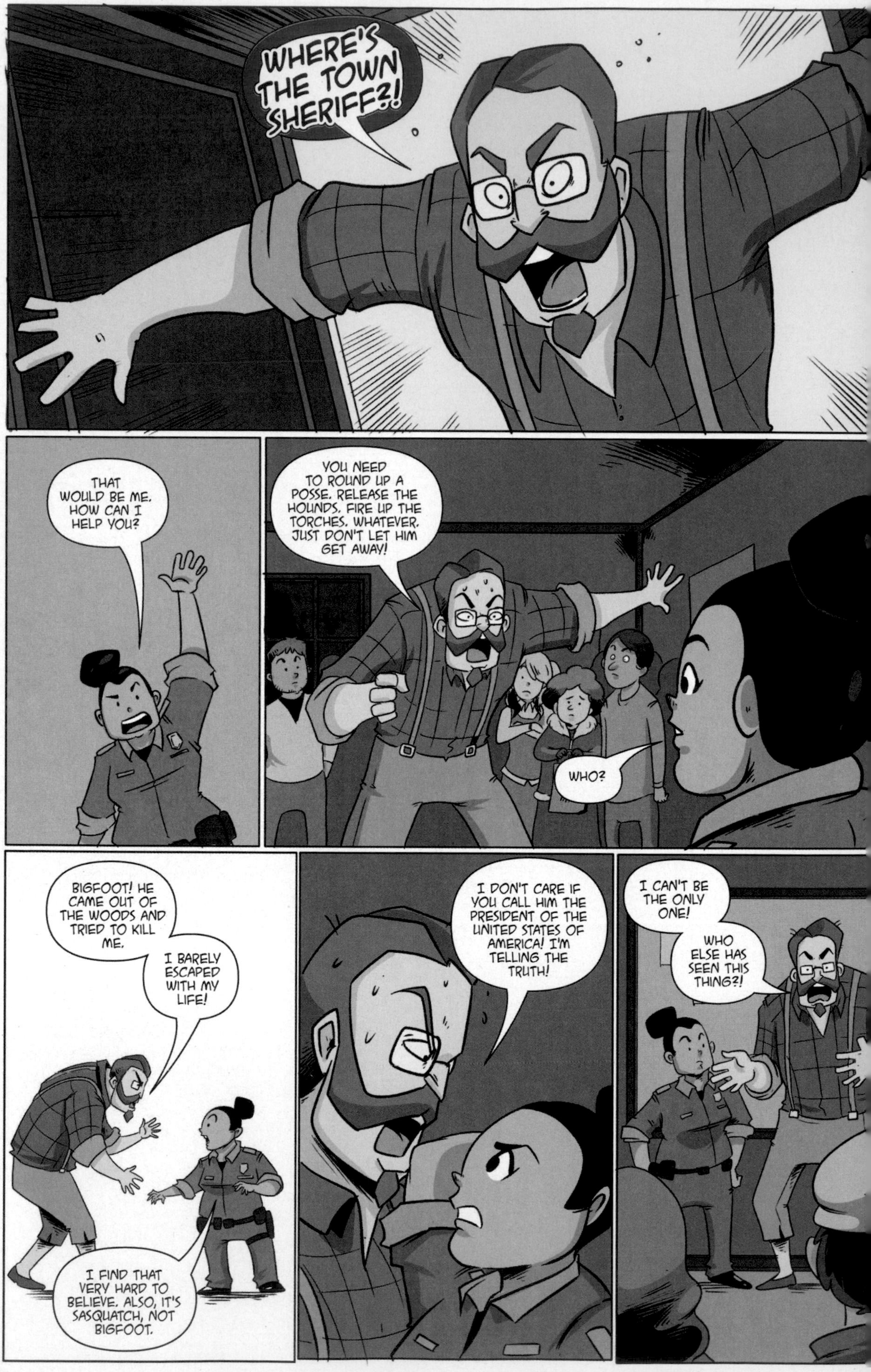
WHERE'S THE TOWN SHERIFF?!
THAT WOULD BE ME. HOW CAN I HELP YOU?
YOU NEED TO ROUND UP A POSSE. RELEASE THE HOUNDS. FIRE UP THE TORCHES. WHATEVER. JUST DON'T LET HIM GET AWAY!
WHO?
BIGFOOT! HE CAME OUT OF THE WOODS AND TRIED TO KILL ME.
I BARELY ESCAPED WITH MY LIFE!
I FIND THAT VERY HARD TO BELIEVE. ALSO, IT'S SASQUATCH, NOT BIGFOOT.
I DON'T CARE IF YOU CALL HIM THE PRESIDENT OF THE UNITED STATES OF AMERICA! I'M TELLING THE TRUTH!
I CAN'T BE THE ONLY ONE!
WHO ELSE HAS SEEN THIS THING?!

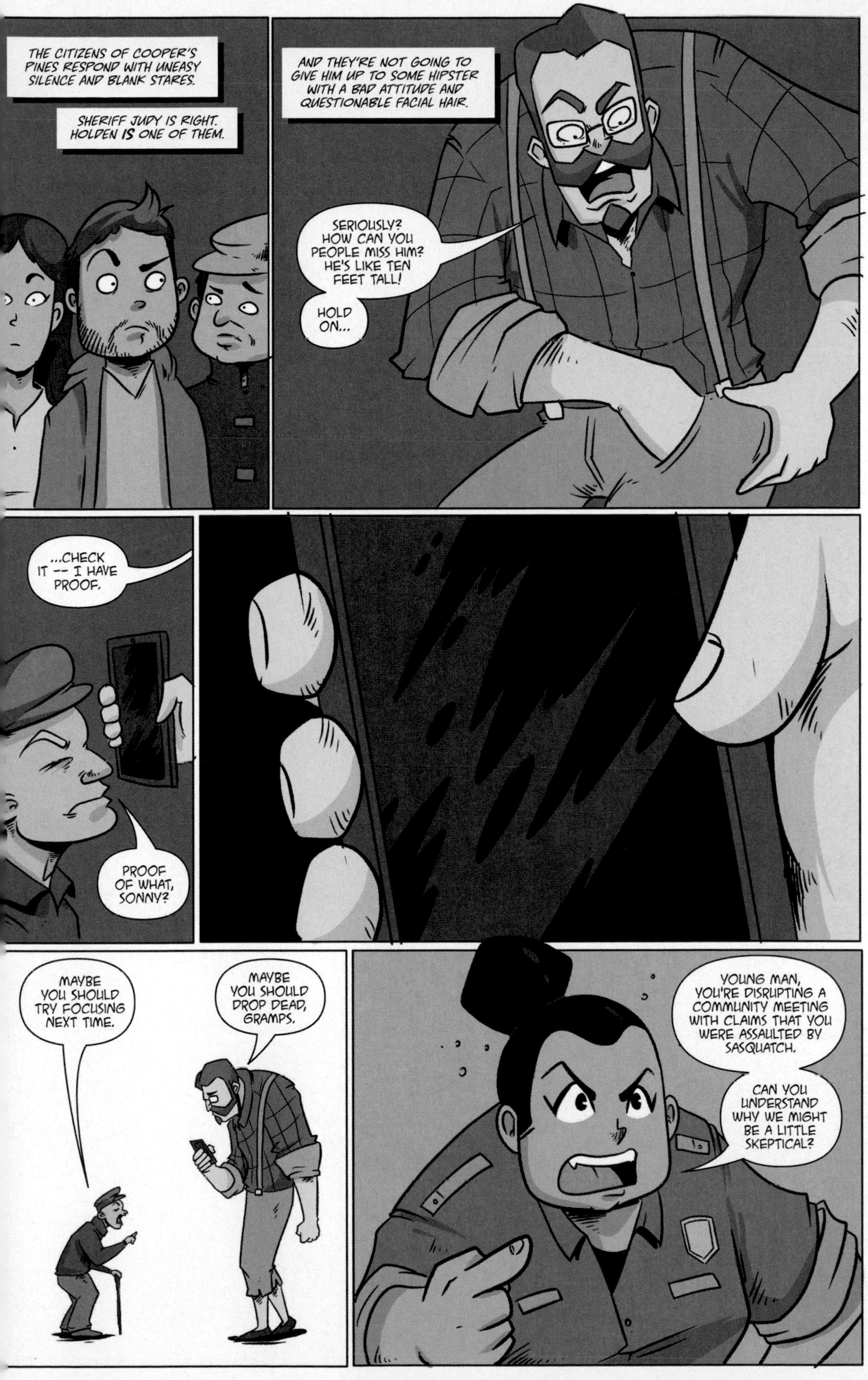
THE CITIZENS OF COOPER'S PINES RESPOND WITH UNEASY SILENCE AND BLANK STARES.
SHERIFF JUDY IS RIGHT. HOLDEN IS ONE OF THEM.
AND THEY'RE NOT GOING TO GIVE HIM UP TO SOME HIPSTER WITH A BAD ATTITUDE AND QUESTIONABLE FACIAL HAIR.
SERIOUSLY? HOW CAN YOU PEOPLE MISS HIM? HE'S LIKE TEN FEET TALL!
HOLD ON...
...CHECK IT -- I HAVE PROOF.
PROOF OF WHAT, SONNY?
MAYBE YOU SHOULD TRY FOCUSING NEXT TIME.
MAYBE YOU SHOULD DROP DEAD, GRAMPS.
YOUNG MAN, YOU'RE DISRUPTING A COMMUNITY MEETING WITH CLAIMS THAT YOU WERE ASSAULTED BY SASQUATCH.
CAN YOU UNDERSTAND WHY WE MIGHT BE A LITTLE SKEPTICAL?

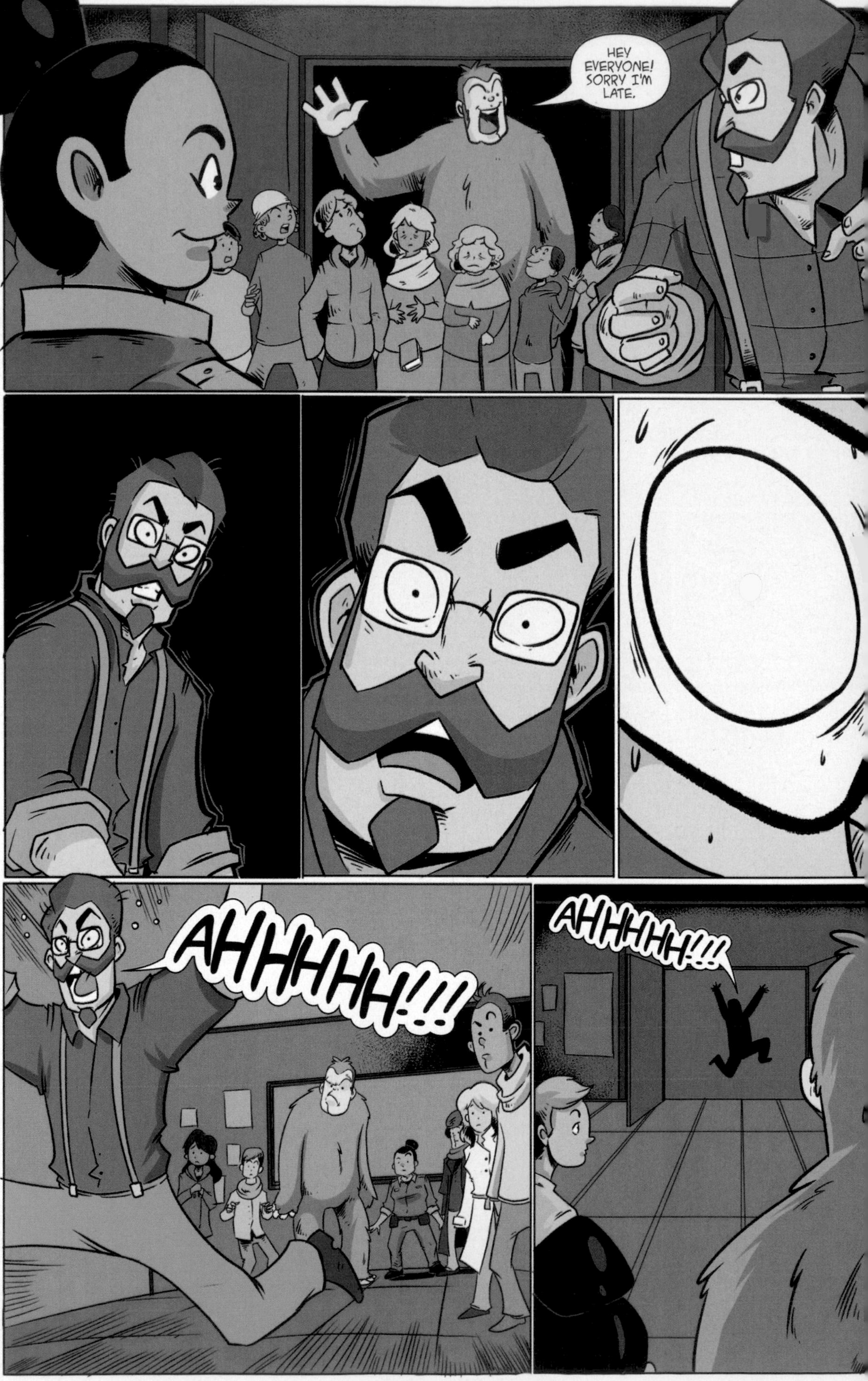
HEY EVERYONE! SORRY I'M LATE.
AHHHHH!!!
AHHHHH!!!

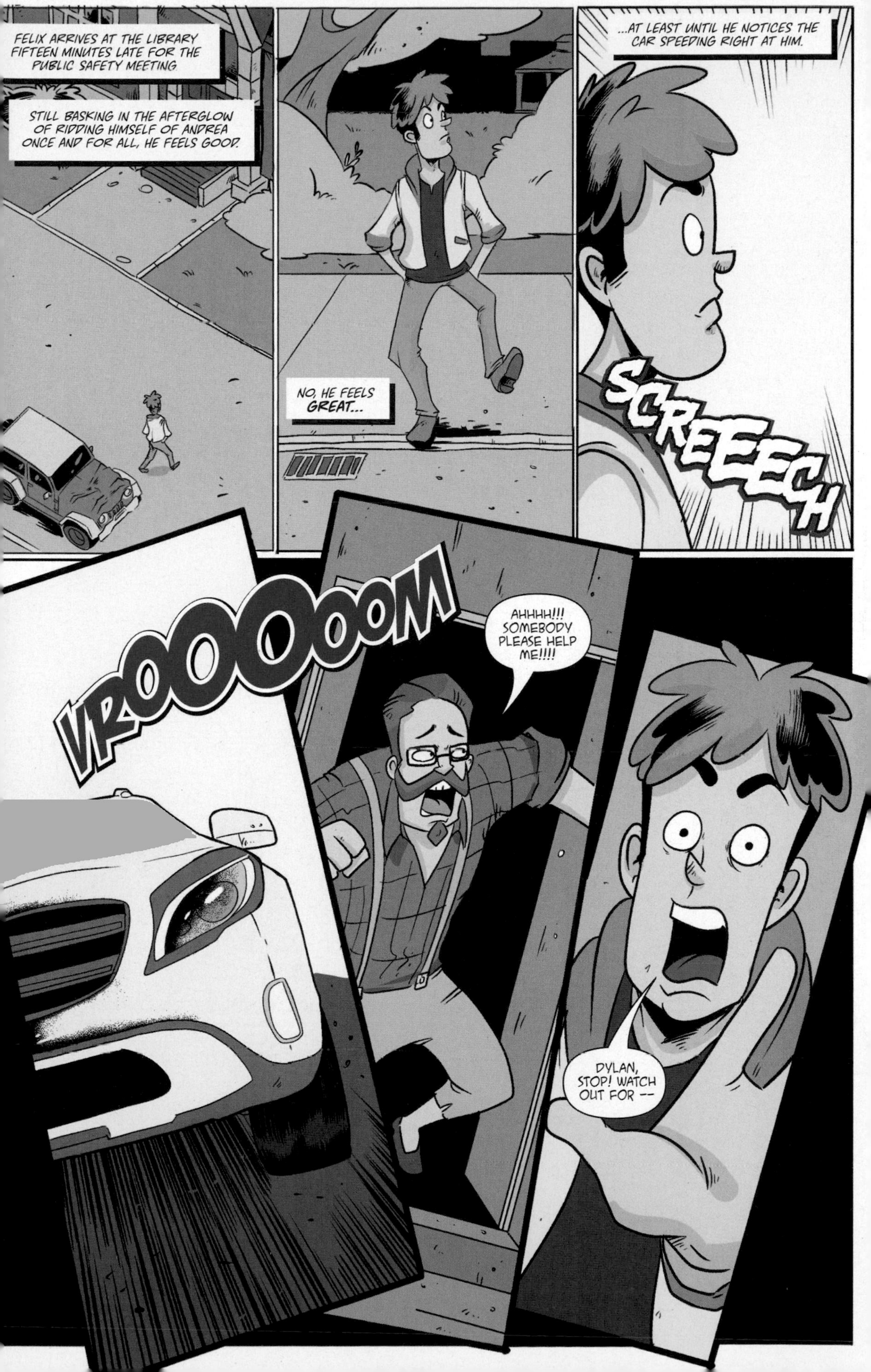
FELIX ARRIVES AT THE LIBRARY FIFTEEN MINUTES LATE FOR THE PUBLIC SAFETY MEETING.
STILL BASKING IN THE AFTERGLOW OF RIDDING HIMSELF OF ANDREA ONCE AND FOR ALL, HE FEELS GOOD.
NO, HE FEELS GREAT...
...AT LEAST UNTIL HE NOTICES THE CAR SPEEDING RIGHT AT HIM.
SCREEECH
VROOOOOOM
AHHHH!!! SOMEBODY PLEASE HELP ME!!!!
DYLAN, STOP! WATCH OUT FOR --

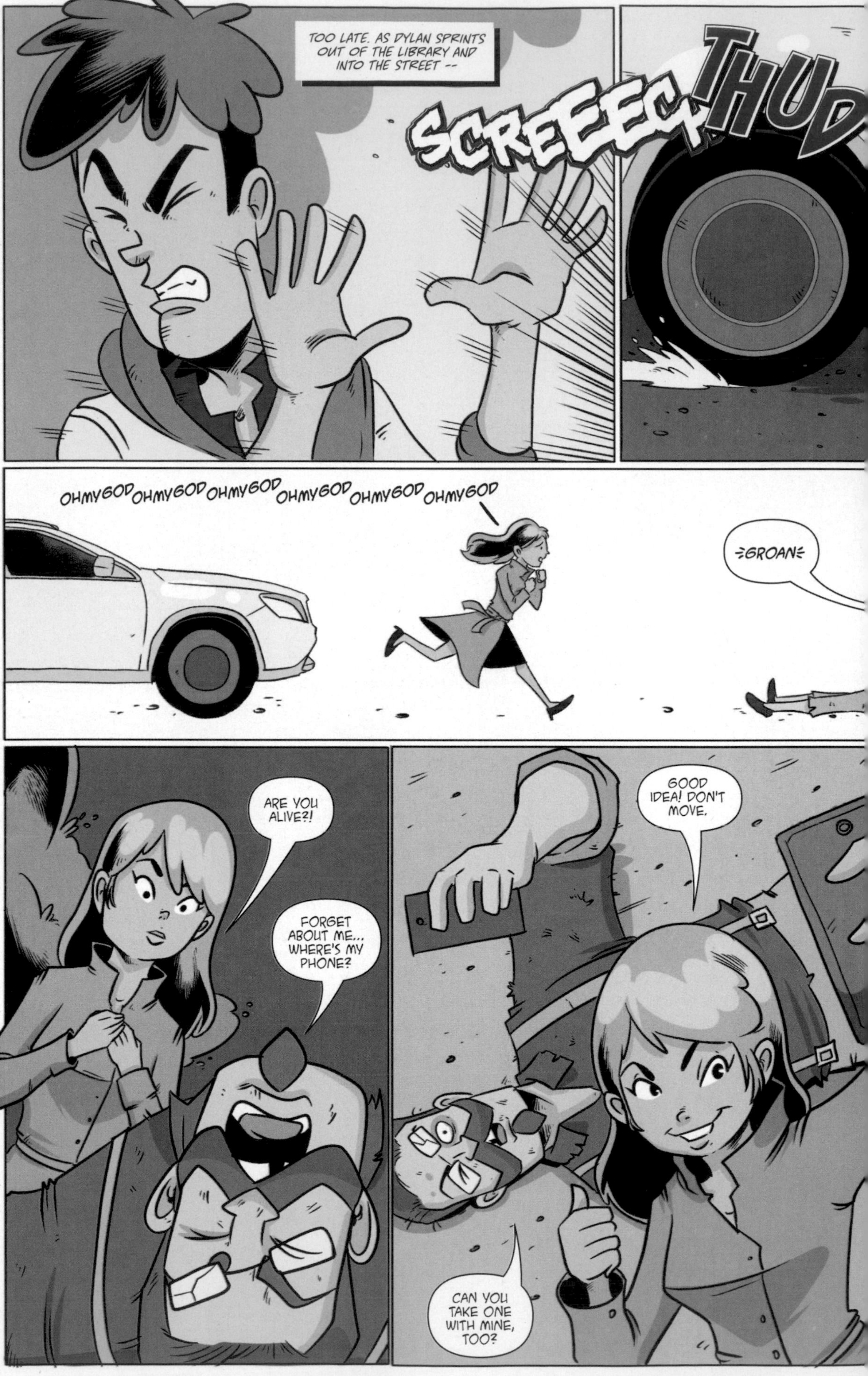
TOO LATE. AS DYLAN SPRINTS OUT OF THE LIBRARY AND INTO THE STREET --
SCREEECH
THUD
OHMYGOD OHMYGOD OHMYGOD OHMYGOD OHMYGOD OHMYGOD
GROAN
ARE YOU ALIVE?!
FORGET ABOUT ME... WHERE'S MY PHONE?
GOOD IDEA! DON'T MOVE.
CAN YOU TAKE ONE WITH MINE, TOO?

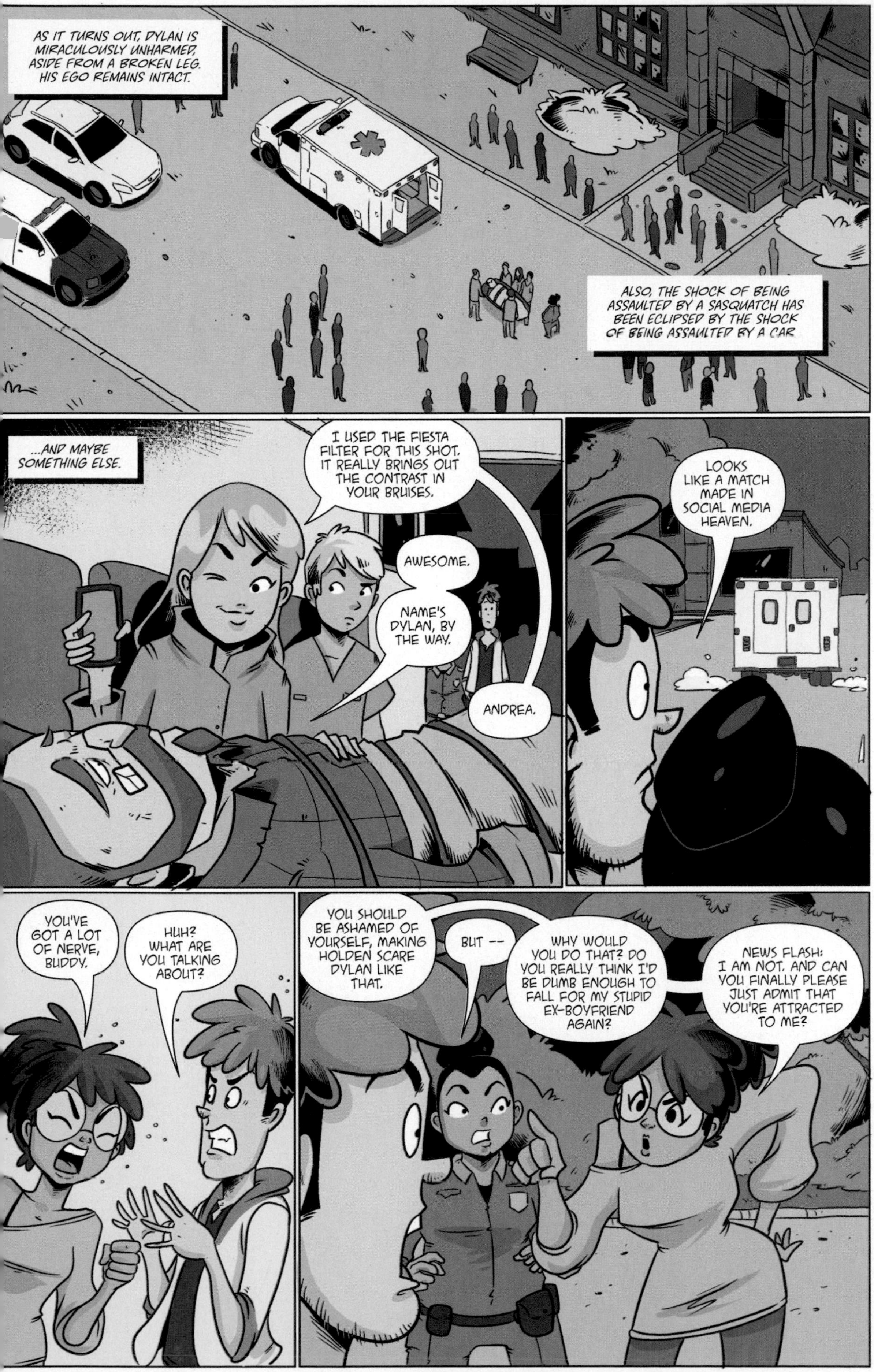
AS IT TURNS OUT, DYLAN IS MIRACULOUSLY UNHARMED, ASIDE FROM A BROKEN LEG. HIS EGO REMAINS INTACT.
ALSO, THE SHOCK OF BEING ASSAULTED BY A SASQUATCH HAS BEEN ECLIPSED BY THE SHOCK OF BEING ASSAULTED BY A CAR
...AND MAYBE SOMETHING ELSE.
I USED THE FIESTA FILTER FOR THIS SHOT. IT REALLY BRINGS OUT THE CONTRAST IN YOUR BRUISES.
AWESOME.
NAME'S DYLAN, BY THE WAY.
ANDREA.
LOOKS LIKE A MATCH MADE IN SOCIAL MEDIA HEAVEN.
YOU'VE GOT A LOT OF NERVE, BUDDY.
HUH? WHAT ARE YOU TALKING ABOUT?
YOU SHOULD BE ASHAMED OF YOURSELF, MAKING HOLDEN SCARE DYLAN LIKE THAT.
BUT --
WHY WOULD YOU DO THAT? DO YOU REALLY THINK I'D BE DUMB ENOUGH TO FALL FOR MY STUPID EX-BOYFRIEND AGAIN?
NEWS FLASH: I AM NOT. AND CAN YOU FINALLY PLEASE JUST ADMIT THAT YOU'RE ATTRACTED TO ME?

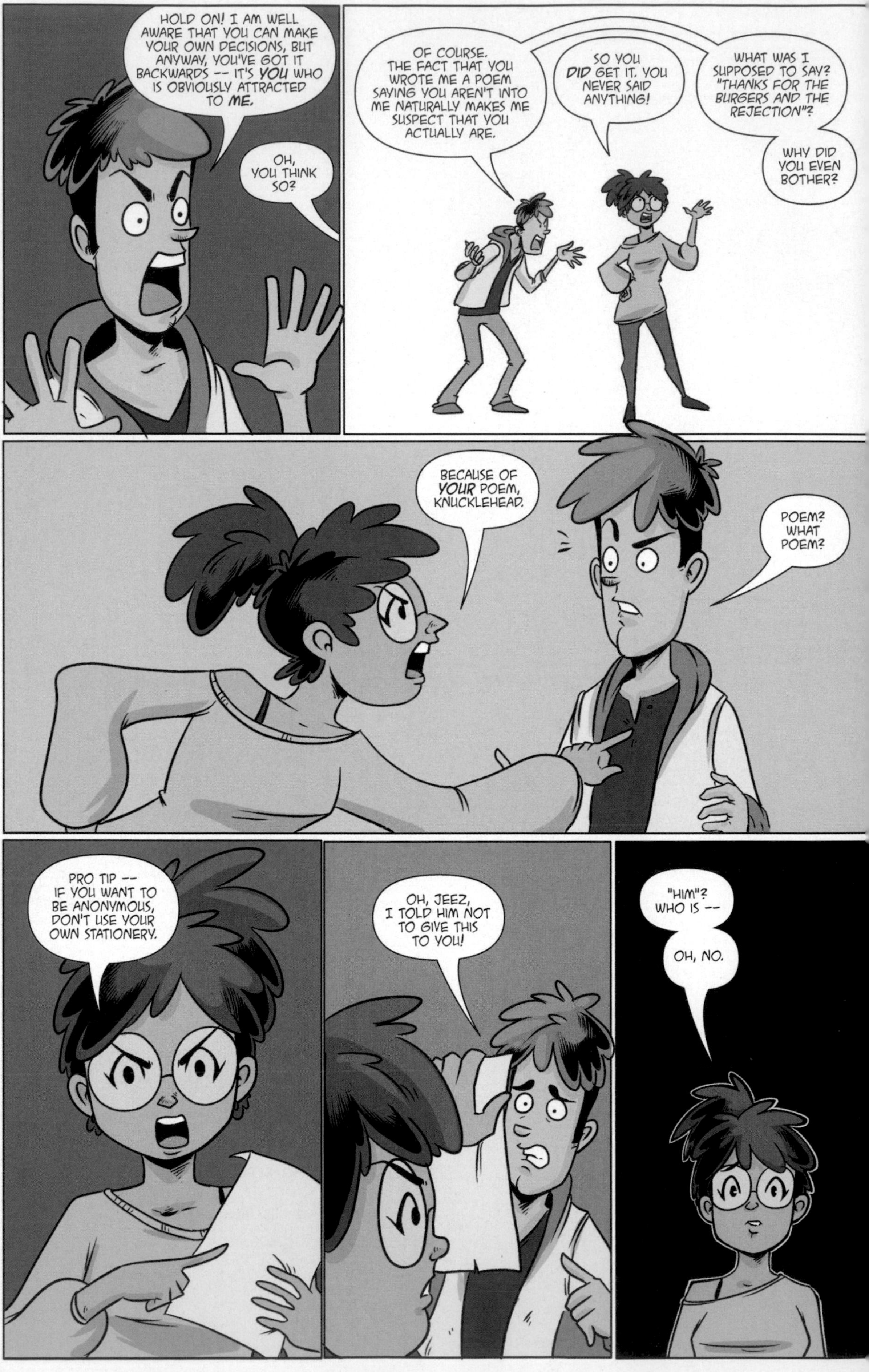
HOLD ON! I AM WELL AWARE THAT YOU CAN MAKE YOUR OWN DECISIONS, BUT ANYWAY, YOU'VE GOT IT BACKWARDS -- IT'S *YOU* WHO IS OBVIOUSLY ATTRACTED TO *ME.*
OH, YOU THINK SO?
OF COURSE. THE FACT THAT YOU WROTE ME A POEM SAYING YOU AREN'T INTO ME NATURALLY MAKES ME SUSPECT THAT YOU ACTUALLY ARE.
SO YOU *DID* GET IT. YOU NEVER SAID ANYTHING!
WHAT WAS I SUPPOSED TO SAY? "THANKS FOR THE BURGERS AND THE REJECTION"?
WHY DID YOU EVEN BOTHER?
BECAUSE OF *YOUR* POEM, KNUCKLEHEAD.
POEM? WHAT POEM?
PRO TIP -- IF YOU WANT TO BE ANONYMOUS, DON'T USE YOUR OWN STATIONERY.
OH, JEEZ, I TOLD HIM NOT TO GIVE THIS TO YOU!
"HIM"? WHO IS --
OH, NO.

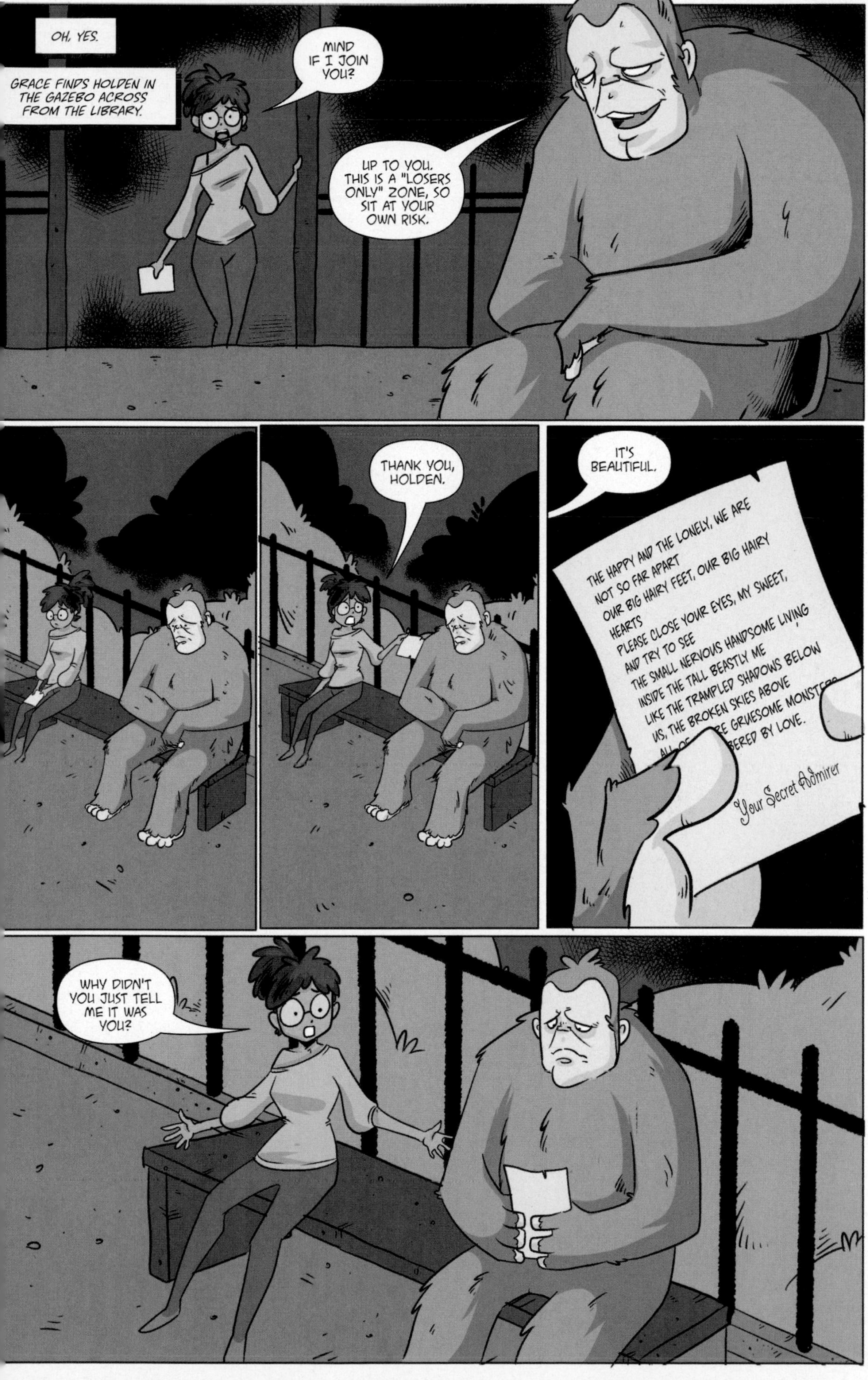
OH, YES.
GRACE FINDS HOLDEN IN THE GAZEBO ACROSS FROM THE LIBRARY.
MIND IF I JOIN YOU?
UP TO YOU. THIS IS A "LOSERS ONLY" ZONE, SO SIT AT YOUR OWN RISK.
THANK YOU, HOLDEN.
IT'S BEAUTIFUL.
THE HAPPY AND THE LONELY, WE ARE
NOT SO FAR APART
OUR BIG HAIRY FEET, OUR BIG HAIRY
HEARTS
PLEASE CLOSE YOUR EYES, MY SWEET,
AND TRY TO SEE
THE SMALL NERVOUS HANDSOME LIVING
INSIDE THE TALL BEASTLY ME
LIKE THE TRAMPLED SHADOWS BELOW
US, THE BROKEN SKIES ABOVE
ALL OF
RE GRUESOME MONST
BERED BY LOVE.
Your Secret Admirer
WHY DIDN'T YOU JUST TELL ME IT WAS YOU?

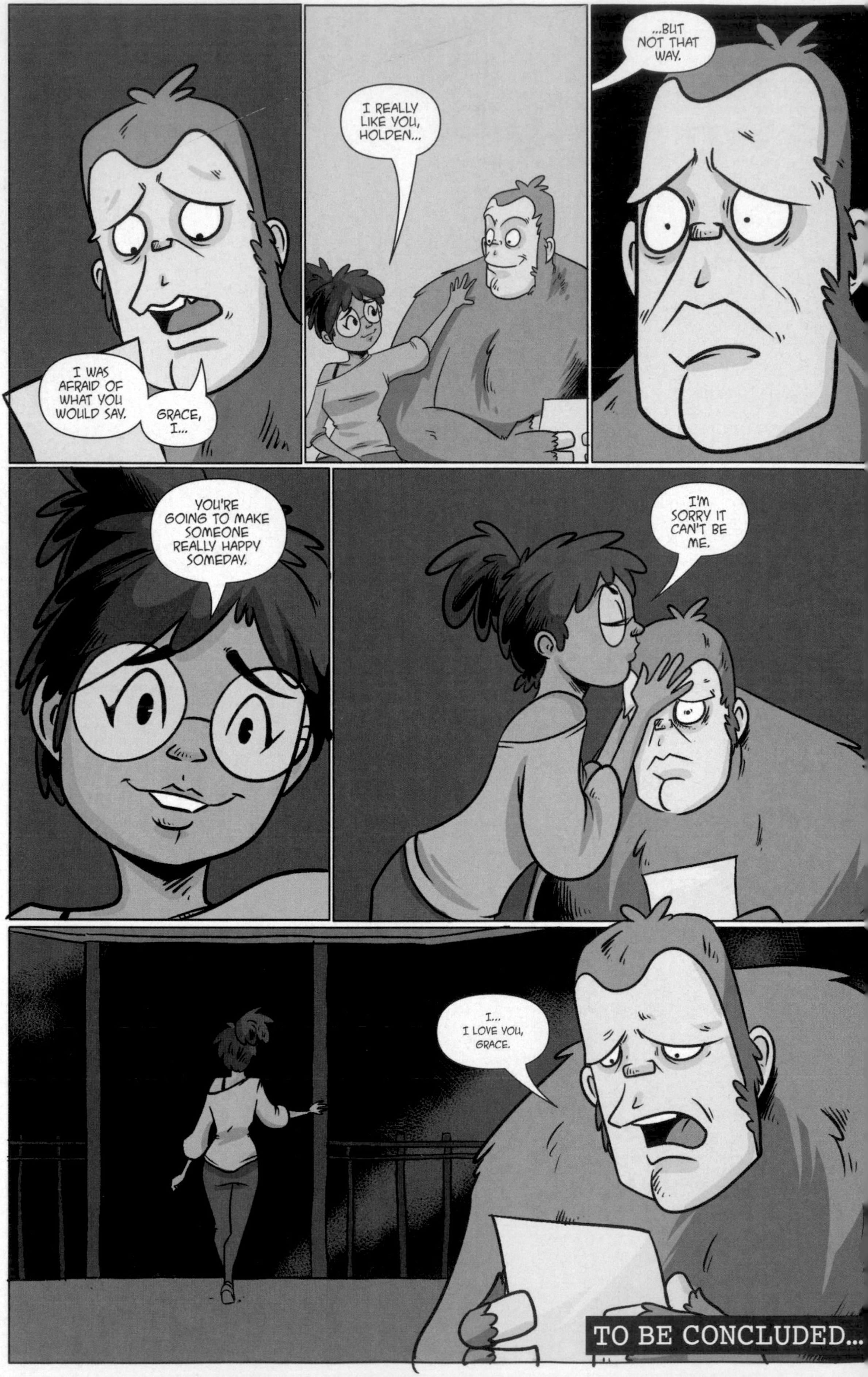
I WAS AFRAID OF WHAT YOU WOULD SAY.
GRACE, I...
I REALLY LIKE YOU, HOLDEN...
...BUT NOT THAT WAY.
YOU'RE GOING TO MAKE SOMEONE REALLY HAPPY SOMEDAY.
I'M SORRY IT CAN'T BE ME.
I... I LOVE YOU, GRACE.
TO BE CONCLUDED...

CHAPTER FOUR: NATURAL SELECTION

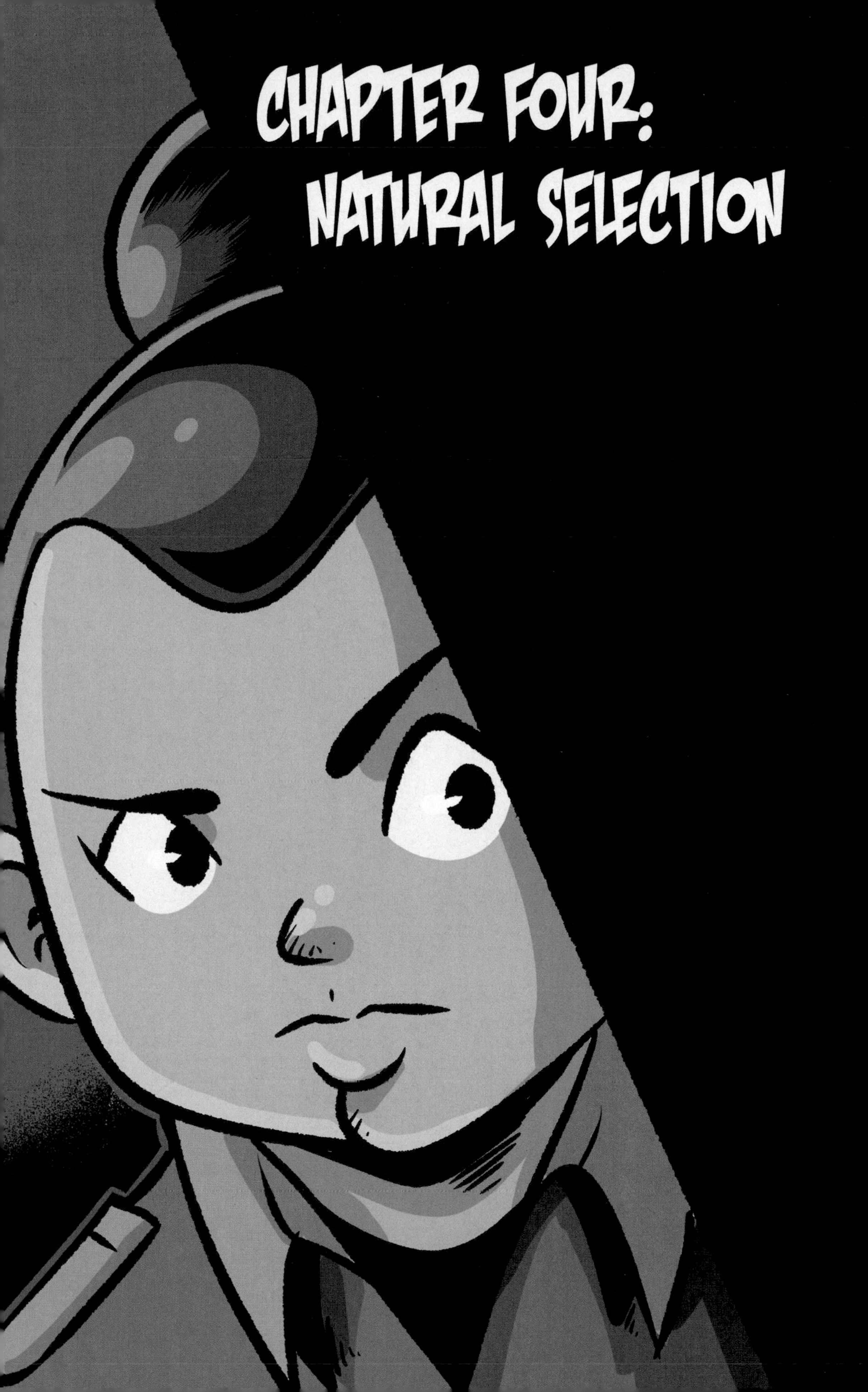

SASQUATCH
IN LOVE

JASON NUTT
Writer

ALEXIS VIVALLO
Artist

JOSH SOUTHALL
Letterer

Bryan Seaton: Publisher/CEO
Vito Delsante: Editor In Chief
Jason Martin: Publisher-Danger Zone
Chad Cicconi: Automotive Stunt Coordinator

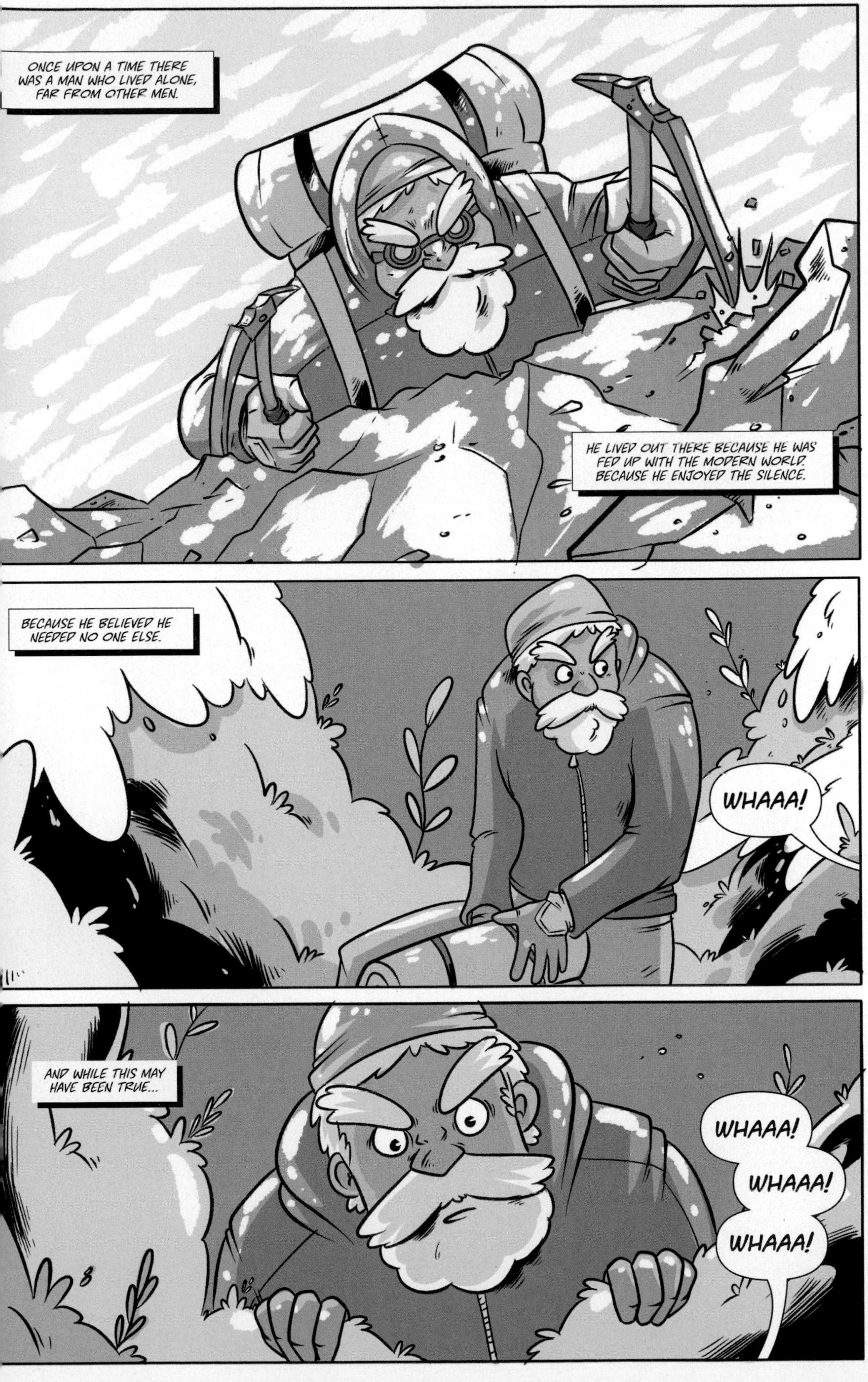
ONCE UPON A TIME THERE WAS A MAN WHO LIVED ALONE, FAR FROM OTHER MEN.
HE LIVED OUT THERE BECAUSE HE WAS FED UP WITH THE MODERN WORLD. BECAUSE HE ENJOYED THE SILENCE.
BECAUSE HE BELIEVED HE NEEDED NO ONE ELSE.
WHAAA!
AND WHILE THIS MAY HAVE BEEN TRUE...
WHAAA!
WHAAA!
WHAAA!

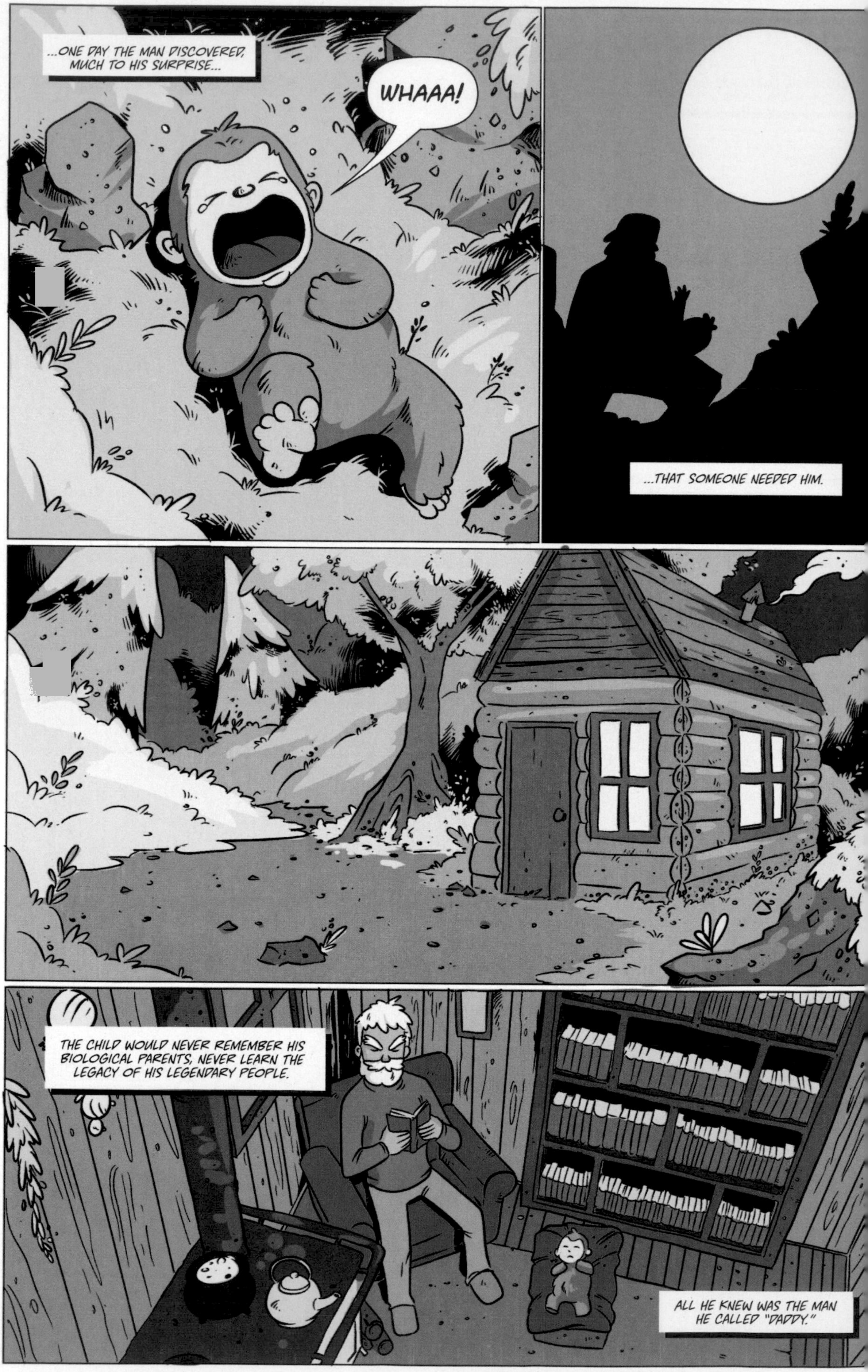
...ONE DAY THE MAN DISCOVERED, MUCH TO HIS SURPRISE...
WHAAA!
...THAT SOMEONE NEEDED HIM.
THE CHILD WOULD NEVER REMEMBER HIS BIOLOGICAL PARENTS, NEVER LEARN THE LEGACY OF HIS LEGENDARY PEOPLE.
ALL HE KNEW WAS THE MAN HE CALLED "DADDY."

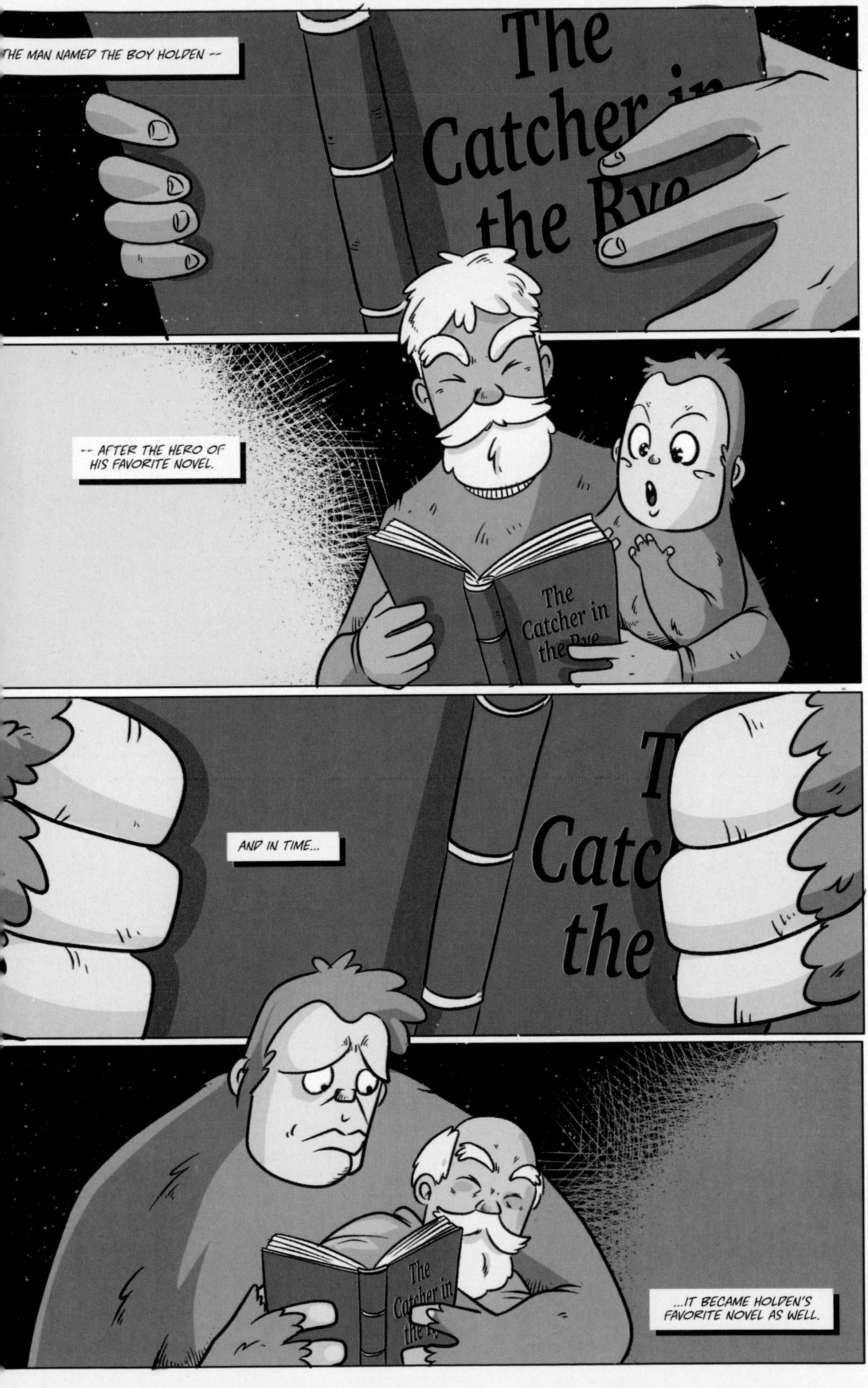
THE MAN NAMED THE BOY HOLDEN --
The Catcher in the Rye
-- AFTER THE HERO OF HIS FAVORITE NOVEL.
The Catcher in the Rye
AND IN TIME...
...IT BECAME HOLDEN'S FAVORITE NOVEL AS WELL.

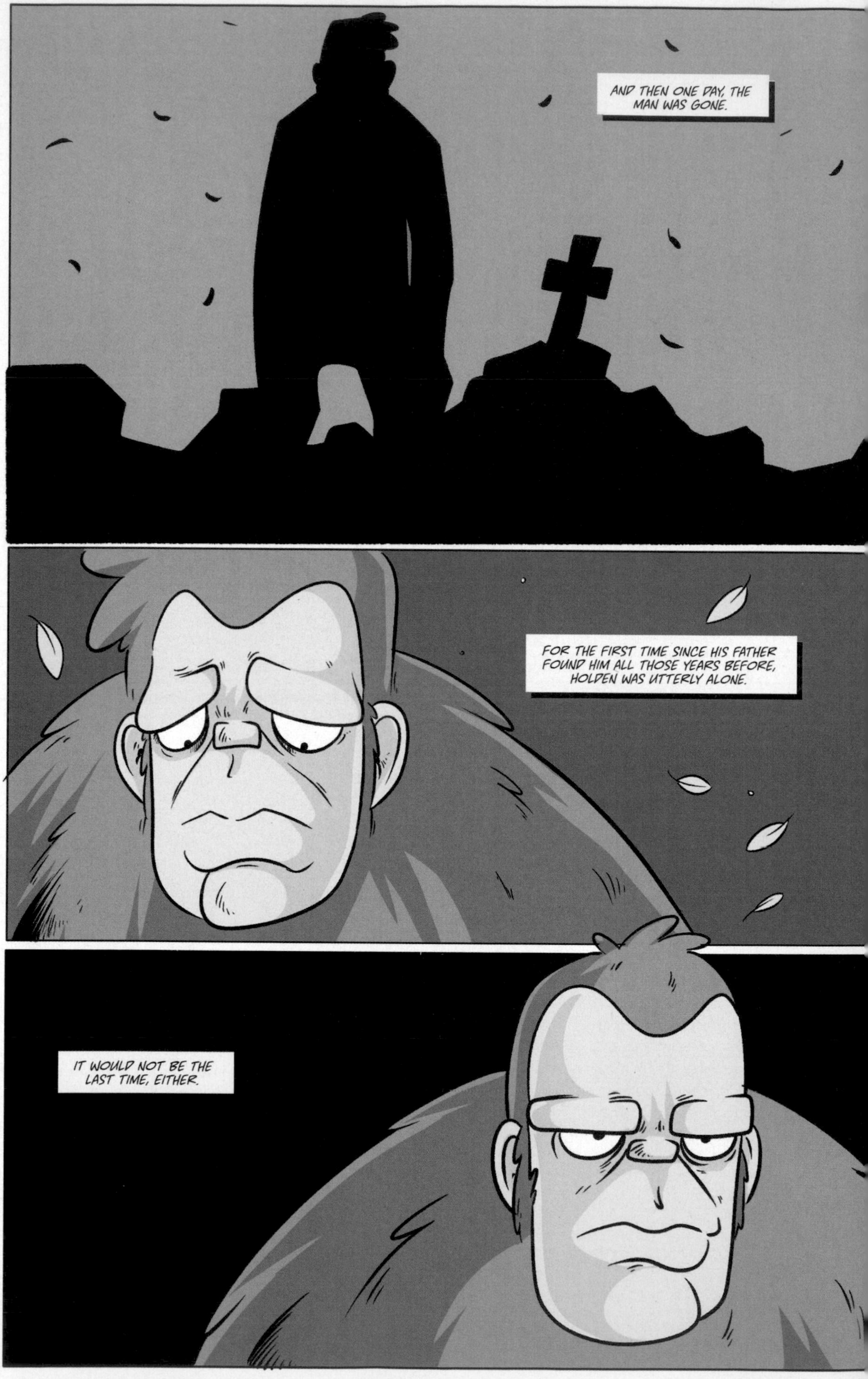
AND THEN ONE DAY, THE MAN WAS GONE.
FOR THE FIRST TIME SINCE HIS FATHER FOUND HIM ALL THOSE YEARS BEFORE, HOLDEN WAS UTTERLY ALONE.
IT WOULD NOT BE THE LAST TIME, EITHER.

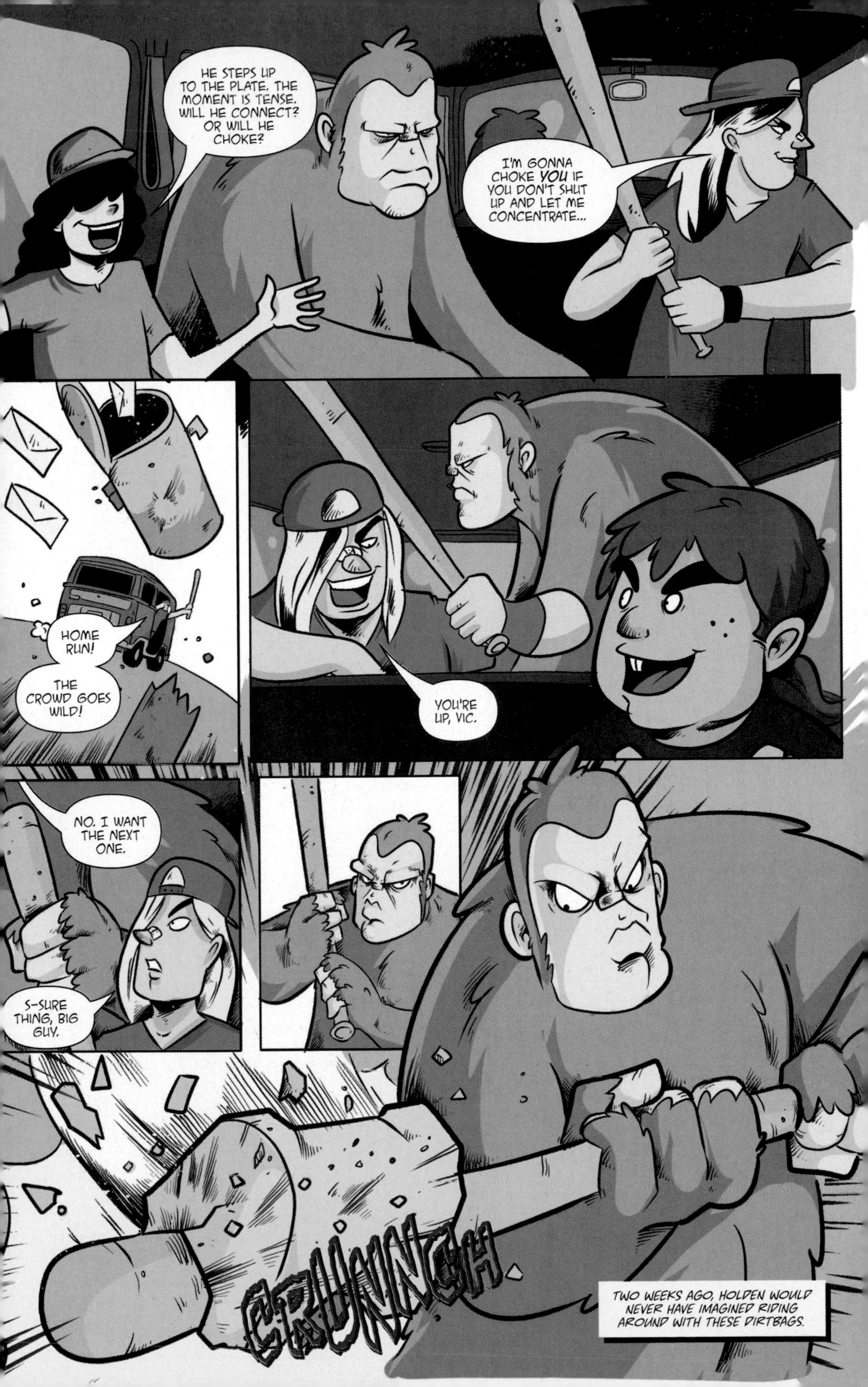
HE STEPS UP TO THE PLATE. THE MOMENT IS TENSE. WILL HE CONNECT? OR WILL HE CHOKE?
I'M GONNA CHOKE YOU IF YOU DON'T SHUT UP AND LET ME CONCENTRATE...
HOME RUN!
THE CROWD GOES WILD!
YOU'RE UP, VIC.
NO. I WANT THE NEXT ONE.
S-SURE THING, BIG GUY.
CRUNNCH
TWO WEEKS AGO, HOLDEN WOULD NEVER HAVE IMAGINED RIDING AROUND WITH THESE DIRTBAGS.

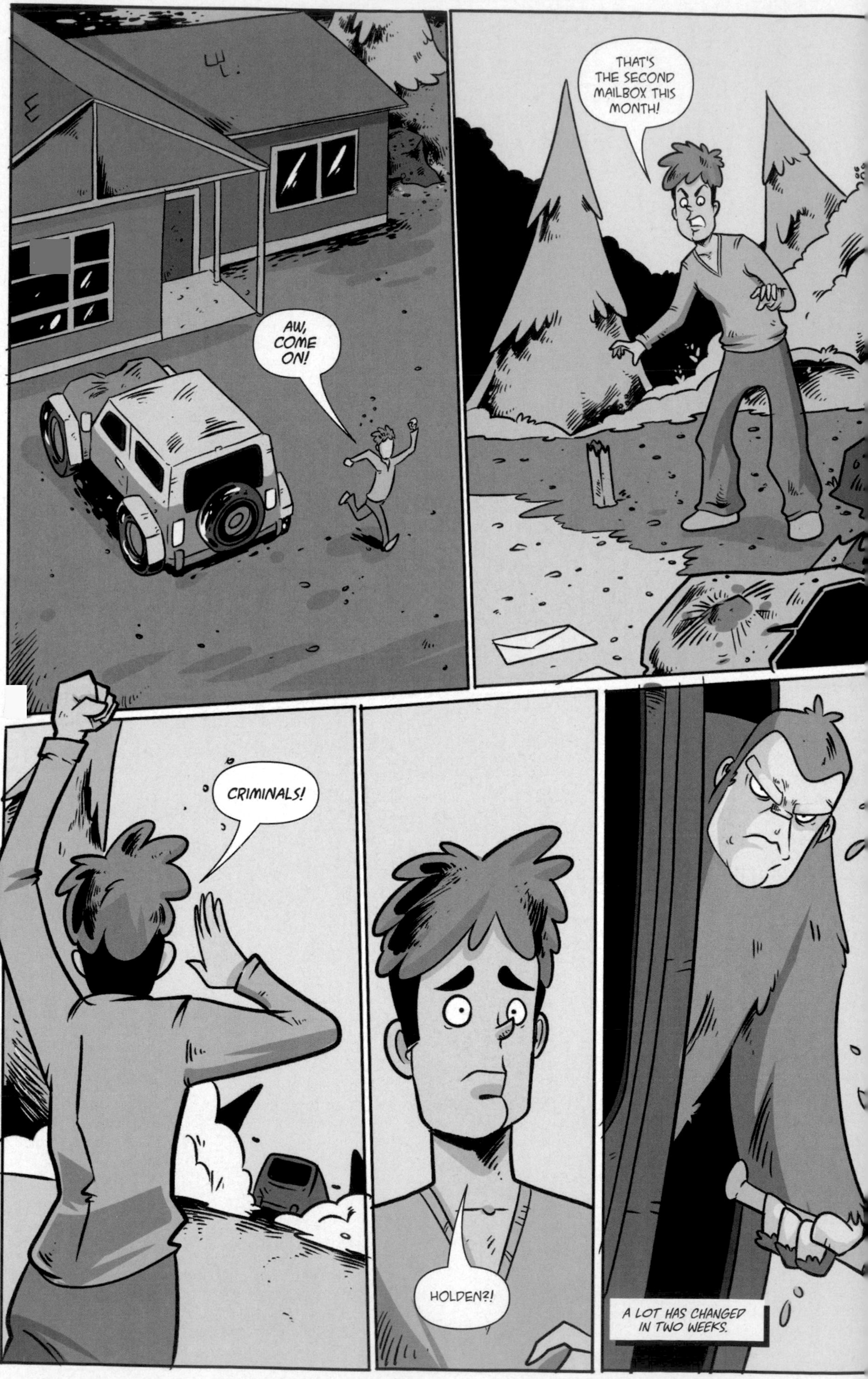
AW, COME ON!
THAT'S THE SECOND MAILBOX THIS MONTH!
CRIMINALS!
HOLDEN?!
A LOT HAS CHANGED IN TWO WEEKS.

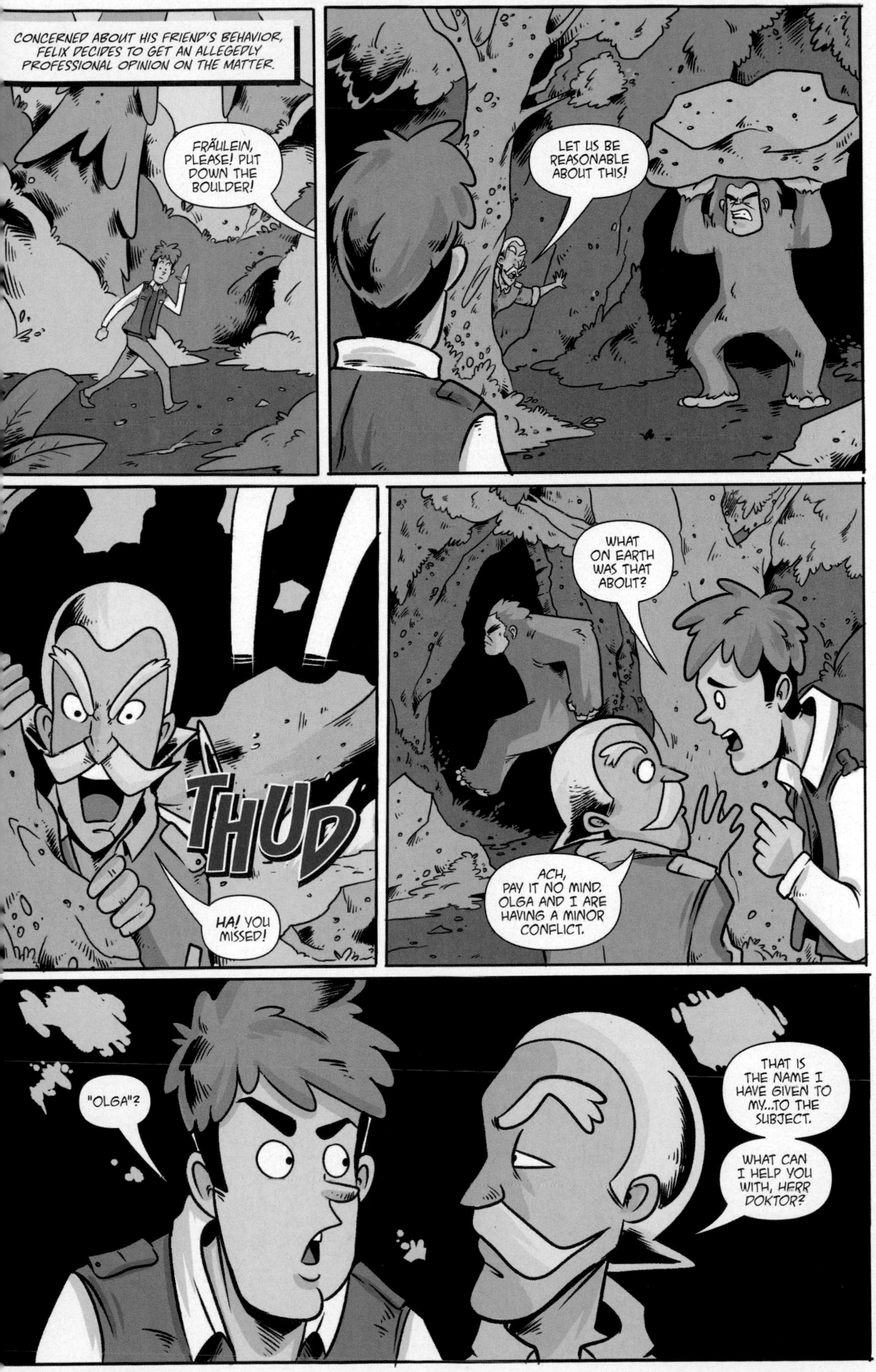
CONCERNED ABOUT HIS FRIEND'S BEHAVIOR, FELIX DECIDES TO GET AN ALLEGEDLY PROFESSIONAL OPINION ON THE MATTER.
FRÄULEIN, PLEASE! PUT DOWN THE BOULDER!
LET US BE REASONABLE ABOUT THIS!
THUD
HA! YOU MISSED!
WHAT ON EARTH WAS THAT ABOUT?
ACH, PAY IT NO MIND. OLGA AND I ARE HAVING A MINOR CONFLICT.
"OLGA"?
THAT IS THE NAME I HAVE GIVEN TO MY...TO THE SUBJECT.
WHAT CAN I HELP YOU WITH, HERR DOKTOR?

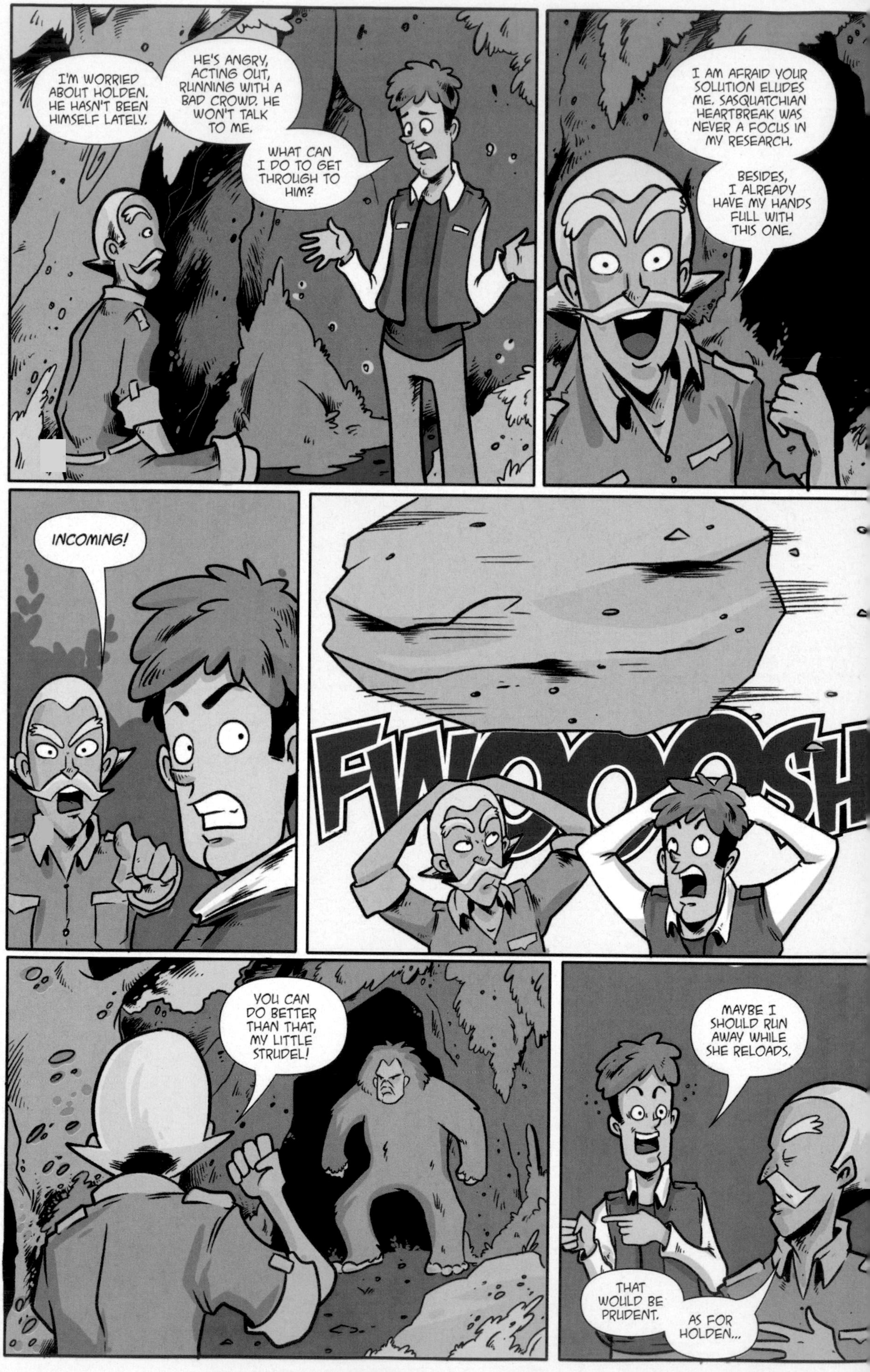
I'M WORRIED ABOUT HOLDEN. HE HASN'T BEEN HIMSELF LATELY.
HE'S ANGRY, ACTING OUT, RUNNING WITH A BAD CROWD. HE WON'T TALK TO ME.
WHAT CAN I DO TO GET THROUGH TO HIM?
I AM AFRAID YOUR SOLUTION ELUDES ME. SASQUATCHIAN HEARTBREAK WAS NEVER A FOCUS IN MY RESEARCH.
BESIDES, I ALREADY HAVE MY HANDS FULL WITH THIS ONE.
INCOMING!
FWOOOOSH
YOU CAN DO BETTER THAN THAT, MY LITTLE STRUDEL!
MAYBE I SHOULD RUN AWAY WHILE SHE RELOADS.
THAT WOULD BE PRUDENT.
AS FOR HOLDEN...

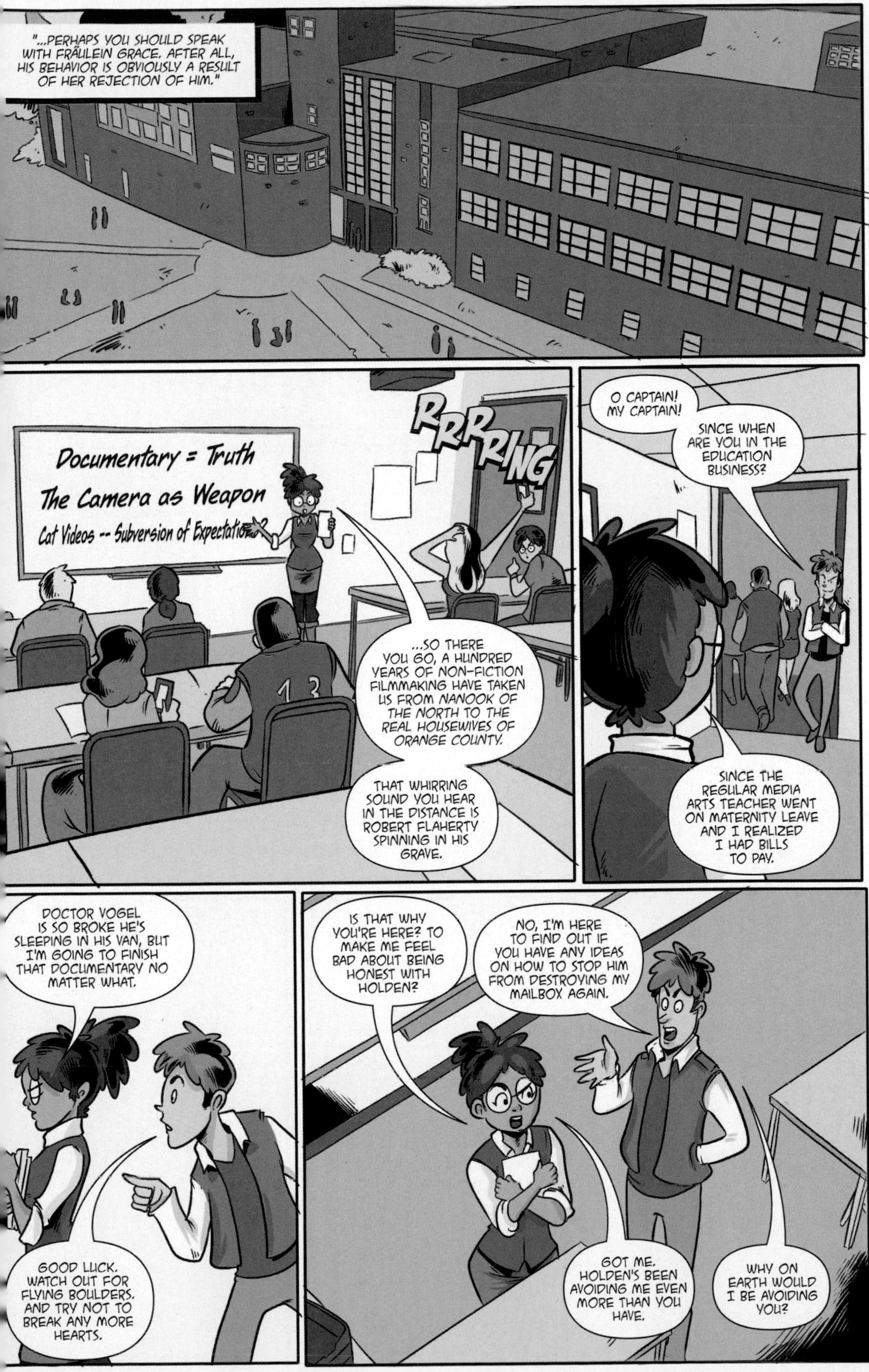
"...PERHAPS YOU SHOULD SPEAK WITH FRÄULEIN GRACE. AFTER ALL, HIS BEHAVIOR IS OBVIOUSLY A RESULT OF HER REJECTION OF HIM."
Documentary = Truth
The Camera as Weapon
Cat Videos -- Subversion of Expectatio
RRRRING
...SO THERE YOU GO, A HUNDRED YEARS OF NON-FICTION FILMMAKING HAVE TAKEN US FROM NANOOK OF THE NORTH TO THE REAL HOUSEWIVES OF ORANGE COUNTY.
THAT WHIRRING SOUND YOU HEAR IN THE DISTANCE IS ROBERT FLAHERTY SPINNING IN HIS GRAVE.
O CAPTAIN! MY CAPTAIN!
SINCE WHEN ARE YOU IN THE EDUCATION BUSINESS?
SINCE THE REGULAR MEDIA ARTS TEACHER WENT ON MATERNITY LEAVE AND I REALIZED I HAD BILLS TO PAY.
DOCTOR VOGEL IS SO BROKE HE'S SLEEPING IN HIS VAN, BUT I'M GOING TO FINISH THAT DOCUMENTARY NO MATTER WHAT.
GOOD LUCK. WATCH OUT FOR FLYING BOULDERS. AND TRY NOT TO BREAK ANY MORE HEARTS.
IS THAT WHY YOU'RE HERE? TO MAKE ME FEEL BAD ABOUT BEING HONEST WITH HOLDEN?
NO, I'M HERE TO FIND OUT IF YOU HAVE ANY IDEAS ON HOW TO STOP HIM FROM DESTROYING MY MAILBOX AGAIN.
GOT ME. HOLDEN'S BEEN AVOIDING ME EVEN MORE THAN YOU HAVE.
WHY ON EARTH WOULD I BE AVOIDING YOU?

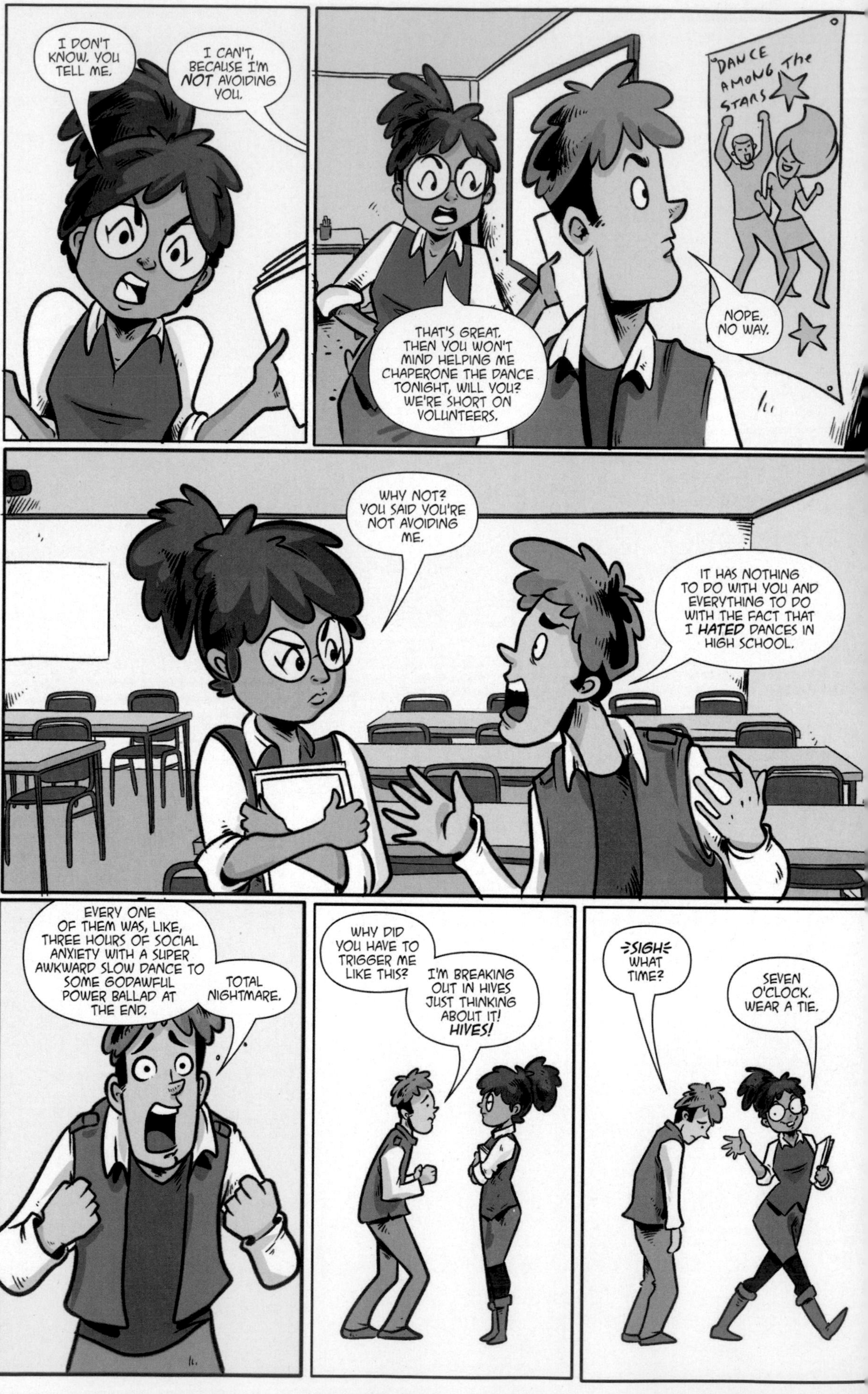
I DON'T KNOW. YOU TELL ME.
I CAN'T, BECAUSE I'M NOT AVOIDING YOU.
DANCE AMONG the STARS
THAT'S GREAT. THEN YOU WON'T MIND HELPING ME CHAPERONE THE DANCE TONIGHT, WILL YOU? WE'RE SHORT ON VOLUNTEERS.
NOPE. NO WAY.
WHY NOT? YOU SAID YOU'RE NOT AVOIDING ME.
IT HAS NOTHING TO DO WITH YOU AND EVERYTHING TO DO WITH THE FACT THAT I HATED DANCES IN HIGH SCHOOL.
EVERY ONE OF THEM WAS, LIKE, THREE HOURS OF SOCIAL ANXIETY WITH A SUPER AWKWARD SLOW DANCE TO SOME GODAWFUL POWER BALLAD AT THE END.
TOTAL NIGHTMARE.
WHY DID YOU HAVE TO TRIGGER ME LIKE THIS?
I'M BREAKING OUT IN HIVES JUST THINKING ABOUT IT! HIVES!
SIGH WHAT TIME?
SEVEN O'CLOCK. WEAR A TIE.

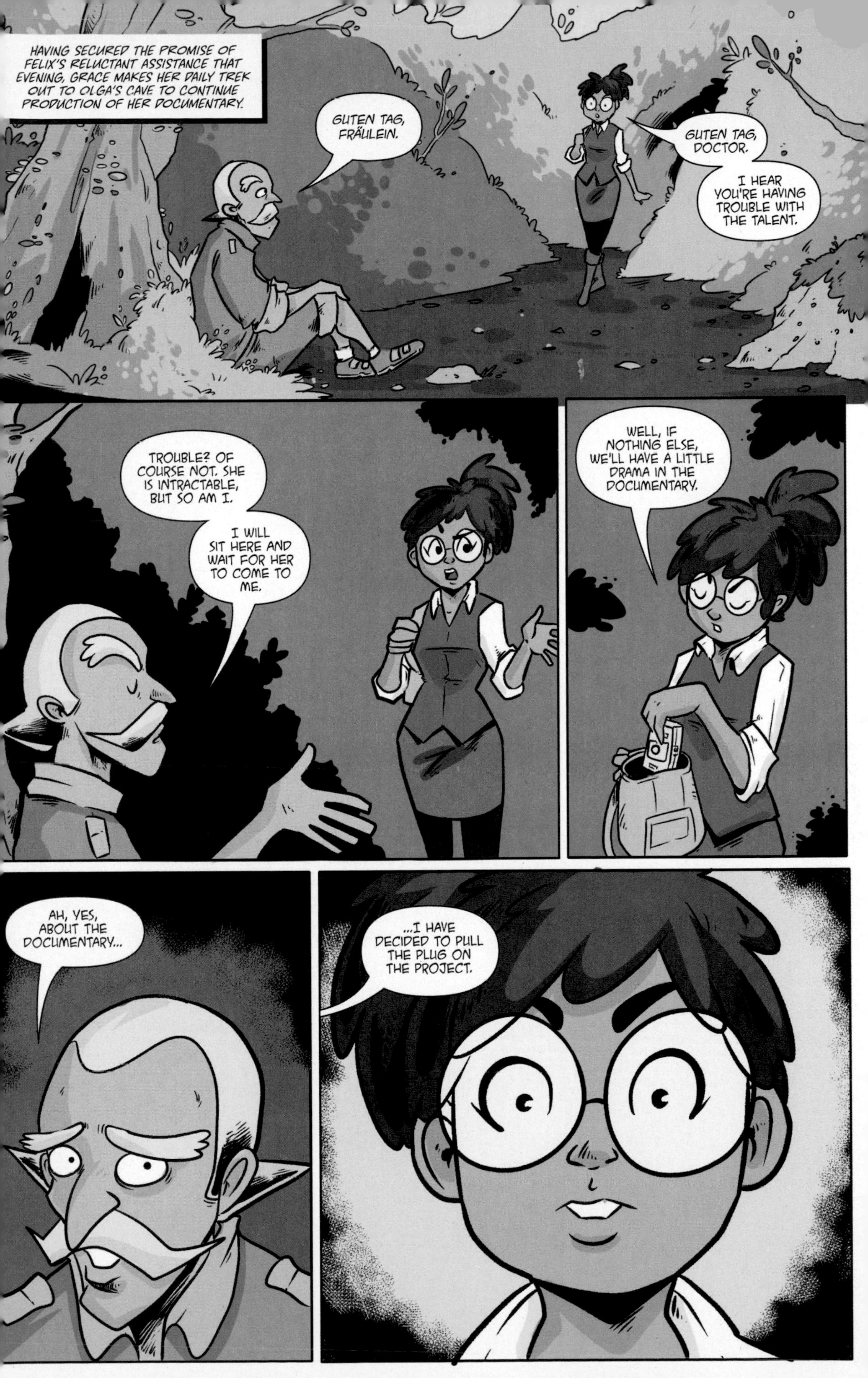
HAVING SECURED THE PROMISE OF FELIX'S RELUCTANT ASSISTANCE THAT EVENING, GRACE MAKES HER DAILY TREK OUT TO OLGA'S CAVE TO CONTINUE PRODUCTION OF HER DOCUMENTARY.
GUTEN TAG, FRÄULEIN.
GUTEN TAG, DOCTOR.
I HEAR YOU'RE HAVING TROUBLE WITH THE TALENT.
TROUBLE? OF COURSE NOT. SHE IS INTRACTABLE, BUT SO AM I.
I WILL SIT HERE AND WAIT FOR HER TO COME TO ME.
WELL, IF NOTHING ELSE, WE'LL HAVE A LITTLE DRAMA IN THE DOCUMENTARY.
AH, YES, ABOUT THE DOCUMENTARY...
...I HAVE DECIDED TO PULL THE PLUG ON THE PROJECT.

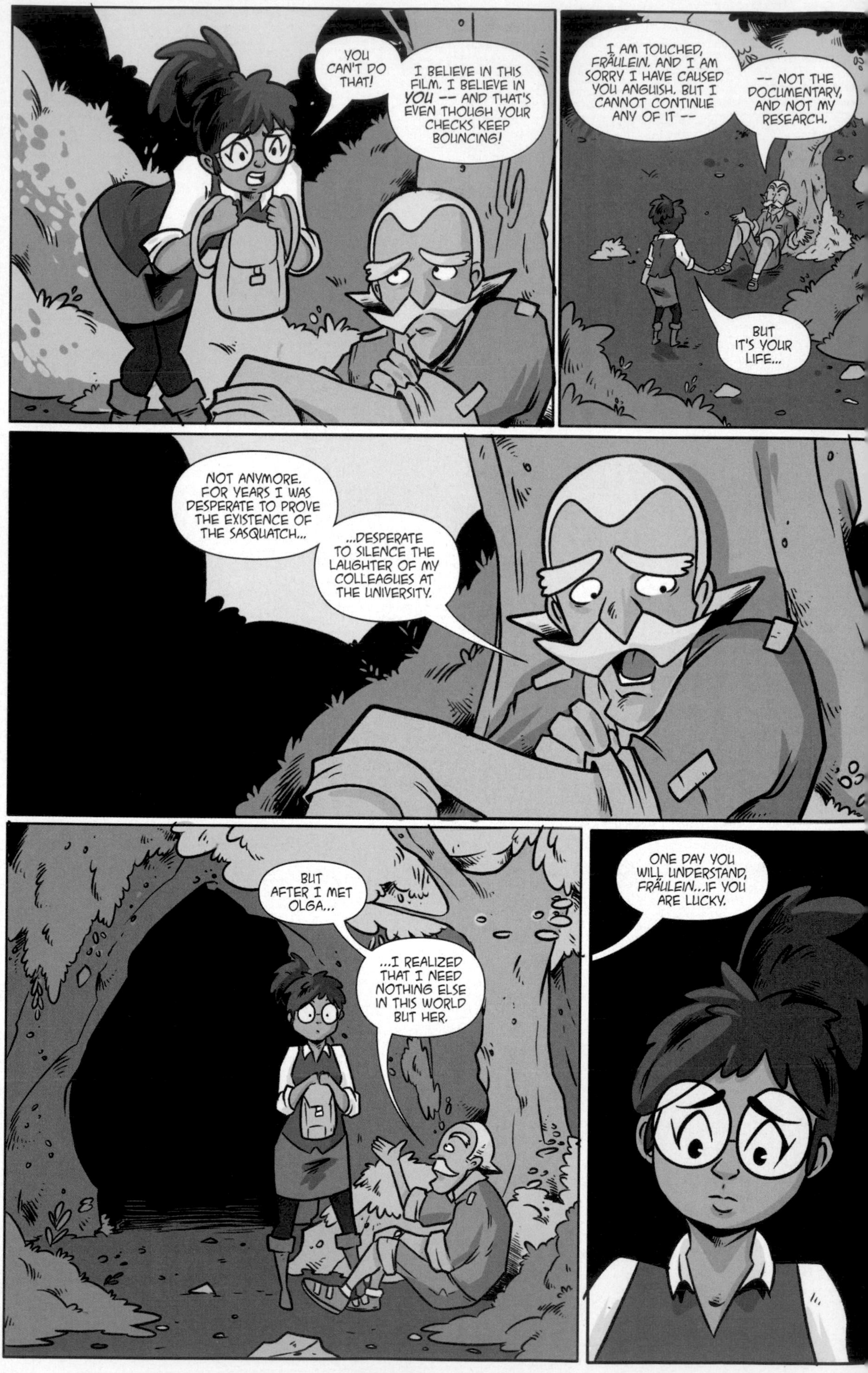
YOU CAN'T DO THAT!
I BELIEVE IN THIS FILM. I BELIEVE IN *YOU* -- AND THAT'S EVEN THOUGH YOUR CHECKS KEEP BOUNCING!
I AM TOUCHED, FRÄULEIN. AND I AM SORRY I HAVE CAUSED YOU ANGUISH. BUT I CANNOT CONTINUE ANY OF IT --
-- NOT THE DOCUMENTARY, AND NOT MY RESEARCH.
BUT IT'S YOUR LIFE...
NOT ANYMORE. FOR YEARS I WAS DESPERATE TO PROVE THE EXISTENCE OF THE SASQUATCH...
...DESPERATE TO SILENCE THE LAUGHTER OF MY COLLEAGUES AT THE UNIVERSITY.
BUT AFTER I MET OLGA...
...I REALIZED THAT I NEED NOTHING ELSE IN THIS WORLD BUT HER.
ONE DAY YOU WILL UNDERSTAND, FRÄULEIN...IF YOU ARE LUCKY.

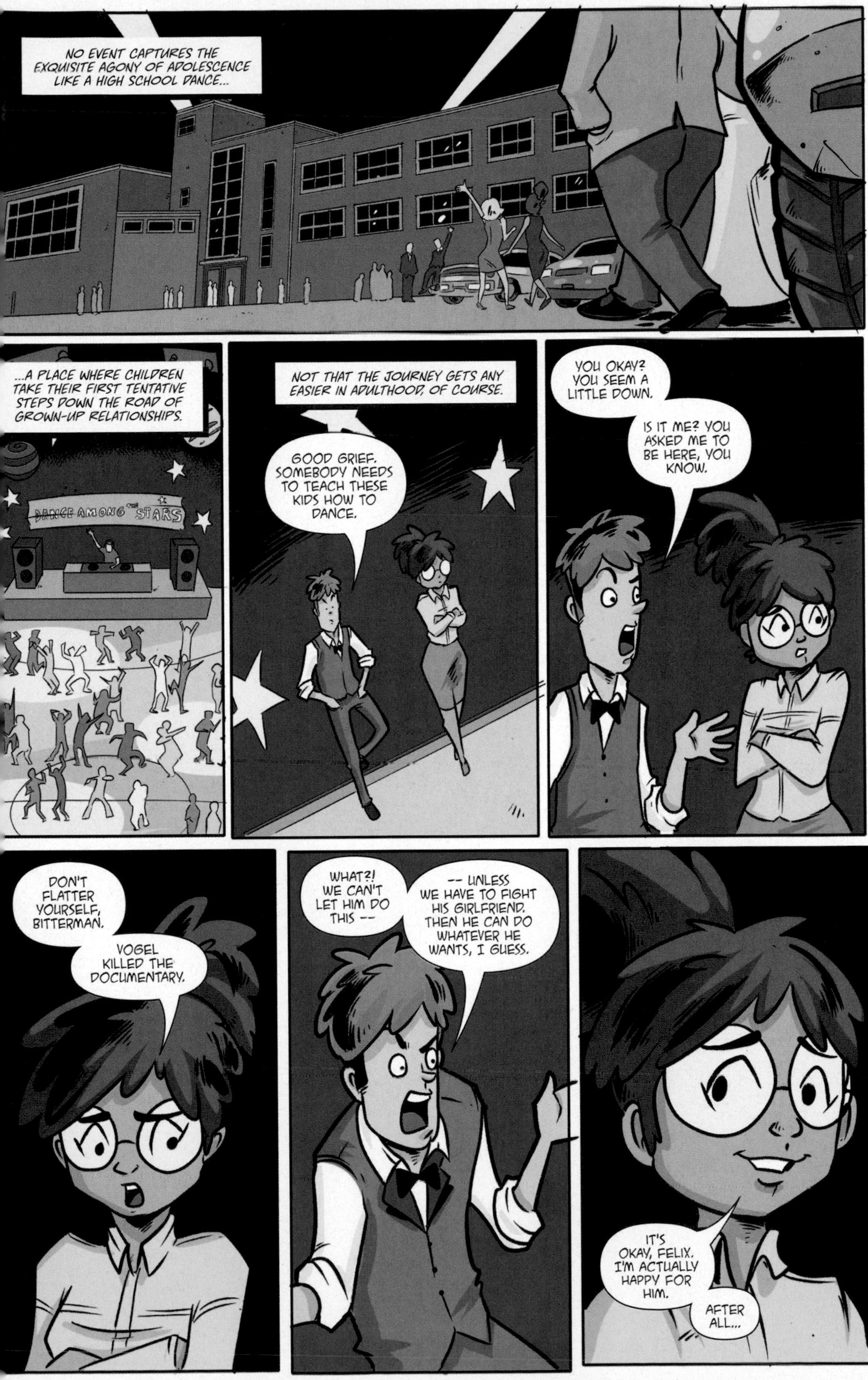
NO EVENT CAPTURES THE EXQUISITE AGONY OF ADOLESCENCE LIKE A HIGH SCHOOL DANCE...
...A PLACE WHERE CHILDREN TAKE THEIR FIRST TENTATIVE STEPS DOWN THE ROAD OF GROWN-UP RELATIONSHIPS.
DANCE AMONG THE STARS
NOT THAT THE JOURNEY GETS ANY EASIER IN ADULTHOOD, OF COURSE.
GOOD GRIEF. SOMEBODY NEEDS TO TEACH THESE KIDS HOW TO DANCE.
YOU OKAY? YOU SEEM A LITTLE DOWN.
IS IT ME? YOU ASKED ME TO BE HERE, YOU KNOW.
DON'T FLATTER YOURSELF, BITTERMAN.
VOGEL KILLED THE DOCUMENTARY.
WHAT?! WE CAN'T LET HIM DO THIS --
-- UNLESS WE HAVE TO FIGHT HIS GIRLFRIEND. THEN HE CAN DO WHATEVER HE WANTS, I GUESS.
IT'S OKAY, FELIX. I'M ACTUALLY HAPPY FOR HIM.
AFTER ALL...

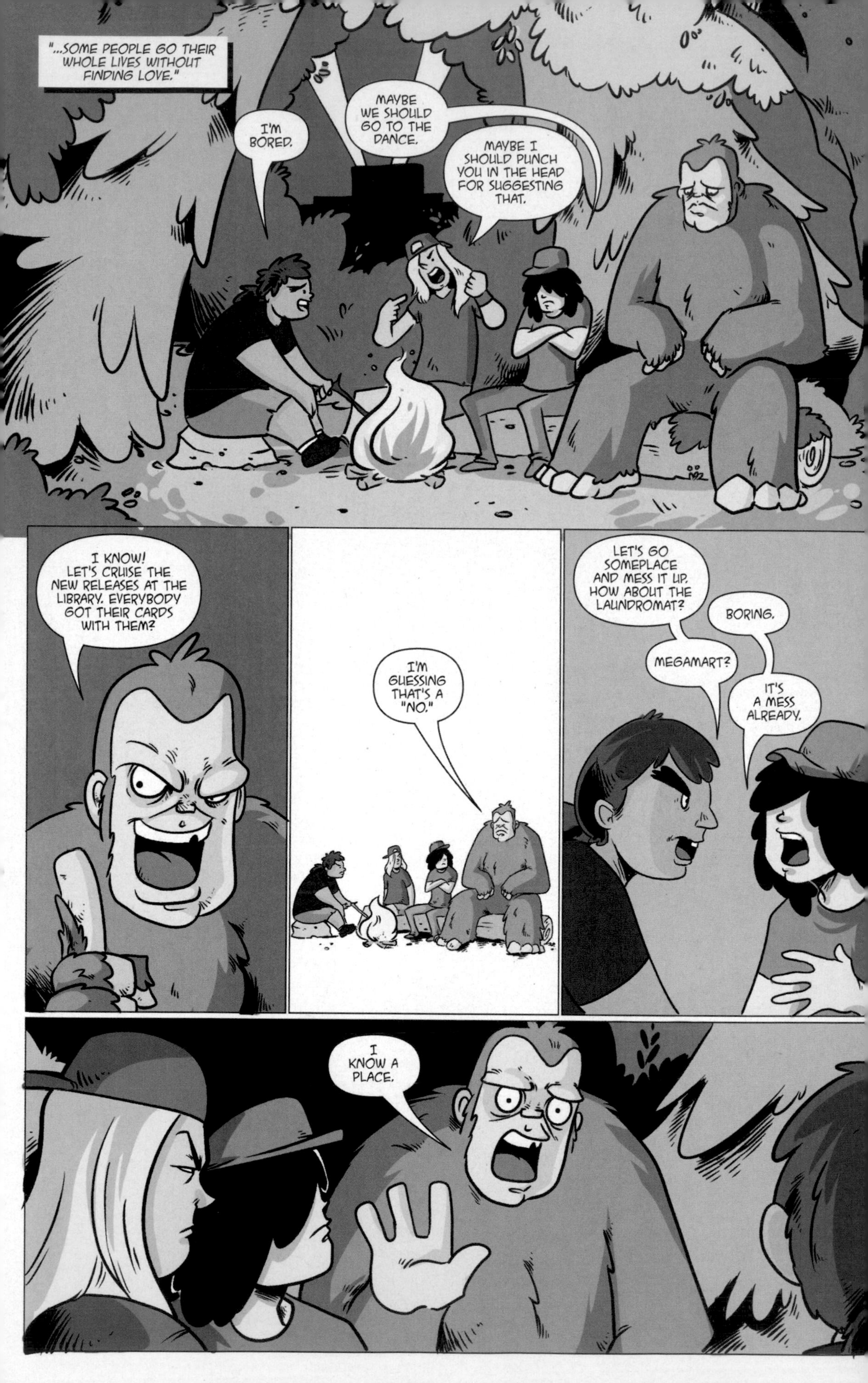
"...SOME PEOPLE GO THEIR WHOLE LIVES WITHOUT FINDING LOVE."
I'M BORED.
MAYBE WE SHOULD GO TO THE DANCE.
MAYBE I SHOULD PUNCH YOU IN THE HEAD FOR SUGGESTING THAT.
I KNOW! LET'S CRUISE THE NEW RELEASES AT THE LIBRARY. EVERYBODY GOT THEIR CARDS WITH THEM?
I'M GUESSING THAT'S A "NO."
LET'S GO SOMEPLACE AND MESS IT UP. HOW ABOUT THE LAUNDROMAT?
BORING.
MEGAMART?
IT'S A MESS ALREADY.
I KNOW A PLACE.

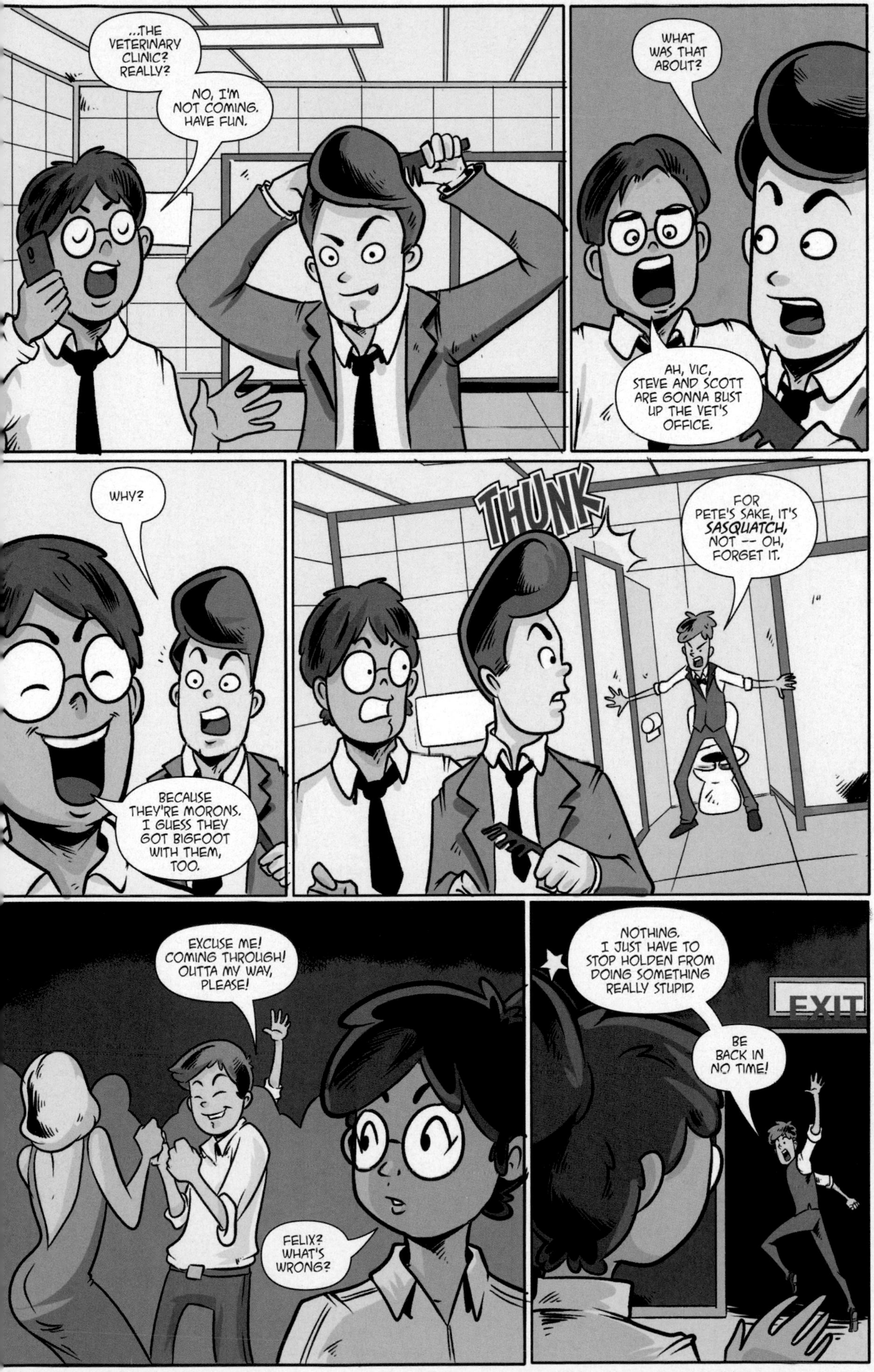
...THE VETERINARY CLINIC? REALLY?
NO, I'M NOT COMING. HAVE FUN.
WHAT WAS THAT ABOUT?
AH, VIC, STEVE AND SCOTT ARE GONNA BUST UP THE VET'S OFFICE.
WHY?
BECAUSE THEY'RE MORONS. I GUESS THEY GOT BIGFOOT WITH THEM, TOO.
THUNK
FOR PETE'S SAKE, IT'S SASQUATCH, NOT -- OH, FORGET IT.
EXCUSE ME! COMING THROUGH! OUTTA MY WAY, PLEASE!
FELIX? WHAT'S WRONG?
NOTHING. I JUST HAVE TO STOP HOLDEN FROM DOING SOMETHING REALLY STUPID.
BE BACK IN NO TIME!
EXIT

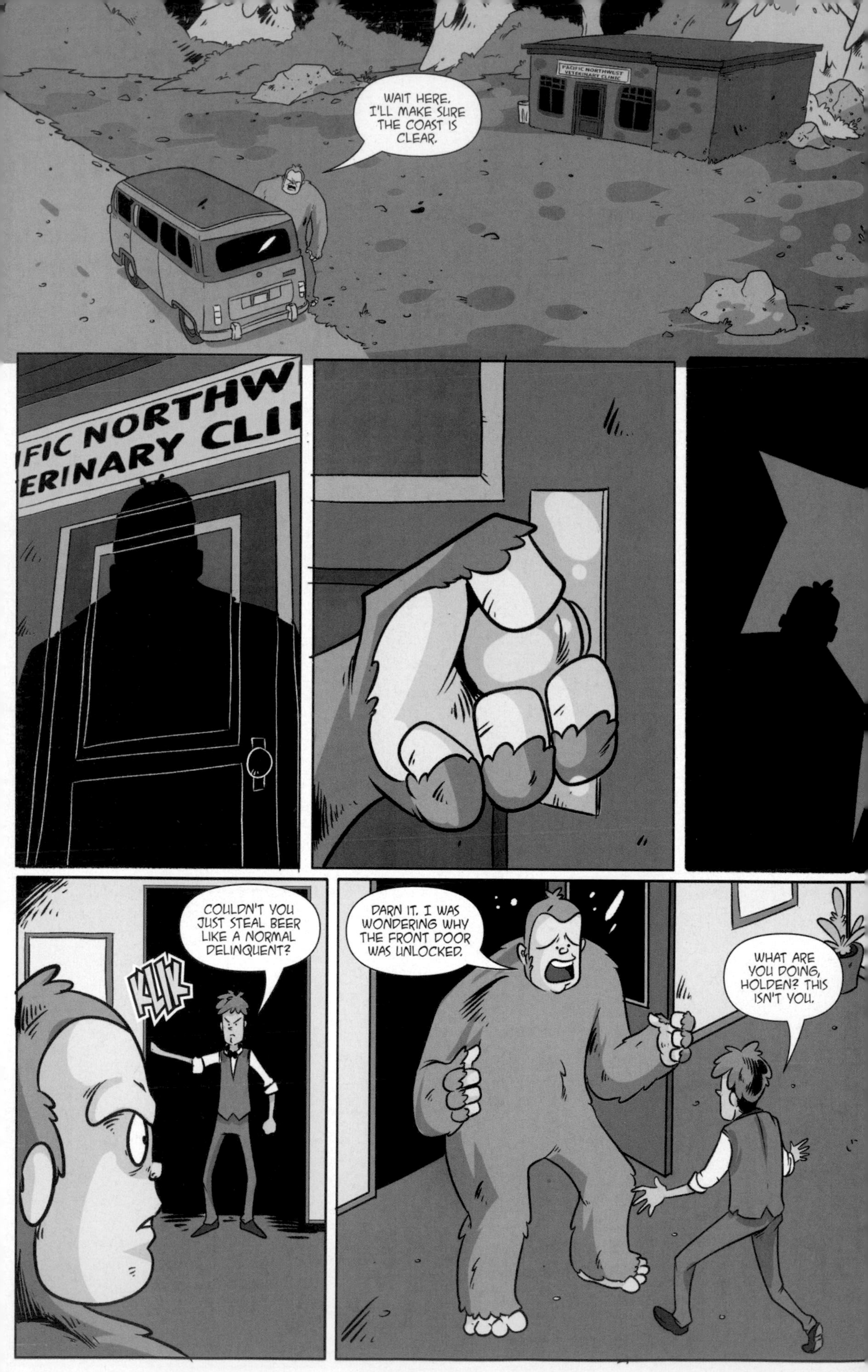
WAIT HERE. I'LL MAKE SURE THE COAST IS CLEAR.
PACIFIC NORTHWEST VETERINARY CLINIC
IFIC NORTHW ERINARY CLI
KLIK
COULDN'T YOU JUST STEAL BEER LIKE A NORMAL DELINQUENT?
DARN IT. I WAS WONDERING WHY THE FRONT DOOR WAS UNLOCKED.
WHAT ARE YOU DOING, HOLDEN? THIS ISN'T YOU.

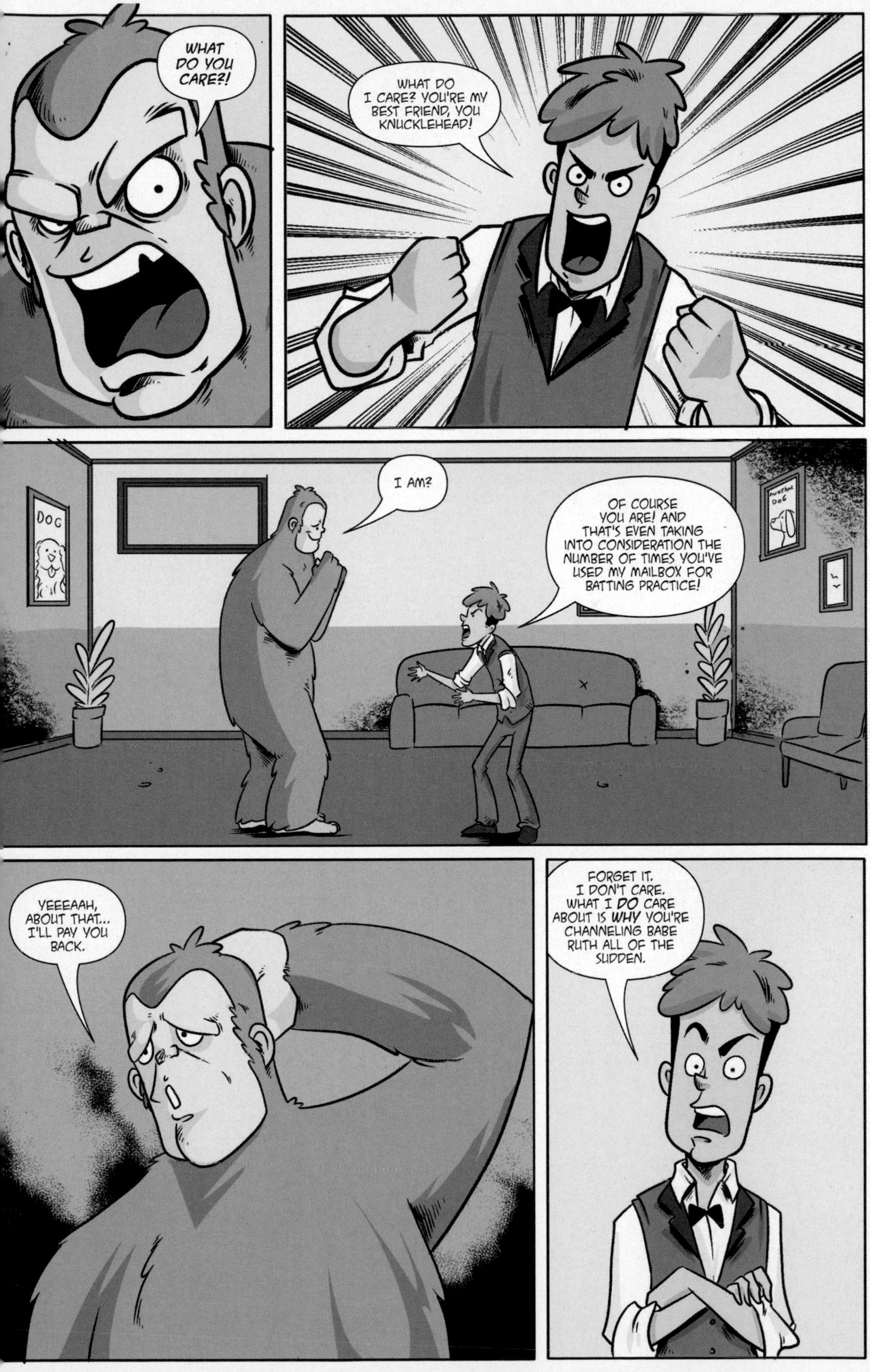
WHAT DO YOU CARE?!
WHAT DO I CARE? YOU'RE MY BEST FRIEND, YOU KNUCKLEHEAD!
DOG
I AM?
OF COURSE YOU ARE! AND THAT'S EVEN TAKING INTO CONSIDERATION THE NUMBER OF TIMES YOU'VE USED MY MAILBOX FOR BATTING PRACTICE!
YEEEAAH, ABOUT THAT... I'LL PAY YOU BACK.
FORGET IT. I DON'T CARE. WHAT I *DO* CARE ABOUT IS *WHY* YOU'RE CHANNELING BABE RUTH ALL OF THE SUDDEN.

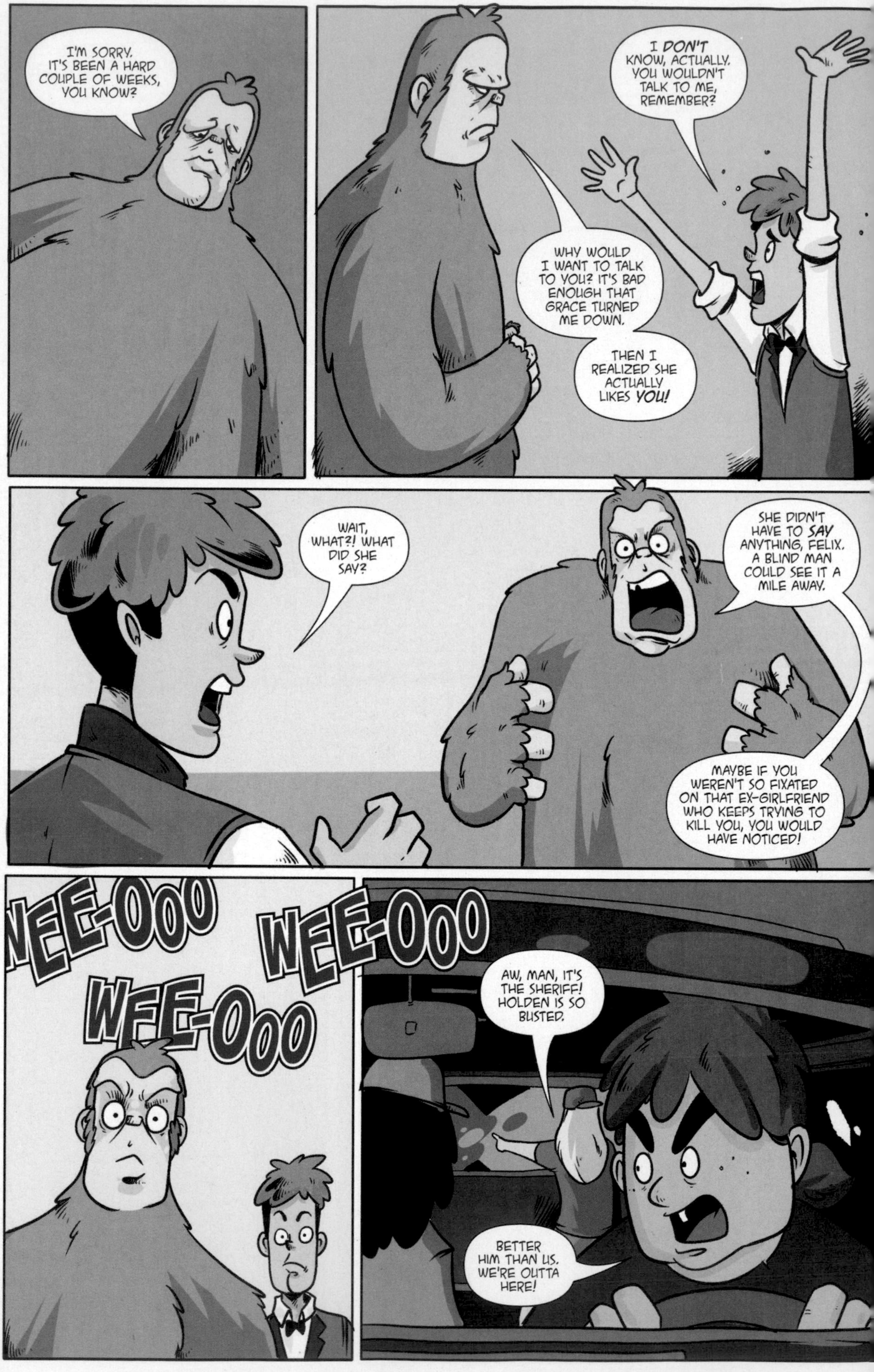
I'M SORRY. IT'S BEEN A HARD COUPLE OF WEEKS, YOU KNOW?
I DON'T KNOW, ACTUALLY. YOU WOULDN'T TALK TO ME, REMEMBER?
WHY WOULD I WANT TO TALK TO YOU? IT'S BAD ENOUGH THAT GRACE TURNED ME DOWN.
THEN I REALIZED SHE ACTUALLY LIKES YOU!
WAIT, WHAT?! WHAT DID SHE SAY?
SHE DIDN'T HAVE TO SAY ANYTHING, FELIX. A BLIND MAN COULD SEE IT A MILE AWAY.
MAYBE IF YOU WEREN'T SO FIXATED ON THAT EX-GIRLFRIEND WHO KEEPS TRYING TO KILL YOU, YOU WOULD HAVE NOTICED!
WEE-OOO
WEE-OOO
WEE-OOO
AW, MAN, IT'S THE SHERIFF! HOLDEN IS SO BUSTED.
BETTER HIM THAN US. WE'RE OUTTA HERE!

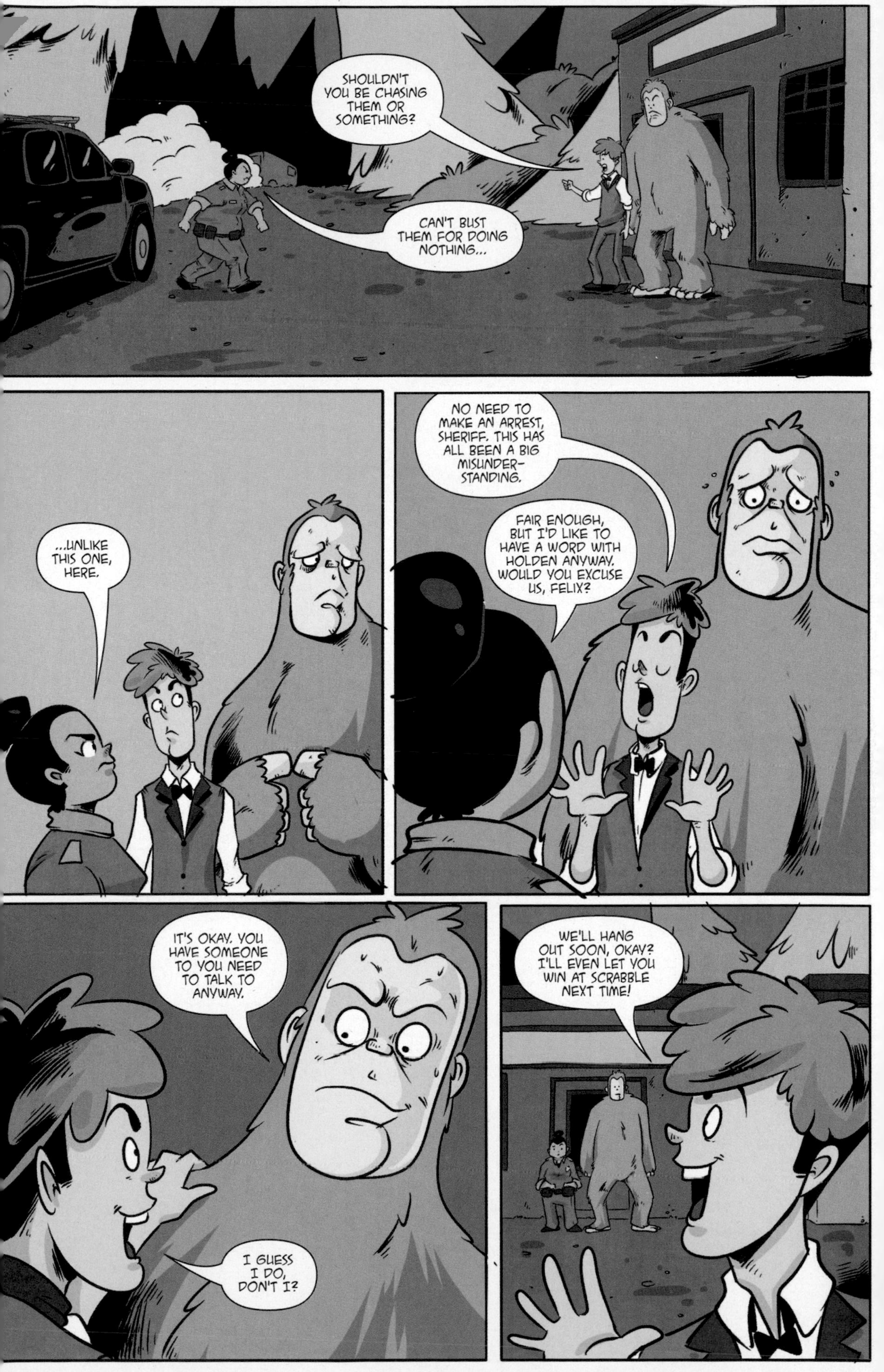
SHOULDN'T YOU BE CHASING THEM OR SOMETHING?
CAN'T BUST THEM FOR DOING NOTHING...
...UNLIKE THIS ONE, HERE.
NO NEED TO MAKE AN ARREST, SHERIFF. THIS HAS ALL BEEN A BIG MISUNDER-STANDING.
FAIR ENOUGH, BUT I'D LIKE TO HAVE A WORD WITH HOLDEN ANYWAY. WOULD YOU EXCUSE US, FELIX?
IT'S OKAY. YOU HAVE SOMEONE TO YOU NEED TO TALK TO ANYWAY.
I GUESS I DO, DON'T I?
WE'LL HANG OUT SOON, OKAY? I'LL EVEN LET YOU WIN AT SCRABBLE NEXT TIME!

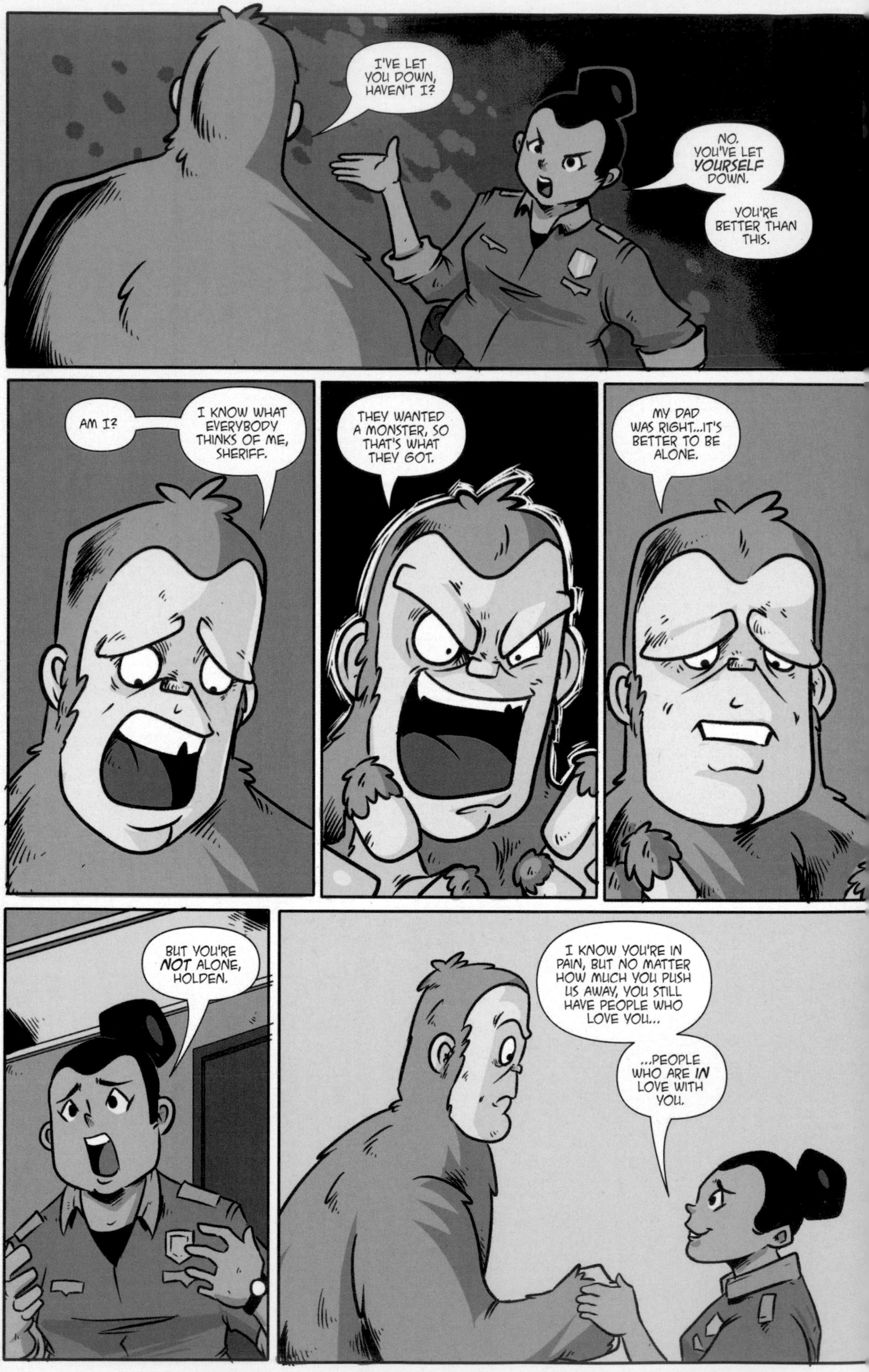
I'VE LET YOU DOWN, HAVEN'T I?
NO. YOU'VE LET YOURSELF DOWN.
YOU'RE BETTER THAN THIS.
AM I?
I KNOW WHAT EVERYBODY THINKS OF ME, SHERIFF.
THEY WANTED A MONSTER, SO THAT'S WHAT THEY GOT.
MY DAD WAS RIGHT...IT'S BETTER TO BE ALONE.
BUT YOU'RE NOT ALONE, HOLDEN.
I KNOW YOU'RE IN PAIN, BUT NO MATTER HOW MUCH YOU PUSH US AWAY, YOU STILL HAVE PEOPLE WHO LOVE YOU...
...PEOPLE WHO ARE IN LOVE WITH YOU.

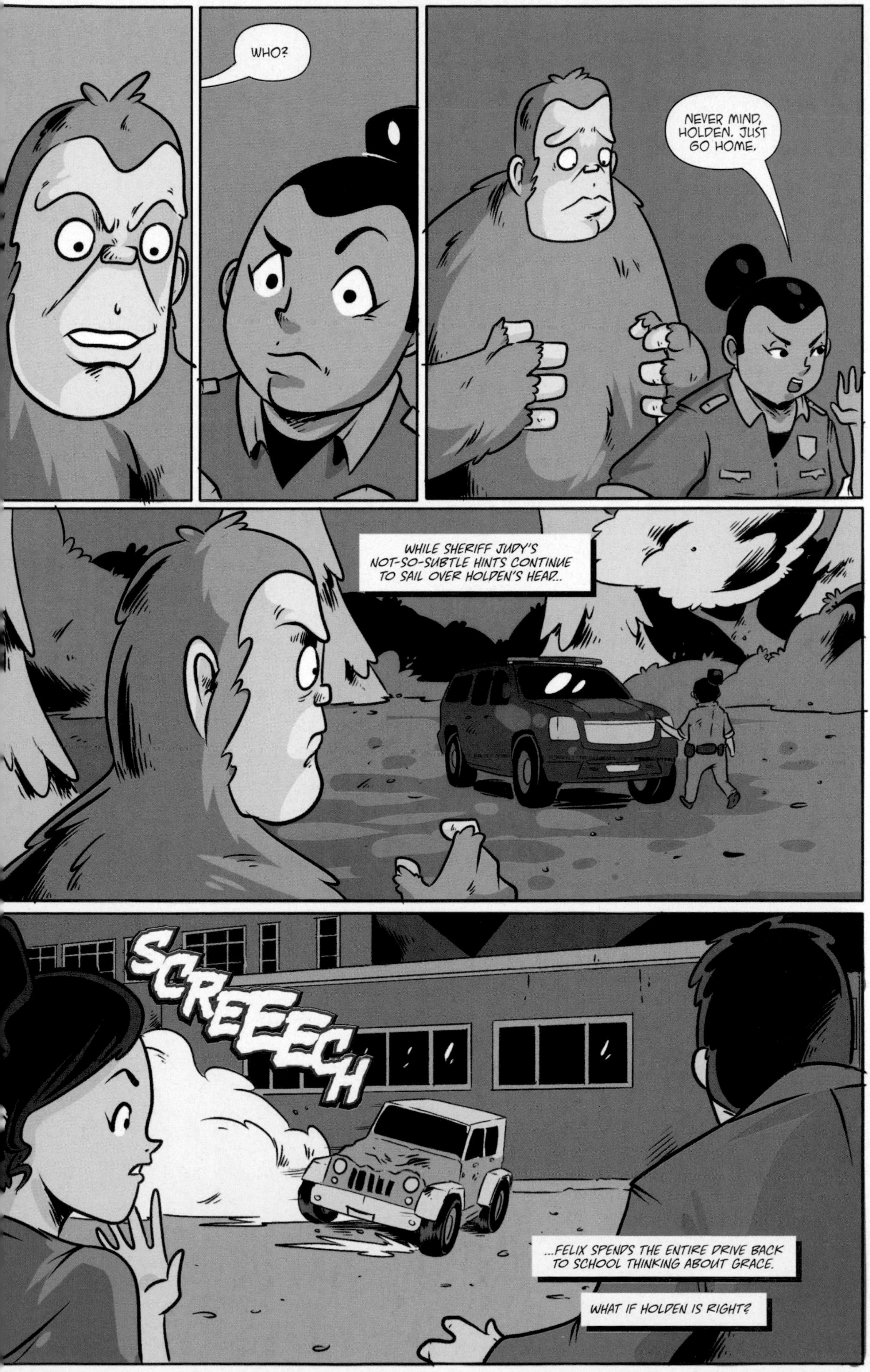
WHO?
NEVER MIND, HOLDEN. JUST GO HOME.
WHILE SHERIFF JUDY'S NOT-SO-SUBTLE HINTS CONTINUE TO SAIL OVER HOLDEN'S HEAD...
SCREEECH
...FELIX SPENDS THE ENTIRE DRIVE BACK TO SCHOOL THINKING ABOUT GRACE.
WHAT IF HOLDEN IS RIGHT?

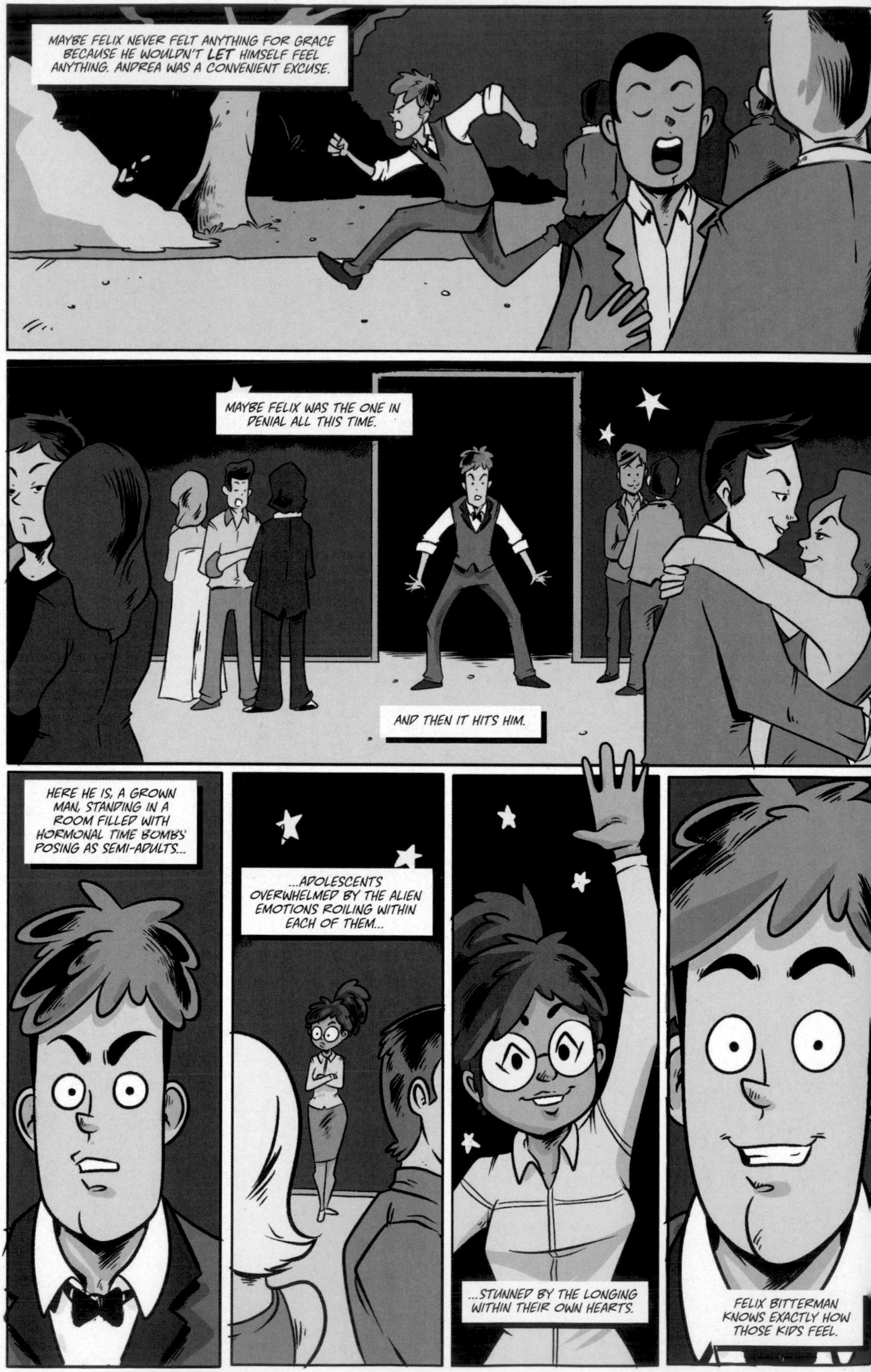
MAYBE FELIX NEVER FELT ANYTHING FOR GRACE BECAUSE HE WOULDN'T **LET** HIMSELF FEEL ANYTHING. ANDREA WAS A CONVENIENT EXCUSE.
MAYBE FELIX WAS THE ONE IN DENIAL ALL THIS TIME.
AND THEN IT HITS HIM.
HERE HE IS, A GROWN MAN, STANDING IN A ROOM FILLED WITH HORMONAL TIME BOMBS POSING AS SEMI-ADULTS...
...ADOLESCENTS OVERWHELMED BY THE ALIEN EMOTIONS ROILING WITHIN EACH OF THEM...
...STUNNED BY THE LONGING WITHIN THEIR OWN HEARTS.
FELIX BITTERMAN KNOWS EXACTLY HOW THOSE KIDS FEEL.

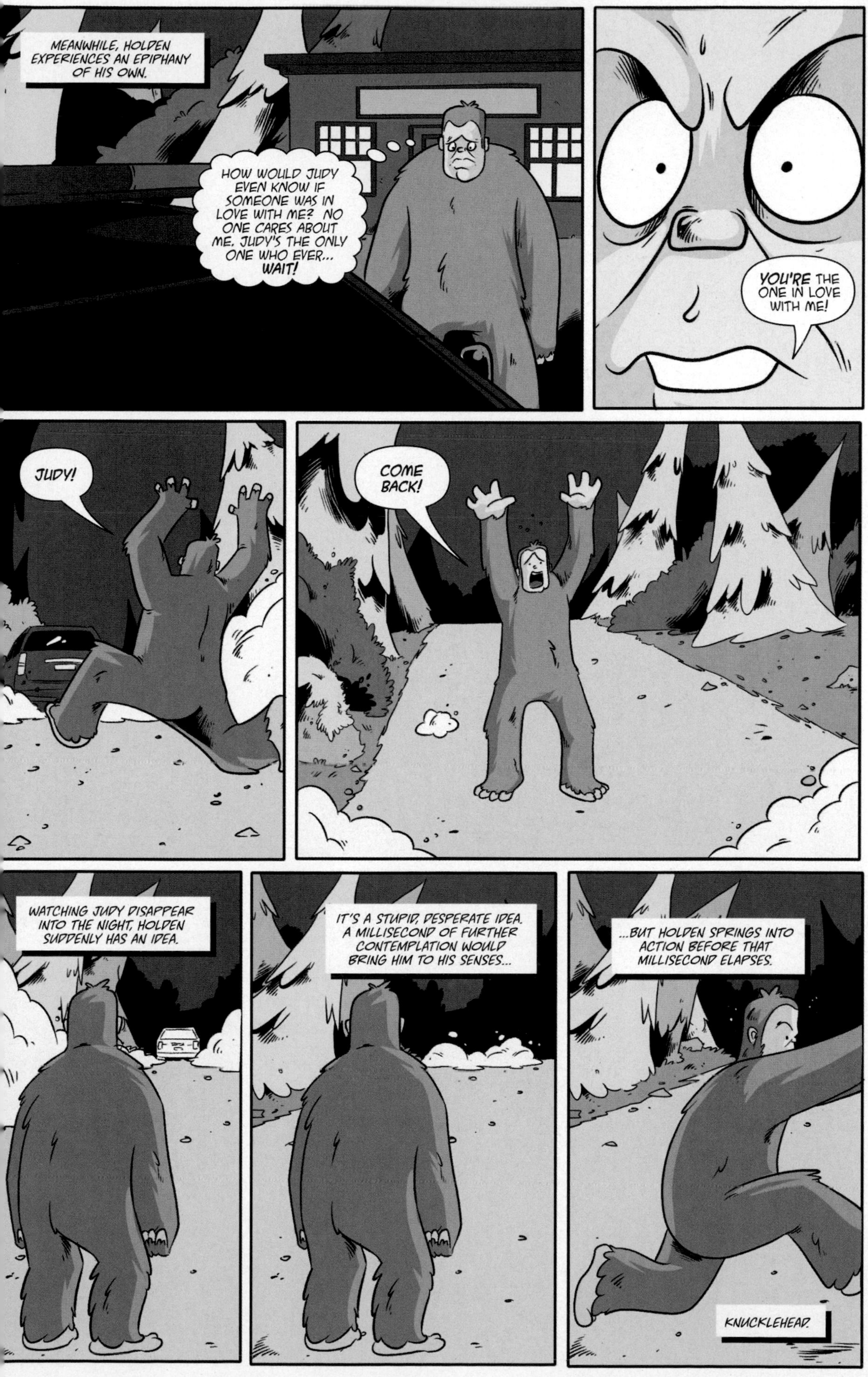
MEANWHILE, HOLDEN EXPERIENCES AN EPIPHANY OF HIS OWN.
HOW WOULD JUDY EVEN KNOW IF SOMEONE WAS IN LOVE WITH ME? NO ONE CARES ABOUT ME. JUDY'S THE ONLY ONE WHO EVER... WAIT!
YOU'RE THE ONE IN LOVE WITH ME!
JUDY!
COME BACK!
WATCHING JUDY DISAPPEAR INTO THE NIGHT, HOLDEN SUDDENLY HAS AN IDEA.
IT'S A STUPID, DESPERATE IDEA. A MILLISECOND OF FURTHER CONTEMPLATION WOULD BRING HIM TO HIS SENSES...
...BUT HOLDEN SPRINGS INTO ACTION BEFORE THAT MILLISECOND ELAPSES.
KNUCKLEHEAD.

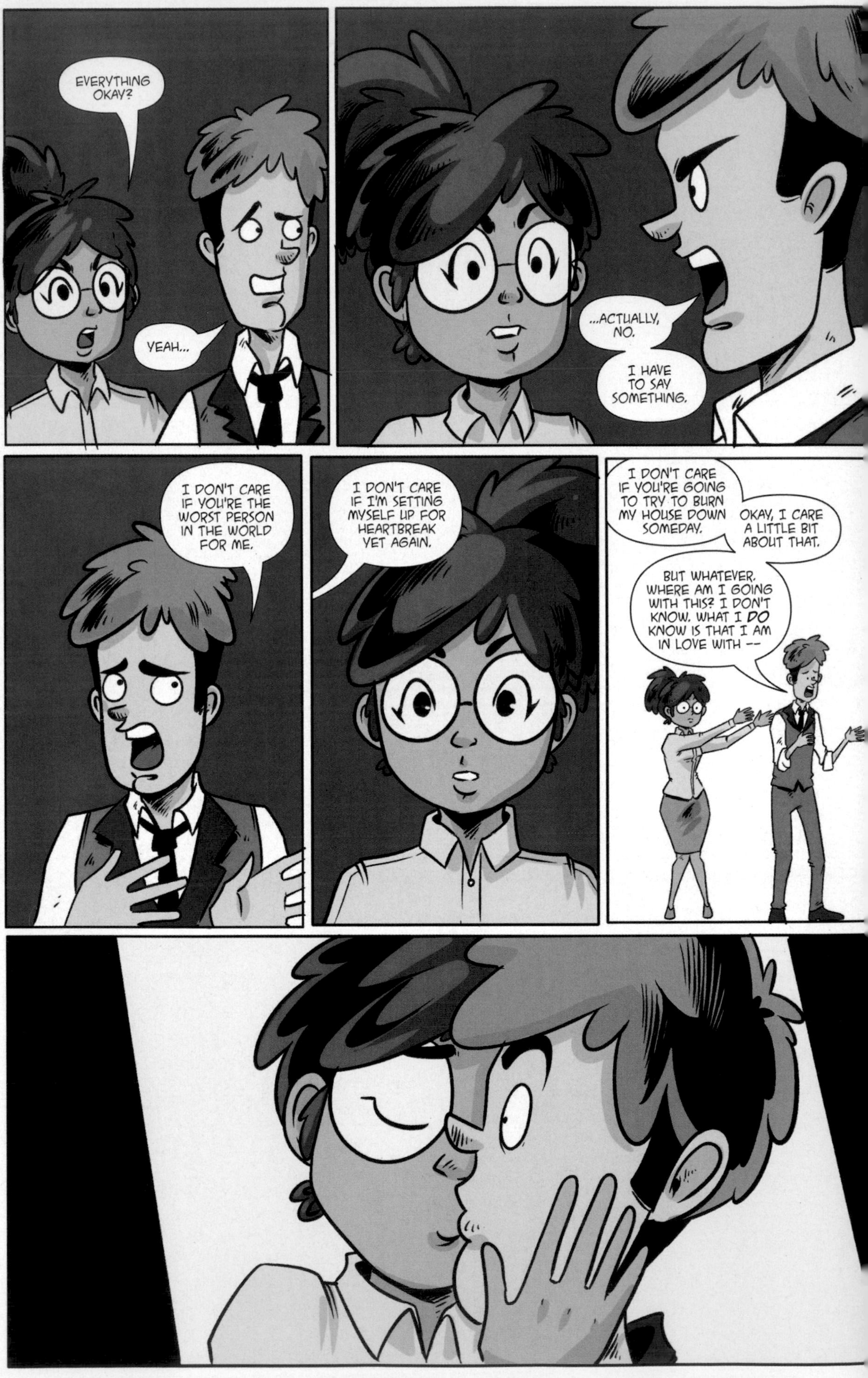
EVERYTHING OKAY?
YEAH...
...ACTUALLY, NO.
I HAVE TO SAY SOMETHING.
I DON'T CARE IF YOU'RE THE WORST PERSON IN THE WORLD FOR ME.
I DON'T CARE IF I'M SETTING MYSELF UP FOR HEARTBREAK YET AGAIN.
I DON'T CARE IF YOU'RE GOING TO TRY TO BURN MY HOUSE DOWN SOMEDAY.
OKAY, I CARE A LITTLE BIT ABOUT THAT.
BUT WHATEVER. WHERE AM I GOING WITH THIS? I DON'T KNOW. WHAT I DO KNOW IS THAT I AM IN LOVE WITH --

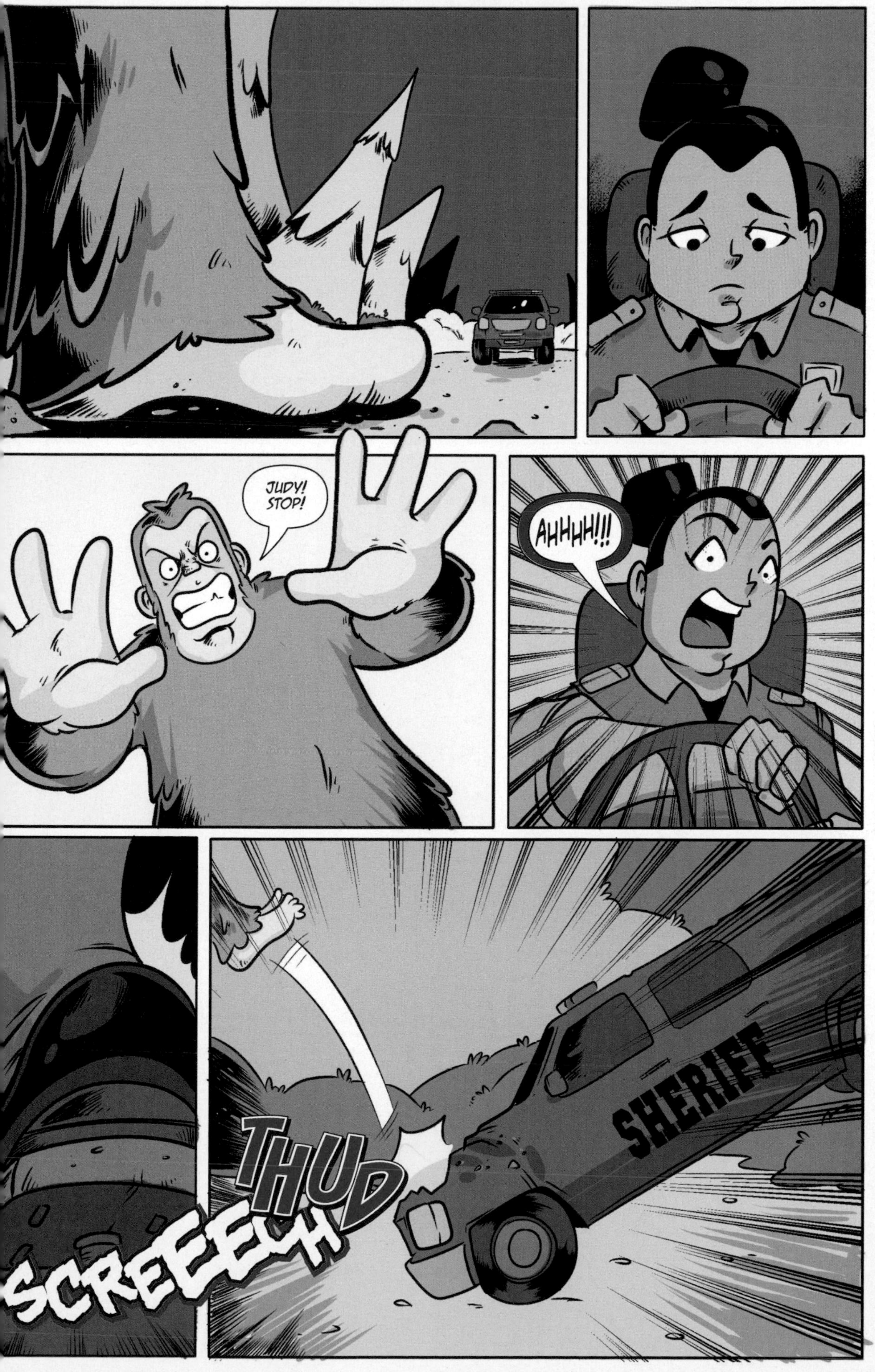
JUDY! STOP!
AHHHH!!!
SHERIFF
THUD
SCREEECH

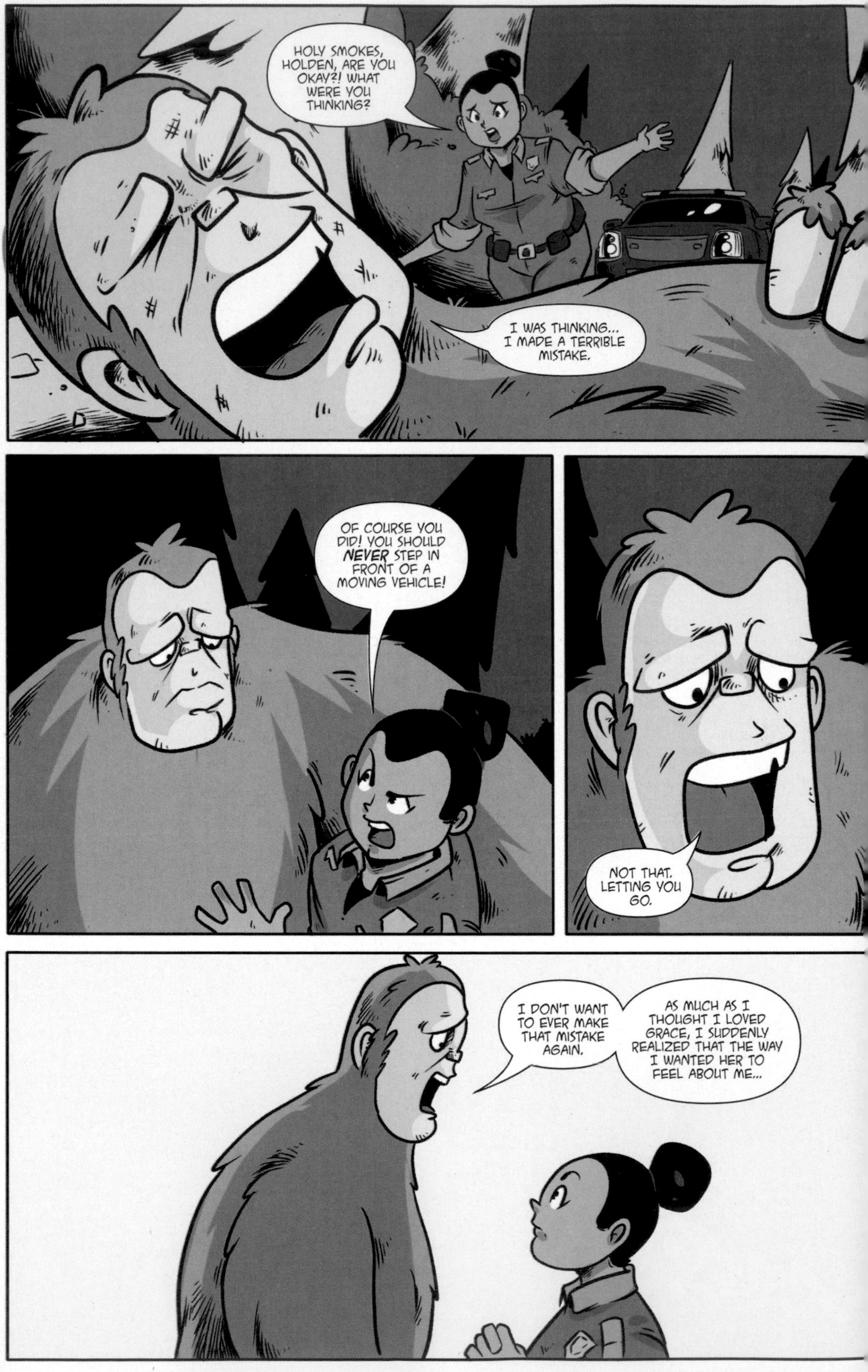
HOLY SMOKES, HOLDEN, ARE YOU OKAY?! WHAT WERE YOU THINKING?
I WAS THINKING... I MADE A TERRIBLE MISTAKE.
OF COURSE YOU DID! YOU SHOULD NEVER STEP IN FRONT OF A MOVING VEHICLE!
NOT THAT. LETTING YOU GO.
I DON'T WANT TO EVER MAKE THAT MISTAKE AGAIN.
AS MUCH AS I THOUGHT I LOVED GRACE, I SUDDENLY REALIZED THAT THE WAY I WANTED HER TO FEEL ABOUT ME...

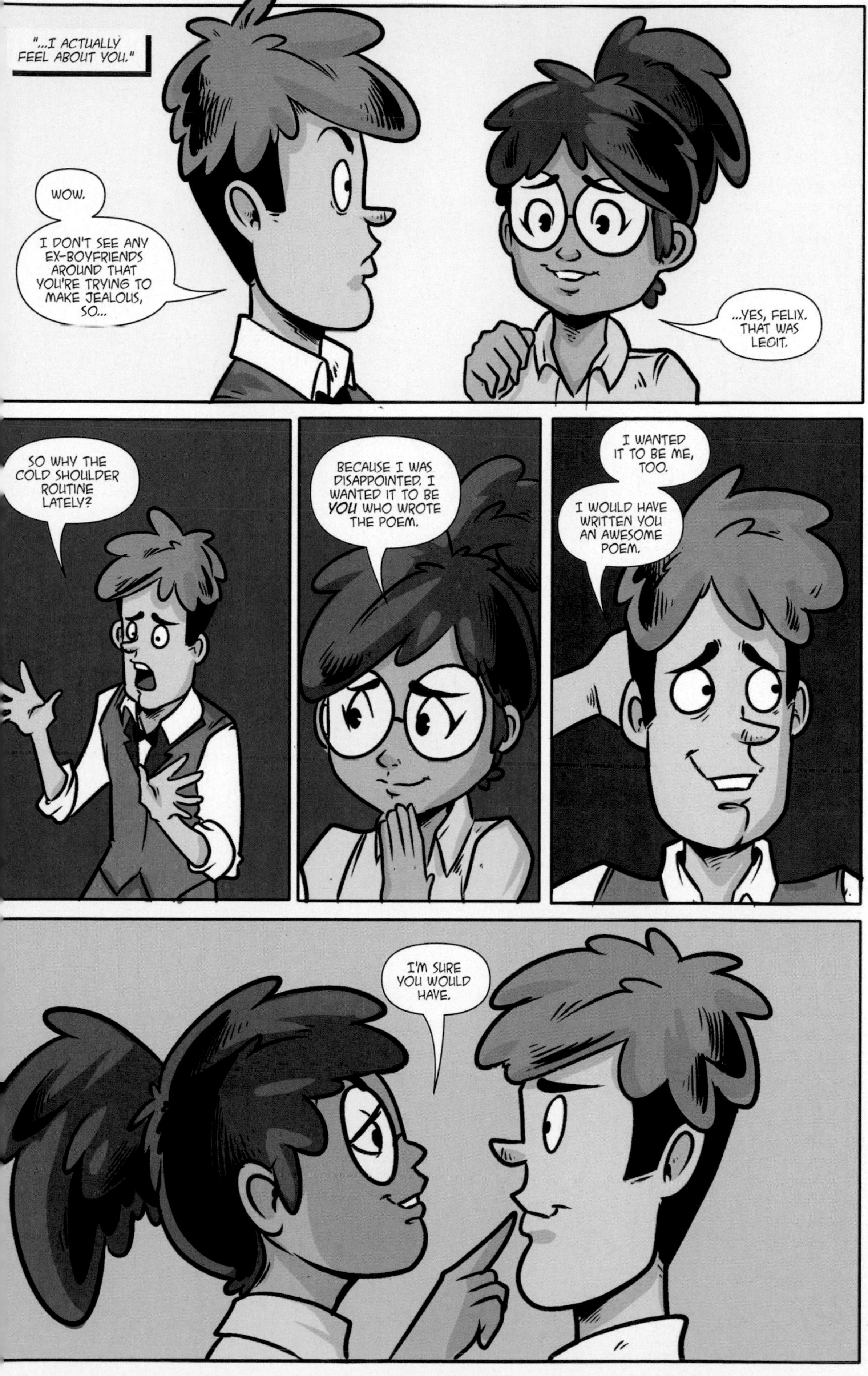
"...I ACTUALLY FEEL ABOUT YOU."
WOW.
I DON'T SEE ANY EX-BOYFRIENDS AROUND THAT YOU'RE TRYING TO MAKE JEALOUS, SO...
...YES, FELIX. THAT WAS LEGIT.
SO WHY THE COLD SHOULDER ROUTINE LATELY?
BECAUSE I WAS DISAPPOINTED. I WANTED IT TO BE *YOU* WHO WROTE THE POEM.
I WANTED IT TO BE ME, TOO.
I WOULD HAVE WRITTEN YOU AN AWESOME POEM.
I'M SURE YOU WOULD HAVE.

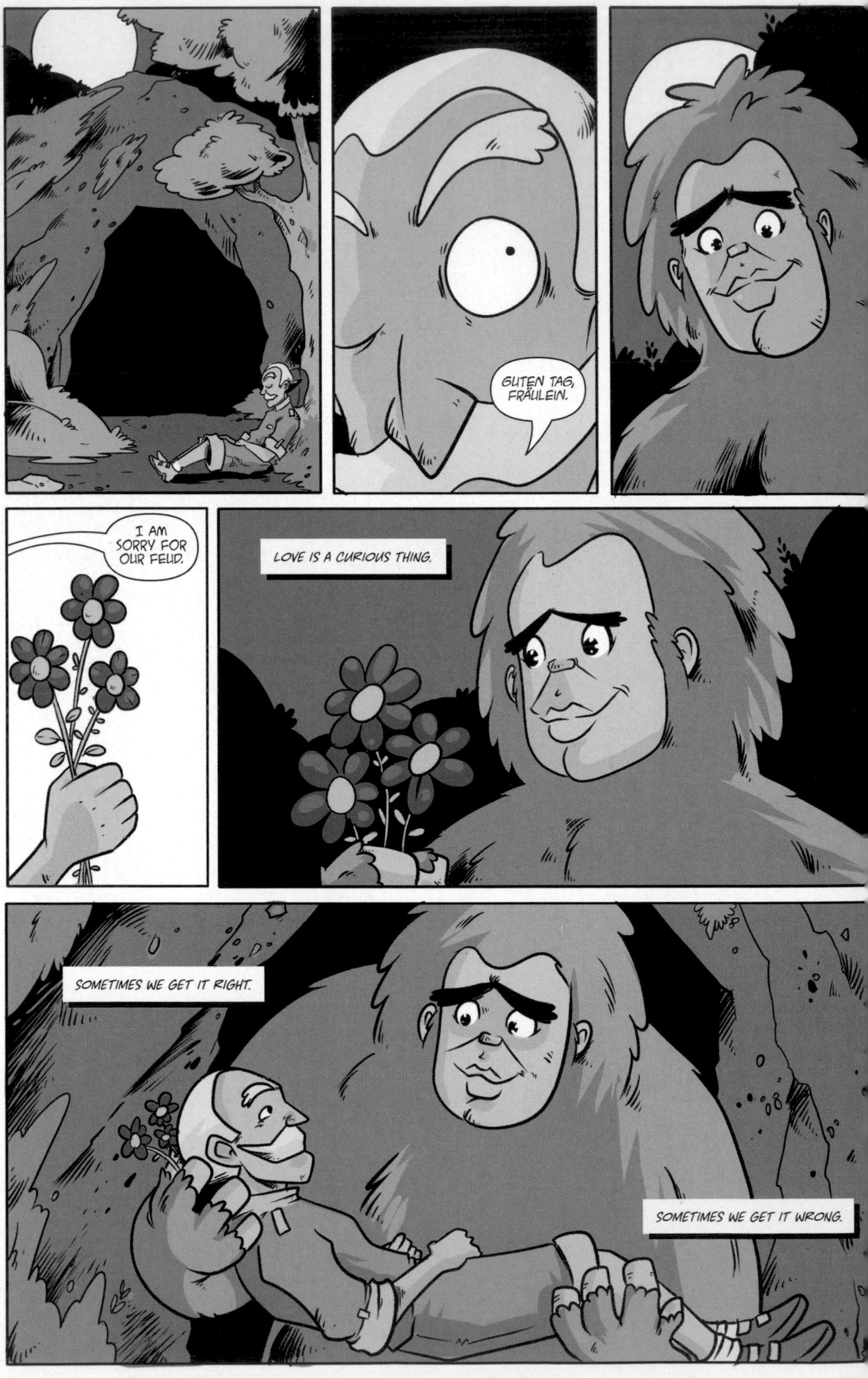
GUTEN TAG, FRÄULEIN.
I AM SORRY FOR OUR FEUD.
LOVE IS A CURIOUS THING.
SOMETIMES WE GET IT RIGHT.
SOMETIMES WE GET IT WRONG.

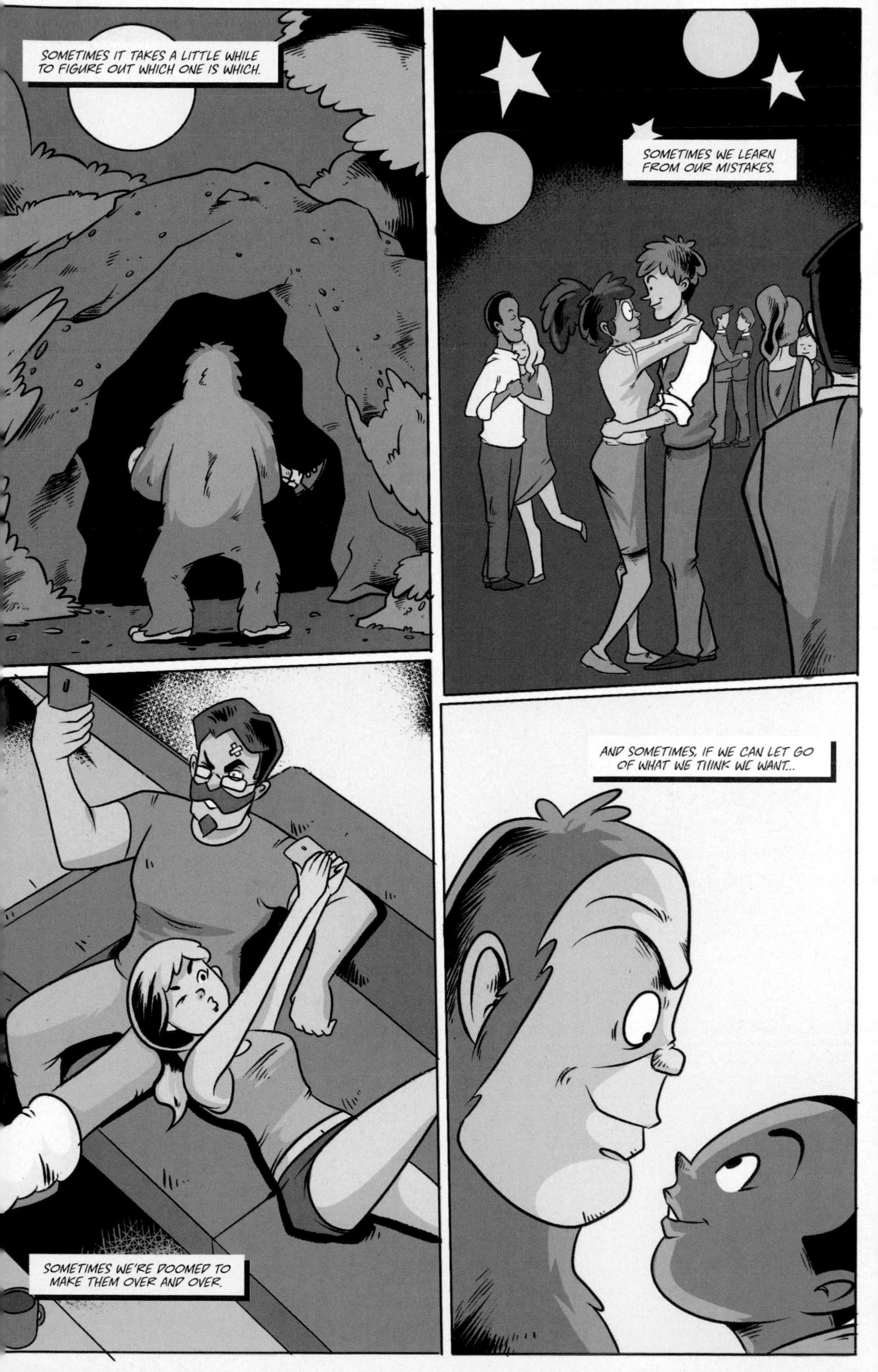
SOMETIMES IT TAKES A LITTLE WHILE TO FIGURE OUT WHICH ONE IS WHICH.
SOMETIMES WE LEARN FROM OUR MISTAKES.
SOMETIMES WE'RE DOOMED TO MAKE THEM OVER AND OVER.
AND SOMETIMES, IF WE CAN LET GO OF WHAT WE THINK WE WANT...

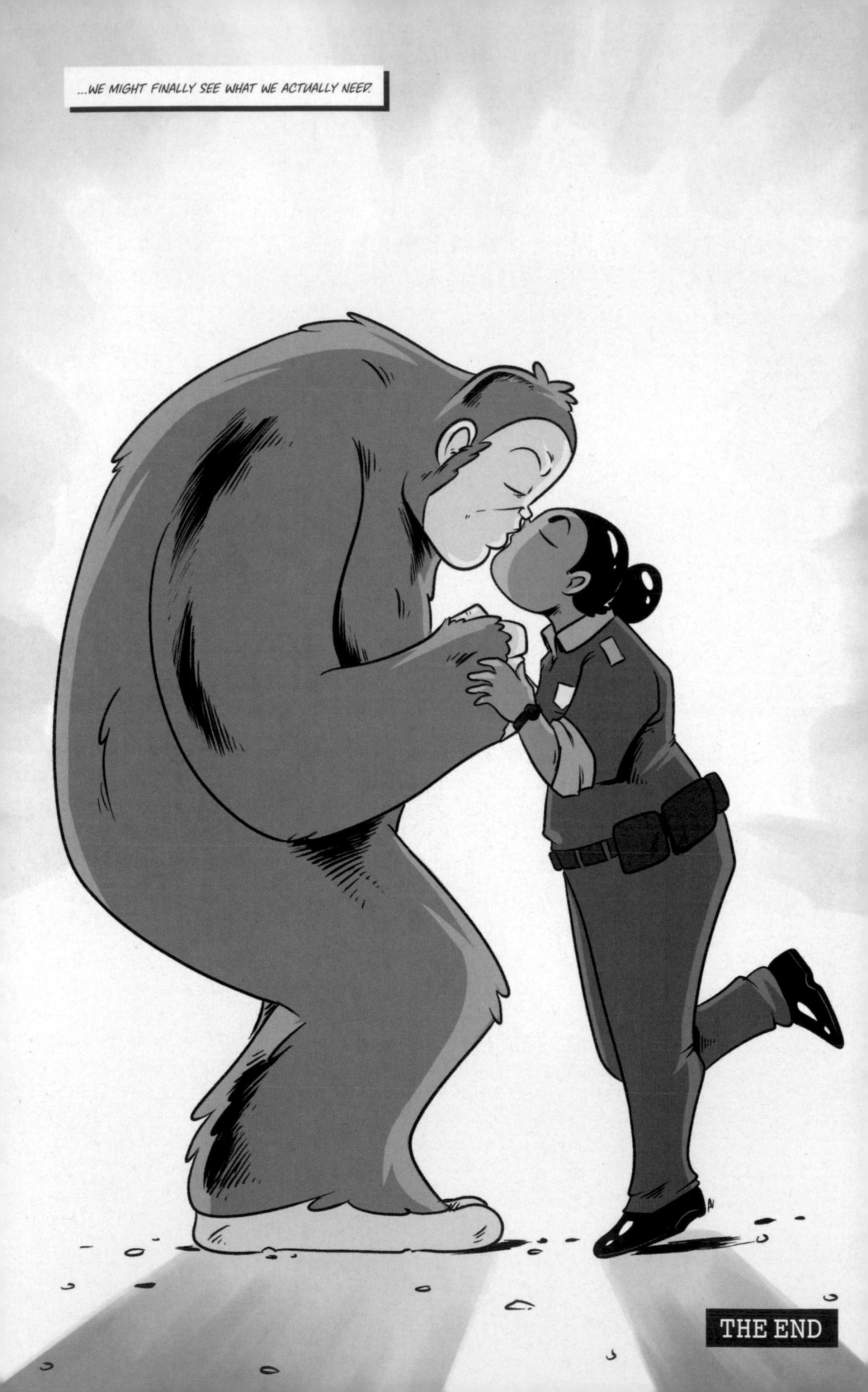
...WE MIGHT FINALLY SEE WHAT WE ACTUALLY NEED.
THE END